Fractured Power

A Novel

By Stephen McGuire

Disclaimer: This is a work of fiction. Unless otherwise indicated, all the names, characters, businesses, places, events, and incidents in the book are the product of the author's imagination or used in a completely fictitious context. Any resemblance to actual persons, living or dead, or actual events is purely coincidental.

This book is published in the United States by SJMcGuire LLC, a Florida business entity, dba Stephen J. McGuire. The publisher and author are providing this book on an "as is" basis and make no representation or warranties of any kind, express or implied, with respect to the accuracy or completeness of the contents of this work, including but not limited to warranties of design, merchantability, or fitness for a particular purpose.

First SJMcGuire LLC Press Edition, 2022

Website: stephenmcguireauthor.com

"It is not in the stars to hold our destiny but in ourselves."

William Shakespeare

Prologue

Lester Kinnard was a troubled, but brilliant young man. He grew up in Bisbee, Arizona, an old mining town located ten miles north of the Mexican border in the southeastern part of the state. He was known for his withdrawn, but witty personality. In high school, he never made a lot of friends and quietly kept to himself most of the time.

He was the only child of Colton and Flora Kinnard, the former, an ex-Army veteran with a reputation for promiscuity and alcohol-fueled violence, and the latter, an aging, long-haired brunette who was a twice-divorced drug addict, hooked on OxyContin and Xanax. At thirteen, Lester discovered from a neighbor that he was illegitimate.

Throughout his childhood, Lester was forced to endure the routine abuse of his stepfather, Colton, but the scars produced from those traumas paled in comparison to the wounds inflicted from the emotional neglect of his mother.

Never did he recall his mother intervening when Colton administered one of his alcohol-induced whippings or worse yet, when he was victimized by his father's periodic sexual assaults.

Despite his being a handsome young man at 6'1" and blondish hair, Lester had difficulty forming relationships, particularly with girls. As a diversion, he dedicated himself to playing basketball for his high school team, which garnered him an athletic scholarship to Cochise College in Sierra Vista, Arizona, a mere twenty miles from Bisbee. Despite his achievements as a player, his parents had never attended one of his games. During his time at the college, he studied psychology, in part, to get a grip on the demons that had haunted him since early childhood.

One sublimely memorable event occurred during the summer of his first year in college when Lester and a classmate went fishing for the day at the Patagonia Lake State Park, an hour's drive southwest from the school. After a day of serious drinking, an argument ensued over who his real father was and after a brief skirmish, Lester angrily pushed the heavily intoxicated young man off the boat. After watching the boy flail in the water, Lester started to reach out to rescue him, but a sudden, profound urge abruptly pulled him back. As if he were in a demonic trance, Lester began to whimsically observe the young man's struggle to stay above the surface and ignored his desperate cries for help.

Just as the boy grasped the side of the boat, Lester, in a moment of callous depravity, reached out and held the boy's head under the water. He intently watched as the young man took a last, desperate gasp of air before slipping beneath the surface into the dark chasm of the bucolic reservoir. As the body slowly spiraled downward into the abyss, his face reflected a look of abject horror and shocked disbelief. It was an expression that Lester would never forget. It made him feel truly alive for the first time in his life.

What a rush it had been! It was as if there was a sudden, psychological break from his outward personality and another entity . . . the real, iniquitous him that he had never fully experienced, had completely taken over. He had been in complete control over whether his friend lived or died and he elected to let him die! Nothing had ever felt so satisfying…it was instant gratification watching the very moment death took the life out of the young man's motionless body.

It was a sensation like he had never known . . . a thrill he replayed in his mind over and over again.

* * * * * * * *

A few years after graduation, Lester found himself employed as a bartender at the Painted Mustang Saloon; a popular, out-of-the-way establishment located on an isolated, two-lane desert road just off Interstate 10, near Wilcox, Arizona, eighty miles northeast of Tucson.

Like most such establishments, the Painted Mustang was a weathered, wooden structure with old-west swinging doors and a shaded, outdoor dining area where transient bikers would drink beer while sitting by their choppers talking shop. The inside walls of the tavern were covered with license plates from every state in the union . . . a testament to the hundreds of transients who passed through the area via the interstate. The long wooden bar had dozens of one-dollar bills tacked to the mantel over the stools and was bounded by neon signs and a prominent old-time Phillips 66 gasoline pump.

A Marlboro cigarette poster accented the wall by a billiards table which rimmed the outer edge of the bar, alongside an ancient shuffleboard game and ten wooden dining tables. Behind the beer taps were shelves loaded with every type of booze imaginable, with a heavy emphasis on whiskey and tequila. The patrons were mostly middle-aged locals, which lent an air of coziness to the otherwise drab interior.

Lester was a reliable enough employee but seemed to have little or no ambition. He had no friends to speak of, men or women. When he wanted to attract a girl, however, he could be downright charming, emitting a vibrant masculinity many young women found most captivating. His cool demeanor and handsome, rugged looks, however, were belied by a deep-seeded melancholy that was noticed by all who worked with him.

He was an extraordinarily intelligent young guy, but outwardly seemed a loner, scarred by a thousand hurts with little purpose or hope for the future.

Little could the downhearted Lester Kinnard have ever imagined the shocking events that fate would soon blindly throw at him; events that would soon predicate his own demise and outwardly, everything he had ever been.

Chapter One

Aiden Fletcher had grown up in Southern California with no parents and no family. He never knew his father and his mother had died at a young age from ovarian cancer when he was six-years-old. He had bounced around the foster care system outside San Diego until he was fourteen, having found himself in over seven group home placement facilities during that time.

The constant reality of being an orphan was never knowing what the future would hold for him. There was little sense of security and a great deal of doubt about what would happen to him next. He would often fall asleep at night and dream of someday being somebody that people knew and liked . . . somebody who made a difference in people's lives.

There were the adoption showings where several of the children were paraded out to prospective parents hoping that someone would want to bring them into their home. After four years of such efforts, which proved to no avail, Aiden began to lose hope of ever having a family to love.

For all the social workers who had entered his life, none of them were around long enough for him to have developed a relationship. There was Denise, a twenty-something grad student who was taking a semester off to learn about the California Child Protection System for her doctoral thesis. She was fun and full of life and got along well with Aiden as he was entering adolescence.

But at the end of her study period, she returned home to Northern California, and Aiden never saw her again. However, she had left an indelible impression on him. He had admired her ambition and the fact that she wanted to use her education to help others. That's when he decided to excel at school.

During his junior year of high school, Aiden lived in a short-term foster home where the husband had been an engineer. Over several weeks, he regaled Aiden with the success stories of people who had come from nothing and had made something out of their lives. It was a lesson Aiden never forgot.

He began studying hard, focusing on English and literature. His grades soon reflected his efforts, and he rose to the top of his high school class.

During the spring of his senior year of high school, Aiden found himself staying with a professor from San Diego State University. Impressed with Aden's intellect and desire to advance, he arranged for Aiden to apply for a special scholarship for underprivileged kids. With the professor's sponsorship, Aiden received a full scholarship, including room and board.

While at San Diego State, Aiden excelled, majoring in pre-law and business, and graduated on the Dean's List. After college, he worked for six years in the University's School of Business, where he showed great promise. Despite a promising career path, however, he decided, once and for all, he wanted to be a criminal attorney; an occupation he had become smitten with after watching scores of episodes of "Law and Order," a highly successful TV legal drama.

Not having the funds to pay his way, he began to apply for academic scholarships to law schools wherever they were available. Only one, the University of Tennessee, accepted him offering what he was looking for . . . a full ride.

The chance he had long dreamed of finally came. Packing his car, he set off on a cross-country trip from Southern California with the wind blowing in his blond hair and the long-awaited opportunity to follow his aspirations.

* * * * * * * *

After the nearly eight-hour drive across the Arizona desert, Aiden arrived in the small town of Wilcox and decided to call it a day. He pulled up to the Painted Mustang Saloon in his old Nissan Pathfinder, filled to the brim with boxes of clothes and personal belongings of every description.

Grabbing a seat at the bar, he ordered a Dos Equis lager and settled into his stool for a well-deserved cold beer.

"Where ya' from, stranger?" Lester Kinnard politely asked, having noticed the Nissan's California tags.

"Escondido," the tall, handsome Fletcher replied. "Just north of San Diego."

Lester had always been curious about people from somewhere else, especially someone his own age. It broke, if only momentarily, the anguish of his otherwise miserable life in the desert of southeastern Arizona.

"Looks like you're making a move somewhere, the way your SUV is loaded down," Lester light-heartedly replied, hoping to continue the conversation.

"Actually, I'm heading to Tennessee," Fletcher replied, repeatedly brushing back his unruly mop of hair and taking a long sip of his beer.

"Tennessee?" Lester quizzically responded. He had never known anyone with a connection to Tennessee. "You have family there?" Lester curiously inquired.

"Nah, actually, I don't have a family . . . no living relatives," Fletcher quietly responded.

"I grew up in orphanages and in several foster homes in Southern California. I'm heading to Knoxville to go to law school on a scholarship at the University of Tennessee."

"Wow!" Lester excitedly replied. "That's pretty cool. How did you manage to get a scholarship to law school? That's something I always thought would be pretty neat, being a big-time lawyer."

"Just lucky, I guess," Fletcher replied. "I always did well in school, and some benefactor set up a scholarship, with housing, tuition, a stipend . . . everything! It's all in here," he casually added, pointing to the small, zippered portfolio bag he had carried into the bar.

"Don't have to be there until the 15th, so I thought I'd take a leisurely trip across the southwest. Always wanted to drive through the Arizona desert," he added.

"Where are you staying tonight?" Lester curiously asked, assuming Fletcher was spending the night in town.

"Don't know yet," Fletcher replied, "any suggestions?"

"Sure," replied Lester. "Try the Del Ray Inn. It's just a couple of miles down the road, affordable, and quite comfortable. Tell them I recommended it; just don't expect any room service."

"I'll do that, thanks," laughed Fletcher. "By the way, what's your name?"

"Lester Kinnard."

"Nice meeting you, Lester. Aiden Fletcher is my name."

Aiden Fletcher, Lester thought to himself. That has a nice ring to it.

The two continued their conversation until the bar's 11:00 p.m. closing time. Fletcher had consumed several drinks when Lester suggested they meet up the road for a nightcap at another dive, which stayed open until 2:00 a.m.

"I always go there after my shift is over," Lester noted. "Gives me a chance to unwind. Let's go have a couple more drinks; I'll buy. You can meet me there and then check into the motel."

"Sounds good," replied the now tipsy Fletcher. "It's still fairly early, and I have nothing better to do."

* * * * * * * * *

The two drove their cars to the Old Saguaro Tavern, a short drive from the Painted Mustang. They continued their conversation over-late night eats and several more beers, with Fletcher responding to Lester's unrelenting questions about his past.

"At this point, I feel you know more about me than anyone in the world," Fletcher jokingly observed.

Lester replied with a slight smile. "Sorry, I didn't mean to be so inquisitive. It's just funny how you meet someone and feel like you've known them your entire life."

Lester's mood was a bit melancholy as he contemplated the new adventure the young Fletcher was about to experience . . . in sharp contrast to his own seemingly hopeless existence.

Fletcher just laughed. By now, he was clearly intoxicated and creating somewhat of a ruckus. The tavern's owner, Alberto Perez, approached Lester.

"Time for your friend to call it a night," Alberto advised him. "We don't want anyone calling the cops on us. We just got approved for keeping extended hours, and I don't need to have my license pulled for overserving my customers."

"No problem, Alberto," replied the subdued Lester. "My friend is here from California, just enjoying himself after the long drive." The two threw down the last of their beers.

"Give me the tab, and I'll drive him to the Del Ray and get him checked in," said Lester. "I'll come back later and get his car for him."

"Sounds good," replied Alberto, knowing his regular customer would understand. "By the way, are you OK? You seem a little down tonight."

"I'm OK," Lester quietly replied, rising from his chair without further responding.

Assisting the staggering Fletcher into his pick-up truck, Lester left the parking lot and pulled out onto the highway driving east toward the Del Ray Inn.

Chapter Two

Early the next morning, Aiden Fletcher left Wilcox and drove his Pathfinder onto the ramp for Interstate 10 toward New Mexico. The night in the desert had been exhilarating. For the first time in his life, he felt he could now be anything he wanted to be. He could leave his broken past behind and dream of his future as an attorney.

The University of Tennessee was going to make everything possible.

He was grateful for this once-in-a-lifetime opportunity. The fickle hand of fate had shone down upon him. A full ride to a noted law school where he could establish himself as one of the community's leading citizens was beyond his wildest imagination, a far cry from his painful past.

Now, anything and everything was there for the taking. Every possibility would now be open for him. He could be the man he always wanted to be, and others would have no choice but to pay deference to his place in society. He was thrilled about the future that lay before him.

* * * * * * * *

Lester, meanwhile, was nowhere to be found. He hadn't been to work in over a week. He hadn't contacted the manager of the Painted Mustang or any of the other employees.

"Wouldn't you think he would at least call us?" said Hootie Simpson, the owner of the bar. "I mean really, you would think he owed us at least that."

It became apparent that Lester had blown the place off and found a new line of work in another town or met a girl somewhere. In the end, it didn't matter. Guys like him were a dime a dozen. They had little ambition and were unaccountable. The Painted Mustang had hired dozens like him over the years, and after three years on the job, it wasn't surprising that he just abruptly left. What irritated Simpson was that Lester had not advised him he was leaving and going somewhere else.

* * * * * * * *

The call came into the Wilcox Sheriff's Office nine weeks later.

"Patrol 18 . . . this is Dispatch. We have a report of an abandoned vehicle near the Dos Cabezas Mine entrance. An inspector for the power company was up in the hills doing his quarterly check of the lines and noticed an unaccompanied pick-up truck. Take a run up there and let us know what you find. Over."

"Patrol 18, here . . . will do Dispatch . . . on my way there now. Over."

Dos Cabezas was a mountain range located just a few miles southeast of Wilcox off Arizona Highway 186. In the 1860s, gold had been mined in the area. Served by the Southern Pacific Railroad, copper mining had been the area's primary industry. Decades earlier, mining operations began to decline, and the railroad ultimately ceased operations. Like many former mining towns throughout Arizona, it was now a deserted and ghostly reminder of its former self.

Within a few minutes, a priority transmission came crackling through to Dispatch.

"Dispatch . . . this is Patrol 18 . . . better send a coroner's vehicle up here . . . we have a body . . . or should I say . . .what's left of it, near the entrance of the mine."

"Roger Patrol 18. Coroner's vehicle on its way," came the somber response.

Within thirty minutes, a cavalcade of two patrol cars and the coroner's medical van drove up an isolated and rarely used gravel road that ended at the entrance to the mine. Behind them were two vehicles from the Homicide Unit and a team of forensics specialists.

Thirty yards from the entrance of the mine lay the badly decomposed body of a young male. Lying beside it was a 12-gauge shotgun with a spent shell casing still in the chamber.

The heat and the coyotes had ravaged the body beyond recognition. A shotgun blast had blown the victim's head off while the skeletal remains contained nothing more than a few tiny clumps of badly-rotted flesh. The keys were still in the ignition of the truck.

"Has anyone run the tags?" Lt. Ernesto Primrose barked.

"Just came in, Lieutenant," responded one of the officers. "The truck belongs to a Lester P. Kinnard, of Wilcox."

"Affirmative Lieutenant," echoed another officer. "We just lifted the victim's wallet and cell phone off the body. He had a Painted Mustang name tag pinned on his shirt. No cash was taken and no blood was found inside the vehicle. It seems pretty clear cut . . . Mr. Kinnard came out here for whatever reason and blew his head off."

Turning to the Coroner, the Lieutenant asked, "any idea how long the body's been out here, Doc?"

"Best estimate . . . at least two months. This amount of decomposition takes quite a while," responded the coroner.

"Any footprints around the truck or the body?"

"None whatsoever," came the reply. "I think the inevitable windstorms would have taken care of that."

"Any other discernible evidence," the Lieutenant asked.

"None that we can visibly see," came the reply.

"Men take another sweep of the area just in case anything else turns up. If not, let's call it a day."

* * * * * * * *

In the ensuing weeks, the forensic investigation confirmed that no blood was in the vehicle; only a few hair samples and prints from several adults were found in the truck, but no definitive DNA matches in any databases. Then again, Kinnard was constantly hauling other people around and loading supplies in his pick-up. The hair samples could have been from anybody.

"We contacted his mother down in Bisbee and showed her a photo of the shotgun," a homicide investigator noted. "She confirmed it was the gun his grandfather gave him when he was thirteen. Probably the only thing he cared about from his childhood. She said he loved that gun."

"Did she mention anything else?"

"Not really," came the reply. "His mother acted like she could care less about him. She struck me as a cold, dispassionate bitch just looking for another pill."

Interviews with his associates at work painted a rather dispassionate picture of Kinnard. None of the Painted Mustang employees were surprised by the news that Lester had taken his own life.

"He was a really tormented guy," said one worker whose words seemed to summarize what most of them thought.

* * * * * * * *

After the conclusion of the investigation, Detective Buzz DeLong, a twenty-year veteran with the sheriff's office, provided a full report during a meeting with the Cochise County prosecutor. Among other things, the forensics team had done a complete extraction of Lester's cell phone data.

"We're guessing early Tuesday morning, August 10th was the approximate date of death," said DeLong. "After that date, no calls were made."

"Anything else of note?" asked the prosecutor.

"We've ruled out robbery . . . no money taken; no signs of a struggle; no blood or DNA evidence; impossible to obtain fingerprints; and no notable dental evidence which could have established an identity, were recovered."

"So, you're comfortable calling this a suicide?" the prosecutor asked.

"Very much so," replied DeLong. "But there was one more thing," Delong added.

"What's that?" replied the prosecutor.

"During the forensics extraction of the cell phone data, we found where the deceased had sent a text to his mother at approximately 1:30 a.m. on August 10th. Oddly enough, she never replied."

"What did it say?" asked the curious prosecutor.

"Something like . . . 'Mother . . . you don't have to be ashamed of me anymore.'"

* * * * * * * *

The extensive investigation into the death concluded, and the verdict was in. The evidence pointed to one inescapable conclusion; Lester Kinnard, at the age of twenty-eight, had committed suicide in the desert of Southeastern Arizona. The prosecutor closed the case, and Lester's remains were privately buried in a family cemetery in Bisbee next to his grandfather, the one person he had cared about growing up.

After years of torment, the troubled life and outward anguish of Lester Kinnard had finally and mercifully been laid to rest . . . never to appear again.

Chapter Three

Aiden Fletcher was enjoying the drive on Interstate 10 eastward from Arizona. He had five days before he had to be in Knoxville and decided to spend a couple of nights in El Paso, Texas, a place he had always wanted to visit.

Since the 1880s, El Paso had been indiscriminately known for its extensive prostitution, gambling, and assorted indiscretions. Located along the Rio Grande directly across from the Mexican border town of Ciudad Juárez, the area had always provided the adventurer with numerous choices for entertainment. With the Army's Strategic Deployment installation at Ft. Bliss and numerous other federal facilities throughout the city, it had become, in recent times, a respectable place to live.

Ciudad, Juárez on the other hand, had long been a lucrative drug and illegal immigrant smuggling route into the United States and, consequently, the site of inevitable turf wars between the Mexican cartels. As such, many individuals were never able to make the crossing, instead falling victim to the attendant violence and murder surrounding the cartels' activities throughout the area.

For whatever reason, Fletcher had always had a natural, distorted attraction for the seamier side of life. Something about the sordid nature of people on the downside of society had a tremendous pull on his intellect, not to mention his sexual fantasies. It was like survival on its most basic level, the observation of which he thought was far more stimulating than surrounding himself with those who spent their non-descript, monotonous lives in the comfort of their cookie-cutter, suburban homes watching sitcoms.

Getting his bearings on his second night in El Paso, an emboldened Fletcher crossed the border into Ciudad Juárez. As he anticipated, it was delightfully run down, even by Mexican standards. He soon ventured along one of the seedier areas of the Avenida Juárez, the main strip through town with innumerable bars, nightclubs, and flashing neon signs. He listened to the beat of lively mariachi ensembles emanating from the numerous shops along the way, as hucksters of all ages and descriptions urged him to come inside to purchase a trinket.

Fletcher passed several maquiladoras, sweat-shop factories, tended by low-paid young women from the outlying towns and villages. He ventured past a reddish-clay looking building with a large painted window proclaiming the "Mango Coyote Latina Grill," a hip, long-established drinkery which provided a cool and eclectic spot for many tourists and locals alike.

It wasn't long before he became noticed.

"Buenas tardes, señor," said the average-looking, cheaply dressed young woman in a black, sleeveless top who was sitting at the far end of the bar. "Cómo estas, señorita," replied Fletcher. "Cómo te llamas?"

"Me llama Lucia," replied the girl.

"Me llama Leo," said Fletcher, figuring it would be the better part of discretion to use an alias.

"Where did you learn to speak Spanish, Mr. Leo?" said the now inquisitive woman, having learned her English from the innumerable American tourists she had encountered.

"I actually grew . . ." Catching himself, he began again. "I actually grew to like it from a couple of Spanish classes in high school. It always came very easy for me."

The evening continued into the wee hours of the morning with numerous rounds of drinks when Fletcher persuaded the now greatly inebriated young woman to let him walk her back to her apartment, just a few blocks away. She agreed, and the two stumbled into the Mexican night, laughing their way to the outskirts of town.

The rest of the evening with Lucia proved to be intensely satisfying. She had made Fletcher feel like a real man, but he had places to be and a schedule to keep.

* * * * * * * *

The nearly 1,500-mile drive to Knoxville from El Paso was long, but had done Fletcher good. It had given him time to think about who he really was and what he wanted to be. Arriving in Knoxville at the campus of the University of Tennessee a few days later, he was tired but delighted to be in a new environment. He drove past the law school and stared. The massive structure reeked of power and authority. Fletcher felt liberated like never before. Here he was . . . this was it! His new life was going to be everything he had ever wished.

Checking into the University Housing Office, he nervously approached the administrator's office.

"Have a seat, young man," said the Assistant Housing Director. "Name please?"

"Fletcher" he stammered. "Aiden Fletcher."

Rummaging through a new student orientation drawer, she located his file.

"Social Security number and driver's license . . .," she routinely requested while combing through the file.

Fletcher laid the license on her desk while simultaneously handing her the previously provided pre-admission documents containing the requested information. She glanced at his California license and looked up at him for an extended moment.

"That's a lovely necklace you're wearing," Fletcher spontaneously noted. "I don't think I've ever seen anything quite like it."

"Well, thank you," she proudly responded, "it was my grandmother's," handing the documents and the license back to him.

"I see you're from California," the assistant noted. "You've come a long way!"

"I sure have," Fletcher replied. "You have no idea," he quietly added.

"How do you like Knoxville?" she continued.

"Well, I've only been here a couple of hours, but so far, it looks pretty interesting!" said a now, more-relaxed Fletcher.

"You'll get a better feel in a couple of days," she added. "It's normal to be a little nervous on your first day on campus. By the way, you should probably go ahead and get your Tennessee driver's license; it'll make things a lot easier for you."

"I definitely intend to do that," replied Fletcher, making a mental note to stop by the DMV as soon as possible.

"Mr. Fletcher, you are assigned to Laurel Hall, Suite 704," the assistant continued, handing Fletcher two access entry cards and room keys. "I think you'll like it there. Rooms are plenty big and relatively quiet."

After another half-hour filling out various admissions documents and getting his meal ticket coupon book for the student cafeteria, Fletcher went to another building where he got photographed for his official law student ID. When he completed his processing, he returned to his loaded car and drove the short distance to his dorm.

There it was . . . his new home! Laurel Hall, a 600-bed red brick graduate dormitory with a computer lab, weight room, and laundry room. A double-private room suite with a den, kitchen, and private bath. Best of all, it was only a short walk down Cumberland Avenue to the law school where he undoubtedly would be spending most of his time.

His roommate would not be arriving until the next day. After dinner and a few beers at a nearby student hangout, Fletcher unpacked his SUV and went to bed early. With the whirlwind of changes that had confronted him, it had been an emotionally draining several days. He fell asleep with a smile on his face staring at his new student ID . . . Aiden Fletcher, University of Tennessee College of Law.

* * * * * * * *

Arising early the next morning, Fletcher took his place in the main auditorium of the law school for orientation and to register for classes. Like most first-semester law students, he enrolled in Civil Procedure, Torts, Criminal Law, Contracts, and

Legal Research. It was a full load, but he was ready to devour whatever they laid on him.

A few weeks into his first semester, his professors had already taken notice of his keen intellect and razor-sharp ability to think on his feet. On more than one occasion, he had already gotten the best of them by posing arguments that even they could not effectively rebut, much to the delight of his fellow first-year students. The latter labored under the tremendous strain of being perpetually under their professors' collective thumbs.

Fletcher flourished in the law school environment where the Socratic learning method allowed him to expose contradictions in the normal thought process to create more solid and logical conclusions.

The case method approach also suited him well. Though it required a lot of reading, he found satisfaction in briefing the myriad judicial opinions from all over the country and then debating the merits of the legal rationale in the classroom, where others might take the opposing position as if in an actual courtroom situation.

He excelled at case analysis and utilized abstract thinking to make critical points in defending his legal positions. Although he made friends in his first-year classes, it soon became apparent that the competition for Law Review and other honorary student journals took precedence. Everyone competed for such acclaim as the more highly desirable employers viewed such achievement as a mandatory credential upon graduation.

Fletcher excelled in his first-year courses and stood near the top of his class. By the end of his second year, he showed a natural adeptness in criminal law which soon brought him to the attention of the Knox County Office of the Sixth District Attorney General, Bob Martin, the county's top law-enforcement officer. He called Fletcher and invited him in for a talk about his future.

"They tell me you're quite the advocate," Martin began, already picking up on Fletcher's commanding presence and calm, collected bearing.

"Well, I don't know about that," Fletcher humbly replied, playing up to Martin's compliment. "I just do what comes naturally, I guess."

"Well, whatever the reason, I think you'd make a great prosecutor," said Martin. "Think you might want to intern here next semester and get a feel for the place? It would give you six credit hours toward your degree."

"Sure! That would really be great!" replied Fletcher, who was genuinely excited by the offer.

"Good," responded Martin. "I'll have one of the staff fill out the necessary paperwork for the school. We'll send you some things to familiarize yourself with, and I'll be in touch."

"Thanks, Mr. Martin. I'm really looking forward to the opportunity," Fletcher replied, arising from his chair.

. . . . What an opportunity it would provide, Fletcher imagined, a widening smile crossing his lips as he walked briskly out of the building.

* * * * * * * *

Fletcher completed his second year of law school with distinction. In addition to making the Dean's List and a top ranking in his class, he was awarded numerous honors for his Moot Court participation; and invited to join the school's Law Review, where he contributed several highly-regarded notes and comments.

Martin encouraged him to volunteer with several law enforcement groups like the Knox County Crime Prevention Committee and the Metro Drug Coalition. He managed to find time to assist twice a week at the Statewide Crisis Hotline office. His calming patience and listening skills provided him with great insight into those vulnerable individuals living on the edge of society.

It was an endeavor that would serve him well in more ways than he could ever realize.

Chapter Four

Sarah McNamara was a tall, career-oriented, 30-year-old physician from a prominent family in Brentwood, an upper-crust community outside Nashville. Her father, Wesley, had established Mid-Alliance Health, which operated eighteen acute care hospitals and nine outpatient facilities in five states with revenue of over a billion dollars per year.

Sarah had graduated with honors from Vanderbilt University with a degree in Psychology. She subsequently acquired a medical degree from Duke University in Durham, North Carolina.

Although she had plenty of opportunities to stay in North Carolina, she decided to return to her home state to ultimately become a part of the Mid-Alliance Health network, which would undoubtedly open up tremendous opportunities for her to establish a practice in Psychiatry.

She completed her residency at the University of Tennessee in the Graduate School of Medicine, afterward undertaking a Fellowship as an Assistant Research Director with the UT Health Science Center. There, she focused on behavioral science, where she gained a broad perspective on human behavior based upon various factors such as emotions, personality, and social interactions.

For as long as she could remember, she had wanted to be a medical doctor, specifically a forensic psychiatrist, a subspecialty of psychiatry that applied scientific and clinical expertise in legal contexts involving civil, criminal, and legislative matters.

As a teenager, she was enthralled by the novels of Thomas Harris and the prominent film, The Silence of the Lambs, which starred Jodie Foster as a young FBI trainee investigating a serial killer who skinned his female victims. In the movie, she seeks out the advice of the imprisoned Dr. Hannibal Lecter, a brilliant psychiatrist and cannibalistic serial killer himself, who helps lead her to the ultimate suspect. The film is cited as one of the most influential psychological thrillers of all time.

Through her early years of practice, she had worked within the court system as an expert witness. As such, she prepared detailed reports and testified in matters such as evaluating an individual's competency to stand trial, defenses based on mental disorders, and the defendant's mental state at the time of the offense.

Her clinical research focused on the assessment and characterization of emergent psychotic illness, including Schizophrenia, and psychotic affective behaviors and how they related to various types of psychological and personality disorders.

She soon became well-regarded in her field, writing articles on criminal violence and the influence of psychotic illness. She conducted numerous workshops throughout the country in cognitive, affective, behavioral neuroscience, and the assessment of attenuated and threshold psychosis. She also assimilated clinical data as Associate Clinical Scientist in the Psychiatry Department at the UT Medical School.

Sarah often spoke at conferences sponsored by the American Psychiatric Association focusing on psychopathology and its association with criminal violence. She also volunteered as a crisis counselor at the Statewide Crisis Hotline. Sarah counseled numerous individuals with anxiety, depression, drug and alcohol abuse, and a host of other psychological issues.

During a routine Tuesday night shift, she met third-year law student Aiden Fletcher. Their first encounter resulted from an extremely heavy call load that had kept all of the counselors tied up for most of the evening. As their shift ended and the call volume winding down, Sarah reached out to introduce herself.

"You're fairly new here, aren't you?" she inquired of Fletcher.

"Yeah," Fletcher casually responded, "I'm Aiden Fletcher. To whom do I have the pleasure of speaking?" he added, with characteristic aplomb and his trademark smile.

"I'm Sarah," she replied, "Sarah McNamara. I'm working here in conjunction with my clinical psychiatric practice, particularly the aspect associated with affective behaviors."

"How interesting," Fletcher replied. "I've always had a great interest in psychology and how it rationalizes people's otherwise destructive behaviors."

"Me too," said Sarah. "I think it's amazing to be able to study the root cause of why people do what they do."

Sarah was about to leave the building when Fletcher made a suggestion.

"Hey, Sarah . . . what d'ya say we go across the street to Kelly's pub and let me buy you a drink? I'd love to continue our conversation."

It didn't take long for Sarah to assess the sincerity of Fletcher's invitation.

"Sure, I'd love to," she replied, with a grin on her face.

The two spent the next couple of hours getting to know each other and exploring their shared interest in psychology.

Despite their busy workloads, the two began to see more of each other over the next few weeks, with greater and greater emphasis placed on how they intended to pursue their mutual careers.

"What type of law do you think you want to practice?" she asked him.

"Definitely criminal law," replied Fletcher. "I want to be a prosecutor . . . you know, be the one who brings the bad guys to justice . . . there's something about it I just find fascinating."

"I understand," replied Sarah, seeing the tremendous potential of Fletcher's ambition. "I feel the same way about my profession. It's all I've ever wanted to do."

"I'm really excited for you," exclaimed Sarah. "Didn't you say you were starting your third-year internship in a couple of weeks?"

"Yeah, in the Attorney General's office," smiled Fletcher. "Can't wait to start."

"You're going to do great," she asserted.

"Thanks," he replied. "I'll let you know how it goes," he said with a loud chuckle.

The two had each found a kindred spirit in the other. Not as much a sexual or romantic liaison, but as individuals who shared their mutual ambitions. They were like trusted advisors who could always rely on the other to advance their respective interests without the usual physical aspects of conventional marriage.

The couple dated for a year before the subject of marriage came up. Fletcher approached Sarah about it, seeing her as a useful partner going forward. Previously, neither had pressed the case for it, as both maintained busy schedules and, were first and foremost, dedicated to their careers, which frequently meant they were engaged in some business-related activity until well into the night. On top of that, Sarah was often out of town, regularly speaking at conferences or attending lectures.

The subject of having children was never a consideration. Given their career ambitions, they simply weren't a priority. However, they concluded that marriage to each other could work if for no other reason because each of them were intelligent enough to understand and assist the other in whatever avenues they were pursuing.

They were married a year later, with a huge wedding near Nashville at The Estate at Cherokee Dock, a 13-acre lakefront property built in 1960, with a nearly 13,000 sq. ft. colonial mansion, the former home of country superstar Reba McEntire. The eight-bedroom, all-white, colonial home had retained all the charm and rustic grandeur of an old southern estate, which it had so tastefully re-created.

After the wedding, the couple flew to The Breakers, a turn-of-the-century Renaissance Revival style luxury hotel located in Palm Beach. They continued with a private cruise to the Turks and Caicos, a British-owned archipelago of forty low-lying coral islands in the Atlantic Ocean southeast of the Bahamas.

There, they basked in the Caribbean sun while enjoying scuba diving and casual dining at the many luxury resorts and restaurants, which gave the islands their reputation as one of the most desirable locales in that part of the world.

Within a few months after their honeymoon, the couple, with financial assistance from Sarah's father, purchased a modest but upscale home in the community of Oak Ridge, where they went about their lives pursuing their budding and promising careers.

The future looked bright for Sarah and Fletcher as they began their journey toward their inevitable destinies.

Chapter Five

Fletcher's internship with the DA's office allowed him to appear in court under the supervision of an Assistant District Attorney and assist in the prosecution of numerous petty offense cases. Although ninety percent of them involved plea deals, he did get to spend quite a bit of time in the courtroom polishing his skills. His prowess was soon apparent to all who observed him in action.

Through his expanding connections, particularly Sarah's father, Fletcher became politically involved in the mayor's re-election campaign, becoming an indispensable strategist. In only a few years, Fletcher quickly became established in Knoxville and seemed destined for a highly successful legal and perhaps political career.

It was a forgone conclusion after graduation that Fletcher would become an Assistant District Attorney. His love of criminal law and prosecution of violent criminals had long before made the decision for him. He began handling misdemeanor, domestic violence, and drunk driving cases. He soon moved up to the major crimes division, where he prosecuted scores of cases from larceny and robbery to criminal sexual conduct and felonious assaults. Before long he was handling major homicide prosecutions and became known for his expertise in forensic and crime scene investigations.

Fletcher made a mark in one of his early murder cases which involved the brutal beating and rape of a young woman who had walked home alone from a bar. When in an extended jailhouse interview with Jace McVee, the prime suspect with a prior arrest record, he broke him down with a powerful and searing interrogation:

"Why don't you tell me about that young girl you killed, Jace," Fletcher began.

"I don't know what the fuck you're talking about," said McVee, an ill-bred, belligerent high school drop-out and day laborer.

"Oh, I think you know a great deal about what I'm talking about," Fletcher cynically replied. "You see, I'm going to give you one chance to admit that you killed that girl, so you can spend the remaining days of your miserable life in the state pen, or I will personally see to it you get the big needle right in your arm and I promise, it won't take twenty years . . . do you understand me?"

"You don't have shit," McVee sneered.

"To the contrary, my friend, I've got an eyewitness that saw you pull the girl off the street and throw her into your car. We're examining the vehicle now for her prints and hair evidence," Fletcher eagerly added, "and when her DNA shows up, you're getting the death penalty, so you can save yourself by confessing now."

The threat didn't seem to faze the callous suspect.

Pushing himself into McVee's face, Fletcher began getting personal and fervently pressing his case. "How did it feel, Jace, when you bludgeoned her in the woods? Did you watch her expression when she breathed her last breath? Did her eyes roll back slowly or all at once?"

“I don’t know what you’re talking . . .” the now visibly agitated McVee tried to speak but was abruptly cut off by the growing intensity of Fletcher’s questioning.

“. . . What a trip it must have been to have forced yourself on her,” Fletcher scowled. “I can’t imagine what a rush it must have been for a low life like you. Do you think she enjoyed it? Her last moments with you? Did it turn you on? Did it make you feel like a real man? You like to feel in charge, don’t you, Jace?”

“Tell me . . . what was it like, man?” Fletcher relentlessly continued, pressing closer. He could tell McVee was growing extremely flustered. He moved in for the coup d’état.

“I guess you had to kill her though, didn’t you?” Fletcher solemnly continued, “otherwise, she would have told everyone how sexually inadequate you were with her . . . just like your mother.”

“Fuck you, asshole! Fuck you!” McVee abruptly screamed, suddenly leaping from the table. “Damn right, I killed that fucking little bitch! She was just like those other fucking skanks I’ve known . . . too good to give me the time of day, even at a bar. Who the fuck was she to refuse to even talk to me! Serves her fucking right . . . goddamn bitch!”

After confessing to a few more details about the assault, McVee, still screaming, was led out of the interrogation room in handcuffs. Fletcher calmly shut off the tape recorder, quickly composed himself, and prepared to leave. His colleagues were taken back at what they had just witnessed.

“How did you pull that off, man,” said one. “I mean, really. It was like you were inside his head the whole time, knowing exactly what buttons to push. He went absolutely ballistic."

"Just lucky, I guess," Fletcher smugly smiled, leaving the room, "just lucky."

* * * * * * * *

Aiden Fletcher's reputation as a no-nonsense prosecutor had grown over the preceding years to where he had fast become one of the leading trial attorneys in the eastern part of the state. His charisma and natural political instincts, not to mention his imposing intelligence, served him well, as did his stature as a behind-the-scenes political confidant.

He had adapted well to the culture in Tennessee, becoming, among other things, an ardent supporter of the Tennessee Volunteers football team. His familiarity with the issues and fundraising expertise got the attention of many of the local political movers and shakers.

As an Assistant District Attorney, Fletcher supervised grand jury investigations and prosecuted numerous cases involving organized crime, political corruption, murder, and various white-collar crimes. He also served as a volunteer adviser to the Knoxville Area Crime Prevention Advisory Commission. He would often confer with local law enforcement officials on active investigations within the Knoxville area.

Fletcher also spent as much time as possible speaking at seminars at the Law Enforcement Innovative Center in conjunction with the National Forensic Academy in Oak Ridge to undergraduate criminal justice students. The classes were part of a three-week program on topics that included crime scene management, shooting incident reconstruction, bloodstain pattern analysis, and forensic anthropology.

He took it upon himself to study the materials to expand his knowledge and better prepare for the ongoing criminal investigations of the cases that came before his office. He soon became a de facto expert in the field.

His successes involved sentencing a long-sought serial rapist to life in prison and a guilty verdict in a highly publicized home invasion and murder case. Fletcher was also responsible for the conviction of a prominent physician for the drunk driving death of a nine-year-old boy and a securities fraud conviction in a case where the University of Tennessee was a victim of a multimillion-dollar scam. He became known for his dramatic courtroom arguments, particularly his cross-examination skills with a hostile witness.

* * * * * * * *

Despite Fletcher's prowess in convicting hardened, violent offenders, the City of Knoxville was experiencing a rash of reported missing young women. The Knoxville police were at a loss as there remained little forensic evidence to identify even a crime scene. For all officials knew, the women had merely runoff, not wanting to be noticed.

However, these cases were of particular interest to Fletcher, who was intrigued by the methodologies of law enforcement to investigate the missing women.

Then, in the early hours of a cool February morning, the largely skeletonized remains of a UT coed; nineteen-year-old long-haired brunette, Miriam Fleming, was discovered partially buried in a little-visited woodland area just a few miles from campus.

Friends had told police she had left her dormitory one evening to attend an outdoor concert at Market Square and had never returned home. Fractures in her jaw and cheekbones indicated she most likely had been brutally beaten. There was insufficient evidence, however, to determine if she had been sexually assaulted.

She was last seen talking to a man at a parking lot, but no one could provide any concrete description of his physical makeup. After an intensive forensic investigation, authorities were unable to identify any DNA which might identify her killer. However, the medical examiner noticed the broken hyoid bone in her neck, which strongly indicated the victim had been strangled, which in his opinion, in conjunction with the evidence of being beaten, was the cause of death.

In the months that followed, two other young women, with nothing in common with each other, were reported missing with little or no evidence of their whereabouts. The cases soon became cold without any significant leads.

The cases, however, did not escape the attention of Fletcher, who turned to the best person he knew to explain the pathologies behind the disappearances.

"So, what kind of person or persons are we dealing with here," he asked his wife one night over a late-evening dinner.

"Assuming we're talking about one guy doing the kidnapping and presumable murders of these women, and I'm not convinced it is, it's difficult to say what the degree of psychopathy might be," she began.

"On the one hand, the killer may just be sensation seeking, with a real need for control or predatory behavior," she explained. "On the other hand, the killer may be mentally ill . . . a psychopath who is suffering from psychotic breaks, which causes him to believe he is a completely different person with internal forces directing him to kill."

"The literature, particularly the theories put forth by Cleckley, called it 'the mask of sanity,' she continued. "The outer persona that they present to the world is the mask which disguises their true, inner self, which is actually the entity controlling their killing."

"Let me guess," said Fletcher. "These monsters all have one common trait . . . a background of being abused when they were young, correct?"

"For sure," replies Sarah. "Most of these individuals came from broken homes and were abused . . . either physically, sexually or emotionally. Maybe all three."

"How they related to their parents and vice versa is how they relate and value other members of society," Sarah concluded. "In the worst-case scenarios, these individuals take their hate and anger toward their parents out on other people who remind them of their parents . . . particularly their mothers."

"So their neglect as children by their parents causes them to seek out a fantasy world, where they are in control, right?" Fletcher astutely surmised.

"That's correct, Aiden," replied Sarah. "The child becomes sociopathic because their emotional and social development was arrested, at a time when they should have been learning the value of empathizing with others."

"In their fantasy world, unlike the world they grew up in, they can do no wrong. Hence, they show no remorse toward their victims," Sarah asserted. "Their actions turn to dominance, control . . . sexual or otherwise, and unfortunately, violence."

"So they dehumanize their victims due to their lack of empathy, right?"

"Correct again," responded Sarah. "It's what allows them to commit the most atrocious violence because, in their fantasies, they have dehumanized their victims to the point they are nothing more than inanimate objects."

"They think nothing of exploiting the very people they have daily interactions with," she continued, "even their own family."

"They use other people to exclusively serve their own purposes without a bit of feeling or regard for them. Everything and everyone serve one purpose and one purpose only; to serve the needs of the psychopath, no matter how insignificant."

"Well, at least we know what we're dealing with, right?" stated the satisfied Fletcher,

"I think you have a very good idea what you're dealing with, Aiden," she replied, admiring his intellectual ability to grasp the psychology of the situation.

"A very good idea indeed."

* * * * * * * *

As summer broke, the skeletonized remains of the two other identified missing women turned up in various parks and wooded areas in and around Knoxville, with little or no forensics to implicate the individual or individuals who had committed the murders.

One of the remains was located in a tree-lined, sparsely-populated area south of Knoxville by a man walking his dog. The victim was identified through dental records as Anna Sue Ellison, a twenty-two-year-old hairstylist, who had disappeared a year earlier in an outlying park known as the Ijams Nature Center, a wildlife sanctuary that offered weekend tourists hiking, rock-climbing, and kayaking. It was also popular for its tree-top canopy courses called the Navitat, a compilation of adventure traverses and zip-lines for all ages.

Like the findings from the examination of Miriam Fleming, the remains of Anna Sue Ellison and the second victim, Ginger Mattingly, age twenty, had clear indications that the victims had been severely beaten and strangled to death. Beyond those findings, however, no DNA evidence was gathered to identify the killer, or the motive for the killing.

Apart from identifying the skeletal remains of the two women, the deaths did not invoke the kind of fierce, immediate public reaction that accompanies the discovery of a freshly, brutally murdered victim, especially a young female. Nor did they provide any fresh clues as who was responsible or what the killer's motivations might have been.

That was all about to change.

Chapter Six

The July summer air was uncommonly cool early on a Saturday morning as the young couple enjoyed their weekend hike at Fort Loudoun Lake, twenty miles southwest of Knoxville. With the backdrop of the Great Smokey Mountains, the lake was a year-round destination and popular weekend getaway for boaters and fishermen alike. Located at the headwaters of the Tennessee River, in the outlying area of Knox County, it was in the uppermost chain of nine TVA reservoirs, providing camping and picnic facilities for all who visited.

The couple had only hiked a few miles when they came upon a semi-secluded rest area where their eyes noticed the semi-nude, bloodied body of a young woman lying in the far corner of the rest area parking lot under a small grove of trees. Alarmed, they made a frantic call to the local 911.

"911 . . . What is your emergency?"

"Oh my God! There's a body in a wooded area, here at the lake!" screamed the young woman.

"Can you tell us where you're located?" came the cool response.

"I'm not sure . . . we're about halfway in on the Ridge Top Trail Loop, near the main camping area," stammered the distraught woman.

"Stay where you are," cautioned the operator. "We're sending the police over now."

"Please hurry! It's horrible!"

As the police vehicles arrived, a small cadre of hikers had assembled in the adjacent parking area where they discovered the body.

" Looks like the killer kidnaped the victim and drove her out here," noted the first officer on the scene.

"Cause of death?" asked Mark Preston, the lead detective in the case.

"Appears to be blunt force trauma to the head, with numerous stab wounds to the upper torso area," the officer responded.

"Victimology?" Preston inquired.

"Looks like our victim is in her early twenties, attractive, blond . . . and sexually assaulted."

"Any sign of a struggle?"

"Judging from her bruises, it looks like she put up a pretty good fight," replied the officer.

"We'll do a routine vaginal swab and check her fingernails for DNA," added the forensic team leader.

After a couple more hours of crime scene analyses, the EMTs loaded the body into the corner's ambulance. The conversation between the investigating officials suddenly became muted.

"Do we have an ID on the victim yet?" asked Preston.

"We ran a check on her cell phone," reported the officer. "It was still in the back pocket of her jeans under the name of Marianne Silvey. We cross-referenced the name, and it appears she is age twenty-four, with an address at a trailer park near Little River."

"This is becoming quite troubling," noted the detective to one of the crime scene specialists. "This is the fourth murder of a young woman in the last few months in this part of the county."

"Same victimology; problem is the MOs don't all quite seem to match," the detective continued.

"Same victim profiles and same blunt trauma wounds to the head, but unlike the prior cases, here we have a sexual assault with multiple stab wounds."

"Maybe our killer is getting a little more aggressive," said a forensic technician.

"Or maybe it's not just one guy," replied the officer.

"Let's not even go there," stated the nearly exasperated detective.

"Any DNA?" an officer asked.

"No DNA possible in the prior cases," replied the specialist. "This one, however, might be a bit different. We'll do a semen analysis and see if there's a match in the database. It's quite possible, however, that even if we identify the presence of DNA, it won't necessarily lead us to a specific individual."

"You mean whoever did these murders might not have any DNA on the books?" asked the detective.

"That's the long and short of it," replied the specialist.

"We're going to have to get a handle on this and soon," noted the detective. "Looks like we may have a potential serial killer on our hands, and God help us if the media starts to connect the dots. We'll have a panic like we haven't seen in these parts in a generation."

* * * * * * * *

After several highly successful years as an Assistant District Attorney, Fletcher had been strongly urged to run for the vacant seat of the retiring Bob Martin as Sixth District Attorney General. After a tough campaign against another seasoned veteran, Fletcher, though relatively unknown to the general public, was elected on a law-and-order platform and became the youngest person, at age thirty-eight, to occupy the seat in over a hundred years.

As the new Sixth District Attorney General, Fletcher was in charge of various courts and administrative divisions that served the multiple functions of the office. In addition to Juvenile and General Sessions courts, he oversaw the Grand Jury and the Criminal Courts Division, the Major Crimes Unit, the Felony Drug Unit, and the White-Collar Crime Unit. In conjunction with these divisions, he supervised the Domestic Violence and Child Abuse offices, along with the DUI and assorted other support offices.

Fletcher had been in the job for just a few weeks when sitting at his desk the early morning of August 16th, he received a call from Sergeant Alex Hopkins of the Knoxville Police Department.

"Sorry to bother you, Mr. Fletcher," said Hopkins, "but Chief Cummings wanted me to call to give you a heads up before the media gets a hold of this."

"Gets a hold of what?" responded the curious Fletcher.

"There's been another body show up this morning," said Hopkins. "It was found down by the river near Sequoyah Park."

Sequoyah Park was in an older area of Knoxville, just south of town on the Tennessee River. It was known for its biking and hiking trails, and surrounded by quaint, well-tended homes, noted for their resplendent display of blooming dogwoods every spring. Adjacent to the park were two waterway accesses to the Tennessee River.

"Have someone call me back as soon as you've got some more information," asked Fletcher, with uncharacteristic urgency.

He flipped on the television in his office. It was too late. WBIR, the most widely-watched station in Knoxville, was already running with the story. On the screen behind the news anchor's desk screamed the early morning headline:

"Are Recent Knoxville Murders Connected?"

"This morning, Knoxville police, called to the scene of yet another horrific murder of a young woman near the Sequoyah Park area," stated the newscaster.

"At this time information, is scarce, but witnesses at the scene tell WBIR News that early this morning, a construction worker discovered the body of a young woman in a portable toilet near an excavation site on the Tennessee River. The victim appears to look as if she had been brutally beaten. Her naked body was taken by authorities and transported to the coroner's office for further identification."

Police spokesman Lieutenant James Carlson was at the scene and interviewed by the various news media about what had occurred.

"What can you tell us about the victim?" asked one anxious reporter.

"We've identified the victim as Nancy Alford of Knoxville. All we know at this time, she appears to be in her early twenties," Carlson stoically replied.

"Any signs of sexual assault?" queried another.

"It's too early in the investigation to determine that," responded Carlson, "but indications could well show that indeed the victim may have been raped."

"What was the cause of death?"

"Again, we'll have to wait for the medical examiner's report, but the victim was severely beaten with multiple stab wounds in the upper torso and head area. But again, nothing is definitive until the coroner's office has had a chance to conduct a thorough examination," noted Carlson.

"Lieutenant . . . this is the now the latest of several identifiable murders in the past few months in the Knoxville area. All of those cases seem to have many similarities," stated one reporter. "Is it possible that a serial killer is terrorizing our community, and should young women be afraid to go out at night?"

"I'm not going to stand here and draw any conclusions as to whether the murders that you speak of have any connection, and I'm certainly not going to surmise at this time that they are the work of a serial killer," responded the now impatient Carlson.

"That's all the questions I'm going to take until we have something more definitive to say," he concluded. "Until then, we urge all citizens to take extra precautions, especially at night, until we have a better handle on what's happening here."

Fletcher watched the entire interview as he sat on the edge of his desk, hand on his chin, pondering the developing situation.

Grabbing his phone, he buzzed his assistant. "Get me Steve Downs at the Crime Analysis Unit ASAP," he barked.

Within moments his assistant buzzed him back. "Mr. Downs on line 1," she said.

"Steve . . . Aiden Fletcher here. How are you?"

"I was doing fine until this morning, sir," replied the somber Downs, a twenty-year veteran of the force.

"Listen, I'm wondering if you could do me a favor," said Fletcher. "I'd like to be kept in the loop on the ongoing investigation of the murders that have occurred recently. I think it's imperative that our offices work closely together until we can get a better handle on what's happening," he declared.

"No problem," responded Downs. "I think that's a good idea. I'll see to it you get a daily briefing from one of our investigators."

"Be sure to include a full update on any forensic findings if you would," added Fletcher.

"Sure thing," replied Downs. "Hopefully, we'll find the sick bastard that's pulling this shit before he strikes again," noted Downs.

"Do you think it's the same guy?" asked the now-curious Fletcher.

"Shit, yes!" replied the animated Downs. "These guys are never happy with just one kill. They're driven by the thrill . . . by the power of it. He'll be back unless we can shut him down."

"The sooner, the better," added Fletcher, pacing behind his desk.

"I'll be in touch," said Downs. "Talk to you soon."

"Much obliged," responded Fletcher.

Hanging up the phone, the TV continued to report on the breaking headline that by now, most of the citizens of Knoxville were just waking up to:

"Is A Serial Killer Stalking Knoxville?"

Slumping back into his chair, Fletcher stared motionless for several long moments at the ceiling fan slowly spinning overhead, deep in thought as the slightest of smirks began to cross his furrowed lips.

A sick bastard indeed, he thought.

Chapter Seven

Fletcher knew after speaking to Downs that things would be escalating and quickly. Picking up the phone, Fletcher buzzed the one person who played an integral part in the meteoric rise of his career. The person who would help orchestrate Fletcher's handling of what would shape up to be a significant public relations event for him as well as the rest of the elected officials in Knoxville.

Brian Asher, only thirty-five, had the legal and organizational skills of an individual much older. As Fletcher's Deputy, they had worked closely together in the Attorney General's Office, where Asher had worked for the Major Crimes Division and Investigations Unit.

Asher had grown up in Boston and had graduated with honors from Yale Law School, but had wanted out of the parochial environment of his New England youth. One of his classmates was a Tennessean and had urged Asher to join him in starting a small firm in Knoxville specializing in corporate work, an area that Asher soon discovered was too mundane for his liking.

On the cusp of accepting an offer as a regulatory attorney in Washington, DC, Asher instead decided to stay in Knoxville and get into criminal law, a field he found much more interesting. He found his way to the Sixth District Attorney General's Office. He had worked with Fletcher on several cases where he had impressed Fetcher with his logic and brilliant investigative skills.

He was an astute young attorney who did his best work behind the scenes while allowing others, like Fletcher, to command the public arena of the courtroom and city hall. Apart from having become friends, they had developed a mutual trust and respect for the other. They had always worked well together to the benefit of each other.

Fletcher made Asher the offer to be his Deputy Attorney General. He knew that Asher would find the work rewarding. Asher had the political skills to run interference to keep Fletcher isolated from the bureaucratic red tape that was part and parcel of his position as Attorney General. They had spent many a night over beers discussing their work and Fletcher had admired Asher's upright principles and courage under fire. He was also loyal to a fault.

"Did you see the news this morning?" Fletcher asked as Asher strolled into the office, reading a news clipping.

"Who hasn't," replied the preoccupied Asher, shuffling the newspaper.

"I just got off the phone with Steve Downs at the Crime Analysis Unit," Fletcher began. "They are going to keep us informed on everything that's happening with these murders, and I want you to liaison with his office on a daily basis."

"Sure," replied Asher. "Good strategy."

"I want to know where they expect the next murder to occur; what stakeouts they may be putting in place; how they intend to investigate the forensics they've collected; their entire strategy," Fletcher added.

"Yeah, I know Jim Jordan in Downs' office. I'll arrange a status call twice a day to discuss everything that's going on,"

Asher responded. "That way, at least we'll be on the same page when it comes to dealing with the media."

"So, what's your take on all this, Brian?" Fletcher asked, knowing Asher would have some pretty unique insights on the events.

"Hard to say, but I'm betting the killer is a long time, down-and-out local whose had some bad things happen recently . . . divorce, wife cheating on him. Who knows? But probably someone with some pretty deep-seated issues who is just recently finding a reason to act on them," concluded Asher.

"That's kind of what I'm thinking," Fletcher replied, pondering Asher's comments. "In any event, we are going to have to think about setting up a trial team once we nab this guy to prepare for what should be a humongous criminal case."

"Undoubtedly," responded Asher. "This will be one time we definitely want to get it right," he added, anticipating the inevitable appeals that would arise from a potential conviction.

"OK then," responded Fletcher, "that is priority No. 1. It takes precedence over everything else we've got going on, at least for the time being. Got that?"

"Yep, you got it," replied the no-nonsense Asher, briskly turning to exit Fletcher's office.

They both understood the significance of the events that had transpired without saying anything more.

For Fletcher, the stakes were huge, and he intended to take advantage in ways that no one but he could have ever imagined.

* * * * * * * *

The murders continued late into the fall, when two more bodies of young women were discovered in various locations in and around the southern part of Knoxville. One body was discovered in a field near a trailer park exit, the victim identified as Marcia Thomas, twenty-four, a waitress at a sports bar off Kingston Pike in Bearden. The other victim, Theresa Abbott, twenty-six, a salesclerk with a home address near the West Town Mall, located directly off Interstates 40 and 75. Her body had shown up in a parking garage nearby.

Both had been severely beaten and stabbed to death, but only Abbott had been sexually assaulted.

Asher had received the latest update from the Crime Analysis Unit and was briefing Fletcher in his office.

"Just got a call from Steve Downs' office," he began. "Looks like the DNA from the semen found in the latest victim, Marcia Thomas, matches the DNA extracted from the two other women who were raped," he began.

"That's encouraging," replied the otherwise nonchalant Fletcher. "Anyone, we know?"

"Unfortunately, not," replied Asher. "Forensics combed the CODIS databases and not a single perp match . . . sorry to say."

CODIS is the acronym for the Combined DNA Index System. DNA evidence collected from a sexual assault victim is categorized by the FBI support program and run against state databases of convicted offenders and arrestee profiles. If the candidate matches an offender profile, the laboratory will go through procedures to confirm the match and if confirmed, identify the suspected perpetrator. CODIS is also utilized against the states' database of crime scene DNA profiles called the Forensic Index, which, if the evidence matches can confirm that the same DNA linked two or more crimes.

"So, we don't have an identifiable perp, but we know at least three of the cases are linked, correct?" concluded Fletcher.

"Correct, boss," replied Asher.

"So, what is the Homicide Unit thinking about what's going on?" asked the inquisitive Fletcher.

"Well, apparently they've had a lot of discussions of who might be behind these crimes," said Asher, "and there appears to be a split of opinion on whether we're talking about one perp or two."

"What's your take?" asked Fletcher, sincerely interested in his assistant's perspective.

"Well, tell you the truth, I can see it going either way," Asher exclaimed. "On the one hand, the odds of having two serial killers in the same area during the same time period seems a little remote, but on the other hand, there appears to be some distinct discrepancies in the victimology," responded Asher.

"For example?" asked Fletcher.

"Well, three of the earlier victims were brunettes, while the latest are all blonds or some variant of such."

"So, you think hair color has something to do with how the perp selects his victims?" said Fletcher.

"It might," replied Asher. "It's not uncommon for serial killers to pursue victims based on similar characteristics of a significant female in their life . . . most often their mother."

"Yeah, but all these women are in the same age range and, from what I've read, quite attractive. Wouldn't that be an equally driving force to the killer, irrespective of hair color, especially a guy rejected by the majority of women he has encountered in his life?" noted Fletcher.

"Of course, that's distinctly possible," admitted Asher. "I'm just trying to examine all the possibilities," he added.

"As we should," commended Fletcher, reaching for the latest victim assessment report.

"But there's something else that bugs me," stated Asher. "The remains of the first two or three victims revealed no evidence of stab wounds, unlike the last two," noted Asher.

"Of course not," countered Fletcher. "They were largely skeletonized. How could they?"

"It's a stretch, I know," replied Asher, "but there might have been a reasonably good chance a plunging knife might have left a chipped bone or something."

"Possibly, but highly unlikely," said the dismissive Fletcher.

"I guess I would have to agree on that point," admitted Asher, "but I'm not quite convinced this is all the work of one guy."

"We'll let the evidence steer us wherever it goes," replied Fletcher, in a tone that indicated he clearly did not expect a different result.

"Well, that's just where we are at the present time," said Asher, not wishing to pursue the point. "So, what's your perspective, boss?" knowing Fletcher had absorbed every detail of the investigation to date.

"I'm pretty well convinced it's one guy," responded the self-assured Fletcher, in an uncharacteristic display of expeditious judgment. The forcefulness of Fletcher's conviction had taken Asher a bit by surprise.

"You seem awfully certain of yourself," said the questioning Asher.

"I've just got a gut feeling about it," replied the confident Fletcher.

"Think about it," he began. "Here we have the remains of several women with nothing in common," Fletcher began.

"This is not an organized killer," he continued. "He is far more impulsive. He murders indiscriminately. He doesn't plan his crimes methodically. Sure, there are common features to his victims . . . attractive young women; but he's into it for a purpose. He probably has few interpersonal social skills sufficient to enable him to develop relationships with women, so he acts far more impulsively. He doesn't think things out. He's most likely a loner, has a low IQ, and there's a good likelihood he's unemployed."

Fletcher continued. "This guy has advanced his rage from the point of going from having beaten and strangled his victims to an up close and personal encounter. His MO is changing as he has become more disorganized in his approach. The more he kills, the more he gets off on it. Merely strangling his victims is not enough. He wants to feel their lives seep out of them as he repeatedly plunges his knife into them. The control is what motivates him; sexual fantasy and otherwise. His killing of these women is a tremendous source of gratification to him, and he develops his MO around that gratification."

Asher sat nearly speechless as he absorbed the clinical-like recitation that Fletcher had just provided. The man is brilliant, he thought. It was not the first time he had come to that conclusion.

Fletcher continued, "I think there is a good chance the killer is a deeply religious type. We are in the Bible Belt, are we not?" Asher just nodded.

"I think the guy suffers from a psychotic break from reality and actually believes that God mandates his killings. I believe he thinks it's his mission to justify his acts by ridding the world of such undesirables because they are not doing God's will, whatever he interprets that as being. For all we know, he might view all women as prostitutes, and the ones he murders are simply at the wrong place at the wrong time."

After a pause to assess Fletcher's comments, Asher spoke. "That's good . . . that's really good . . . the best summation I've heard anyone give regarding these crimes. I think you're really on to something," he added.

"Tell the investigators we need to focus the search on one guy and one guy only. I'll bet you my next paycheck, I'm right on this," Fletcher asserted.

"I'm not taking that bet," said the now clearly converted Asher. "You've convinced me." He sat in his chair, taking in the tour de force argument that Fletcher has just propounded. He was in awe of Fletcher's command of the psychological peculiarities of the still at-large murderer.

Leaving Fletcher's office, Asher couldn't process the depth of Fletcher's analysis. It was almost as if he had gained access into the killer's head, and he chuckled to himself. Then again, his wife was a forensic psychiatrist, and he might have received substantial insight from her.

Whatever the case, Fletcher had convinced him and law enforcement that beyond any reasonable doubt, one guy was responsible for the swath of murders that was now terrorizing Knoxville. Fletcher, working in conjunction with the Knoxville police, would proceed forward, operating exclusively on that basic assumption.

Chapter Eight

The unsettling nature of the random, ongoing attacks was terrorizing the City of Knoxville. The public uproar over the murders grew by the week as law enforcement officials seemed clueless about the identity of the perpetrator. The warnings began as admonitions that the public exercise a heightened sense of caution and soon escalated to a feeling of abject fear. Young women all but ceased going to the bars or engaging in other activities that took them into the city at night and numerous activities were canceled.

Numerous leads came pouring in, all of which had to be checked out, with none providing any credible evidence that led to anything other than a dead end. The police explained to the elected officials that they were at a loss as to where the investigation was headed.

TV stations were running stories and editorials nearly every evening condemning the police department for "dragging their feet" on the investigation. At the same time, man-on-the-street interviews displayed an ever-increasing frustration with what appeared to be a lack of progress in the cases. Soon, it appeared the coverage was as much about the police ineptitude to protect the public and capture the killer as it was about the killer himself.

It seemed for a while that more journalists were reporting on the events than law enforcement officers who were investigating them. The media seemed obsessed with the story. Between the reporters, camera crews, and photographers, they produced an overwhelming amount of content that saturated the airwaves and the newsprint to the near exclusion of practically everything else. Some questioned whether the all-pervasive media coverage didn't escalate the fear and apprehensions of the citizenry beyond what they should have been. They called on the general managers of local television stations to temper their nearly non-stop coverage of the story in their daily broadcasts.

The authorities set up a toll-free number for anyone with information that could lead police to the killer's identity, which resulted in scores of "leads," all of which seemed to feed the media frenzy for information on the murders. Forensic psychologists and behavioral analysts soon became regular guests on the morning and evening news broadcasts as people tuned in to their evolving speculation as to what type of person might be committing the heinous acts.

Soon the public's demand for answers reached the boiling point. At a regularly scheduled news conference of the local media and concerned citizens with the Mayor and Police Chief, the pressure grew to a fever pitch:

Reporter: "Mr. Mayor, Jack Taylor of WBIR-TV. The citizens of this community have been told for weeks now that law enforcement has been hotly pursuing numerous leads in the murders of several young women in the Knoxville area. Still, to date, nothing has been presented to the public which gives them confidence that the investigations have progressed."

"What do you say to the citizens of Knoxville who have the right to be informed as to what is occurring in their community?"

Mayor Whitley: "I will have to defer to Chief Cummings on where the investigation currently stands. I can assure you of this . . . we are using every tool at our disposal to see to it that the individual or individuals responsible for these reprehensible crimes are taken off the streets and held responsible for their actions."

Reporter: "That's well and good, Mr. Mayor, but what does that mean exactly? You aren't giving us any useful information that will provide the general public with any confidence that this killer will soon be apprehended. The public demands more!" the near-screaming Taylor concluded. The audience then burst into spontaneous applause.

Mayor Whitley: "Folks . . . believe me, I understand the frustrations that people are feeling. I have a family here too. No one is safe until the person responsible for these grisly murders is locked up, and we are working overtime to see that happens as soon as possible," said the beaten-down Whitley. "But let me turn this over to Chief Cummings for a few words."

Gladly stepping off the podium, the flustered Mayor turned the dais over to the Chief of Police.

Chief Cummings: "Ladies and Gentlemen; members of the media, I echo everything the Mayor has just said about the ongoing efforts that the Police Department, in conjunction with the Mayor's Office, and the District Attorney's Office have undertaken to identify and arrest the person or persons responsible for these murders. I would like to share with you some of the tactics we are undertaking in pursuit of those responsible, but that simply is not possible. Rest assured, in the coming days, we expect to make an arrest and return our streets to the citizens of this community."

Reporter: "Chief Cummings . . . you just mentioned the idea that you may be dealing with the prospect of more than one killer. Is that an accurate assessment of where the evidence is now leading?"

Chief Cummings: "We cannot exclude any possibility at this point, but the prevailing feeling within the Department and especially the Attorney General's Office is that we are dealing with a single killer who is responsible for all the murders which have taken place during the past year."

Reporter: "So is your investigation proceeding principally on that assumption?"

Chief Cummings: "Yes. Most definitely."

Reporter: "So are you ready to officially confirm that we have a serial killer in our midst here in Knoxville?"

Cummings paused ever-so-briefly and spoke candidly. "Yes. I'm afraid we do."

The admission only seemed to intensify the audience's anxiety.

Suddenly an agitated, middle-aged man leapt from his chair in the audience and yelled.

"You people had better get to the bottom of this, or we will find someone that will!" he screamed. "I've got a nineteen-year-old daughter who has to commute on city transportation every day and night to go to work, and I'm scared to death for her well-being."

The audience again erupted in hoots and howls. The entire room was on the verge of disorder. Sensing that the meeting needed to end quickly, Chief Cummings brought it to an abrupt conclusion.

"Bear with us, folks," he requested. "We are doing our best, and I promise you we will bring those responsible for these heinous crimes to justice. You have my word on that."

Watching the news conference from his office, Fletcher was generally pleased with how it had gone. The fervor over the continuing threat was ratcheting up, and the Chief had managed to convey the critical notion to the public that authorities were searching for a single killer.

Everything was shaping up exactly the way it needed to, he calmly thought.

* * * * * * * *

It was nearly 11:00 a.m. two days later when the phone rang at the Knoxville Police Department.

"Central Dispatch, where can I direct your call?" said the operator.

"Uh . . . I'd like to talk to someone about the . . . uh . . . murder of the girl up near the West Town Mall," the voice stated.

The operator, sensing something different about this call, put the female caller directly through to Detective Michael Rossi, who was leading the investigations into the murders of the young women.

"Detective Rossi," he quickly asserted, grabbing the phone. "Who is this I'm speaking with?" He could tell the person on the other end was quite nervous.

"This is Carolyn," replied the anxious woman.

"Can I get your last name, Carolyn?" Rossi politely asked.

"Chapin," she said, "Carolyn Chapin."

"OK thanks, Carolyn," responded Rossi.

"Can you tell me why you called today?"

"It's about that young girl that you found in the parking garage up near the West Town Mall," the edgy woman responded.

She now had Rossi's full attention. "What did you want to tell me about that Carolyn?" he cautiously asked.

"I think I may have seen who the man was that killed her," she nervously replied.

The hair on the back of Rossi's neck stood on end. "Carolyn, listen to me," said the exuberant Rossi. I'm going to send a patrol car to pick you up and bring you down to the station. Here you'll be able to tell us everything you have to say. Is that OK, Carolyn?"

"Sure, I guess," she said. "I don't want to cause any trouble."

"Believe me, Carolyn, you're not causing any trouble," responded the animated Rossi. He got her address and dispatched a patrol car to pick her up.

Within the hour, a female officer was escorting a middle-aged woman with long, brown hair and little makeup into the police conference room, where several investigators had gathered to hear what she had to say. After introductions, Rossi turned on a tape recorder and broke the ice:

"Tell us, Carolyn, what did you see in the garage? Don't leave out a single detail."

"Well, I work at the Chipotle Mexican Restaurant in the Mall. I've been working there for seven years."

"Yes, go on," replied the eager Rossi.

"Well, I got off work after we closed at 10:00 p.m., actually it was closer to 10:30 p.m. after we cleaned up for the night," she added. "So, I got in my car, parked right outside the restaurant next to the parking garage."

"Is that where you saw something?" interjected Rossi.

"At first, I didn't think much about it because the garage is almost always empty that time of night," she continued.

"As I was getting ready to start the engine of my car, I saw a man drive past me in an old, beat-up pick-up truck with a woman in the front seat who was all bloody. She wasn't moving at all," Carolyn said.

"Now tell me, Carolyn, did you get a good look at the man?" exclaimed Rossi.

"Well, I was getting ready to leave, but I knew there was something that just wasn't quite right with the situation. So I got out of my car and hid behind a dumpster nearby. I was watching as he drove his truck to the end of the entrance of the parking garage and went up the ramp."

"What did you do next?" asked one of the investigators.

"Like I said, I waited a couple of minutes, and sure enough, here comes that pick-up back down the ramp, only this time the woman wasn't in the front seat with him," she asserted.

"Just as he drove right past me, one of our clean-up crew was throwing a trash bag from the kitchen into the dumpster. The driver turned unexpectedly right toward me, but I don't think he ever saw me."

"Did you get a good look at him?" asked the inquisitive Rossi.

"Oh, I got a very good look at him," responded Carolyn, now growing in confidence.

"How would you describe him?" asked another investigator as everyone at the table was hurriedly taking notes.

"I would say mid-forties, kind of a rough-looking dude," she said. "Looks like he wasn't very clean . . . wearing overalls, and had a beard. He had on a red shirt and a black baseball cap."

"Could you tell what kind of truck he was driving?" Rossi asked.

"Looked like an old Ford F-150, like a mid-eighties kind of truck."

"Do you remember what color the truck was?"

"Red with white stripes down both sides," she replied.

"Anything else you may have noticed about the truck?"

"Yeah," she volunteered. "It had a Bass Pro Shops decal on the window and a bumper sticker in the back that said, "Country Boy."

"Carolyn, let me ask you a very important question," began Rossi. "Would you be able to describe this guy to a police sketch artist?"

"I think so, yes," said an assured Carolyn.

"What if we gave you a bit of a break and then let you spend some time with the police sketch artist. Do you have time to do that for us?" Rossi asked

"Well, I was going shopping with my daughter this afternoon, but yeah, I can do that later," said Carolyn.

Carolyn gave her daughter a call and after a snack, sat down with Julia Shelby, a police artist who had been providing suspect sketches for fifteen years.

Nearly two hours later, the two emerged and presented Rossi with a composite drawing of the man Carolyn had said she had seen. He had a receding hairline and a squinty, dull-looking expression and what looked like a four-day-old beard. He had a bulbous nose, and his hair was medium brown with flecks of gray and uncombed. The most noticeable aspect, however, was his dull and dark eyes.

* * * * * * * *

Homicide detectives wasted no time getting the composite sketch of the man on the local news. The airways pasted the image across every TV screen in Knoxville with the admonition: "If you think you have seen this man, contact the Knoxville Police immediately. Do not try to apprehend him as he is considered armed and very dangerous."

Within twenty-four hours, numerous tips came into investigators, each claiming they might have seen the suspect. Then the one they were waiting for finally made contact.

"Homicide Division may I help you?" asked one of the investigators.

"Yes, sir, I think I may know who the serial killer is," announced the voice.

"Who do you think it is?" asked the excited investigator.

"I think the man in the sketch is Otis Stamper," he continued.

"And why do you think you know that?" inquired the investigator.

"Because he lives on a small farm right down the road from me."

Chapter Nine

Otis Stamper was born in the backwoods of East Tennessee to Ruby Stamper, an uneducated, overwhelmed single mother and a father who had abandoned them soon after his birth. Initially raised by his mother until he was five, the two of them moved to Boyds Creek to live with his grandparents who were hard-shelled Baptists.

His mother worked part-time as a check-out clerk at a local farmer's supply store to augment her SSI disability check. She had an array of short-term boyfriends who always seemed to follow the same pattern . . . abusive and alcoholic.

Otis was of low to medium intelligence with an undistinguished school record and few friends. At the age of seven, in the wee hours of the morning, he was found banging loudly on the mailbox in his grandparent's yard. Otis later recalled he did it to "scare away the meanies." Although he engaged in illusions for years, he was never referred for psychological counseling by either his mother or his school. At age nine, he set the family's chicken coup on fire, which killed several chickens and a family goat.

Shortly thereafter, his grandfather died, leaving his upbringing to an often shacked-up and boozy mother and a completely incapable grandmother, who regularly called his philandering mother a "whore who was doomed to hell."

Through his high school years, he played tackle on his school's football team. Despite his large physical frame, he never committed enough time to the endeavor to earn a college scholarship, which his coach and several others thought, with a little effort, he was capable of getting.

He was suspended from school on several occasions for fighting and cited for simple marijuana possession at age fourteen. As a juvenile, he engaged in numerous petty offenses, including drunk and disorderly charges, and had gotten an out-of-town girl pregnant by the time he was fifteen. He spent an inordinate amount of time viewing sadomasochistic pornography and he often fantasized about running a brothel full of young, beautiful whores.

After years of misdirection and an unstable family life, Otis dropped out of high school. He left home, living in several out-of-the-way towns throughout the Tri-State area of Tennessee, Virginia, and North Carolina. While working as a day laborer and car mechanic, Otis lived at a subsistence level. Otis' pay was augmented by selling marijuana, which he grew in an isolated field in the back acreage of a friend's farm.

He married at age twenty-three to a restaurant worker and lived in Bristol, Tennessee, in a quaint trailer park. The marriage lasted two years until the wife ran off with another man and was never seen again.

Stamper spent the next several years banging around the area of Asheville and Hendersonville, North Carolina, before finding steady and lucrative work as part-owner of a small carpentry shop. Over this period of time, he enjoyed a relatively peaceful existence with very few run-ins with the law.

At age forty, he met a forty-five-year-old woman with two grown children. She convinced him to cash out his small share of his carpentry shop so the two could move to her hometown of Kingsport. After finding reliable work at a mill, the two married and rented a small home on the northern outskirts of the city near the Virginia state line.

For two years, the couple lived in modest tranquility until the wife began to lose interest in Stamper, which according to friends, stemmed from his lack of social skills and far-right ideals. There were rumors of her sexual infidelity as well.

Finally, while driving through a section of Kingsport, Stamper noticed his wife's car parked in a lot near a local motel. Parking across the street near a used car lot, he waited until his wife left the motel in the company of another man, who Stamper immediately recognized as one of her colleagues from work. Arriving home later that afternoon, he confronted her about her infidelity, and when she attempted to lie about the encounter he beat her severely, repeatedly calling her a "dirty whore."

After the police were called, they charged him with domestic abuse and a thirty-day restraining order was issued. Grabbing what few belongings he could pack in his truck, instead of finding a temporary place to stay in Kingsport, Stamper just kept driving on I-81 southwest.

Stamper arrived back in Boyds Creek, the small farming community where he had grown up and rented a small, rundown caretaker's house on a two-hundred-acre corn and soybean farm. He lived essentially as a recluse, going into Knoxville only when necessary and spending most of his day after working in the fields drinking Jack Daniel's whiskey on his front porch.

He was constantly in a dour mood, still angry at his wife's infidelity. All the young women he noticed at the Knoxville bars were attractive and seemed to have something going for them, unlike himself. None of these women, who he inevitably referred to as "whores," would ever be inclined to associate with him, and he could feel their disdain whenever their eyes met.

After years of feeling alienated by women, Stamper stumbled into his truck late one night after a heavy round of drinking at a local pub south of town. He soon noticed an equally inebriated blond woman wobbling across the parking lot behind the bar, saying goodbye to her friends. As they drove off, the woman went to enter her car when a sudden and uncontrollable urge came over Stamper. Sneaking quickly up behind her, he hit her on the head with a brick and carried her back into his truck.

He drove off with her bloodied and unconscious in the front seat as he made his way to a deserted area near Ft. Loudon Lake, where he had spent many weekends during his youth. When he found a secluded spot in a deserted rest area, he pulled her out of the cab and began to rape her repeatedly.

Coming to, she began to scream loudly, repeatedly calling him "a filthy animal," when Stamper, in an abject rage, pulled out the large serrated knife he kept on his belt and stabbed her over and over. When done, he drove his truck back to his farm in Boyds Creek. Once there, he wiped the front seat and floor with water and a crop herbicide in an attempt to eliminate the modicum of blood she had left after he knocked her unconscious.

Afterward, Stamper sat on his front porch in the warm air of the Tennessee night with his dog and pornographic magazines and drank copious amounts of whiskey. He felt an overwhelming sense of power and liberation. No longer a victim of women . . . his mother, his wife, all the women who had rejected him . . . those "dirty whores." They were now his victims, and he had an invigorating feeling of control over them.

It was a feeling he wanted to experience again.

* * * * * * * * *

Boyds Creek was a small, unincorporated community in Sevier County, Tennessee, located about twenty miles southeast of Knoxville. It was nothing more than a collection of small farms in the rolling countryside of East Tennessee. The townspeople would venture into Knoxville for their more serious shopping beyond the local Home Depot and Dollar General Store. At the same time, a John Deere dealer and Dairy Queen provided what little local employment there was in the sparsely populated area.

A few miles north of Boyds Creek was Indian Warpath Road, off the French Broad River, a small, two-lane state road that intersected with Route 3336, a one-lane road which led to a series of small parcels of land, primarily used to grow corn, hay, and soybeans.

The Knox County Sheriff's Department, the Sevier County Police, and the Tennessee State Police responded to the caller's tip and, after nearly an hour of tactical strategy calls, assembled a few miles west of Boyds Creek and immediately blocked off Indian Warpath Road in both directions.

A tactical SWAT team proceeded within a few hundred yards of a small, rundown farmhouse with two vehicles in front. One was a flatbed hay-hauling truck and the other, a red and white Ford F-150. Running a check on the pick-up's tag indicated the vehicle was registered to Otis Stamper, a long-time Boyds Creek resident who lived alone on the edge of one of the fully planted soybean fields.

As the SWAT team surrounded the house, a nearly wild dog began to bark incessantly at their approach. Suddenly a shot rang out from inside the house, hitting one of the SWAT members directly in the front of his bulletproof vest. The impact knocked him down but otherwise caused no harm.

A second shot hit one of the officers in the arm, and the other members immediately carried him off to safety. The unit opened a barrage of fire on the house with their assault rifles, pummeling the façade and obliterating the front door. Within moments, the firing ceased and the SWAT leader raised a megaphone to his lips.

"Otis Stamper . . . This is the police. Drop your weapon and come out with your hands up!" bellowed the leader.

"I repeat . . . drop your weapon and come out with your hands up!"

For what seemed like an inordinate amount of time, nothing happened. Then, just as the tactical team was going to tear gas the structure, a man's voice echoed from inside the house.

"OK . . . OK . . . I'm coming out!" Otis screamed. "Don't shoot!"

"Hands up . . . drop your weapon, or you're a dead man!" ordered the leader of the SWAT team as a half-dozen rifles were aimed at the front door.

Slowly, the door began to rattle and nearly disintegrated as Stamper deliberately moved to exit the dwelling.

Stepping outside to the front porch with his hands in the air, Stamper was instantly surrounded by the SWAT team. After being thrown to the ground, he was immediately handcuffed by an officer while another slammed his knee into Stamper's spine.

Escorting him to a police vehicle, the SWAT leader sought to ascertain his identity.

"Are you Otis Stamper?" demanded the terse-sounding officer.

"What the fuck is it to you?" replied the caustic suspect, whose body odor was palpable.

"I'll ask you again," repeated the officer, twisting his cuffed arms in a most painful way. "Are you Otis Stamper?"

"OK . . . OK, I'm Otis Stamper . . . so the fuck what?"

The SWAT leader pushed the suspect into the back of a patrol vehicle after reading his Miranda rights and announced, "You are under arrest for suspicion in the murder of Theresa Abbott in Knox County."

"Theresa, who?" asked the seemingly confused suspect. "I didn't fucking kill anybody named Theresa," replied Stamper, as the door to the squad car closed and it sped off. Three other vehicles, sirens blaring, escorted Stamper on the twenty-mile trip back to Knoxville.

* * * * * * * *

The SWAT leader immediately called Chief Cummings office, who anxiously awaited word on the arrest along with Mayor Whitley. A collective cheer went up in Cummings' office as the official word was given that Stamper was indeed in police custody. An immediate call was made to the media to announce that a major press conference would be convened regarding the serial murders within the hour.

In the meantime, police-scanner radios in the cars of numerous crime-beat reporters had already made their way to Stamper's farm in Boyds Creek to get first-hand interviews with the remaining arresting officers at the scene. As TV cameras began rolling across the front of the house, one focused on a close-up of Stamper's pick-up. The camera quickly zoomed to the bumper on the back of the truck, where an oversized sticker blurted the soon to be famous phrase

"Country Boy."

* * * * * * * *

The hastily called press conference convened in the main auditorium of City Hall as the TV cameras rolled.

The Mayor confidently approached the podium and announced:

"Ladies and Gentlemen, excuse the impromptu nature of this press conference, but I am delighted to announce that the prime suspect in the Knoxville serial murders has been arrested and taken into custody. His name is Otis Stamper, forty-three, of Boyds Creek in Sevier County; an eyewitness identified Stamper in connection with the murder of Theresa Abbott, twenty-four, just a few weeks ago."

"Do you have evidence tying him to any of the other murders, Mr. Mayor?" came the immediate first question from one of the assorted newspersons gathered.

"We have DNA evidence that we believe will tie him directly to at least two of the other murders you reference, and we have probable cause to believe he is most likely responsible for the remaining four murders as well."

"So, you expect indictments in all seven of the recent murders in Knox County?"

"We'll wait and see what evidence is presented to the Grand Jury," responded the confident Mayor. "In fact, Attorney

General Fletcher's office will be presenting evidence to the Grand Jury this afternoon, and we fully expect indictments to be returned in all seven of the outstanding cases."

"What can you tell us about the suspect?" asked another reporter.

"Well, as I described in my opening comments, Mr. Stamper was arrested today at his farm after engaging in a shoot-out with sheriff's deputies and the State Police. We've conducted a preliminary review and apart from a few minor run-ins with the law as a juvenile, Mr. Stamper does not have an active criminal record," the Mayor asserted.

"Is your review confined to the Knox County area?" asked another reporter.

"No, sir," replied the Mayor. "We are in contact with other jurisdictions both in Tennessee and surrounding states. We are investigating whether he may have been arrested under another name or in connection with some cold cases that have yet to be solved. We are awaiting information on those inquiries."

"At this time, all we know from talking to a few neighboring farm owners and locals in the area is that Mr. Stamper attended Seymour High School in Sevier County. He was believed to be single and was considered to be somewhat of a recluse. Apart from frequenting some local markets and bars in the area, he is not known to have socialized with many people in the community."

After another forty-five minutes of extensive questioning, the news conference terminated, leaving many more questions for the media and public alike. Though such inquiries remained unanswered, they quickly gave way to an immediate and enormous sense of relief that resonated throughout the city. After months of trepidation, people felt they could wander outside their homes and even meet in public places in safety for the first time in ages.

By the afternoon, the mayor's press conference continued to broadcast on every TV and radio station in Knoxville. The story was picked up nationally as well. Video from the arrest at Stamper's farm was shown over and over again and seemed to inevitably focus on the bumper sticker of his truck which had given its name to the entire episode. Later that night, the official mug shot of Stamper was disseminated to every news outlet in Knoxville under the now all-pervasive moniker:

"Arrest Made in 'Country Boy' Murders"

Chapter Ten

Watching every moment of the mayor's news conference while holding a phone to his ear communicating with the homicide investigation team, Brian Asher ushered his way into Fletcher's office as he was taking one call after the next regarding the arrest of Otis Stamper.

"Martha . . . hold all my calls for the next half hour," Fletcher barked to his legal assistant.

"What d'ya have, Brian?" he anxiously asked Asher.

"I'm in touch with the General Sessions Court Clerk," Asher responded. "She thinks we can impanel a Grand Jury this afternoon, sometime after four."

"Has the suspect retained counsel yet?" asked Fletcher.

"Apparently there's not a reputable criminal defense attorney in Knox County who'll touch this case," replied Asher. "Although most would like the publicity, they know damn well if they took it, their standing in the community would turn to shit, so hardly anyone will touch it."

"Not hard to understand," replied Fletcher. "Doesn't matter. The court has probably already appointed a Public Defender," he smirked, knowing the second-tier quality of some of the local attorneys at the Public Defender's Office would make a conviction much more likely.

"Get in touch with Homicide," ordered Fletcher. "Make sure they have Carolyn Chapin ready to testify. Also, I'm going to need the investigative files and the forensic data for all seven of the cases to present to the Grand Jury."

"You're going for indictments on all seven cases?" exclaimed the greatly surprised Asher. "I know we have the DNA matches for three of them, but the others . . . I don't know about that boss."

"No time to argue," asserted Fletcher, taking control. "We have enough circumstantial evidence to seek indictments on all of them."

"Aiden, I know you want to get this guy and close these cases out, but I think you may be jumping the gun," stated a now slightly flustered Asher. His boss rushing to judgment seemed distinctly out of character for the normally judicious Fletcher.

"We're going after all seven," demanded Fletcher. He was in no mood to hear anything to the contrary.

"What if we only get convictions on some of the murders? If he's acquitted on other counts, the public's fear that there may be a second killer on the loose is going to start up all over again. Why not wait until we can get more evidence before charging on all counts?" Asher logically asserted.

"Like I just said, we have enough circumstantial evidence to pull them all together," repeated the confident Fletcher.

It was soon obvious to Asher that his boss was not taking no for an answer on his intention to seek indictments on all seven counts. His best judgment told him Fletcher's motivations were well beyond merely getting Stamper the death penalty. As usual, his instincts were correct as Fletcher began to preview his strategy.

"Don't you see," stated Fletcher. "We're going to make this the biggest trial this part of the state has ever seen," he began. "It's going to be historical."

"Why don't we just pressure Stamper to cop to a plea in trade for a life sentence with no possibility of parole?" Asher logically deduced. "It would spare the public all the emotional angst that the type of trial you envision would inevitably stir up."

"You don't get it, do you, Brian?" said the now impatient Fletcher. "The type of all-in scenario I'm contemplating is exactly what this community needs . . . and wants!" he exclaimed.

Fletcher continued. "For the better part of two years, the people out there have been paralyzed with fear for themselves and for their children. They want revenge . . . they want blood. They want to see that the monster that did these horrible slayings gets the death penalty. It's primal for them. They want to set an example for other would-be freaks that if you pull this shit in Knox County, rest assured, you're going to die."

Asher was taken back by Fletcher's emotional investment in the case. Almost like it was personal, there was more to it for him, a lot more. Nevertheless, he felt it was his ethical responsibility to persist.

Committing to the tried-and-true approach that he and Fletcher had always practiced, Asher continued to assert his position when his assistant handed him an unopened note.

"In my professional opinion boss, I still believe it is our first and primary legal responsibility to pursue the prudent course and go with what we've got and let the evidence in the other cases develop. Who knows, maybe others will come forward and tie the cases together. He'll be in prison in any event. The threat will be gone."

"Enough!" demanded Fletcher. "I've made up my mind . . . we're going forward." Asher had never seen Fletcher so wound up and so demanding. There had to be something else about Fletcher's insistence that just wasn't adding up. For a moment, the thought of resigning crossed his mind.

Why the hell was he so adamant about this? Asher thought to himself.

"What does your note say?" Fletcher asked, changing the subject.

Opening the folded piece of paper that he had been handed, Asher spoke.

"You were right," he quietly began. "The Court has appointed a Public Defender, and he has just indicated he will not pursue a preliminary hearing."

"Good," replied Fletcher, "saves us a lot of effort and time. We can go straight to the Grand Jury this afternoon."

"OK," said Asher, still stinging from Fletcher's rebuke of his otherwise compelling legal advice.

"Have you thought about who you're going to appoint to lead the prosecution?" Asher asked. "Andrea Mattingly would be outstanding. Born and raised in Knoxville, a top-flight prosecutor, and a mother; a keen mind who would have a real connection to the community at large."

"I have," responded Fletcher, "I've already selected someone."

"Who might that be?" asked the curious Asher. He knew Fletcher almost always discussed such assignments with him and usually relied on his recommendations.

"Me!" retorted the grinning Fletcher. "I'm going to prosecute this case."

Asher couldn't suppress his surprise. The Attorney General never tried cases, especially big ones like this. It kept politics out of the equation. Then he realized what Fletcher had already surmised. It was the politics of the situation that made Fletcher want to lead the case.

"Any objections?" asked the now somber Fletcher, knowing his adamant rejection of Asher's previous advice meant his question was merely pro forma.

"Would it matter if I did?" responded the deflated Asher.

"No," Fletcher tersely responded. After a long pause, he stared directly at Asher.

"Look, Brian . . . you're just going to have to trust me on this. It's not that your advice wasn't prudent. I just have to do what I think is best, and sometimes that means you have to buck conventional wisdom."

"Your call, boss," conceded the now recovering Asher, knowing that he was undoubtedly beaten.

"OK then," stated Fletcher, "get your team prepared to go, and let's get ready for the Grand Jury."

Sitting back in his overstuffed, comfortable chair for a brief respite from the hustle-bustle of the days' events, Fletcher deliberated intently about the capricious hand of fate that had made this moment possible. He shook his head in solitude as he wondered about the meaning of it all . . . about everything that had ever happened to him.

After what Fletcher had been through in his life, the stage was set, and like a highly confident, much-acclaimed actor, he was about to enter stage right.

* * * * * * * *

The Grand Jury room was just down a secluded hallway from Fletcher's office in Suite 152 of the City County Building on Main Street in Knoxville. The thirteen citizens impaneled to determine whether there was "probable cause" to bring formal charges against the accused were typical, everyday men and women from the community with no particular ethnic, or economic make up. Twelve votes were necessary for an indictment, also called a true bill.

Although there was no particular determination of what generally constituted "probable cause," for Grand Jury purposes, it was commonly thought of as evidence which supported a reasonable suspicion of guilt, without the necessity of demonstrating, as in the actual trial of the matter, proof "beyond a reasonable doubt." After they had assembled in the Grand Jury room, Fletcher presented his opening statement.

"Ladies and Gentlemen," he began. "Thank you for being here today. I'm Aiden Fletcher, Sixth District Attorney General." Fletcher made for a commanding presence in the hearing with his well-modulated voice and impeccable attire.

Watching as the members of the Grand Jury listened intently to Fletcher's every word, Asher could now understand why it had been a mistake for him to think that anyone else could have better served as lead prosecutor in the cases before him.

Fletcher began his statement.

"Ladies and Gentlemen, as most of you have undoubtedly been aware, the City of Knoxville for the past couple of years has had a vicious serial killer in our midst." He extended his right arm, pointing to where Otis Stamper sat in leg-irons guarded by three sheriff deputies and continued.

"That serial killer is sitting right in front of you . . . Otis Stamper," Fletcher exclaimed, his arm still outstretched. As he spoke, he was casually eyeing the jury as several of the impaneled women visibly recoiled.

"Today, I will present evidence for your consideration which clearly ties Mr. Stamper to the deaths of seven young women in this community," Fletcher confidently began. "Women who, for lack of any other explanation, were simply at the wrong place at the wrong time."

"I am today offering you the eyewitness testimony of Carolyn Chapin, who can positively place Mr. Stamper in the parking garage where he dumped the body of Theresa Abbott. The forensics evidence will show, she died of numerous stab wounds and was sexually assaulted by Mr. Stamper."

"I will also present evidence which will indicate beyond a reasonable doubt that Otis Stamper sexually molested two of the other victims in this case. We know from forensic testing that Mr. Stamper's DNA was found on the two additional victims, the names of whom are included in the packet I have provided." Fletcher was on a roll.

"But Ladies and Gentlemen, there are four other victims named in this case who demand justice in their own right," he continued. "With the exception of Marcia Thomas, whose body was recently found in a field beaten, and stabbed to death, but not sexually assaulted, all of the remaining victims showed similar injuries and circumstances that coincide with the three victims we just described."

"What are we to make of the fact that the first three victims had no evidence they had been raped or stabbed like the victims who were found more recently?" asked one of the grand jurors.

"That is the essence of our case, Madam Juror," replied the collected Fletcher. "Please keep in mind that the first three victims' bodies were not discovered until some while after their deaths. In fact, they were mostly skeletonized by the time they were found, and it was thus, physically impossible to ascertain whether they had been stabbed or raped, as there simply wasn't sufficient flesh remaining on the body to run those tests," Fletcher postulated.

"We strongly believe and will prove that the same perpetrator . . . Mr. Stamper, killed those women. Their victimology, as well as the circumstances and location of their remains, tie in quite nicely to the locations and the MO of the killer who was responsible for the more recently discovered bodies," Fletcher assuredly explained. "We have little doubt that in addition to being beaten and perhaps strangled, that the earlier victims were stabbed and raped as well."

"How about Marcia Thomas, whose body was recently found in a field?" another juror asked. "She had been stabbed, but had not been sexually assaulted. How should we interpret that situation?" she inquired.

"That's an excellent question, and to answer it, we are going to offer the testimony of our forensic psychologist who will testify that serial killers do not always follow the exact same MO," answered Fletcher. "It might be that he simply just didn't have the time to rape her," he added.

"Just keep in mind Ladies and Gentlemen, that all the victims who have been identified, were between the ages of nineteen to twenty-six and all of them resided in the same general vicinity at the time of their deaths. The odds of two or more serial killers operating in such a tiny defined area as this at the same time are frankly, beyond calculation," asserted the confident Fletcher.

The forcefulness of his presentation was clearly impacting the jurors, as evidenced by many of them nodding their heads in full agreement.

"In any event," Fletcher continued, "there are numerous similarities in the Thomas murder to align it with the previous evidence we have presented in all the other cases."

"And don't forget, Ladies and Gentlemen, the people who kill like this aren't above throwing off the authorities by manipulating the crime scene to serve their own dastardly purposes." That line seemed to resonate with everyone in the room, including Asher.

After wrapping up his presentation, Fletcher presented the testimony of the prosecution's criminal psychologist and Carolyn Chapin, after which Otis Stamper was asked if he wished to say anything in his own defense.

"Y'all just making this shit up," he coarsely began. "You got nothin' on me. I may have fucked a couple of those women, but I didn't kill nobody," he drawled. "I didn't fuckin' kill nobody."

After follow-up remarks by Fletcher, the Grand Jury repaired to their conference room for consideration of the evidence presented. They didn't deliberate long.

* * * * * * * *

An hour later, Asher came charging into Fletcher's office just as Fletcher was getting off the phone.

"We did it!" Asher excitedly proclaimed. "The Grand Jury just returned seven true bills! Seven fucking true bills!"

The men high-fived and congratulated each other on the office's extensive work to get to where they were. Several attorneys down the hall heard the commotion and rushed into Fletcher's office to join the celebration. After a few moments of jubilation, Fletcher put a hiatus on the festivities.

"OK, folks. We've accomplished what we set out to achieve, but now the real work begins," Fletcher announced. "We are not going to stop until we get seven convictions in this case . . . understand? Seven convictions. So thanks again for all your efforts, and let's get back to work."

* * * * * * * *

After another hastily called press conference, this one presided over and masterfully choreographed by Fletcher, the media immediately began to immerse the airways with the now breaking news. Headline after headline led with the same notorious lead:

"Boyds Creek Man Indicted on Seven Counts in 'Country Boy' Murders"

Like a master artist, Fletcher had taken advantage of the entire landscape before him. He had provided the assembled news media with the only sub-heading they would possibly need. It was so brilliantly simple and immediately resonated throughout the community of Knoxville.

In a quietly terse, but emphatic response to one final question as to how confident he felt about the day's events, Fletcher looked straight into the camera and in a Lawrence Olivier moment, gave a discreet smile that spoke a thousand words as he confidently uttered:

"We Got Him. Rest easy my fellow citizens . . .We Got Him!"

* * * * * * * *

"WE GOT HIM," became the rallying cry for a city that had for far too long endured the horror of such senseless killings. It came to represent a new day when the people reclaimed their independence and were no longer afraid to venture outdoors at night. It allowed the citizenry to recapture their sense of everyday security. It represented the new reality that when people came together for a common cause, nothing . . . especially evil, could ever defeat them. It had bonded the community like nothing anyone had ever seen.

Soon bumper stickers began to appear throughout the city, simply stating, "WE GOT HIM."

One ingenious entrepreneur who owned a local sports pub had a bi-plane fly over Neyland Stadium during a UT-Ole Miss football game with a "WE GOT HIM," banner followed by an advertising logo with the bar's name on it. The stadium erupted in a tumultuous roar and the crush of business to the man's establishment over the next several weeks was simply beyond imagination. Another brave soul hung a sheet over the mid-section of the Henley Street Bridge, proudly proclaiming to all who drove past that, "WE GOT HIM."

Even an obscure little Baptist church got in on the commotion by proclaiming on its outdoor bulletin board, "WE GOT HIM," followed by a nifty but humorous little twist on the trend by stating on the second line in smaller print, "That Would Be Jesus of Course!"

"WE GOT HIM," soon dominated the airwaves as the story simply wouldn't go away, it was a phrase that had given the local community a strength of spirit that would never be forgotten.

As for Aiden Fletcher, it was the beginning of something that he could never have imagined.

Chapter Eleven

The trial of Otis Stamper would be the biggest event to hit Knoxville in a generation. Soon, the local media was covering every aspect of his arrest and upcoming prosecution.

At his arraignment hearing, the courtroom was packed with curious observers and a throng of assembled media.

Standing before the arraignment judge and an Assistant District Attorney in an orange jumpsuit and leg-irons with a four-day-old beard, Stamper was a fearsome sight. His course demeanor only added to his menacing persona. But there he was . . . a monster in the flesh!

The public got their first frightening look at the man they felt confident had been the serial killer that had been haunting their lives for so long.

Stamper stood motionless with his attorney, Bradley Foster, a highly capable attorney in the Public Defender's Office until the judge spoke.

"Counsel, have you and your client had the opportunity to review the charges against him?"

Foster: "We have Your Honor."

Staring directly at Stamper, the judge spoke, "If so, how does the defendant plea to the charges contained within the indictment relating to the alleged murders of the seven individuals listed?"

Stamper: "I didn't kill all those people judge."

Judge: "You will be given time to present your case, Mr. Stamper. Right now, I need to know how you plea to the charges against you. After a brief conversation with his attorney, Stamper responded:

Stamper: "Not guilty, but I still didn't kill all those people."

On the question of bail, the judge turned to the Assistant DA and spoke:

"What is the State's recommendation regarding bail in this case?"

"Your Honor, the State strongly argues that bail be denied given the evidence in these cases. The defendant is a clear and present threat to the community-at-large, and we believe he will kill again if not incarcerated immediately."

Turning to Foster, the judge spoke: "What is your response counsel?"

Knowing the chances of getting his client released on bail were zero, Foster didn't even waste time making a case for bail.

"We defer to the court's judgment in this matter, Your Honor," he somberly conceded.

Without a moment of thought, the judge replied, "Bail denied . . . the defendant will be remanded to custody pending trial."

"Trial in this matter will be set for the week of April 19th before Judge Kent Blaine, in Division One of the Sixth District Criminal Court. Hearing adjourned."

That was it. The appearance lasted all of two minutes. Stamper would now be put on trial for the murders of all seven women as charged under the indictment.

* * * * * * * *

In the weeks that followed, the attorneys engaged in extensive discovery and exchanged their lists of witnesses they planned to call, including their expert and character witnesses. After exchanging the investigative reports with Stamper's attorney, the prosecution stood prepared to proceed to the preliminary evidentiary hearing before Judge Blaine.

After addressing several motions filed by the Assistant District Attorney, Judge Blaine turned to Foster:

"Counsel, do you have any motions for the Court's consideration?"

"Yes, Your Honor. We have three motions we'd like to present," Foster replied.

"Proceed," responded the stern Blaine.

"First, Your Honor, the defense moves to dismiss the charges against the defendant as the state's evidence in this case is insufficient to demonstrate guilt on behalf of my client, particularly the evidence presented with respect to at least the first three victims listed in the indictment. . . Mses. Turner, Ellison, and Mattingly. Finally, we ask the same as it relates to the sixth victim named in the indictment, Ms. Thomas," stated Foster.

Blaine had studied the investigative record anticipating the numerous motions filed on behalf of the defendant. He prepared to rule and rule decisively.

"Motion denied, counselor," responded Blaine. "Both you and the State will have an opportunity at trial to address the sufficiency of the evidence against your client. What's your next motion?"

"Your Honor, the defense asks that the Court sustain our motion to suppress certain evidence recovered by the authorities on my client's property shortly after his arrest. This evidence will be used by the state to assert that Mr. Stamper was complicit in the execution of the crimes for which he has been charged. We believe that the police did not have a sufficient search warrant to conduct the full range of its search, and thus any evidence acquired as a consequence should be ruled inadmissible," Foster asserted.

"The fact that certain evidence was seized from an outbuilding on the property where the defendant resided which was not included in the initial warrant should, under the State v. Lindsey Brooke Lowe precedent, be ruled inadmissible," he concluded.

Turning to the Assistant DA, the Judge inquired, "Counsel, what is the State's response?" he queried.

"Your Honor, the warrant, in this case, was more than sufficient as it authorized a search of the defendant's home and the 'surrounding premises,'" replied the ADA. "The fact that the evidence in question, in this case, was discovered in an out-shed located elsewhere on the farm where the defendant resided is insufficient to exclude it as evidence against the defendant, as the wording of the warrant clearly meets the prohibition against an unreasonable search and seizure enunciated under the Lowe exclusionary rule standard," concluded the ADA.

Anticipating the defense's motion, Blaine was ready to rule.

"Although the Lowe standard does prohibit the admission of evidence obtained from an unreasonable search and seizure, the evidence in question was still contained on the property leased by the defendant. Even if not located within the house in which he was residing, it is sufficient to fall under the general 'surrounding premises' description authorized by the warrant. On that basis, the defendant's motion is denied," he firmly concluded.

"Anything else counsel," replied Blaine, turning to Foster.

"Yes, Your Honor," responded Foster. "The defense wishes to file a motion for change of venue," he added. "We have presented this to the court along with a memorandum of law in support of the motion."

"For the record counsel, what is your chief argument for this motion," stated Blaine, fully anticipating the answer. Everyone in the courtroom leaned forward to hear the discussion knowing this was the one motion that stood a real chance of being sustained.

"As the court is well aware, the publicity in this case, is unprecedented. There is not a person in this community who has not been bombarded by the local media with the image of my client and the accompanying dialogue of having a serial killer within our midst. The fact that the man-in-the-street has been inundated with the "WE GOT HIM" campaign has solidified, at least in the mind of the public, that my client is guilty, not just of one murder, but of seven murders, which precludes him from obtaining a fair trial in Knox County," concluded Foster.

"May the State be heard on this Judge?" intervened the anxious ADA.

"Proceed," directed Blaine.

"Your Honor, the State acknowledges the media's extensive coverage of this case," the ADA began. "However, despite counsel's assertion that the community bias against his client would preclude him from receiving a fair trial, the state, in anticipating such a motion, has conducted public opinion surveys of the previous jury pool which we have shared with counsel. While there may be substantial prejudice against the defendant, there is still a sizeable contingent of people in this community who indicate that they could consider the evidence presented at trial and make a decision on the defendant's guilt or innocence based exclusively on that evidence."

"As a result, we believe that careful and prudent voir dire in the jury selection process would eliminate the prospect of bias against the defendant and therefore ask the court to dismiss the motion on those grounds."

Blaine paused momentarily. He was aware that the massive public outcry to the murders that had been ascribed to the defendant presented a real question of whether a fair trial could be accorded to him.

However, Blaine was also a savvy, veteran judge who knew the political repercussions that might well impact his career if he agreed to transfer the case to another county within the state and deprive the people of Knoxville of a say in the biggest criminal case of their lifetimes.

He also knew the healing effect the trial could provide to the citizenry and the resulting positive exposure he would personally receive for presiding over the case. In the latter instance, it was evident what that might do to secure his future as an elected official within the community. It was thus clear that he had to do and what he was going to do.

"Rule 22 of the Tennessee Rules of Criminal Procedure," he began, "allows a party to request a change of venue if the evidence indicates that the party could not otherwise receive a fair trial in the jurisdiction where the case is brought."

"However, after careful consideration of the issues raised in this motion, the court is of the opinion that a fair trial may be had by the defendant if judicious oversight of the jury selection process is accorded."

"In addition, the court takes notice of the fact that the length of time that will have elapsed since the initial coverage of this case until the actual trial on the merits is sufficiently long enough to allow the defendant to be accorded a fair trial."

"The Supreme Court has noted that passage of a significant period of time between the media reports and the defendant's trial can have 'a profound effect on the community and, more important, on the jury, in softening or effacing opinion.'"

"The court concurs with the State's position that judicious use of voir dire will go a long way to eliminate any potential bias that might otherwise present itself in the trial on the merits of this case. Moreover, the court notes that the elapsed time since the initial onslaught of media coverage in this case to the time of the scheduled trial on the merits is sufficient to allow the defendant to receive a fair trial in Knox County."

"Accordingly, the defendant's motion for a change of venue is denied. Trial will be set for April 19th, as scheduled.

"Any further issues that need to be addressed?" asked Blaine

"No, Your Honor," said both counsel in union.

"Then this hearing is adjourned," announced Blaine.

Chapter Twelve

After a few years of marriage, Sarah and Fletcher had developed a comfortable, but not particularly intimate relationship. They got along with each other, but both were deeply ensconced in their respective careers. Their marriage was not so much centered in love, but more out of convenience.

Because of their professional commitments, they were used to spending several days apart. When they were together, the conversation was most often centered on the more practical aspects of their lives and not on things they shared as a couple. In many ways, their relationship was more akin to being roommates than living as man and wife.

The Stamper trial served as an intersection of interests for both of them, and Fletcher began to bounce notions off his wife that pertained to the evidence accumulated in the Stamper investigation.

"What are you reading?" asked Fletcher of his wife as he and Sarah lounged in their den one night over the remnants of a post-dinner bottle of wine.

"Just another forensic psychology article," she smiled. It was a private joke between the two about her ongoing involvement in behavior science and how she was constantly investigating academic articles for use in her consultant practice.

As the Stamper trial was fast approaching, Fletcher had long realized that his wife might well serve as an informal sounding board to assist him in his understanding of the forensic evidence gathered regarding the seven victims for which Stamper had been indicted.

Here, Fletcher had an expert in forensic psychology living under the same roof with whom he could bounce ideas off without having to worry about her discussing their conversations with anyone connected with the case. And what a sounding board she was! Soon Fletcher began sharing the psychological profiles with Sarah that the state's expert witnesses had provided, which formed the basis of the arguments Fletcher was planning to employ at trial.

Fletcher devoted fifteen hours a day preparing for trial digesting all the evidence in the case. He particularly focused on the earlier murders and how he was going to tie them in with the murders where Stamper's DNA was found on the victims. In fact, he seemed possessed in his focus on the earlier homicides, feeling that the other three were clearly a slam dunk.

After presenting much of the collected evidence to Sarah, he was curious about what the forensics indicated to her.

"So, what do you think of the cumulative evidence in the Stamper case?" he asked her.

Not wanting to come across too strongly and knowing his propensity to get very upset when things weren't going his way, she responded in very general terms.

"Well, I think most of the forensics would support a finding that Stamper undoubtedly murdered several of the women involved," she casually remarked, "but I'm not convinced the evidence is such that it would prove beyond a reasonable doubt that he committed all seven of them," she calmly concluded.

"Only several?" Fletcher questioned, beginning to show some irritation with his wife's conclusion.

"Yeah," she replied. "The evidence pertaining to at least four of the victims does not, in my opinion, clearly support a finding that Stamper conclusively committed those murders," she repeated.

"What do you mean does not clearly support a finding that Stamper did not commit some of the murders," he asked, with a tinge of disgust. "The Grand Jury had no trouble connecting them."

"Calm down, Aiden. You're acting like you have a personal stake in this," she said. "In any event, all I'm saying is I think you're going to have to tie him into those murders employing circumstantial evidence because the forensics, at least at this point, do not conclusively establish a clear connection to your defendant."

"How can you so cavalierly conclude that?" he fumed. He was not happy that even his own wife was not accepting that Stamper had committed all the murders.

"Easy Aiden . . . the forensics indicate what they indicate," she responded, with an all-knowing smugness.

"You might well get a conviction on all counts, but you're going to have to be awfully persuasive to be able to prove it on these forensics," she reiterated.

"Are you saying you're not convinced he committed all seven murders he's been charged with?" asked the now nearly incredulous and clearly flustered Fletcher.

"I'm saying the forensics show what they show," she again asserted, somewhat irritated.

"Perhaps you can tie Stamper into those murders by other means, but if you're going to rely on the forensics to prove his guilt, I think you're going to have an uphill battle."

Her matter-of-fact conclusions had taken him by surprise and perhaps even brought him a bit down to earth. He had been operating under an inflated sense of the evidence and the blind faith that he could convince a jury that Stamper was indeed the murderer of seven different women.

"I'm going to bed," Sarah abruptly announced. "I have to catch an early flight tomorrow to Washington to attend a two-day conference," she stated.

"Before you go, tell me more," responded Fletcher, having calmed down a bit. "What is this conference pertaining to?" he inquired.

"It should actually be quite interesting," she noted. "It's going to address the biological and sociological aspects behind why some people commit violent crimes," she added.

"That sounds interesting," stated the now calmer Fletcher. "Explain to me some of the basics behind all that."

"Well, it is somewhat complicated," she replied, "but distilled down to the basics, it's going to be a discussion of whether violent criminals are born that way, or are simply created as a result of their social environment."

"So in other words," Fletcher responded, "it's not just about whether some killers are born with a screw loose. It may be a much deeper issue as them simply never developing normal attachments toward people and thus can't help their anti-social behavior, right?"

"Pretty much like that," replied Sarah. "There is no scientific statement that can be made concerning the exact role of biology or environmental factors as the determining factor of a violent criminal's personality."

"However, there is a growing view in academic circles regarding what is being called the 'Fractured Identity Syndrome,' which basically suggests that a traumatic social event or series of such events during one's childhood can result in the fracturing of the base personality of the child, which can ultimately create a violent killer."

"It's a relatively new theory proposed by Holmes, Tewksbury, and Holmes, which combines aspects of Cooley's 'Looking Glass Self' and Goffman's 'Virtual and Actual Social Identity'" theories, she added. "Their research is actually gaining a lot of traction in the literature on the psychology behind serial killers."

"Kind of like a split-personality?" Fletcher asked. He was most intrigued about what his wife was now saying.

"Yes, basically," she replied. "But the term "fractured identity" is defined by the authors as a small breakage of the core personality, which is often not visible to the outside world and is only felt by the criminal himself," she concluded.

"Fractured identity," Fletcher repeated. "That really sounds interesting," scratching his chin in contemplation. He had never thought of it in those terms.

"It actually is," Sarah replied. "Their literature is showing that psychopathic behavior may account for someone who actually experiences these types of psychotic breaks that cause them to believe they are actually another person or are compelled to murder by other entities which they believe control their homicidal rages," she concluded.

Fletcher listened intently. "So, what you're saying is that this inner entity takes over and controls the outer person to commit an act of violence, and that is the only thing that can temper the inner rage?"

"That's it in a nutshell," replied Sarah.

"So, it's not so much a mental illness, but circumstantial situations . . . most likely in childhood that creates these breaks?" Fletcher asked.

"That's now how we're now approaching it," Sarah answered. "The research data I just cited is clearly indicating that the genesis of such a fractured identity seems to have occurred in many cases from the sexual or emotional abuse suffered as a child," Sarah stated.

"We know that all children want to develop social relationships with their parents and their peers," Sarah asserted, "but the relationship a child has with its parents is of critical importance as to how the child values other members of society."

"The literature I quoted tells us when a child is raised in a broken home and has suffered abuse . . . physical, sexual or emotional, they endure a tremendous amount of neglect, and that leads to a loss of self-esteem, which becomes the origin of their fantasy world where they are in complete control."

"So we now know that having not experienced relatively normal socialization from their parents, the child is unable to form healthy relationships with other members of society, and their unaddressed traumas can lead to psychopathic behaviors, right?" responded Fletcher.

“That’s what the research is telling us,” responded Sarah. “Such abuse might cause a killer to engage in otherwise deviant behaviors such as fetishism or necrophilia,” she added. “Moreover, children who are helpless to control their own abuse might create a fantasy world or new reality to which they can escape . . . one which they have total control over their environment and the people who occupy it.”

“So, what you are saying is that by creating this artificial reality, the fantasized child can now have complete power over others, and having developed sociopathic behaviors, they are unable to be guided by the normal concepts of right or wrong,” Fletcher remarked.

“According to the literature, that’s right,” responded the smiling Sarah.

Fletcher continued. “So, by not being able to perceive the difference between right and wrong, boundaries are lost, and the individual utilizes dominance, sexual conquest, violence, and ultimately killing to satiate this formidable need for control, correct?”

“Exactly, correct, Aiden,” smiled Sarah, impressed with Fletcher’s innate understanding of the issue. “Other academic research, particularly the work of Giannangelo, describes the situation as ‘allowing the serial killer to leave the stream of consciousness for what is, to him, a better place.’”

“So you’re describing psychopathic behaviors, such as lack of remorse or the need to control, to describe the outward characteristics of such individuals, right?” retorted Fletcher.

“Correct,” Sarah responded. “But unlike people with major mental disorders, such as schizophrenia, psychopaths can actually seem normal and often-times quite charming.”

"Sounds like some breakthrough research," responded Fletcher. "I'd like to talk to you some more about that when you get back."

"Sure," replied Sarah, "it might help you understand what your guy Stamper is all about," she responded.

"It just might," he slyly replied. "It just very well might."

Chapter Thirteen

Two weeks before Stamper's trial was scheduled to commence, his attorney, Bradley Foster, found himself ensconced in Fletcher's Sixth District Attorney's office. He, with Brian Asher and a bevy of Assistant DAs, was attempting to reach an agreement on several of the discovery motions still outstanding. After most of them had been resolved, Foster and Fletcher focused their attention on the subject of a potential plea

"So, what are we looking at?" asked Foster, in a somber voice.

"You're looking at seven counts of first-degree murder," responded the collected Fletcher, not opening the door even a crack.

"What are you prepared to offer?" Fletcher added out of curiosity.

"My client has agreed to plead guilty to three counts of second-degree murder," replied Foster.

"Three counts?" responded the cynical Fletcher, "he has been charged under seven counts."

"My client didn't commit the other four murders," replied Foster, matter-of-factly.

Fletcher stood his ground. "Your client committed all seven of these murders, and you and I both know it," he retorted, as his aids looked anxiously on.

"You and I know no such thing," replied the now aggressive Foster. "You've got no DNA in the first three cases and one of the latter cases," he added. "All you have is a circumstantial argument, which I don't think is going to cut it."

"By the time I'm through with your client, he's going to look like the Zodiac killer," responded the cocky Fletcher.

"If your boy wants to plead to seven counts of second degree, we'll take a look at it," offered Fletcher, but anything else, and we're going to trial." The absoluteness of Fletcher's position had taken everyone by surprise, including some of his staff.

"You seem awfully bent on getting all seven of these murders tied up in a neat little bow, Aiden," stated Foster. "What gives? You know the evidence on the other four victims is shaky as can be."

"I know one thing Bradley . . . we've got the guy who perpetrated all seven of these crimes," Fletcher smugly replied.

"I don't think so," Foster curtly responded. "We're going to bring in evidence of a second killer and put all four of those counts in question," he added. "Who knows? We're going to raise enough doubt to put all these counts into question."

"I'll throw it out on the table again," Foster proclaimed. "Three counts second-degree murder, fifteen to sixty years per count, no death penalty . . . deal?"

"No deal," replied the now immovable Fletcher. "See you in court."

"You seem awfully damned anxious to lay these other murders on my guy Aiden," snarled Foster as he grabbed his briefcase to leave. "Awfully damn anxious indeed."

After Foster left, Fletcher and Asher met in Fletcher's office to discuss the meeting.

"I thought you were a little hasty in declining Foster's plea deal," replied Asher, matter-of-factly.

"Why do you think I was hasty?" Fletcher abruptly replied.

"Because you had three guilty pleas on the only cases where we could actually tie Stamper to the victims," responded the frustrated Asher, somewhat taken back by Fletcher's refusal to negotiate.

"We had him cold on those counts, Aiden," yelled Asher. "Why are you risking it all on the other cases which frankly, many of us believe might well have been committed by another perp," he noted.

"We could have always brought him up on those charges when we acquired further evidence to do so," Asher added. "Tell you the truth, half the staff doesn't even understand why you even presented those other cases to the Grand Jury . . . at least not why now?" he exclaimed.

Fletcher erupted. "Because I'm the one who decides what's tried and what isn't," screamed a now furious Fletcher. "Not you, not the third-year guys down the hall . . . ME! Do you understand that?"

Fletcher's wrath was something Asher had never experienced. His rage had consumed him. It was as if he had become another person, all because his trial strategy had been questioned, something that was a routine discussion in most of the criminal trials the two had ever worked.

"Whatever, you say," replied the defeated and now highly-contemptuous Asher, turning to leave. "Whatever the fuck you say."

As Asher repaired to the confines of his office, he slammed the door and stewed silently at his desk.

What on earth was Fletcher trying to do? He pondered. All these years they worked together, he had never seen Fletcher make such an arbitrary and capricious decision. It didn't make sense!

What in the hell was he doing?

* * * * * * * *

April 19th had rolled around, and the City of Knoxville was in a frenzy. Otis Stamper was about to be tried for the murders of seven local women and the terror he had unleashed on the city. Aiden Fletcher, now the most visible and admired person in Knoxville, was prosecuting the case. For weeks, the talk shows had been absorbed with the storyline that everyone in the community was now well-versed in. The excitement, as well as the tension, was palpable.

Television reporters encircled the courthouse and scrambled like a hive of bees. Respective counsel managed their way through the throng of media, onlookers. They walked up the twenty-two steps to the distinguished front entrance of the stone and mortar courthouse building. Atop, flew both the American flag and state flag of Tennessee.

"Do you expect to see your client convicted?" screamed one of the reporters to Foster.

"We expect a fair trial on the evidence presented," replied Foster, forcing his way through the masses.

"Are you seeking the death penalty?" yelled another as Fletcher hurriedly walked by. He declined to answer.

The frenzy of activity continued for the long-awaited beginning of one of the biggest trials ever to be conducted in the State of Tennessee, and the community-at-large was consumed with it.

During voir dire jury selection, the attorneys had struck numerous individuals whose bias would not have allowed them to judge the case presented on the merits. After much examination and legal maneuvering, the jury had been selected . . . seven men and five women. Their identities were kept confidential, so neither they nor their family members would be inundated by the news coverage of the trial.

In a packed courtroom with cameras perched in all directions, it began . . ..

Judge Blaine: "Will the clerk call the case at bar?"

Clerk: "State of Tennessee vs. Otis P. Stamper, Docket No. C76420," he announced. "In Division 1, Sixth District Criminal Court, Knox County Tennessee."

Judge Blaine: "Will counsel, please enter their appearances for the record."

Fletcher: "Aiden Fletcher, Sixth District Attorney General, for the State of Tennessee, Your Honor."

Foster: "Bradley Foster, representing the defendant, Otis Stamper, Your Honor."

Judge Blaine: "Upon ruling on the various pre-trial motions in this case, are counsel prepared to make their opening statements?"

In unison, the attorneys announced, "We are, Your Honor."

Judge Blaine: "Very well, let's hear first from the State of Tennessee."

Fletcher: "Your Honor, I stand here this morning representing the great people of Tennessee in a matter of utmost importance to our local community. Over the past couple of years, seven women . . . seven contributing members of our society, were brutally murdered by the man who sits before you, Otis P. Stamper."

Fletcher extended his arm and, for the longest of moments, pointed directly to the defendant.

"Mr. Stamper, the defendant in this case, has a long and troubled history, not only as a member of this community but in his relationships with women. As the evidence we will present clearly indicates, the defendant, Mr. Stamper, brutally beat, strangled, stabbed, and/or raped each of the murder victims for which he is being charged in this case."

"In three of the counts this jury is being asked to consider, the evidence shows the defendant's DNA, gathered at the scene of these crimes, either through blood and tissue evidence, or semen analysis, was, in fact present, which proves conclusively that he was at the crime scene and that he in fact murdered the victims in question."

"In the other four counts of murder for which he is charged, the time span between when the murders were committed to the time the victims' bodies were discovered, was of such long duration that given the natural decomposition caused by exposure to the elements, it was impossible to recover DNA of any type or ascertain precisely how the victims were in fact murdered. However, the prosecution will show beyond a reasonable doubt that the location of these murders and MO behind each one was fully consistent with the actions of the defendant, Otis Stamper."

Fletcher's opening statement continued for another forty-five minutes, outlining what the State intended to prove at trial. In the end, his summation was brief and to the point.

"Ladies and Gentlemen. I have tried to provide an overview of the case against the defendant, which will demonstrate beyond a reasonable doubt that his actions amount to nothing less than the cold-blooded, pre-meditated murder of seven innocent young women in our community."

"As a consequence, know from the outset that the State is fully committed to seeking the death penalty in each and every one of these cases, and the evidence will fully support such a finding. Thank you very much."

Judge Blaine: "Thank you counsel . . . and now for the defense."

Foster: "Thank you, Judge Blaine. Ladies and Gentlemen, the prosecution has just presented to you a rather flimsy argument as to why my client was, in fact, the person who killed the seven women for whose deaths he is now being charged. Mr. Fletcher has just conceded that in four of the counts presented, the prosecution has little to absolutely no evidence which would involve my client in those murders at all, yet they seem to be of the opinion that merely by force of argument, you should find him guilty nevertheless."

"Not only that, but he asks that you sentence my client to death for the murders of those that the evidence will clearly show, my client did not commit. Nothing could be more of a travesty under the laws of the great state of Tennessee."

"In the three cases where Mr. Stamper's DNA was found, the defense will argue that although Mr. Stamper may have had consensual sex with those women, he was not responsible for their deaths. Even if you were to find that he was, the State's argument that he committed these killings with premeditated intent sufficient to support murder one charges is certainly not supported by the record."

"In conclusion, the defense will argue that the prosecution's case has been over-charged and, at the least, tainted by the public pressure that has surrounded these killings to filing indictments in an attempt to bring all these cases to a close, regardless of whether they have the right guy. As we will show during the course of this trial, they most certainly do not. Thank you, Your Honor."

Judge Blaine: "Counsel, you may call the prosecution's first witness."

Fletcher: "Thank you, Your Honor. The State calls Carolyn Chapin to the stand."

Fletcher ran through the entire litany of Chapin's testimony, from how she had observed Stamper's truck drive to the garage with a bloodied, seemingly lifeless body in the front seat to how minutes later she saw the truck leave the garage with the woman no longer in it.

She went on to give chilling testimony as to how Stamper looked directly at her as he was leaving the scene, which left the audience, as well as the jurors shaken.

Over the course of the next few days, Fletcher followed the testimony of Ms. Chapin with that of a forensic expert, which tied the murders of the three women with Stamper's DNA to the irrefutable fact that he was indeed at the crime site at the moment the murders occurred. Following that testimony, Fletcher called two medical witnesses, who tied the first three murders to death by strangulation based on a finding that the victim's hyoid bone in their neck had been broken, an event that can only be caused by strangulation. However, each made the point that due to the decomposition of the bodies, they could not rule out that each of the first three victims could have been stabbed to death as well.

After each of those witnesses offered compelling testimony in support of Stamper's guilt, Fletcher then called in detectives to testify as to the relatively close proximity of where each of the murders occurred and the seeming consistency between the victims' ages and physical appearances.

Finally, Fletcher called a forensic psychiatrist to explain the various methodologies behind the murders, from the initial beatings and strangulations to the stabbings and sexual assaults. The psychiatrist made a compelling presentation on how serial killers often change their methods of killing in order to throw off authorities from their MO. Citing the proximity of the discovered bodies, she concluded that all the murders in question were the result of the same killer.

Sarah Fletcher attended the trial during the psychiatrist's testimony for her own benefit. She wanted to hear how another professional in the field assessed the psychological evidence, even if they were a witness for the prosecution.

For her, at least, it had been an interesting presentation.

Foster had cross-examined each of the prosecution's witnesses, attempting to raise even a modicum of doubt in the jury's mind. The dialogue had been riveting.

Foster (to Carolyn Chapin): "Ms. Chapin, you testified that you observed Mr. Stamper driving his pickup truck up the ramp with a lifeless, bloodied woman in the front seat. Is that correct?"

Chapin: "That is correct, sir."

Foster: "How would you describe the amount of blood covering the woman? Was it a small amount, a medium amount, or was she covered in blood?"

Chapin: "Oh, she was covered in blood, no doubt about it."

Foster: "So, she was covered in blood, yet you were able to identify her from police photographs as Theresa Abbott, is that correct?"

Chapin: "That is correct."

Foster: "Well, Ms. Chapin, I'm trying my best to understand how you could positively identify the victim when by your own admission, she was covered in blood."

Chapin: "Well, I just did," she adamantly insisted.

Several jurors nodded in agreement as Chapin had responded in a good ole' Tennessee straight-talking way.

After tiptoeing around the DNA evidence for which he had little defense other than his assertion that Stamper had engaged in consensual sex, Foster subsequently proceeded to cross-examine one of the detectives who testified as to where the various bodies were found.

Foster: "So Detective Harris, you've testified that the bodies of each of the seven victims, in this case, were found in the quote 'same general area' as each other, which led you to believe that they were all killed by the same person, correct?"

Detective Harris: "That is correct counselor."

Foster: "Would you define for this jury what you meant by the 'same general area?'"

Detective Harris: "Well, all seven bodies were discovered within ten to twelve miles of each other."

Foster: "Within ten to twelve miles of each other. Was that the only criteria that you analyzed in trying to piece together these killings . . . the distance within which you discovered the bodies?"

Detective Harris: "Of course not. We looked at the victimology of the women. They were all about the same age, attractive, working women."

Foster: "So did it cause you any concern that the first three victims and one of the last two victims discovered were brunettes, while the others were mostly blondes?"

Detective Harris: "We considered that, whether there might be two killers involved, but we concluded along with the forensic evidence and our psychological profile, that those distinctions did not rule out a single killer. In fact, we concluded from the totality of the evidence gathered that all the killings before us were committed by the same individual."

Foster could sense he wasn't making much progress with the jury, despite what appeared to be real questions about the credibility of the evidence.

Finally, Foster cross-examined the prosecution's forensic psychiatrist, Dr. Nancy Bunner, about the disparities in the victim's method of murder and the psycho-pathology of such a killer.

Foster: "Dr. Bunner, you've testified before this court that the fact that even though some of the victims, in this case, appeared to have been killed by different means, i.e., strangulation vs. stabbing and sexual assault vs. no sexual assault, that you ultimately concluded all the victims were killed by the same person; is that correct?"

Dr. Bunner: "That's correct. We came to that conclusion after a thorough review of the forensic evidence."

Foster: "Could you explain to this jury exactly how you came to that conclusion?"

Dr. Bunner: "Certainly. In the case of most serial killers, we tend to see a pattern . . . not only of victimology, but of methodology. Serial killers can either be organized in the deliberation of their killings or disorganized; i.e., they kill perhaps on the spur of the moment. Here, we saw the same organized pattern of killing in all seven cases. The killer presented himself at a location where a young victim might frequent; a bar, a restaurant, a hiking trail, etc. There is no doubt that the idea of killing the individuals in these cases was premeditated; it was just a matter of who the victim would be."

Foster: "OK, that may explain motive, but it certainly doesn't explain methodology, does it?"

Dr. Bunner: "Well, you have to understand that killers are not machines. Whether their killings are based on rage, fantasy, or whatever, they are, in the end, crimes of opportunity. Thus, in some of the cases before us, where the method of killing may have varied, it could well have been that at the time of the particular incident, the killer may not have been in a position to sexually assault the victim. There may not have been time, or there may have been potential witnesses in the area. It just doesn't always turn out the same way each time."

Foster: "What about stabbing a victim vs. beating and strangulation. Does that inform your conclusions when there are disparate methodologies used in various killings?"

Dr. Bunner: "Well, certainly, that gives us pause, but at the end of the day, the culmination of all the evidence, in this case, we felt, pointed to one killer."

Foster: "One final question Dr. Bunner. How many cases have you testified in as the prosecution witness, especially in violent crime cases tried by Mr. Fletcher?"

Fletcher: "Objection, Your Honor . . . relevance!"

Foster: "Your Honor, to the contrary, we think it's quite relevant as Dr. Bunner has a long history of testifying on behalf of the prosecution, particularly in these types of cases where Mr. Fletcher was the prosecutor. One might make an argument that such an expert has at least an unconscious bias toward the State, which routinely hires them as an expert."

Judge Blaine: "Objection overruled. Could you repeat the question, Mr. Foster?"

Foster: "Certainly, Your Honor . . . Dr. Bunner, how many times have you served as a prosecution witness, especially in one of Mr. Fletcher's cases?"

Dr. Bunner: "Oh, I don't know, maybe twenty-five, I imagine."

Foster: "If I told you the record shows you've testified in 33 criminal cases where Mr. Fletcher was the lead prosecutor, would you find that correct?"

Dr. Bunner: "That could very well be true . . . but at no time did I . . ..

Foster: "No further questions, Your Honor."

After five days of trial, the prosecution finally rested its case. For the most part, they were satisfied that the jury was on their side as far as how they explained the evidence should be interpreted.

Now it was the defense's turn.

Foster called his own experts, particularly a forensic psychiatrist, Dr. Hannah Brown, to testify.

Sarah Fletcher sat upright and listened with keen interest.

Foster: "Dr. Brown, we've established your expert credentials as a forensic psychiatrist.

You have thoroughly reviewed the evidence in this case, have you not?"

Dr. Brown: "I certainly have."

Foster: "From the totality of the forensic evidence that you reviewed, what is your conclusion?"

Dr. Brown: "My conclusion is that there is a high probability that more than one person committed the murders in question."

Foster: "And what do you base that conclusion on, Dr. Brown?"

Dr. Brown: "From the fact that in the first three murders, the manner of death appeared to be by blunt force trauma and strangulation, and in the four other murders, death was caused by blunt force trauma and stabbing. I would also add that in only three of the latter four cases, were the victims sexually molested."

Foster: "What does the variation in the manner of death indicate to you, having assessed all of these cases?"

Dr. Brown: "Well, it's hard to say, but it is my strong impression that not only was there a second killer, but he was a copycat."

The jury shifted uneasily in their seats and stared at each other.

Foster: "What do you mean a copycat?"

Dr. Brown: "I mean, someone who was trying to cover up his own murders, to look like someone else's."

Fletcher: "Objection! The witness is offering nothing more than gross speculation . . . copycat, come on!"

Fletcher rolled his eyes upward and threw his pen across his table in a show of abject disgust that it was even conceivable a copycat killer might still be on the loose.

Judge Blaine: "Please be seated, Mr. Fletcher . . . now."

Foster: "Your Honor, in response to the State's objection, I would argue that the witness is testifying as an expert and in that capacity, she is entitled, within reason, to express an opinion as to what the forensic evidence indicates."

Judge Blaine: "Objection overruled. Proceed, Mr. Foster."

Foster: "So, Dr. Brown, if your professional opinion is that you believe a copycat killer may have been responsible for some of the murders charged in this case, it would have to follow the defendant could not, and did not, commit all the murders he has been charged with, correct?"

Dr. Brown: "That's correct."

Foster: "Could you expand on that, please?"

Dr. Brown: "Certainly. It is my professional opinion that with respect to at least Marcia Thomas, the victim whose body was found beaten and stabbed in a field, the evidence indicates that she was not sexually molested like any of the last four victims."

Foster: "So what does that tell you from a forensic pathology perspective?"

Dr. Brown: "That tells me there's a reasonable possibility that whomever committed that murder did not want his DNA identified."

Foster: "Why would such a killer not want his DNA identified?"

Dr. Brown: "Apart from the obvious reasons, it would be because that would demonstrate unequivocally that there was another killer involved."

Foster: "So if a copycat killer was operating at large, it might not explain his motivation to kill, but certainly would indicate he took great pains not to expose his own identity. Correct?"

Dr. Brown: "Correct, but it might also explain that the killing was well thought out ahead of time. Maybe even to the point of providing a diversion."

Foster: "What do you mean providing a diversion?"

Dr. Brown: "I mean, it might have been done in an attempt to throw authorities off the scent and toward another individual."

Foster: "Conversely, might you also conclude that a copycat killer who had not previously stabbed his victims might have stabbed his last victim for no other reason than to make it look like it was someone else?"

Dr. Brown: "That is a distinct possibility. That scenario certainly entered my mind. Particularly where a murderer had previously beaten and strangled his victims."

Foster: "Thank you, Dr. Brown. No further questions, Your Honor."

Sarah Fletcher was absorbed with the testimony being given and was taking copious notes.

Judge Blaine: "Mr. Fletcher, you may cross-examine the witness."

Fletcher: "Gladly, Your Honor."

Fletcher's disdain for Brown's testimony was palpable. Walking briskly to the witness box, he confronted her immediately.

Fletcher: "So you want this jury to believe that a copycat imitated the murders of the defendant. Is that right?"

Dr. Brown: "That's groping a little counselor. What I said was that I think from the empirical evidence a copycat might have been covering for his own murders by changing his methodology of killing to match other identified killings."

Fletcher: "But that's just speculation, right?"

Dr. Brown: "An educated guess."

Fletcher: "But a guess nevertheless."

Dr. Brown: "As I said, an educated guess."

Fletcher: "Dr. Brown, would it make any sense to you for a second killer to kill someone just for the purpose of throwing the police 'off his scent' as you proposed?"

Dr. Brown: "It would if he was a serial killer."

Fletcher: "What do you mean by that?"

Dr. Brown: "I mean if the killer was a serial killer by pathology, rather than someone who just happened to kill someone haphazardly, the odds are very great that he would be driven to kill . . . again and again. If that was indeed the case, then our second killer was using the methodology of another killer to camouflage his own murders, which would allow him to continue doing what he was doing without fear of being captured."

Fletcher: "Are you throwing that out as a remote possibility, or do you seriously believe that?"

Dr. Brown: "What I believe is that the evidence indicates that is, in fact, a distinct possibility in this case."

Sarah Fletcher just sat and stared as she pondered the legal ramifications of Brown's testimony.

In an attempt to offset the drama of Brown's confident testimony, Fletcher used a bit of staged theatre to dissuade jurors that anything she had said was worthy of consideration.

Approaching Brown as if to follow up with another question, Fletcher suddenly stopped and threw up his hands in disdain and just stared at Brown in disbelief.

"You can't be serious!" he mocked.

"Objection!" shouted Foster. "Counsel is ridiculing the witness."

Judge Blaine had seen every courtroom trick in the books and was having nothing of it.

"Sustained," Blaine bellowed. "Do you have another question for the witness Mr. Fletcher?"

Fletcher continued his animated disdain for Brown's testimony for another long moment.

Fletcher: "No . . . nothing further, Your Honor."

Judge Blaine: "Then sit down! Dr. Brown, you are excused. Thank you."

As Dr. Brown stepped down from the witness chair, Fletcher turned and gave her a genuine hostile look that no one could miss. It was a look that transcended the matter before them . . . a look of rage.

Foster: "Your Honor, may we take a short break? I need to have a discussion with my client."

Judge Blaine: "Sure. I think we could all use a break. Let's reconvene at 2:30 p.m."

As Foster gathered his materials from his desk and the jury filed out to their jury room, Fletcher stormed out of the courtroom, oblivious to all around him. He was livid . . . angrier than any of his colleagues had ever seen him.

* * * * * * * *

During the break, Foster and Stamper convened in a small conference room in a holding area behind the juror's room and discussed the next phase of their case.

"Otis, let me tell you where I think we are," Foster began. "After all the testimony so far, despite the fact that I think we've made some inroads, I think the jury is probably siding with the prosecution on all counts. What Brown just testified to is too much for them to comprehend. Do you understand what I'm saying?"

"Yeah, I understand," replied Stamper. "They just want to pin it all on me."

"We've presented all of the evidence that we have in your defense, and frankly, I think they have you cold on the three cases where your DNA is involved," concluded Foster.

"That part doesn't look good . . . I agree," said the dejected Stamper.

"At this point, we're just fighting to avoid the death penalty," Foster asserted. "Between the two of us, I don't see any way you're acquitted on all counts . . . nor in my opinion should you be."

"Yeah, I know," responded the solemn Stamper.

"I do have one last card to play," continued Foster.

"What's that?" replied the now curious Stamper.

"Putting you on the stand to testify that you did not kill those other four women," said Foster, looking Stamper right in the eye.

"I didn't!" yelled Stamper. "You have to believe me!"

"It's not about whether I believe you. It's about whether the jury believes you," replied Foster.

"Are you agreeable to testify in your own defense?" asked Foster. "I think it's all we got left. If you do, Fletcher is going to rip you apart on cross-examination. Do you understand what I am saying?"

"I understand," said Stamper, eager to proceed.

"You're going to have to convince those jurors; not only did you not intend to kill the three women you did, but you had nothing to do with those other murders. Can you do that?" stated Foster.

"I'll try," responded Stamper.

"Try your best, Otis. Your life depends on it," concluded Foster.

* * * * * * * *

After the break, the parties reconvened in the courtroom. The trial was in its eight-day of testimony.

Judge Blaine: "Counsel, are we ready to proceed?"

Counsel: "We are, Your Honor."

Judge Blaine: "Mr. Foster, does the defense wish to call any further witnesses?"

Foster: "We do, Your Honor. The defense wishes to call the defendant, Otis Stamper, to the stand."

The audience gasped as Stamper was led from the defense table to the witness stand by sheriff's marshals. Here he was. After months of terror, the community would see . . . and hear . . . up close, the ogre who had so haunted their lives.

After preliminary questions regarding Stamper's difficult background and brief attempt to make a life for himself, Foster got to the meat of his examination. He tried to humanize him for the sake of the jury.

Foster: "Otis, did you kill any of the women who've been identified in this trial?"

The jury was taken back by the directness of the question. After a long pause, Stamper began to weep uncontrollably. Foster allowed sufficient time for him to recover and asked again.

Foster: "Otis, let me ask you again. Did you kill any of the women for which you've been indicted in this case?"

Stamper: "Yes," he quietly stammered. "I killed three of the women involved."

The audience, as well as the jury, gasped at the unexpected admission.

Foster: "Which three did you kill Otis?"

Stamper: "I killed the woman who's been identified as Marianne Silvey, whose body I left at Ft. Loudon Lake. She was the first," he admitted.

Foster: "Who else?"

Stamper: "After her, I killed Nancy Alford at Sequoyah Park."

Foster: "And who was the third?"

Stamper: "After those two, I killed Theresa Abbott, whose body I put in the parking garage."

Foster: "So you don't challenge the testimony of Carolyn Chapin, who said she saw you at the garage with Ms. Abbott's body do you?"

Stamper" "No, I was there with her."

Foster: "So Otis, did you kill these same women the same way?"

Stamper: "Yes, I stabbed them."

Foster: "Did you stab all three of them?"

Stamper: "Yes, all three. The same way."

Foster: "Did you sexually molest any of these women?"

Stamper: "Yeah, all of them."

Foster paused to let the impact of Stamper's testimony sink in with all in the courtroom. Everyone, including the Judge, was transfixed on Stamper and awaited Foster's next question. The drama was overwhelming.

Foster: "Otis . . . before this trial began, you offered to plead guilty to the deaths of the three women you've just described, is that correct?"

Stamper: "Yes, sir. That's correct."

Foster: "But the prosecution didn't accept those pleas, did they?"

Stamper: "No, sir. They didn't."

Foster: "Do you know why they didn't?"

Stamper: "Because they said they wouldn't accept my pleas unless I plead guilty to killing all seven of the women involved?"

Foster: "So why didn't you plead guilty to killing all seven of them?"

Stamper: "Because I didn't kill the other four! Even the three I did kill was just in the moment. I just lost my head. I never set out to kill anybody. You have to believe me! I never even came across those other four women. I have no idea who they are. I didn't even know who the three were."

Foster: "So Otis, is it your opinion the prosecution just wanted to pin all these murders on you, for the sake of convenience to assure the public that the killer of all these women had been caught?"

Fletcher: "Objection, Your Honor! Calls for a conclusion. This witness is in no position to discern what the prosecution's motives were."

Judge Blaine: "Sustained."

Foster: "Otis, I want you to think very, very carefully before I ask you again. Did you kill or molest any of the other four women that you've been charged within the indictment?"

Stamper: "No sir . . . I did not! You have to believe me! I killed the three of them but no one else! I didn't even mean to. Please! As God is my witness!"

Foster: "No further questions, Your Honor."

Judge Blaine: "The State may cross-examine the witness."

After pondering the dramatic effect of Stamper's testimony on the jury, Fletcher knew he had to do something and do it fast. He strode across the courtroom to the witness box with the same contemptuous look he had shown Dr. Brown. His plan was clear, and he jumped on it as he approached Stamper. Without a moment of hesitation, he let loose.

Fletcher: "You're a goddam liar . . . you worthless piece of horse shit!"

Foster: "Objection! This is outrageous! Counsel is deliberately trying to inflame the jury, Your Honor!"

Judge Blaine: "Sustained. Counsel, in my chambers . . . Now!"

The trial was temporarily recessed as Judge Blaine angrily stomped out of the courtroom toward his chambers. As counsel followed, Blaine slammed the door shut. Looking directly at Fletcher, he let go.

Judge Blaine: "That was one of the most dishonest things I have ever seen in my thirty years on the bench, and I know why you did it. I'm this close to calling a mistrial!"

Fletcher: "Your Honor. . . "

Judge Blaine: "Quiet! I'm not done with you. If you so much as sneeze throughout the remainder of this trial, I will cite you for contempt, and I will personally file an ethics complaint with the state bar association. Do you understand me?"

Fletcher: "Yes, Your Honor."

Judge Blaine: "When we go back in there, you are going to apologize to the jury, and it better be good, or I may yet call a mistrial. Are we clear counsel?"

Fletcher: "Perfectly clear, Your Honor."

After another few minutes of dressing down, Fletcher, Judge Blaine with the attorneys in tow, headed stridently back into the courtroom. Staring directly at Fletcher, he began:

Judge Blaine: "Mr. Fletcher, I believe you wanted to make a statement to the jury."

Fletcher: "Thank you, Your Honor. Ladies and Gentlemen. I have asked the judge for an opportunity to address you to apologize for my outburst just before the break. That was uncalled for, and I deeply regret it. The pressure of a proceeding like this for that one moment got the best of me, and I lost my normally good judgment. I want to apologize to each of you and ask that you please disregard it and any implications that may emanate from it."

Walking back to his table, Fletcher looked briefly to Blaine, who discreetly nodded his approval. Taking his seat, Fletcher allowed the slightest of smiles to cross his lips. His strategically-timed outburst had achieved its intended effect and had done so beautifully.

Judge Blaine: "You may continue with your cross-examination of the witness counsel."

Fletcher: "Thank you, Your Honor. Mr. Stamper, you testified that you deliberately murdered three of the women in this case. Is that correct?"

Stamper: "That's not correct. I never said I deliberately murdered them."

Fletcher: "That's because you know if the jury finds your killings were premeditated, regardless of whether you killed three or seven of the victims that you're eligible for the death penalty. Isn't that correct?"

Stamper: "That's what I've been told. But I never set out to kill any of those women. It just happened. They pissed me off, and it just happened. I didn't go looking for them."

Fletcher: "You didn't go looking for them, but you just happened to be where they were located. Quite the coincidence, isn't it?"

Foster: "Objection. Here he goes again, Your Honor."

Judge Blaine: "The reporter will strike that last comment. Need I remind you, Mr. Fletcher, of what we discussed in our chambers meeting?"

Fletcher: "Sorry, Your Honor. It won't happen again."

Judge Blaine: "It better not."

After concluding his cross-examination of Stamper, Foster called no further witnesses.

Judge Blaine: "Does that conclude the presentation of the defense's case?"

Foster: "It does, Your Honor. The defense rests."

Judge Blaine: "If that's the case, court is adjourned until 9:00 a.m. tomorrow morning when closing arguments will be heard."

As Fletcher packed his briefcase and turned to exit the courtroom, he stopped and stared at the jury box. Tomorrow was going to be the second biggest day of his life.

Chapter Fourteen

Fletcher had a sleepless night thinking about how he was going to present his closing statement. He knew Foster had planted the seed of doubt in the jury's mind when he discussed the forensic evidence with respect to the four victims who had neither been stabbed nor raped. He would have to skirt around the fact that Stamper hadn't left any DNA at the scene of four of the murders and play on their collective angst that everyone in Knoxville had been feeling for the past several months. That was going to be the key.

As trial reconvened the next morning for closing arguments, the courtroom was abuzz. The tension within the tightly packed crowd was electric. After eight days of trial, the matter would come down to how persuasive the attorneys could be summarizing the evidence. The jury looked particularly ready for the big show to begin.

"All rise!" the clerk announced abruptly.

"The Honorable Judge Kent Blaine presiding," he continued.

Judge Blaine: "Please take your seats, ladies, and gentlemen. Just so there is no confusion, I wish to remind the audience that at no time during today's proceedings will any demonstrations, yelling, or applause be tolerated. Anyone who fails to abide by these rules will be removed from the courtroom. Are we clear on that?"

The audience offered a collective nod of understanding.

Judge Blaine: "In that case, I would now ask the prosecution if they are ready to present their closing argument."

Fletcher: "We are, Your Honor."

Judge Blaine: "Then you may proceed, Mr. Fletcher."

Fletcher: "Thank you, Your Honor."

Fletcher had dedicated a tremendous amount of time contemplating how he was going to present his closing argument. He knew his whole case, at least as he perceived it, might well hinge on how persuasive he could make this final performance . . . the performance of a lifetime . . . and he was ready.

Dressed in an impeccable dark gray suit with a crisp white shirt and blue tie, he arose from his table and slowly walked over to the jury box. With great deliberation, he turned and stared for an inordinately long time and pointed directly at Stamper.

Fletcher: "Ladies and Gentlemen of the jury, the man you see at the defendant's table . . . that man is a murderer . . . a cold and calculating serial murderer."

"We know he's a murderer, not just because he has admitted to it on the record in this courtroom . . . but because the evidence speaks to us as clearly as it can . . . the evidence is telling us as well . . . and in no uncertain terms . . . that man is a murderer!"

"All of us, myself included, our children . . . have lived in terror for the last couple of years because of that man. The families of the seven young women who were his victims, in this case, are screaming out to you . . . that man is a murderer!"

"The forensic evidence which you have heard so much testimony about is clear and speaks to you beyond a reasonable doubt. Otis Stamper, with deliberate and calculating effect, murdered seven women because he is a monster. The monster of Knoxville sits here before you, and . . . WE GOT HIM!"

"The evidence speaks in a clear and discernible voice and says Otis Stamper is an ogre . . . a monstrous ogre who has an insatiable need to destroy lives. A brute who can only find control and purpose in his own miserable life by killing young women . . . no matter whether they are blondes or brunettes. It makes no difference. He kills women to satisfy his rage. Maybe his mother, maybe his wives, maybe even his girlfriends, made him feel this way. Maybe they created his sense of inadequacy. But for whatever reason, it really doesn't matter. Otis Stamper is a cold and heartless killer! Killers like him live in a self-centered, fantasy land. They have no empathy for their victims or their families."

"His methodology may not always be the same, but he abducts and kills these women before disposing of their bodies all within the same general vicinity. Carolyn Chapin was an eyewitness to his brutality. She saw it through her own eyes. Otis Stamper is what Dr. Bunner called an organized killer. One who deliberately sets out to kill someone and plans their crime methodically."

"As Dr. Bunner further testified, the defendant most likely suffers from psychotic breaks from reality. In his case, he might view it as his mission to rid the world of certain types of women. Women who are young and attractive and would normally have nothing to do with a man like him. A man who has done nothing his whole miserable life but to break the conventions of civilized people. People like you and I who wish to live in a safe and prosperous society, in a community like Knoxville."

"Whether he kills for lust, resentment or simply derives pleasure from watching people suffer, we can't say. What we do know, however, is that Otis Stamper, deliberately and with malice, killed the seven women at issue in this proceeding."

"The defense wants to make a big deal about the fact that the first three victims showed no sign of being stabbed or raped. Thus, such evidence shows a different MO from the latter killings, which would indicate there has to be some doubt about whether there might have been two serial killers involved in these murders."

"Ladies and Gentlemen, they are grasping at straws. They are grabbing onto the only thing they have to keep him from getting the death penalty. It's all they have. They have tried to convince you that not all the parts of the puzzle fit together in a neat, little, tidy package. Therefore, it had to be different killers!"

"Oh really! The only reason why the first three bodies didn't show evidence of stabbing is because they were so badly decomposed it was impossible to determine whether they had indeed been stabbed to death. Our forensic expert, tells us there is an overwhelming prospect it's the same murderer who committed all these crimes. Even with respect to one of the last four victims who was shown not to have been raped, that in no way means a second murderer killed her. Our psychiatrist testified it might have been nothing more than in that one incidence; the killer did not have the time nor the opportunity to rape the victim as he had the others."

"Ladies and Gentlemen, the defense would have you believe that two serial killers have been operating in Knoxville over the past couple of years. Do you really believe that? Do you really think two different serial killers just happened to pop up here at the same time? In the same area? Do you know what the odds of that happening are? They are beyond calculation."

"Tennesseans have a long and well-deserved reputation for good, old-fashioned, common sense. If you exercise that today with respect to the evidence that has been produced in this trial, I have little doubt that you will return a verdict of guilty in each of the seven counts presented."

"Let's send a message. A loud and clear message that Knoxville is a community that will not tolerate this type of criminal conduct. Let's send a message to the people waiting outside this courtroom and those in their homes and offices who are counting on you to do them and this town justice."

"Together, let's send a message to the families of those who lost their lives that we are a law-abiding community. We hold the perpetrator of such crimes accountable to the full extent of the law and that no amount of legal finagling or made-up courtroom arguments will ever change that."

Fletcher abruptly turned and pointed his finger at the defendant.

"Let's send a loud and clear message that we are a community of laws that protects our citizens and our children from monsters like Otis Stamper!"

Walking over to the exhibit table, Fletcher grabbed the 8" inch serrated knife that forensic experts speculated was the type of knife used in the murders and approached the jury. Pointing the knife toward Stamper, he continued.

"The man that sits in this courtroom accused of these heinous killings is a monster . . . a monster who showed no mercy to his helpless victims as he repeatedly and viciously stabbed them to death in a horrific, demonic blood-letting," Fletcher began. "No mercy at all!"

Walking toward the prosecutor's table where a thick law book lay, he suddenly turned and began to repeatedly stab the law book uncontrollably with his arm up-raised and with all his might.

Fletcher continued to stab the book time after time, without let-up, as his countenance took on a fierce and horrific expression that shocked the courtroom observers with his unbelievable display of mad, psychotic terror. As he finished his quivering, merciless assault on the law book, he paused to catch his breath and continued his narrative.

"The man that sits before you is a monster that could do this to innocent, young women. A monster who could inflict the pain and the abject paralyzing fear into a dying young woman whose last moments on this earth be filled with horror. A monster whose rage was so profound that he could thrust a knife into them over and over and over and over and over . . .."

Exhausted from his frightening demonstration of physical violence, Fletcher dropped the knife to the floor in a dramatic fashion. The jury recoiled in a stunned reaction to what they had just observed. The display had been incredibly powerful and emotionally gripping. Imagining the violence and horror that the young victims experienced in their final moments were simply too riveting to ignore. Exhausted from his performance, Fletcher's evil expression, which had seemed so absolutely genuine just moments before, began to subside as he brushed back his ruffled hair and turned one last time to the jury.

"It's in your hands Ladies and Gentlemen," he solemnly asserted, still breathing heavily. "The future safety and health of all our citizens is in your hands . . . here today . . . right now." He paused to stare at each of them for the longest moment and concluded.

"The people of Knoxville are counting on you. Thank you very much."

All eyes were on him as he deliberately walked slowly back to the prosecutor's table in a self-conscious continuation of his remarkable performance; his deportment crumpled from the fearsome exhibit of horror he had just provided.

The audience and jury simultaneously exhaled from Fletcher's dramatic demonstration. It was the performance of a lifetime. Not a word was said afterward, as the stunned audience groped to gather their composure after such a dramatic display. It was like they had actually witnessed a real, brutal murder right in front of them.

Several women in the audience were dabbing tears from their cheeks after what they had just witnessed. Fletcher's weary look symbolized the months-long emotional fatigue they had all experienced. They were tired . . . tired of the fear . . . tired of the disruption . . . tired of having their lives turned upside down.

Sensing the fragility of the moment, the Judge allowed the audience and himself to gather their collective breath before continuing. After what seemed the longest of time, he spoke.

Judge Blaine: "Thank you, Mr. Fletcher. We will now hear the defendant's closing statement."

Foster approached the jury box deep in contemplation. He knew Fletcher's presentation had had a tremendously powerful effect on the jury. He could not allow it to be the last imagery they would take into the jury room. Walking a few steps toward the prosecution table, Foster began to clap his hands in a forceful manner.

Foster: "Bravo!" he exclaimed. "Bravo! That was a compelling performance, Mr. Fletcher."

Turning back toward the jury, having attempted to redirect some of the effects away from what they had just seen, he spoke.

Foster: "Thank you, Your Honor. We have just witnessed an astonishing, if not laudable, demonstration by Mr. Fletcher, which was no doubt offered to evoke a great deal of emotion from the jury. I myself was taken back by the drama of it all. Quite a performance indeed."

"However, Ladies and Gentlemen, we are not here to be entertained. We are here to discern cold, hard facts, and the truth is, the prosecution has provided insufficient facts to warrant guilty verdicts on each of the seven counts in this indictment. It certainly has not met the standard of proof of my client's guilt that the law requires . . . proof that is demonstrated 'beyond a reasonable doubt.'"

"No matter how much you might be inclined to want to hang all the murders in this case on Otis Stamper, the reality is that the evidence just won't support it. The evidence simply does not demonstrate that Otis Stamper, 'beyond a reasonable doubt' . . . murdered all seven women at issue in this proceeding."

"The testimony of Dr. Brown makes this abundantly clear. Her testimony is that forensics don't lie and, in this proceeding, there are at least four cases where there is no evidence whatsoever that Otis Stamper had anything to do with the women that were killed."

"Let me repeat that. The forensics in this, case, do not establish whatsoever that Otis Stamper had anything to do with at least four of the murders in question."

Fletcher and several of his team began to fidget uncomfortably in their seats. They knew Foster was making a compelling argument.

"Moreover, Ladies and Gentlemen, there is insufficient evidence to establish, 'beyond a reasonable doubt', that my client acted in a premeditated way, even with respect to the victims he has admitted to the killing."

"The prosecution's witness described the killer as an organized murderer who planned his killings methodically. As someone who maintained a high degree of control over the crime scene. I ask you, Ladies and Gentlemen, does leaving your DNA on the bodies illustrate a high degree of control over the crime scene?"

"Unless the prosecution can demonstrate 'beyond a reasonable doubt' that Mr. Stamper acted in a pre-meditated fashion, you simply cannot find him guilty of murder in the first degree. Not only on the four counts we have contested but on the seven counts before us."

"At the end of the day, Ladies and Gentlemen, we all want the same thing. A safe community for our families and our children. But we want to assure that result by being a community that values the rule of law, and not one which acts on impetuous emotion for the sake of relieving ourselves of whatever anxieties that may still exist as a result of the horrible murders; we have experienced these past two years."

"My plea to you Ladies and Gentlemen is to do the right thing in this case and acquit my client of the contested crimes for which he has been charged. Crimes which no matter how you look at it, are overcharged and unsupported."

"If this community stands for anything, it is that we are judged by a jury of our peers, and but for different scenarios, any of us could be on trial here . . . on trial for our lives. I ask you to give the defendant the same basic rights you would demand . . . to be tried based on what the evidence and the evidence alone illustrates. We ask for no more and certainly no less. We're simply asking you to do the right thing. Thank you very much."

Like Fletcher, Foster had done a remarkable job making his case in his closing argument. After hearing evidence in the case for over a week, it came down to the forcefulness of the arguments both attorneys had made.

Judge Blaine: "Thank you, Mr. Foster. Does that conclude the presentation of the parties?"

Attorneys: "Yes, Your Honor."

Judge Blaine then instructed the jury on what they could and could not determine as a result of the evidence presented and admonished them about discussing the case with anyone but themselves.

Judge Blaine: "Does counsel have any further questions before we adjourn?"

Attorneys: "None, Your Honor."

Judge Blaine: "If there are no further questions, this proceeding is adjourned until a verdict has been reached."

Slamming his gavel, that was it. The biggest trial East Tennessee had ever seen was all but over.

The courtroom quickly vacated as the assembled throng of spectators and media alike swarmed around the front entrance hoping to get a brief interview from the respective attorneys. Neither would comment. People milled around for the next hour or so until the crowd had pretty much dispersed from the area. Some repaired to the tavern across the street to keep the conversation about what they had just observed going over drinks.

It was late afternoon when the jury received its instructions from the judge and retired for deliberations. No one knew when they would return with a verdict, but everyone realized that whatever it was, it was going to shake the City of Knoxville to its core.

* * * * * * * *

At 11:00 the next morning, the attorneys were notified by the court that the jury had reached a verdict and that court would reconvene at 11:30 a.m. The news quickly spread to the media, who once again surrounded the courtroom with cameras and news vans. The anticipation was palpable.

Inside the courtroom, the atmosphere was electric, as throngs of spectators quickly filled the allocated seats. The first two rows were cordoned off with rope that held signs that said "VIPs ONLY." After just a few short minutes, it began.

As Judge Blaine entered behind the bench, the clerk stood and, with a determined voice, cried, "All Rise!"

After a seemingly endless several moments to allow himself to get organized and an equally interminable amount of time deep in conversation with the clerk, Blaine leaned over the microphone and spoke.

Judge Blaine: "Will the clerk please escort the jury to their seats?"

One by one, the jury filed into the courtroom with stern expressions on their faces. Expressions that everyone strained hard to try to interpret. As they took their seats in the jury box, the courtroom became eerily quiet.

Looking directly at the jury foreman, Blaine spoke:

"Has the jury reached a verdict in the case at bar?" The foreman stood and, in a deliberated cadence replied, "We have, Your Honor."

Pulling out a slip of paper, the foreman handed it to the clerk, who walked it over to the Judge. The courtroom was deathly quiet. Blaine opened the paper and took his time scanning the results before he finally spoke.

Judge Blaine: "Mr. Foreman, in Docket C76420, State of Tennessee vs. Otis P. Stamper, how do you find on the seven counts contained in the indictment?"

The tension in the room was crushing.

Jury foreman: "Your Honor, we the jury, find the defendant . . . GUILTY of first-degree murder on all seven counts contained in the charging document."

A collective gasp emanated throughout the courtroom.

Fletcher, upon hearing the verdict, suddenly took on a look of tremendous relief across his face.

Several spectators started hugging, and the loud conversation began to be heard. Attorneys at the prosecutor's table began hugging in celebration as families of the dead women wept in joy.

Judge Blaine: "Order in the courtroom!"

The conversation immediately ceased.

Judge Blaine: "Does counsel wish to poll the jury?"

Foster: "We do, Your Honor."

Stamper slumped in his seat as Foster conducted the routine survey of each member of the jury to assure that they had supported the announced verdict on each of the seven counts. After the poll was completed, Blaine looked at Stamper.

Judge Blaine: "Will the defendant, please rise?"

Stamper slowly took to his feet and hung his head.

Judge Blaine: "Do you have anything you'd like to say before I pronounce sentence?"

Stamper: "Your Honor, all I want to say is that I apologize for killing the three women that I killed. To their families, I ask for their forgiveness, though I don't think I deserve it. I'm just a poor man who has fought demons my whole life. I've never set out to kill those women, I was just in a bad place, and it happened. But I want to say one last time. I never killed those other four women. As Jesus is my personal savior, I swear I didn't kill those women. Honest to God!"

Blaine paused before he pronounced the sentence. The spectators were glued to what he would say next.

Judge Blaine: "In that the jury has found the defendant, Otis P. Stamper, guilty of first-degree murder on the seven counts contained in the indictment, I sentence you to be incarcerated at the Riverbend Maximum Security Institution in Nashville, until such a time as all appeals have been exhausted and at that time you are hereby sentenced to be put to death by lethal injection."

Judge Blaine: "Are there any last formalities that need to be addressed?"

Attorneys: "No, Your Honor."

Judge Blaine: "Then if there are no further matters before me, this proceeding is adjourned."

Stamper was being led out of the courtroom by three deputies when he began to yell to the jury. "I didn't kill those four people! I swear to you I didn't!"

He was quickly detained and led out the side door to a holding cell behind the courtroom as the spectators left the courtroom to the scores of cameras waiting outdoors.

Foster sat slumped in his seat, trying to understand what had just happened. He knew his client was guilty of the three murders but was absolutely convinced he hadn't committed the other four.

Fletcher celebrated quietly with his legal team and prepared to meet outside with the assembled media. Walking out of the courtroom, he paused for a long moment staring at the now nearly empty chamber contemplating the significance of what had transpired.

Once again, fate had intervened. More than he could ever imagine, his life would never be the same again.

* * * * * * * *

Making his way down the steps of the courthouse, Fletcher was mobbed by the assembled media.

"Are you surprised you got convictions on all counts?" asked one.

"Not in the least," replied the coolly confident Fletcher. "We knew we had the evidence."

"Do you think your dramatic closing statement sealed the case for you, Mr. Fletcher?"

"The closing argument was nothing more than an expression of what the evidence clearly showed . . . that Otis Stamper was guilty on all counts," Fletcher smugly replied.

"Was there ever any concern that the jury might find on behalf of the defendant?" asked another.

"Well, you're always concerned until the final verdict is read, but my team and I had faith in the notion that the jury would interpret the evidence the way we believed they should. It gives us a great deal of confidence and reaffirms our trust in the justice system."

The media onslaught continued as they mobbed Foster outside the courthouse.

"What are your thoughts on the jury's verdict, counsellor?" asked a reporter.

"Well, we are quite disappointed in the fact that they found my client guilty on all counts. Frankly, I don't see that verdict holding up on appeal, but we'll have to wait and see," he replied.

"Are you saying the jury didn't have sufficient evidence to support their verdict?"

"That is certainly the rationale we will be using in the appeal of this matter. There's no doubt about it," Foster responded.

"Are you saying your client didn't get a fair trial?" asked an inquisitive reporter looking for a titillating quote.

"You said that, not me," replied Foster, with a slight smirk. The implication was that was exactly what he thought.

"Do you think the prosecution's closing demonstration impacted the verdict announced?" asked another reporter as Foster attempted to squeeze by.

"Yes, I do," Foster honestly responded. "I think it unduly influenced the jury in an attempt to deflect their focus off the real evidence," he noted.

After several more questions from the assembled throng, Fletcher jumped into a waiting car with Sarah for the trip back to his office. He was met with thunderous applause by a group of spectators on the sidewalk.

"You're getting the rock star treatment," she laughed. It had been a good day for her husband, even if she had her doubts about the quality of the evidence submitted.

"I could get used to being a hero," joked Fletcher, jumping into the car.

Back in the office, the entire staff threw a celebration in Fletcher's honor. With balloons and party favors galore, the partying continued until mid-afternoon, when Fletcher stood on a desk to acknowledge his staff.

"Speech, speech" yelled several in unison. After having been such a pain in the ass to them for so long, Fletcher saw this as a chance to make amends.

"First of all," he began, holding a glass of champagne in his hand, "I want to thank the entire staff for their efforts in getting this case to trial. Were it not for everyone in this room; we would not be standing here today. I particularly want to thank Brian Asher for his enormous insights in the procedural strategies we employed, which allowed us to win several critical pretrial motions which help shape the trial to our advantage."

Asher stood alongside Fletcher as the two embraced. Despite his earlier frustrations with Fletcher, Asher let bygones be bygones and was genuinely excited as to what it might all mean for Fletcher's future.

There had already been some scuttlebutt that Fletcher might be drafted by some local party officials to run for Congress; a proposition that up until then, Fletcher had repudiated. Whatever his future held, however, today was a day to celebrate and celebrate they did.

* * * * * * * *

It wasn't just Fletcher and his staff who were rejoicing in the big court victory. Every media outlet in Knoxville was touting the only story anyone had an interest in throughout the day. The TV channels and online newspapers all led with the same headline:

"Stamper Gets Death Penalty in 'Country Boy' Murders"

The bars and parks throughout the community were overflowing with revelers. It looked like St. Patrick's Day without the green.

For the first time in months, the City of Knoxville could take a deep breath, now that they were assured that the guy who had committed all the murders, they had been reading about was safely behind bars and no longer a threat. No more would they have to go out at night wondering if Otis Stamper was the only mass killer in their community. No more would they have to look their children in the eye and tell them not to worry.

It was literally Independence Day to a community, who for the greater part of two years, was afraid to go out at night to fill-up their cars with gasoline. It was a tribute to Aiden Fletcher that the city felt free again. Because of his courageous stand in prosecuting the one man who had been terrorizing their city, he was quickly becoming the talk of the town.

As Fletcher and Sarah returned home for the evening, they celebrated with a quiet dinner and drinks. Listening to some new age piano on their Pandora station, they reflected on the day's events.

Sarah: "So how does it feel now, Mr. Big Shot," she chuckled. She knew instinctively that the events of the day were most likely going to change their lives forever.

"Feels pretty damn good," replied Fletcher, exhausted from the trial. "What did you think about it all?" he asked.

"Well, I'm very happy for you, Aiden, but I think you were the recipient of a great deal of luck," Sarah responded.

"Luck . . . how so?" said Fletcher.

"I think you know as well as I do that the forensics were not there to establish Stamper's guilt on all seven counts," she replied matter-of-factly.

Respecting her expertise in the field, Fletcher tried to placate her.

"Look, Sarah, I know you're the authority on the subject, but I think we established enough of a connection with the evidence to secure the guilty verdicts. I really do," Fletcher confidently stated.

It seemed, for a moment, he was making his closing statement all over again.

"I know that," she replied. "I'm just looking at it purely from a forensics perspective. If it makes you feel any better, I thought your closing performance was magnificent. Foster was right . . . bravo!" Sarah offered Fletcher a warm smile.

"So let me ask you this, sweetheart," Fletcher queried. He never called her sweetheart. "If you had been on that jury, how would you have voted?"

"In all honesty, leaving the emotion out of it, I would have returned guilty verdicts only on the three cases where his DNA was found," she said. "I don't think I would have had any other choice."

"Glad I didn't have you on the jury," Fletcher laughed. Inside, however, he begrudgingly had to accept that Sarah was probably right.

Contemplating the trial's outcome, he knew he had been lucky . . . very lucky indeed.

Chapter Fifteen

In the weeks after the guilty verdicts came in, Fletcher became an extraordinarily wanted man. Every TV station, news magazine, and public service organization wanted him to appear before them to either give a speech or merely make an appearance.

The cases kept coming into the Sixth District Attorney's office, but he assigned them to his trial staff for prosecution as he had done before the Country Boy murders. He spent the majority of his time speaking in and around Knoxville to civic and volunteer groups. Even the Mayor's Office was constantly seeking to appear with Fletcher at business luncheons in hopes that perhaps some of Fletcher's popularity might rub off on him.

It soon became apparent to all who surveyed the scene that Aiden Fletcher could just about name his tune when it came to his future career. Nothing could ever approach the popularity he had enjoyed after securing the guilty verdicts against Otis Stamper. As such, Fletcher himself began to ponder his next career move.

The offers were coming in fast and furious. Every big-name law firm in town wanted Fletcher to come aboard as a named partner. Just having his name on the firm masthead would ensure an outpouring of new clients and a certain public image boost. That meant big bucks to the firm, and they knew it.

Most of the corporate big-wigs were also encouraging him to work with them, usually with the idea of making him a highly visible public spokesman to promote their brand throughout the region.

Opportunities were also presenting themselves from out of state, as large corporations from Atlanta and Charlotte began to contact him about opportunities there. It wasn't long before Fletcher became one of the most visible, if not most popular, individuals in the state of Tennessee.

Fletcher and Sarah began to discuss some of the offers he was receiving. Their conversations were quite enlightening.

Fletcher: "What do you think about the senior partner offer from Kirkland & Ellis in Atlanta?" he calmly asked Sarah over dinner.

"To be honest, I'm not that crazy about the prospect of moving to Atlanta," she said. "Too much traffic and not enough opportunities for someone in my field."

As always, Sarah's personal ambition was a significant part of her motivation.

"It's just one potential option," Fletcher replied, sensing Sarah's less than enthusiastic response to the question.

In fact, he was glad to have her shoot down the idea. Atlanta didn't have much appeal to him either. The idea of practicing law with a big firm seemed like a monotonous way to spend the rest of his career . . . doing the same damn thing day after day.

Besides, Sarah was hoping to one day land a position with the FBI where she could focus her professional efforts exclusively on forensic analysis. It was something she could never get enough of, and it was a field where she honestly thought she could have an impact.

Fletcher had a few conversations with his trusted aides about his future as well. As Asher came in one morning for his usual briefing, Fletcher sought out his wisdom.

"Brian, where do you think I should take my act from here?" he said with a laugh.

"I not sure you should give up being a prosecutor," replied Asher. "You're at a point where you can get a conviction just by showing up," he jokingly responded, a clear reference to Fetcher's rising popularity in the community.

"I thought about it," replied Fletcher. "I could probably keep this job as long as I wanted," he truthfully asserted.

"Or until you fucked up the next big case," Asher laughed.

"I don't know," Fletcher said. "After the Country Boy case, I'm not sure I could ever top that," he truthfully admitted.

"I'm not sure anyone will ever top that," Asher replied with blunt assurance. "At least not in these parts."

Asher was right. The Sixth District Attorney's job was Fletcher's for as long as he wanted it, and nothing would probably ever take it from him. Almost overnight, he had become an iconic figure in that part of the state.

"Have you thought about politics, Aiden?" Asher inquired, sincerely curious as to his answer.

"Politics?" responded Fletcher in a quizzical tone. "Why would anyone think I'd make a good politician, for Christ's sake?"

"Don't deceive yourself," Asher replied. "There's a lot of people in this town who'd like to see you get into politics."

"Actually, that's why I came in to talk to you. Ole Ambrose Cooper called this morning and invited you to lunch tomorrow. He says he has a couple of important things to talk to you about."

Ambrose Cooper was a legendary figure around Knoxville. He was the founder of the Titan Construction Group, an enormous conglomerate of companies that built commercial buildings throughout the South. The company was headquartered in Knoxville where Ambrose had spent his entire life. He was usually seen in his box at a UT football game where he had long been known as the University's biggest donor. Often the president of the University and other big-name celebrities would accompany him. It was said Ambrose had built half of downtown Knoxville, an assertion that wasn't too far from the truth.

He was known to be a man of his word and one who, when he set his mind on something, didn't stop until he got it.

"Do I have anything on the calendar for tomorrow?" Fletcher asked Asher.

"A couple of meetings in the morning and one at 11:30. After that that nothing until 2:30 p.m. If you're inclined to go to the Ambrose luncheon, I can reschedule the 11:30 for another time," said Asher.

"Where did Ambrose want to meet?" Fletcher inquired.

"Pine Wood Club at noon," Asher quickly replied.

"Well, I guess it wouldn't hurt anything," Fletcher commented, knowing full well this might prove to be an intriguing opportunity.

"Sure," exclaimed Fletcher. "Tell his office I'll meet him there."

* * * * * * * *

The Pine Wood Club was perhaps the most exclusive country club in Knoxville. Founded in 1928, it was a club of first rank among the elite of Knoxville. With a five-year waiting list to become a member, it was known for its generational influence with the movers and shakers of the extended community.

Ambrose Cooper had been a member for as long as anyone could remember. The running joke within the club was that he had been one of its founding fathers. Cooper himself would play up to the joke, letting members know that the club was waiting for him to die before commissioning an oil portrait of him but that he wasn't about to do them a favor.

Fletcher had never met Cooper but had certainly known about him. He was a man you didn't want to have as an enemy.

Pulling up to the winding driveway by the front portico entrance, a valet immediately presented himself as Fletcher stepped out of his dark blue Audi.

"Good day, sir," the well-mannered middle-aged gentleman exclaimed. "Beautiful day today, is it not?"

"That, it most certainly is," replied Fletcher, handing the man his keys and a ten-dollar tip.

"Thank you, sir," said the man. "Enjoy your meeting."

Fletcher turned as the valet drove away in his car. How did he know I had a meeting? He chuckled.

Walking into the front entrance of the club, a well-dressed porter introduced himself.

"Aiden Fletcher here to see Mr. Cooper," he announced.

"Right this way, Mr. Fletcher. The group is waiting to meet you."

The group? What group? I assumed this was just going to be Ambrose and myself, Fletcher thought.

Escorting Fletcher into a private dining room overlooking the immaculate terrace and putting green, Fletcher was a bit taken back when he saw several renowned big-wigs from within the state sitting around an enormous table. At the center of it all sat Ambrose Cooper, flanked by two of his top corporate people.

"Aiden!" Cooper yelled. "Come on in and meet the boys."

Before sitting down, Fletcher slowly circled the table as Cooper introduced the individuals at the table.

"Everybody. This is Aiden Fletcher," announced Cooper. "Aiden, let me introduce you around."

Pointing to the man closest to him, Cooper began.

"First, we have Paul Bowling, Chairman of the Republican Party of Tennessee," Cooper announced.

"Nice to meet you, Aiden," Bowling exclaimed. "We've been hearing an awful lot about you lately."

"Here, here," said the others, almost in unison.

"Pleasure to meet you, Paul," Aiden politely replied.

"Next we have Steve Shepard of the Congressional Liaison Office, and Larry Dumenil from the Republican National

Committee in Washington." Two other prominent business leaders with active political interests filled out the table.

"Nice to meet all of you," said Fletcher in a calm voice, as he took a seat at the table.

If there was any doubt about the gist of the meeting, it was no longer in question.

"Aiden, I'll cut to the chase," announced Cooper in a characteristically direct fashion. "There's a number of us around this table that would like to see you run for Congress. I know you probably don't think you're a politician at heart, but believe me, I'm confident you have what it takes."

The directness of Cooper's proposal had caught Fletcher off guard.

"Well, that's quite an opening line, Ambrose," he joked. "Do you ever just get right to the point?" The others around the table laughed.

"Run for Congress, wow!" said Fletcher. "That's quite a leap," he added. "I've never been involved in national politics."

"Don't worry," assured Cooper, "all politics is local anyway."

"We think you should announce you're a Republican candidate for the Second District congressional seat," announced Cooper. "The men at this table could sure give you some powerful backing."

"I never imagined such a thing," stated Fletcher, obviously caught off guard by what was discussed. "I just don't know quite honestly whether that's my cup of tea."

"Just think about it, Aiden," replied the matter-of-fact Cooper. "We still have several weeks before you have to make a decision," he added.

"But what about Prentice Malone?" asked Fletcher, in reference to the Democratic incumbent who represented Knoxville's Second Congressional District.

"I'm not overly concerned about him," said Cooper. "It'll be a tough race, but it's a fluke he's even in there, to begin with," he concluded. "If it weren't for his rich ole daddy basically buying him the seat last time, he wouldn't even be an issue."

"But he is an issue, Ambrose," interjected Bowling. "A big issue. You know the power of incumbency." Prentice had been the first Democratic incumbent in the Second District seat in a generation. Still, his having campaigned on more federal assistance to farmers and an enhancement of rural entitlement programs was beginning to get people's attention.

"He's a country boy first and foremost and shouldn't be getting too comfortable in that slick ole' congressional seat," chuckled Cooper. "Especially if we can get Aiden to run against him."

"Prentice isn't a bad guy," asserted Bowling. "He's just not one of us."

Being 'one of us' was what politics was all about in this part of the country. Elected officials acted for and on behalf of the big agricultural and commercial interests throughout the state. What was good for them was good for the people . . . like it or not.

The key was getting the right man on the inside; someone who could steer favorable legislation into the various appropriations bills to get the feds to fund most of the projects that the private interests would be making their money on. Malone had never been a loyal soldier in the sense that his political leanings were increasingly drifting more toward social issues than what was important to the business

"Another term or two, and we'll have a hell of a time prying his ass out of that chair," commented Shepard, whose job it was to keep in constant contact with the pulse of Congress.

"Isn't that the truth," seconded Bowling. "You know the power of incumbency is a difficult obstacle to overcome. We can't afford to let Malone get too comfortable up there. After all, some other corporate interests will sneak in and make him theirs, and we'll be left emptyhanded," he added.

Several at the table nodded in agreement.

"This is a critical election, boys," piped Cooper. "We need a strong candidate like Aiden. Someone who will seize the bull by the horns and run."

"Gentlemen, I appreciate your confidence in me," announced the humbled Fletcher. "But this is something I'm going to have to give a great deal of thought to," he continued. "First of all, I don't even know if my wife would be up for this," he said. "After all, she has her own career to think about."

"Take your time Aiden. This was a preliminary meeting. Just so we can gauge your interest. You don't need to commit now in any event," replied Steve Shepard, comfortable with how the meeting had gone.

The truth is, the men assembled for lunch at the Pine Wood Club had been discussing Fletcher's name ever since the Country Boy trial had concluded. Almost overnight, Fletcher had become a luminary in Knoxville. Suave, handsome, and smart as a tack.

The leaders seated around the table were looking for a new leader who might help them advance their agenda in Washington, and push the issues important to the folks at home. Both of the state's Republican senators were well into their late seventies and had held their respective seats for over thirty years. They were tired, but would never give up their seats short of a life-threatening condition.

"Let me tell you some other local issues that are important to the people of East Tennessee, Aiden," intervened Paul Bowling of the state Republican Party. "Take the opioid epidemic throughout this part of the state. It's terrible! We need someone like yourself to really crackdown."

"These fly-by-night pain clinics are popping up like flies and distributing painkiller meds like it was popcorn," replied Dumenil. "People are becoming hooked on that shit every single day."

"After that, they turn to Fentanyl, and I don't have to tell you what that does to people. You can walk anywhere in the east Tennessee mountains and see people on that shit walking around like zombies," Cooper noted. "I don't even want to go there."

"Most of all, we need someone who can work with the pharmaceuticals and the state authorities to ensure a cleaner distribution and more accountable path for dispensing prescription pain killers," said Bowling, who seemed to have studied the issue at length.

"Moreover," he continued, "we need to get a handle on the state's budget deficit, particularly the state pension plan. Ever since the recession, the state budget deficit has severely impacted the already crucial rural provider shortages and hospital closures."

"We've also got to address the health care access challenges here in East Tennessee," Bowling added. "With a nearly ten percent uninsured rate in these parts and the tremendous need for additional treatment facilities, we're going to have to come up with something substantial or write off half the population, which you know will destroy the local economy."

"Bottom line Aiden," Cooper interjected. "We're going to need a strong voice in Washington to advance our priorities, especially for a much-needed online sales tax for goods purchased in Tennessee. We think that could bring in as much as $15 million a year in revenue to the state."

"We hope that strong voice will be you," said Dumenil of the RNC.

As the meeting drew to a close, Fletcher was encouraged by the outpouring of support from such a distinguished list of party operatives. All in all, it had been a very stimulating conversation.

"Gentlemen," he began solemnly, "let me take some time to digest what has been said here today. I will have to re-assess a few things, both personal and professional. As I said, there's also the prospect that my wife, who's a Tennessee girl, not wanting to pick up and leave," he added.

"I'm sure you understand how that goes," he said with a laugh.

"Tell her we'll get her invited to some Georgetown cocktail parties; that'll keep her interested," laughed Dumenil.

"What it may really take is a position with the feds where she can pursue her psychiatric career," Fletcher said seriously.

He knew Sarah would never abandon her career, even if it meant a big jump for Fletcher. That's just not the way they were. Her career was everything to her, even if it meant Aiden had an opportunity he couldn't refuse.

"Well, I wouldn't worry too much about that," said Shepard. "We might be able to make that happen." Hell, once you're a congressman, you should be able to make that happen," he added with a laugh, knowing the rampant nepotism that existed in Washington.

With that, most of the individuals who were sitting at their table got up to bid each other adieu. After several continued conversations, they followed each other out the front door to retrieve their cars from the valet.

Ambrose Cooper stayed behind for a few more words with Fletcher.

"You know Aiden, I'm an old man, and I've seen a lot of things," he began. "Some good, some not so good. But the one thing I know is that power is fluid. It doesn't reside in iconic old musty buildings and statehouses. It manifests itself in the hearts and courage of men, special men, who want to achieve things. Men who want to make things better. I believe you're that kind of man."

"Powerful men can shape events to their own liking," he continued. "You're in a position now to command the kind of respect and support where you can damn near achieve anything you want to."

Cooper's confidence in him was most rewarding, Fletcher thought.

"You've demonstrated to a great many people with the Country Boy trial that you are the type of man who can take on big issues and convince his fellow citizens that he is working on their behalf. I think you have a natural political demeanor," Cooper concluded. "I'd call it a certain political prowess," he added with a glint of a smile. "You're vibrant and instinctively understand the everyday man's mentality," Cooper continued. "Especially those who are down and out. You seem to have a real knack for relating to them. I think you are truly someone who the public at large could gravitate to. You bring an energy to the equation that's infectious. An energy that can inspire others."

Despite his outward concerns, Fletcher realized full well that this was the next big step in his truly remarkable life. If Cooper and the other big boys were willing to sponsor him, it would be damn near impossible to turn them down.

Chapter Sixteen

"How did your meeting with Ambrose go today?" Sarah asked with a certain amount of curiosity. "It's not every day you get to hob-nob with a big shot like him," she added.

Sitting down to a hastily prepared Chinese dish she had quickly thrown together after a long day of work; Fletcher took a long sip from his wine glass and dabbed his mouth with his napkin.

"He wants me to run for Congress," he nonchalantly murmured, eating a bite of his chow mein. Fletcher waited an extended moment to see how his wife would react.

"What!" she exclaimed. "Are you serious?"

"Of course, I'm serious. Would I lie to you?" Fletcher smiled.

"Really? They want you to run for Congress? In Washington?" she proclaimed.

"Ah . . . yeah. That's where the Congress is located . . . in Washington, DC," Fletcher responded with a growing smirk.

"Why you?" Sarah asked in all sincerity. "I know you're a smart guy and all that, but there must be ten other connected people in this town who would give their right arm for that job," she replied.

"That's probably right," Fletcher agreed. "But the party guys I met with today think with my newfound popularity and the threat of Prentice Malone possibly winning a second term, they don't want to take any chances."

"So, they think you're their best shot to re-take the seat?" she asked.

"Apparently so," replied the assuming Fletcher. "Apparently so."

"So, what did you tell them?" Sarah inquisitively asked.

"I told them I'd talk to you and a few other people and get back to them," he casually replied.

"How long do you have to make up your mind?" she asked.

"No big rush," Fletcher responded. "But if I'm going to do it, I probably need to let them know in the next couple weeks."

"There's a lot to consider, Aiden," said Sarah. "Not just if you get elected, but moving; finding another place to live; always being in the public eye. Are you sure you really want that?"

"It would require a lot of sacrifices," Fletcher acknowledged.

"And what about me?" Sarah urged. "You know my career is everything to me. I'd go bat-shit crazy if I couldn't practice psychiatry."

"Pardon the pun," Fletcher laughed. She managed to crack a smile as well with his lame retort.

"I know, I know," he repeated. "It's a big decision. There's a lot more to it than just getting elected to Congress."

“The long days; the endless fundraisers; the travel and speaking engagements; the whirl of people always around you. We might not even get to spend as much time with each other,” he noted.

Sad to say, but neither of them were overly concerned with the latter issue. During the course of their loveless marriage, they had each gravitated to their respective work and found the other’s company only superficially enjoyable. Most of the time they spent together was usually around the dinner table for the occasional meal or at a public event where it was useful to have the other there.

“Wow, Aiden, this is a really big decision,” stated Sarah. “Do you think I would be able to find something interesting up there in my line of work?”

“I promise you if we get elected, I’ll find you something you’ll enjoy. Maybe with the NIH or the FBI. I would think there would be a ton of opportunities for someone like you,” he asserted.

“The FBI!” she exclaimed. “That’s something I would really be interested in. Their forensics work would be something I could really get my teeth into,” responded Sarah. She was now becoming energized by the whole notion of Fletcher going to Washington.

“Can’t promise anything,” replied Fletcher, “but I’ll do my best to make that happen.” In the back of his mind, it occurred to him that Sarah being in the FBI might work to his real advantage.

“There’s a lot to think about, Sarah,” concluded Fletcher. “A lot indeed. Let me talk it over with Brian and a few more people and see where we are in a couple of weeks, OK?”

"OK," said Sarah, now with a bit of optimism that it might just possibly work out assuming they won the election.

* * * * * * * *

Over the next week, Fletcher spoke to many people about the prospects of running for Congress. Enough people wholeheartedly supported the idea, which began to make him feel like it might, in fact, be doable. In addition to some prominent businessmen in the city, Fletcher called Cooper several more times to iron out lingering questions he still had about committee assignments and what he could expect as a first-year Congressman.

The more he thought about it, the more he came to the conclusion it would be like his first-year at law school, where the basic premise was to keep your mouth shut until called upon and just find a way to survive.

Getting off the phone several days later in his office, Fletcher called Brian Asher in for a late-morning meeting.

Since the end of the Stamper trial, the Sixth District Attorney General's Office had been flooded with requests for media and magazine interviews with Fletcher. Knoxville was still abuzz with the afterglow of getting Stamper locked up and sentenced to death.

"Close the door behind you, would you?" he directed Brian.

"Sure, what's up?" asked Asher, sipping on his coffee.

"Just wanted to pick that Yale brain of yours," replied Fletcher. "What d'ya think if I told you I was being asked to run for Congress?"

"In Washington?" Asher responded.

"That was my wife's first reaction!" Fletcher chuckled. "Of course, in Washington."

"Wow! That's quite a load before I even have my first cup of coffee," Asher commented."Is this something you've been thinking about for quite a while?"

"No, not at all," responded Fletcher. "A group of Republican Party people only approached me a week or so ago and encouraged me to run. I told them I would think about it."

"Well, have you decided anything?" Asher inquired.

"Not yet," replied Fletcher. "I'm still trying to sort it all out."

"What do you think of the idea, Brian?"

"Well, of course I have never really dwelled on it, but now that you bring it up, absolutely . . . why not?" he excitedly proclaimed.

"Being a first-term Congressman isn't the greatest, but there's a process in place where you'll be taken care of," Asher said. "Honestly? I think you'd knock it out of the park, Aiden. I really do."

"Plus, you'd get to live in Washington, DC," added Asher. "That's certainly something I would enjoy."

"Well, if things work out alright, we might just be able to find you something to do up there," Fletcher chuckled.

"Seriously, Aiden, I think you should give it a shot. You just never know what it could lead to," Asher asserted. "It sounds like a once-in-a-lifetime opportunity."

They continued their conversation regarding some case matters, and Asher left Fletcher sitting alone in his office.

. . . . A once-in-a-lifetime opportunity, Fletcher pondered. Indeed, yet again!

* * * * * * * *

The Second Congressional District of Tennessee is located in the eastern part of the state and included Knoxville and the surrounding areas. It borders North Carolina to the south and Kentucky to the north. Knoxville's greater metropolitan area pretty much etched its boundaries.

Apart from being the home of the University of Tennessee football team, it was the headquarters for the Tennessee Valley Authority (TVA). For over a hundred years, it was a dyed-in-the-wool Republican district with an occasional Democrat sneaking in to fill a seat. But the way the country was heading, many of the historical trends, especially in the Old South, were beginning to erode away and no longer predictable as the younger generation became enamored with left-leaning policies.

Contemplating whether to throw his hat into the ring, Fletcher spent the next several days talking to the party men he had met at the luncheon with Cooper. More and more, the talk shifted to the necessary fundraising to launch a campaign.

"Ambrose is willing to put up half a million and a couple of his business associates another half a mil," asserted the finance head of the Republican National Committee, Brent Sullivan; a seasoned political pro. "But that is just a start. If you decide it's a go, we will have to go on a rigorous fundraising tour throughout the state."

"My guess is we're going to have to personally raise $5 million and hope another $5 million comes in from outside the state. That's means a lot of exposure and eighteen-hour days from here on in."

"Are you up to that challenge?"

Fletcher wasn't yet ready to commit. He still had numerous questions about how it would all unfold.

"Where would the campaign staff come from?" Fletcher inquired, unsure how to assemble a competent group of political advisers on such short notice.

"Let me take care of that," replied Sullivan. "I'll see that Bowling puts together a crack staff in very short order. He has connections to several top political operatives who would be itching to take on Malone this fall."

"In the meantime, I'll be arranging for the money men to get organized and on the phone. All we need is the final word from you."

"I'll get back to you, Brent," replied a genuinely excited Fletcher. "I just have to tie up a few loose ends before I can give it the all go."

"Before you decide anything, I want you to talk to Sander Percival," said Sullivan. "You know the former Senator from North Carolina. Talk about a treasure trove of knowledge! I think he held that seat for forty years. He can tell you everything about Washington. You owe it to yourself to speak with him before you give us the go-ahead."

"I most certainly will," Fletcher assured, grateful for the suggestion.

"Great!" said Sullivan. "I'll have him call you tomorrow."

"I'll very much look forward to it," responded Fletcher.

* * * * * * * *

The next afternoon at two o'clock sharp, the eighty-two-year-old Percival called Fletcher's office.

"Kathy, I do not want to be disturbed for the next hour, understand?" Fletcher barked to his assistant.

"Yes sir, Mr. Fletcher," she promptly replied.

"Aiden Fletcher speaking," he announced, picking up the phone.

"Mr. Fletcher, this is Sander Percival calling from Charlotte. How are you today?"

Fletcher was immediately absorbed by Percival's melodic southern drawl.

"I'm doing fine Senator, thank you for taking the time to call," responded Fletcher.

"I understand you're thinking of getting into the firestorm of Washington," laughed the old man.

"I am, but it's not too late to opt-out," joked Fletcher.

"Well, let me tell you, my boy. Politics can be the most putrid example of human organization, but it can also be the most satisfying," Percival began.

"Are you willing to give up most of your principles in exchange for power? That's the real question you have to ask yourself," Percival intoned.

"I hadn't quite thought about it that way," responded Fletcher with a sudden, uncertain look on his face.

"If you'll indulge me, let me explain a few of the facts of life of official Washington," Percival continued.

Fletcher slumped back in his chair and waited for what promised to be a most enlightening lecture.

"In most parts of the United States," Percival began, "people are only interested in the overall direction of the country, and they expect their representatives to feel the same way."

"When elected officials get to Washington, they soon come to see how the process really plays out. Issues are no longer debated on their merits; they are merely pieces in the overall game that's being played."

"That's really all it is . . . a game. A political sleight of hand." Percival added. "Issues are merely moved around and traded by the lobbyists, the special interests, and the politicos in exchange for money and power."

"That's a bit more cynical than even I had imagined, Senator," noted the now doubtful Fletcher.

"Just remember this," responded Percival. "That's all it's really about," Percival continued, "money, power, and the ability to manipulate the system. Everything else is make believe. It's not real."

Percival's words hung over Fletcher like a heavy cloak. They resonated like nothing else he could ever remember. Lost for a moment in thought, he let a smile slowly cross his lips as he mimed the words to himself.

. . . . *Make believe. It's not real* . . ..

Percival continued. "The real art of politics is convincing your constituents you're working on their behalf when in reality you're working for your corporate sponsors, who are the real people you owe your allegiance to."

"So, are you saying there's no place for principles?" asked Fletcher. "There has to be a secret to advancing issues that are important to you?" asked Fletcher.

"The unwritten rules of Washington are that Congress places a heavy emphasis on political loyalty, not lasting principles. So don't ever try to buck what the party leaders want, even if you think it may be good for the country. If you do, they will relegate you to the backbenches and the outer reaches of influence. Just be sure to tow the party line, and you should be OK."

"Is that why there's such a gridlock in Washington?" asked the ever-curious Fletcher.

"It's not the so-called political gridlock that's the problem," replied Percival. "Hell, if anything, the parties actually work pretty closely together, but not for the reasons you may think.

They do it to fleece the American public while running up obscene budget deficits and lining the pockets of their sponsors."

"Remember," Percival noted, "the democratic system in this country is nothing but a two-headed hydra. You have two diametrically opposed groups both working the same game. Everything is pay-to-play. Proposed legislation is nothing more than the vehicle by which the big dollars trade hands. Every step of the legislative process costs money . . . every single step."

"So, how does a first-term Congressman achieve any success?" asked Fletcher, not sure how he would become established in the game.

"Everything is about the fundraising," continued Percival. "That's the key. Ingratiate yourself with leadership. Try to get on one of the major committees like Ways or Means or Appropriations. Then spend every waking hour raising money . . . for yourself and for the party. That's what will get you noticed. Learn to play the money game, and you'll succeed."

"It's nothing more than a house of cards, my boy, and if the American people weren't so out to lunch, bat shit stupid, they'd have figured it out decades ago," concluded Percival.

"That was quite an education, Senator, but what was the satisfying part of it you previously mentioned?" asked Fletcher, hoping to find at least some morally redeeming aspect to the work.

Percival paused and let his hair down a bit.

"For all the money-grabbing aspects of life on Capitol Hill," he began, "I will say there are moments when I actually feel my sins might be forgiven," he chuckled.

"Like when we pass a public works bill, for instance, and I'm able to one day see the new park that the money helped make possible. To see young people and the average family who doesn't have much out having a good time, that touches my heart," Percival confessed.

"I've even supported some foreign exchange educational programs where I've gotten to meet some really bright, young minds who've made their way to the U.S. to try and better themselves. To make it possible for them to reach for the stars and achieve their dreams; that's pretty special for me," he admitted.

Fletcher was taken back by the soft spot in Percival's heart. "That's great, Senator. Any last words of advice?" Fletcher asked, pleased with the wisdom he'd been offered.

"Remember one thing, my boy," Percival noted in a now serious voice. "America is a capitalist country. Washington, DC, is nothing but a microcosm of the nation at large. Fortunes are won and lost every day on Capitol Hill, and elected officials are nothing more than the intermediaries that help make it all happen."

He continued. "The Founding Fathers most likely didn't anticipate the type of unfettered greed that exists today, but they did understand human nature. My guess is that they realized it wouldn't take long before open access to the public treasury would become an industry unto itself," remarked Percival.

"If you're lucky enough to gain a seat in Congress, you will become a member of one of the most exclusive clubs in the world," he concluded. "A club that extends its deserving members more privileges than you can ever possibly imagine. Money, power, fame, and let's not forget the women. My goodness sakes!"

"In a nutshell," Percival concluded. "It's the best job in the world. Once you have it, you'll fight to keep it and you'll never let it go."

Percival's words had given Fletcher newfound inspiration: money, power . . . fame!

They had touched a raw nerve in Fletcher's inner psyche. He had never allowed himself to dream this big . . . even as a child.

* * * * * * * *

That night Fletcher and Sarah found themselves at home together after their respective days' work. The subject of running for Congress had been at the forefront of their minds for the past several days.

"Did I tell you I talked to Senator Percival from North Carolina today?" Fletcher said as they sat down to dinner.

Pouring some wine, Sarah was curious about their conversation, knowing it would have a significant effect, one way or another, on Aiden.

"Did he sell you on Washington?" she inquisitively asked, knowing it wouldn't take a lot for Fletcher to close the deal.

"He was quite enlightening, actually," Fletcher began. "Beyond all the bullshit games you have to play, he said there are actually a lot of rewards that go with the job," he added.

"Like what?" Sarah curiously asked.

"Oh, like just helping people generally. He said you could make a difference in people's lives."

"That's nice," she replied. "So, what do you think?" she asked.

"No, what do you think?" Fletcher threw the question back at her, knowing she would have to be all-in on the decision.

"I think on the one hand it would all be quite exciting," Sarah pronounced. "But I'm a little worried about what I would do . . . you know my career is important to me, Aiden."

"I know it is," he replied, "and I wouldn't want you to be unable to pursue it."

"Sarah . . . if I can make this happen," he began, "I promise you we'll get you situated in a position you will really like. My being in Congress should open a lot of doors for you."

She knew what Fletcher was saying was true. If she ever planned to make a big leap in her career, this would be the opportunity to do it.

She paused before responding. "If this is what you really want to do, Aiden, I'll be behind you and help make it happen," she exclaimed. "Have you made up your mind about it?"

Now it was Fletcher's turn to pause. "It's going to be a hell of a lot of work," he announced. "There's going to be a lot of dirt flung at me, which won't be pretty."

"You can handle it," she responded. "Besides, you put away the Country Boy. If you can do that, you can do anything!"

After Fletcher swirled around his sip of wine, he got a look of determination on his previously non-committal face. Her words had closed the deal.

"OK, then let's do it! He excitedly shouted . . . Hell yes! Let's do it!"

The couple gave each other a rare, amorous look and toasted.

"To Congressman Aiden Fletcher!" Sarah exclaimed as the couple raised their glasses in an enthusiastic salute. The smiling Fletcher began to laugh giddily.

"You know, "I'm beginning to like the sound of that. I don't mind saying, I think I could get used to it."

Both smiled as they finished their wine and prepared for the busy days to come.

* * * * * * * *

The next day Fletcher was busy at the office when he grabbed the phone.

"Brian, could you stop in my office for a minute?" Fletcher said over the office intercom.

Within a few moments, Asher walked through Fletcher's office and was instructed to close the door behind him.

"Brian, I want you to be the first to know . . ." Fletcher paused. "I've decided I'm running for Congress," he calmly noted, waiting for Asher's reaction.

"What can I say?" said the now exuberant aide. "I think that's great! I think you'd make a great Congressman."

"Well, it won't be easy. That's for sure," replied Fletcher. "I'm going to need some top people around me. I want you to be my campaign manager . . . how about it?"

"I've never run a campaign Aiden, you know that," said Asher.

"You've got a Yale law degree," responded Fletcher. "Not to mention you're one of the brightest and most perceptive people I've ever been around."

"How'd you like to go to Washington?" exclaimed Fletcher. "If I win this thing, I'll bring you on board with me. It'll be great."

Asher could clearly see the enthusiasm on Fletcher's face. He quickly flashed back on when he had almost gone to DC several years earlier. He was excited by the prospect then, and he was excited now.

"I'm in!" Asher gleefully announced.

"OK, that's what I wanted to hear," Fletcher responded.

"I'm calling Ambrose Cooper this afternoon and get the ball rolling. Get ready for the roller-coaster ride of your life!"

Asher rushed out of his office as Fletcher pondered the reality of it all.

If he won, it would provide a life he could never have imagined. The kind of life only he could truly appreciate.

Chapter Seventeen

"Ambrose Cooper, please. This is Aiden Fletcher calling."

Fletcher twitched as he nervously awaited the response on the other end of the line. This was the call that would initiate it all.

"Aiden, my boy! How are you?" asked the energetic Cooper. "I've been thinking a lot about you."

"That feeling is mutual, Ambrose," responded Fletcher. "I've been thinking a lot about you too," he chuckled.

"Well, that can only mean one thing, right, Aiden?" the wise old bird surmised.

"You're always a step ahead of me, Ambrose," Fletcher extolled.

"So what's the verdict, my boy?" asked the inquisitive old man.

"The verdict is that I'm in, Ambrose," Fletcher excitedly replied. "I've decided to run for Congress."

"That's the news my associates, and I have been waiting to hear," Cooper exclaimed. "That's some good news to these old ears. Very good news indeed"

"So, what's the next step?" Fletcher curiously asked.

"Leave that up to me, Aiden," Cooper responded. "Give me a few days, and I'll put the whole team together; campaign guys, pollsters, media marketing guys, and not the least of which the fundraisers."

"I've heard all about them," replied the now enlightened Fletcher, recollecting his call with Senator Percival.

"Do you have anyone in mind for campaign manager?" asked Cooper.

"Sure do," responded Fletcher, "my deputy, Brian Asher. Yale law and a very bright guy."

"I've met him," replied Cooper. "Sharp guy, alright, but I'm going to suggest we give him a little campaign expertise. I have the perfect guy in mind . . . Joe McCoy. That guy knows more about Tennessee politics than anyone around," responded Cooper.

"He ran the Governor's successful campaign last year and is just itching to get back in the game."

"He sounds like a godsend," replied Fletcher. "What does he want for his trouble?"

"Probably what most people would want," answered Cooper. "A position in Washington after the election. He's a political animal and would just thrive in DC."

"That shouldn't be a problem," said Fletcher. "He would be in a candy store up there. Anything else?" Fletcher inquired.

"Well, I'll check in with the boys," said Cooper. "I expect they are going to want you to make a formal announcement in the next few days, once we get the organization up and running."

"I'll start writing my announcement speech," Fletcher remarked. "I have a few ideas I'd like to convey."

"That's great, Aiden," smirked Cooper. "Just make sure you mention the Country Boy murders everywhere you go. Got that?"

"Of course!" exclaimed the grinning Fletcher, wistfully pondering the comment.

One thing was for sure . . . wherever he was going, the Country Boy was going with him.

* * * * * * * *

The big day soon came when Fletcher was to make his announcement that he was running for Congress. The story had leaked to the mainstream media in the days preceding the event, and the energy was palpable. The citizens of Knoxville had the first real opportunity to publicly acknowledge Fletcher for all he had done to rid them of their murderous nemesis Otis Stamper, and they weren't about to shy away.

The speech was scheduled to be made on the steps of the Sixth District Courthouse, with American flags surrounding him. A dynamic photograph of Fletcher was on the podium that read "Tennessee Loves Aiden" and "Aiden for Congress." It would be a short speech, but one packed with emotion and hope.

Cooper's legions had made sure the turnout was enormous. A pep band was playing patriotic themes while banners and streamers littered the ground beneath them. Small children were playing with their party favors while adults mulled around to get a glimpse of their hero.

By having rid Knoxville of the most heinous episode in its recent history, Aiden Fletcher had become nearly a rock star. He was undoubtedly the city's favorite son, and it seemed anything the citizenry could offer him, they would. With his handsome countenance and commanding bearing, he was the personification of what a popular political figure would look like.

As Fletcher and his wife made the long, choreographed walk down the courthouse steps, it looked like he had already won. Thunderous applause broke out as the Mayor gave a few remarks before introducing Fletcher. The anticipation was electric.

Approaching the dais, Fletcher soaked up the genuine and unrelenting applause from the massive group of citizens. Folks in dress attire and folks in overalls all came out to show their respects to the man who had liberated their city and their lives. The moment for him to speak had arrived.

"Ladies and Gentlemen," he began, "I'm Aiden Fletcher, and I'm formally announcing my candidacy for Tennessee's Second District seat in the United States Congress."

The raucous applause again broke out along with numerous yelps, howls, and foot stomps as the audience bestowed their deafening and uncompromised approval.

"I'm running for Congress because I want to stand up for America!" he began. "Who is with me?" The applause was immediate and enthusiastic. "Who's ready to send a message to the elites in Washington that the voice of East Tennessee is no longer going to be ignored?" The roar from the crowd intensified even further.

"You know, I'm running against an incumbent who seems to think that taking more money out of our local businesses and sending it to Washington is somehow going to make our lives better. Do you honestly believe that?" A cascade of boos rained down from the masses as Fletcher shook his head in disdain.

"Ole Prentice Malone wants you to think that if you just pay a little higher tax that he'll make our health care system in East Tennessee a whole lot better. Do you think he's telling you the truth?" A collective 'NO . . . OOO!' rang out from the audience.

With perfect comedic timing, Fletcher then let off a zinger. "Folks, Prentice and his ilk can't even make the Postal Service run right. Under his watch, he'll turn it back into the Pony Express!" The crowd roared with laughter.

"Folks, in all seriousness, this election boils down to a few basic issues that most of us in these parts, no matter what our political affiliation, can agree on. First, my most basic priority is to ensure that the streets of Knoxville continue to be safe for our children to play in during the day and for our wives and daughters to go out into at night."

A tumultuous applause spontaneously erupted as the line was meant to tweak the pulsating fervor of the crowd's weeks' long jubilation stemming from the recent conviction and incarceration of Otis Stamper, the "Country Boy" murderer.

"Country Boy! Country Boy!" began the deafening and incessant chant.

"If you send me to Congress, I can assure you that never again will we allow a vicious monster to roam our streets and terrorize our citizens . . . never again!" Fletcher was playing the Country Boy sentiment for all it was worth.

"Ladies and Gentlemen, with your help, we can get Tennessee and the country at large back on track with two simple things," Fletcher asserted. "1) Your common sense, and 2) an abiding faith in God." The applause was relentless as

Fletcher had touched a deep and long-held belief in the Bible-thumping crowd.

"I'd like to propose a few common-sense solutions to the problems facing East Tennessee and this great country of ours," Fletcher continued.

"First, to help grow the economy, get the danged government OUT . . . OF . . . THE . . . WAY!" In approval, the crowd leaped out of their chairs as several pulled out their flasks and began swigging away.

"Second, let's do something about unfettered spending in this country. Let's get people off the hopelessness of welfare and into good-paying, rewarding jobs!" Another roar was let loose by the audience.

"Why is it that my opponent only seems to want to talk about all the good things your higher taxes are going to bring?" Fletcher yelled. "Before we even begin to talk about raising working people's taxes, don't you think we ought to be talking about cutting the waste, fraud, and abuse that accompanies most of our federal spending? What happened to that conversation Prentice?" he scolded.

The applause vigorously continued as the people enthusiastically looked at each other and mutually nodded their approval.

"Folks, if I accomplish nothing else in my role as your representative, I'll make you one promise here today," Fletcher assured. "That is, I will do everything within my power to help ensure the bloated budget in Washington gets cut before one more, hard-working Tennessean pays a nickel more in taxes!"

Wholesale pandemonium broke out among the now deliriously partisan crowd.

"There's a couple more issues I'd like to speak to that are important to the people of East Tennessee," he continued, keeping the vibes hopping.

"First, on illegal immigration, I'll fight to keep the hard-working folks in, while I'll support any and all measures to keep the lawbreakers out!" Fletcher asserted. The roar of the crowd continued unabated as their whoops and hollers continued to grow in intensity.

"Finally, when it comes to the federal courts, I'll see to it that the next President appoints real judges . . . those who understand their role is to simply interpret the law . . . not just a phalanx of cultural warriors to the bench. Judges that instinctively know that late-term abortion is immoral. Judges that understand their role and respect the Constitution. Judges who will honor judicial precedent."

He paused to let the impact of his words sink in.

"Folks, if you feel the same way that I do on these issues, then I humbly ask for your support. I need to have you get out there and do your part. We need volunteers to spread the word of our campaign. We need fundraisers to help us raise enough money to take on Prentice Malone and his gang of Washington bureaucrats. We need local activists to support our campaign by handing out campaign literature so we can share the word with all the citizens of Knoxville."

"Ladies and Gentlemen, it will take all of us to stand up and take back our state and take back our country. We can do it with your help . . . and God's."

"Thank you all, and God bless America!"

Moving off the podium, Fletcher embraced Sarah and gave her a huge kiss for the cameras. The crowd was ecstatic.

"Aiden! Aiden! Aiden!" began the rhythmic chant.

Turning around, Fletcher caught a glimpse of Ambrose Cooper in the VIP section of the makeshift bleachers. He was clapping loudly and gave Fletcher an enthusiastic thumbs up. He knew he had just witnessed the making of a political star. His instincts had proven him right. Aiden Fletcher was the man who would lead him and his associates back to the corridors of power.

Thinking back on the events of the afternoon, Fletcher was pleased. He had enthusiastically inspired the crowd with his thoughts and emotion. The speech had achieved its intended results. Virtually overnight, he had become the prohibitive favorite for the Republican nomination for the Second District congressional seat.

It was a great speech and a great moment. For Aiden Fletcher, the future he could never have imagined in his youth was coming true before his eyes.

Chapter Eighteen

The primary election was held that June and Fletcher had laid waste to his Republican opponents. Two had dropped out in the days following Fletcher's announcement, and the other three offered but token opposition. As the final tally came in on the primary night, Fletcher had secured the Republican nomination with a staggering seventy-eight percent of the vote.

Immediately after the results poured in, many operatives with the other campaigns made efforts to secure a position with Fletcher and his now hitting-on-all-cylinders team. Within a relatively short time, Cooper and his associates had ponied up the initial money raised and set up a cadre of campaign advisors to keep Fletcher's message in the limelight.

A finance director was soon appointed to secure an ongoing flow of contributions. They identified the highest-performing network of donors and continuously solicited campaign funds from fundraising events and town hall meetings.

An opposition research director was appointed to scrutinize every aspect of Prentice Malone's life and tenure in Washington. Like most such investigations, sufficient dirt was uncovered and kept Malone and his compadres from creating a false narrative about his gleaming childhood and successes as a young man. His numerous businesses and associations with special interests would soon become a major issue in the campaign, as would his tax and business records.

As Fletcher was combing over some position papers one afternoon, Brian Asher approached him on some personal research he was doing.

"Aiden, the research team is trying to organize a comprehensive biography on you, not just for our own benefit, but to see where the opposition might try to exploit you. Can we talk a little bit about your early background?" Asher asked.

"Sure," responded the leery Fletcher. "Not much to say that you don't already know," he calmly added.

"Yeah, I know the basics," Asher responded. "Just thought you might like to fill in the blanks."

"Well, Brian unfortunately, the basics of my early life are all I have," Fletcher earnestly began. "As you know, I grew up in foster homes and state orphanage facilities throughout Southern California. I have no family whatsoever, and other than my college years at San Diego State, I have nothing worth sharing about my younger days."

"Nothing else about your early life that you think might be important for people to know about you?" Asher asked. "Like, what were the names of a couple of the foster care facilities you stayed at? Maybe we could contact them, and someone may still remember you. Maybe they might even share some anecdotes from your youth."

Not wishing to expound on the topic, Fletcher abruptly replied. "Nothing except some childhood anxieties that I don't think are worth mentioning, nor do I particularly want to re-live," Fletcher responded, hoping to end the inquiry.

"Well then, let me ask you this," Asher added, getting the hint but still not quite satisfied.

"Is there anything about your early life that we wouldn't want the opposition to know about because I can guarantee they'll be digging for any dirt whatsoever they can find on you?" Fletcher contemplated the question and paused ever so slightly before he answered.

"Brian, you have to understand something," Fletcher solemnly began.

"As an orphan, I simply didn't have a lot of opportunities like most people. I didn't play on sports teams. I don't have a recorded family background, and there aren't a lot of people who knew me growing up. At least not anyone that I've kept up with. Other than a couple of professors that helped me in college, there isn't much about my early background to talk about . . . I wish there was," he wistfully replied.

"So, where do you think we should begin in telling the people about your life story?" asked the now curious Asher.

"Tell them my life began in Tennessee," replied Fletcher, realizing he hadn't given Asher a lot to work with.

"OK, at least we'll make that part look good," said the somewhat disappointed Asher, turning to leave Fletcher's office.

Contemplating the discussion that had just concluded, Fletcher let the slightest of grins cross his lips.

Yeah . . . at least make that part look good.

* * * * * * * *

As the campaign geared up, much time was spent by the team's policy director filling out the innumerable questionnaires offered by potential endorsing groups who wanted to be associated with Fletcher's campaign. Shortly thereafter, the grassroots organizing unit geared up by hiring a field director and organizing the various phone banks and door-to-door canvassing efforts.

A considerable amount of money went to building up a communications effort that focused on newspapers, radio, and online interviews. One assistant was brought on board exclusively to handle Facebook, Twitter, and Instagram accounts while Snapchat editors worked to spread the campaign's message on a daily basis.

With the assembly of highly skilled campaign operatives, Brian Asher transitioned to the role of communications director and doubled as the campaign's press secretary. His quick wit and intelligence, combined with his astute ability to think on his feet, made him indispensable to the overall effort. He was considered Fletcher's right hand-man and sat in on every meeting of any importance, often making decisions for Fletcher when he could not attend.

The most important aspect of Asher's job was to manage Fletcher's backbreaking schedule. Fletcher was putting in nearly eighteen-hour days throughout the last weeks before the election, between the requests for interviews, policy pronouncement meetings, and fundraising efforts.

Most of the strategic decisions were guided by the polling and focus groups, which influenced the advertising and mail solicitations. Donor databases and text messaging efforts aided voter contact initiatives, not to mention the campaign merchandise arm, which provided the thousands of campaign T-Shirts, hats, and bumper stickers seen throughout Knoxville.

During a lull in the campaign, Fletcher and Sarah were able to share a quiet evening alone just weeks before the election.

“What a crush!” remarked Sarah as the two collapsed around their outdoor fireplace.

“Did you ever think it would be like this?” she asked, trying to get a handle on Fletcher’s mental health after the toll the long weeks had taken.

“Well, we knew it wouldn’t be easy,” he replied. “They don’t just give out these congressional seats like popcorn, after all.”

“You know, I hope you do win,” she casually remarked. “I think I’m finally ready for something new. Maybe DC might do us both some good.”

“Sounds like you could use a change of pace,” Fletcher responded.

“Yeah, I probably do,” she replied. “I think I’d like to be a smaller fish in a bigger pond for a change,” she said.

“Well, if we get to Washington, that’s definitely going to be a bigger pond,” Fletcher remarked.

“How about, you Aiden? Have you had enough of Knoxville?” she inquired, not knowing his response.

“You know, I’ve never really thought about it before,” he answered. “These last two years with the trial and now the campaign have been an absolute whirlwind. I’ll just cross that bridge if I come to it. He knew there was a lot of work ahead before he even imagined finding himself in Washington.

As Sarah went to bed, leaving Fletcher sitting in front of the dying embers of the warming fire, he contemplated Sarah’s question.

Knoxville had been very, very good to him. He had been lucky to have found so many fulfilling opportunities during the last several years. If all went well . . . Washington, he imagined, would provide so many more.

* * * * * * * *

As the last weeks of the campaign geared up, Fletcher prepared for the state-wide televised debate with Prentice Malone. It was always a nerve-racking time for candidates as they never knew what zingers the moderator or the opponent might throw at them.

Fletcher, however, was confident as the telecast drew near. He knew he could deflect anything that Malone might try to throw at him and maybe even turn it on him to his own advantage.

The debate was to be held in the town hall in front of an audience of 150 people. Fletcher's policy advisors pummeled him in the waning days before the debate with the latest facts and figures in an attempt to catch Malone off guard and make him appear to be unprepared.

Despite the optimism of his chief supporters and his campaign team, Fletcher knew the odds of defeating Malone were not in his favor. In a startling statistic, ninety-eight percent of all congressional incumbents were re-elected. Such congressional stagnation had been the norm for decades, and despite an opponent's popularity, most incumbents simply had the advantage in money and exposure. The fact that incumbents had won the previous election meant that they had at least some appeal to the local electorate. Incumbents usually also had a well-oiled campaign team that could simply overwhelm a first-time candidate's efforts.

The most significant advantage for incumbents was simply the pork-barrel spending they had most likely been able to procure for their district. Fortunately for Fletcher, Malone himself was but a first-term Congressman whose footprint in the district was not yet fully established.

Nor at this point was he even a household name. With all of Malone's advantages, Fletcher knew he would have to win by mere force of personality. That and by making Malone look bad. Even better . . . to make him look inept. Like a stumbling neophyte by comparison.

It was a tall task, but Fletcher was prepared.

Chapter Nineteen

The debate began at 8:00 o'clock on a Wednesday night one week before the election. The moderator was a local newscaster with a long tenure on the city's airwaves. The panel of questioners included a representative from the local teacher's union; the president of the Knoxville Chamber of Commerce; and a member of a citizen's group for racial equality.

After opening statements, where Fletcher presented a confident self-image, the candidates debated the Affordable Care Act, Immigration, and the economy. The panel opened the questions up to the televised audience who had texted their concerns to the moderator.

Malone was quick to get out of the gate.

"Ladies and Gentlemen, my opponent, would have you believe that I am single-handedly responsible for the entire national economic recession," he said to a mild chuckle from the audience. "Fact is, the Second District of Tennessee has one of the most enviable records in the nation on economic progress during these difficult times," he proudly proclaimed.

Fletcher jumped right in to respond.

"Need I remind Congressman Malone that he is not speaking on the floor of the House of Representatives where the Constitution guarantees him immunity from any lies or falsehoods asserted during congressional debate," said Fletcher with a debonair smile.

The audience immediately broke into laughter as Malone grew visibly uncomfortable.

"You mentioned the facts. Let me tell you what the real facts are, Congressman," Fletcher continued in an all-out frontal assault. "The Second District has the second-lowest per capita income of any district in the Tri-State area. The people of East Tennessee are, in actuality, not seeing the increase in economic opportunities that the Congressman would have us believe."

Malone was taken back. "I think the people of Tennessee can certainly look forward to improved working conditions in the very near future," he optimistically replied.

Fletcher saw his opening. "Now that's something I can agree with, Congressman. As soon as you are defeated for the Second District congressional seat, I think the economic opportunity in these parts will improve tremendously."

The audience roared with approval.

Malone knew it was time to pull out the heavy ammunition. "My opponent seems to act like he knows what is best for the fine people of Tennessee, yet he has only lived here for a relatively short period of time," he announced.

"In fact, he refuses to give us much information on his background other than he grew up an orphan in Southern California. I think the people of Knoxville have a right to know more about someone who just showed up here out of nowhere. Care to enlighten us, Mr. Fletcher?"

Fletcher had prepared for the question. "Congressman Malone . . . you come from a very prosperous, family and you've had opportunities most people in these parts could never dream of. I, like many of the people watching this debate, came up the hard way. I never had a father. My mother died at a very early age. I had no one to take me in."

"The fact that I'm standing here today is a testament to the good, old-fashioned values we like to teach our kids . . . hard work . . . a moral compass, but most of all, a respect for those underprivileged individuals who weren't born with a silver spoon in their mouth." He peered directly at Malone for an extended pause to let the assertion sink in.

With a cool, collected bearing, Fletcher continued staring at the camera as if he were directly speaking to the people watching at home.

"I have no background or noted family history that I can offer the good people of Tennessee that might legitimize me as a contributing member of society," he continued. "I can only offer them the values that I came to adopt for myself. The values of wanting to make something of my life, to put myself in a position to help others, and if the time ever came, to set an example for all young people, who perhaps like me, have had nothing or nobody to look up to."

"So yes, I am new to Tennessee, but the values I bring with me are as old as the Smoky Mountain hills, which many of our fine citizens call home. They are the values of community, courage and respect for our fellow man." He concluded with a flourish.

"Ladies and Gentlemen, this election is not about who can utilize federal resources to better our personal benefit. It is about giving folks the opportunity to carve out a meaningful and fulfilling life for themselves and their children."

"It's about sitting out on your porch at night after a satisfying meal, pleased that you've been able to provide for your family for another day and holding the promise that you will be able to provide for their futures in the days to come."

"That is what all of us strive for. It is what all of us aspire for our children. It is what has made this country great for over 200 years. It is what it means to be an American. To live in a free and prosperous country where all of us, no matter what our upbringing, are all free to make our own way to the best of our ability."

The moment was electric. Fletcher's passion and good old-fashioned, down-home values resonated with all who watched the debate. It became the talk of the town in the days leading up to the election. His soliloquy was replayed over and over on every media outlet in the region.

Fletcher had come to represent all that was good about the community of Knoxville. In a matter of a couple of years, he had risen from being an unknown prosecutor to the favorite son for a large segment of the local population. Would it be enough to see him through the election?

Only fate would determine the outcome.

* * * * * * * *

It was Tuesday, November 3rd, and the polls opened at 6:00 a.m. The latest vote counts showed Malone leading Fletcher by 4,000 votes by mid-day, before the eastern part of Knox County tabulations began to come in. By 5:00 p.m., the race was neck and neck as both candidates garnered support from their most loyal constituencies. Finally, by 6:00 p.m., Fletcher surged into the lead as a higher-than-expected vote tally from the more rural parts of the county begins to trickle in.

Finally, by 8:00 o'clock, with nearly 350,000 votes cast, the TV stations called the race for Fletcher, who was declared the upset winner with 51% of the vote or 178,000 votes. Fletcher's campaign retinue had been encamped in the main ballroom of the Hyatt Place Downtown Hotel where over 2,000 loyalists and campaign workers fretted away the hours until the results were considered official at 9:00 p.m.

Jubilation was rampant as the six-piece band broke out in a snappy rendition of "Happy Days Are Here Again." Asher and the rest of the senior campaign officials danced uninhibitedly to the strains of "Rocky Top Tennessee," and local luminaries made their way into the ballroom to hear the winner give his much-anticipated acceptance speech.

As his senior aides exalted around the stage waiting for their candidate to make an appearance, Fletcher and Sarah, sipping on French champagne and munching on appetizers that the hotel had provided, were upstairs on the phone taking congratulatory calls from supporters throughout the country.

Finally making their way down to the main ballroom amidst a phalanx of security officers and hotel personnel, the confetti flew, and the cheers erupted as the couple strode across the stage to receive their ecstatic supporters.

* * * * * * * *

At the Riverbend Maximum Security Institution in Nashville, Otis Stamper and the other forty-eight death row inmates watched the gala from their prison cells. Amidst the constant chatter and yells, Stamper watched as Fletcher arrived at the podium to make his acceptance speech.

"Goddamn sum bitch," screamed Stamper as Fletcher was introduced.

"Hey, Otis! Ain't that the mutha that put you away?" laughed an inmate in the cell next to him.

"Hey man," yelled another, "you made his ass famous!"

"Shut the hell up, you dirt bags!" screamed Stamper. "That lyin' piece of crap set me up," shrieked Stamper.

"I didn't kill all the women he said I killed," Stamper continued. "He just made that stuff up to make himself look good."

"I didn't kill all those women, and he had them give me the death penalty, anyway," Stamper added.

"That bastard is going to get his if it's the last thing I ever do," Stamper asserted, throwing his cup at the TV. The other inmates laughed upon hearing Stamper's empty threat.

"That no good, lying prick is nothing short of evil," Stamper asserted to anyone who would listen.

"I'm telling you, he's an evil son-of-a-bitch."

* * * * * * * *

As Fletcher stepped to the microphone with Sarah by his side, he forced a pause as the celebratory cheers continued unabated. After several of the officials on stage motioned for the raucous crowd to calm down, Fletcher finally was able to speak.

"To everyone here tonight," he began, "I want to thank you from the bottom of my heart. Sarah and I would not be standing on this stage if it were not for the dedicated efforts of each and every one of you."

After another extended round of applause, he continued.

"This was a tough campaign, and I want to particularly thank Brian Asher and Ambrose Cooper for putting together a campaign staff that got the job done and put us over the top."

After thanking numerous other state and party officials, he said what was in his heart.

"As Sarah and I head off to Washington, we take with us the hopes, dreams, and aspirations of the multitude of Tennesseans who have placed their confidence in us to represent them in a way that they will be proud."

"We intend to do just that," Fletcher continued. The applause started up again.

"Although we will be spending a great deal of time in that god-forsaken place they call Washington, DC . . ." he paused for the crowd to break out in laughter, "we will never forget our roots right here in Knoxville."

"So again, for everyone who is here tonight, thank you from the bottom of our hearts and let's get to work!"

The band broke out again in a celebratory tune as revelers continued their festivities for a couple more hours until the hotel bar finally closed down.

Fletcher walked slowly through the crowd and thanked as many individuals as he could before fatigue finally set in, and he and Sarah found their way to the top floor of the hotel to their suite. There, with a half-empty bottle of champagne, they toasted his victory and sat just staring at each other.

"We did it!" exclaimed Fletcher.

"We sure did," Sarah replied, with a broad smile on her face.

"What now?" she added, with an uncertain expression on her normally confident face.

"We go to Washington and figure it all out once we get there," replied the chuckling Fletcher, not seemingly having a clear answer to her simplistic question.

"We'll take it one step at a time," Fletcher assured her. "There's a whole mechanism that will help us make sense of it once we get ourselves situated."

"Goodnight, Congressman," said the exhausted Sarah as she finished her last sip of champagne.

"I like the sound of that," replied Fletcher, sitting for a few more minutes trying to put the evening's event into some kind of perspective.

After reveling in the excitement of his election, Fletcher paused as he stared out the window of the suite into the peaceful Knoxville night.

His mind reflected on what had brought him to this moment and what it would mean to his future.

The image of Otis Stamper flashed through his brain as Fletcher thought back on the Country Boy phenomenon and how perfectly everything had managed to work out. Pulling out his pen, he scribbled, "Congressman Aiden Fletcher" on a notepad and contemplated his new legislative persona.

Next to it, he wrote the name of Otis Stamper and laid back on the sofa. After a few moments staring poignantly at the names on the pad, he got up to turn off the lights as a recurring thought occupied him.

Together, the two of them had made it all possible.

Chapter Twenty

In the days following the November election, Fletcher was busy with the transition to Washington. In addition to selling their house, he and Sarah had a hundred things to take care of before the big move.

Asher assisted Fletcher in interviewing a few key congressional staff positions with people from Tennessee he could trust. After a third straight day of interviews, Asher was about to leave for an appointment when Fletcher called him into his office.

"I guess that pretty much wraps up most of the key staff positions, Brian," Fletcher said. "We've got commitments from some top people for our legislative director, administrative assistant, and press secretary, which ought to put us in pretty good shape going into January."

"Yeah, that ought to take care of the staff appointments," Asher stated, "at least for now."

There's still one more thing on the agenda," responded Fletcher.

"What's that?" replied Asher.

"I need you to say yes to be my chief of staff," Fletcher said nonchalantly.

"You know, I was hoping you might ask me about that," remarked Asher, breaking into a huge smile.

"You've always had an itch to go to Washington, haven't you, Brian?" Fletcher exclaimed.

"You know I have," Asher responded.

"Well, here's your big chance," Fletcher smiled. "What 'ya say?"

"Thanks, Aiden. It would be an honor," Asher humbly replied, excited about the prospect of a career in Washington.

"I think we can accomplish some great things together," Fletcher remarked, putting his arm around Asher as the two men engaged in a warm hug.

"I'll always be there for you," said Asher, in a sincere show of loyalty.

"Likewise," replied Fletcher. "We'll always have each other's back."

"Something tells me that's going to be a full-time job," responded Asher with an ominous laugh.

* * * * * * * *

Fletcher and Sarah began making short jaunts up to Washington to do some house hunting and get a feel for the lay of the land. After receiving advice from nearly everyone about where to live, they settled on an old brownstone near Dupont Circle in the District near 20th and Massachusetts Avenue N.W.

It was located a block from the Woodley Park Zoo. It was only four short Metro stops on the Red Line to Judiciary Square, a short walk to the Capitol and the various House Office

Buildings where Fletcher's congressional office would be located.

Fletcher kept busy during their short stays, in Washington meeting with national party leaders and various lobbyists who were already wining and dining with him in order to seek his support on favorable legislation in the House.

In what seemed like a nonstop cycle of introductions to senior House members and party leaders, Fletcher made acquaintances with committee members and their key staff assistants, people who Fletcher soon discovered were almost as powerful as the congressional members themselves.

Arriving in December for freshman orientation, Fletcher mingled with fellow new congressional members and the Capitol Hill press corps. There he was given a short tutorial on life as a member of Congress and was able to bring on board a transition aide who would oversee setting up operations and managing logistics in the new office.

Fletcher soon found himself crowded into a committee room at the Rayburn House Office Building for a ritual known as the office lottery, where new members drew numbered disks from a silk-lined box. The number drawn would determine the order in which the new member would be allowed to choose from the available office spaces.

Fletcher's lottery number came up, and after an exhaustive search of available offices, selected Suite 204 in the Longworth Office Building, which housed approximately 250 congressional offices. Thereafter came the Steering Committee assignment process, and Fletcher was fortunate enough to be appointed to the House Financial Services Committee; a powerful entity which controlled a great many of the money matters in the House. In addition, he received an assignment to four lesser subcommittees.

It was late December, Fletcher and Sarah had made final preparations for their move to Washington. With assistance from some of Fletcher's political operatives, Sarah had received a two-year study appointment as a senior psychiatrist at the National Institutes of Health and left for Washington a couple of weeks early while Fletcher wrapped up their affairs in Knoxville. "Happy New Year Aiden," said Sarah, catching an Uber to the airport, knowing they would be apart for the holiday.

"Happy New Year to you Sarah," responded Fletcher. "It's going to be a great year," he added.

* * * * * * * *

Asher and Fletcher got together for dinner in Knoxville on December 31st at the Lion's Head restaurant a couple of nights before they were scheduled to depart for Washington. While enjoying a bottle of Burgundy, and thick, Wagyu steaks, they had extended discussions regarding staffing, orientation plans, and political policy. It was a grand last evening together in the town that had made it all happen.

"Have you found a place to live yet, Brian?" asked Fletcher, over after-dinner drinks.

"Sure did," he replied. "Nice little basement apartment on Capitol Hill. It's off First Street and Independence Avenue, not far from the Cannon House Office Building."

"Are you sure that's a safe area at night?" asked Fletcher, having heard about the historical crime rate in that part of the city after dark.

"Oh, I think it will be fine," replied Asher. "There used to be some issues with some robberies and break-ins, but I'm not overly worried about it."

"Well, just be careful, nevertheless," responded Fletcher.

"I will, mother," Asher jokingly responded. "See you in DC in a couple of days."

"See you then," smiled Fletcher. Turning to leave, they gave each other a warm embrace in celebration of all they had achieved together.

"Don't forget what I said," reminded Fletcher. "You never know who's out there roaming the streets at night."

Chapter Twenty-One

The early-morning sun slowly inched its way above the glistening dome of the U.S. Capitol as dawn broke across the grayish, January sky to introduce Washington, DC, to a blistering-cold, winter day.

Fletcher had arrived in Washington with a full schedule before him. On January 5th, he was sworn into office and allowed on the floor of the House for the first time. He and Asher immediately began with their fundraising efforts which they soon learned was not only a full-time effort but the most important aspect of Fletcher's job as a newly-elected Congressman.

His schedule was a perpetual round of appearances, fundraising, lunches, and nonstop telephone requests by special interest and party leaders alike. Occasionally, he would take a moment to meet with a visiting constituent and have his picture taken with them.

"That's a guaranteed vote," he would always say after such an impromptu meeting.

His nights were usually filled having dinners with lobbyists and interest groups wanting to bend his ear for something or another. The schedule allowed him minimal downtime to contemplate all that was going on around him. Learning the ropes was not an easy task and it required an almost immediate allegiance to the money game.

It was during a fundraising call with one of the state party leaders, that Brian Asher had first learned of a stunning occurrence in Knoxville shortly before he and Fletcher had left.

"Brian, I heard it on the Q.T. that there's been another suspicious murder in Knoxville," the source had told him.

"Oh really!" exclaimed the shocked Asher. "Where was it?'

"Over near the Civic Auditorium and Coliseum in the Old City," said the source.

"What happened?" The curious Asher asked.

"Don't know exactly," said the source, "all I heard was a young woman had been strangled to death."

"I can't believe it," a dejected Asher responded. "Just when it looked like we had things under control."

"Well, it could have been a domestic abuse situation, a drunken assault gone over-board, or some random killing . . . who the hell knows? There is some evidence of it being a robbery, however. The victim's purse was strewn on the ground beside her with no money or credit cards inside. But I think the Police Chief and the Mayor are not letting this one out of the bag. They certainly don't want the public catching wind of it this time around."

"I can see why," replied Asher, still scratching his head. "I'll be sure and tell Aiden."

"Tell me what?" Fletcher queried as he burst through the door of his office suite, reading yet another policy paper.

Asher gently closed the door to his office and spoke in a soft tone.

"You won't believe this Aiden, but there's been another strangulation murder in Knoxville," Asher slowly began.

"My God! What!" replied Fletcher, visibly shocked hearing the news. "When? Where?"

"Downtown, near the Civic Auditorium, apparently just a few nights ago," replied Asher.

"New Year's Eve?"

"Ah . . . yeah," Asher answered, finding Fletcher's response a bit prescient.

"Any further details available?" asked the intently curious Fletcher.

"Signs point to a robbery, but even that is not for certain. That's about it right now," advised Asher, "but I'm sure we'll be hearing more."

Fletcher chewed on the news for a few moments and rendered his opinion on the matter.

"An isolated event . . . had to be," replied Fletcher.

"Let's hope so," responded the still shaken Asher.

"I'm just glad it's someone else's concern now," announced the sullen Fletcher.

"Yeah," replied Asher. "I just hope it doesn't cause the whole 'Country Boy' thing to blow open again."

"That, I'm not worried about," responded the confident Fletcher. "We nailed the right guy, and his name is Otis Stamper."

"Keep me abreast about it," Fletcher ordered, ending the conversation as he turned for the door and briskly walked down the hall.

* * * * * * * *

That night at home, with moving boxes still strewn in all directions, Fletcher had a rare evening alone with his wife.

"How's the new job going?" he inquired.

"Not bad," she replied. "I'm getting in on a new psychiatric research study which is actually pretty intriguing," she said.

"Tell me more," said the interested Fletcher.

"Well, it's actually about the psychopathic behavior of abused children and how it impacts their relationship with other people into adulthood," she announced.

"Sounds like fertile ground," replied Fletcher with an all-knowing expression.

"You know it is," Sarah responded.

"How was your day?" she asked.

"More of the same," Fletcher chuckled. "Fundraising, fundraising, fundraising."

"I did hear something interesting today, though," he continued. "Apparently, there was another murder in Knoxville a few nights ago," he stated. "Young woman . . . strangulation apparently."

"My God!" exclaimed Sarah. "Not again!"

"It has to be an aberrant event . . . maybe a robbery. Knoxville is a big town after all," said Fletcher.

"I've got a bad feeling about this, Aiden," Sarah promptly announced. "You know I always had my doubts about Stamper killing all those women."

"What are you saying? That there is still a serial killer loose in Knoxville?" an incredulous Fletcher asked.

"I'm saying I think there's a very likely prospect parallel killings are going on, and it was premature to lay them all on Stamper," said Sarah.

"Come on, Sarah, let's not go there again," Fletcher testily responded. "We had Stamper cold, and you know it."

"Not on all of them you didn't," she argued, recalling their previous discussion on the subject. "You did a masterful job utilizing the public angst, but the forensics didn't prove it all out."

"Well, who's to say?" Fletcher retorted.

"I'm sure Otis Stamper sitting on death row would probably have a say," she curtly replied.

"Well, in any event, we can't worry about it," Fletcher deferred. "It's not our problem anymore."

Sarah wasn't so sure.

* * * * * * * *

The investigation into the latest murder was quietly being undertaken in Knoxville. In the local papers, the only mention of it was a brief description of the victim, Annabel

Locum, 22, a single, tall-brunette, nail salon employee from just north of town. Her manner of death wasn't mentioned in the article.

Unlike the most recent Country Boy victims, Locum was not beaten, stabbed, nor sexually assaulted. Initial forensics indicated the cause of death was strangulation but offered no indication of who her assailant might be. From all indications, it appeared to be a drunken domestic assault, or a robbery gone awry. The lack of forensics, however, had stumped investigators. Either her killer was awfully lucky or knew what he was doing. They prayed it was the former.

Friends had indicated Locum had been drinking for an extended period of time at one of the downtown bars off Henley Street in Market Square until just after 1:00 a.m. on New Year's Eve. Earlier in the evening, there had been a throng of inebriated young people in the area making their way home after a night of indulged celebration.

An unconfirmed report indicated that a woman matching her general description was seen getting into a car with a man around 1:30 a.m., but neither could be described with any certainty.

The investigation would forge ahead with what little evidence was found, but without the intense media focus that the city had been recently inundated with.

The less said on this one, the better.

Chapter Twenty-Two

Time flew by, and over the next couple of years, Fletcher and Asher became more and more accustomed to their work on the Hill. Growing his influence with party leaders, Fletcher was appointed to a seat on the powerful House Judiciary Committee where he became well-acquainted with some of the most influential members in Congress.

In Knoxville, no further developments had evolved in the case of Annabel Locum and to the relief of city officials, nor had any other similar such murders occurred in the city to cause any public consternation. The two-year-old Locum murder had since been relegated to the category of an isolated killing, as police resources were re-directed to more pressing matters.

When Fletcher returned to Knoxville for business every few weeks or so, he was treated as an up-and-coming Congressman with a bright political future. The Country Boy moniker, along with the notoriety of the previous murders, had all but faded away, much to his great relief.

Sarah's two-year study appointment was about to expire, and she had earned her way to a position where she was being considered for an Associate Director position for the FBI's Violent Criminal Apprehension Program (VICAP), which was responsible for the analysis of violent and sexual crimes, particularly those committed by repeat offenders. Although the Unit was based in Quantico, Virginia, Sarah was in line to lead a psychiatric sub-unit to study the psychopathic patterns of such offenders at the agency headquarters in Washington.

When she mentioned the position to Fletcher, he contacted a colleague on the House Judiciary Committee, which had oversight of the FBI. Using his growing influence, the member was happy to endorse her candidacy to the Office of the Director, which promptly offered her the position with a sizeable staff of psychologists and data analysts. The offer had caught Sarah by surprise, and it made her deliriously happy.

"This is what I've always wanted to do, Aiden," she excitedly announced. "Did you have anything to do with this?" she curiously asked, with a fake frown.

"I made a call, but you earned it, my dear," he truthfully replied.

"Well, this is something I'm going to eat up because forensic pathology is exactly where I want to be," she indicated.

"I know that, Sarah. I told you I thought you'd find something once we came to Washington," responded Fletcher. "I'm so proud of you."

Fletcher had more than one reason to be happy for his wife. Now he had someone on the inside to help him stay abreast of the latest killings and how law enforcement was tracking unsolved murders.

"Let me know when anything interesting comes up," Fletcher calmly added.

* * * * * * * *

Sarah began her new life in Washington by attending several meetings around town which pertained to her work and that of the Bureau in general.

At one particular luncheon, she sat with Diane Johnson, an attractive, super-personable lobbyist from one of DC's largest firms, Boyd-McKensie, LLP. The two hit it off immediately. Like sorority sisters at a long-delayed reunion, they opened up to each other, usually laughing along the way.

Over the course of the next several months, the two would often meet for lunch or dinner dates when their husbands were occupied with their own schedules. They soon discovered their immense loyalty to each other and their ability to listen to whatever problems that had crept into their respective lives.

Sarah felt that with Diane, she could truly be herself. Something she had never really experienced with Aiden, who had spent the majority of their marriage following his own, driven aspirations. In time, Sarah came to feel that Diane would always have her back, no matter what was going on. If nothing else, she would always be there with a shoulder to cry on, real or metaphorical.

She had no way of knowing how important a role Diane was about to play in her life.

* * * * * * * *

Sarah began her new appointment by analyzing long-cold cases by tracking and correlating accumulated information on violent crimes, especially murder. By utilizing the agency's web-enabled software, it allowed federal, state, and local users to directly enter data into the national database located at the FBI.

As such, users were able to retrieve and analyze cases, query against the database, and run reports. VICAP records included known forensics, victim and offender descriptive data, lab reports, crime scene photographs, and news media references.

Sarah's team communicated with state and local law enforcement in an attempt to connect cases with similar patterns in the hopes of identifying violent serial offenders.

Among the potential violent criminal investigations brought to her attention, was one a member of her staff had been working on for over a year which related to a couple of similar murders in the Washington, DC area. The killings had not stood out in a region known for having 160-200 homicides per year. Nor would they draw a lot of attention in a town known for its daily broadcast of national political coverage and international news, not to mention the ever-present coverage of the local Washington professional sports teams.

The cases were interesting, nevertheless. Both of the victims were young women, who had been beaten and strangled to death, without any evidence of sexual assault. They were both in their early twenties, with one having brunette and the other dark-colored hair.

The first of the victims' bodies was discovered floating in the Washington Channel just down from the Tidal Basin on the southwest waterfront near the Ft. McNair army installation. A police patrol boat had pulled the body out of the river, which exhibited deep abrasions around the neck and numerous skull fractures. The noticeable tissue loss was most likely caused by an army of feasting crabs, as the body had been determined to have been in the water for several days.

No semen or other DNA of any kind had been recovered, and the body had not yet been identified from any of the missing person's reports. The victim had high amounts of drugs in her system leading investigators to believe she may have been assaulted during a late-night attempted drug buy near the S. Capitol Street overpass . . . an area well-known for such illicit activity. She, later identified as Selma Thornton, a twenty-three-year-old office worker in Rosslyn, Virginia.

More recently, the body of another young woman had been recovered near Gravelly Point on the Virginia side of the Potomac, off the George Washington Parkway just a couple of miles from Crystal City and Reagan National Airport. This victim had been beaten severely, most likely with a metal pipe, and strangled so violently that her hyoid bone not only was broken, but had nearly disintegrated. She, was subsequently identified as Elise Baker, twenty-five-year-old, convenience store clerk from Chevy Chase, Maryland.

As was routine with many such cases, the particulars of the Washington murders were assessed in the VICAP database and discussed among the staff. It was suggested Sarah include a segment about serial murders in her speech before the upcoming National Sheriff's Association Annual Education & Technology conference in Washington.

"I think that would be a timely presentation," agreed Sarah. "I think it's imperative to share what we've assembled with local law enforcement."

When the date of the conference rolled around, Sarah had prepared an overview of investigative methodologies in tracking serial killers throughout the United States.

Her piece on the psychological gratification that serial killers get when killing their victims received the most attention. During a follow-up question and answer session, the discussion was illuminating.

"Dr. Fletcher, can you tell us what kind of psychopathology distinguishes someone who sexually assaults his victims before killing them and someone who doesn't? In other words, what does the sexual aspect of the killing say about the killer?"

“That’s an excellent question,” replied Sarah. “It’s one aspect of the pattern of killing that we look at very closely.”

“Psychological gratification can take many forms,” she said. “From anger, sensationalism, sexual predilections and financial gain to merely demographic or ethnic similarities, any of which may determine where and with whom the serial killer may engage.”

“As to the pattern of behavior that involves sexual assault, the research tells us a great deal,” she continued. “In cases where killers have been abused as children, they might see forcible sex as a vehicle to satisfy their fantasies of lust or the psychological need to have absolute control, domination, and power over their victims. Something they didn’t have in their everyday lives. Such fantasies allow the killer to leave their reality for what for them is a better place.”

“Do you see clear distinctions in those cases where sex is not a component of the murder?” asked another attendee.

“In those cases, where sex is not the primary motivation, the research tells us that most such killers operate out of long, borne-out hatred for someone in their past, such as a parent or a spouse. In those situations, the killer might select his victims based on similar physical traits or age, and the method of killing is usually up close and personal. These types of killings are typically by stabbing, strangulation or just beating their victims to death, which expresses the innate rage of the killer toward whatever it is that the victim represents.”

“On the other hand, we can’t discount the possibility, especially with more organized killers that they abstain from a sexual assault for no better reason than they simply don’t want to leave their DNA on the victim.”

"Are most serial killers easily identifiable in everyday life?" came the next question.

"That's another great question," replied Sarah.

"Keep in mind that not all serial killers are ogres who would frighten women and children on the streets. Some can seem quite normal, lead exemplary lives, and actually be quite charming. Some might even be leading citizens of the community who show no signs of being a psychopath."

"Some of the more intelligent killers can even be the perfect husbands and fathers without anyone, including their spouse ever realizing the monster that lurks beneath their exterior."

"One thing is clear," Sarah continued. "Most serial killers have experienced some sort of breakage from childhood norms. Most of our models indicate how early childhood trauma inevitably sets the child up for deviant behavior and perhaps violence in adulthood."

The conference ended with a group of attendees gathered around for another half-hour of questioning. For Sarah, it had been a great success and one she could build her unit's reputation on.

At home, she and Fletcher spoke of the day's events and how her engagement had gone.

"I take it your conference was successful," Fletcher commented, judging from Sarah's upbeat mood that evening.

"Very much so," she responded, pleased he was taking an interest in her work.

"Any new information on the Washington cases you mentioned the other night?" he casually asked, mixing a drink at the bar.

"Well, no DNA on either body," she replied. "I think this guy is pretty sharp. He doesn't leave a lot of clues."

"Then what do you think it will take to catch him?" Fletcher curiously asked.

"Probably an eyewitness or a victim who escapes from his clutches," she noted. "Either way, it's not going to be easy getting a handle on this guy."

"Maybe he'll screw up and make it obvious," Fletcher opined, picking up some briefing papers and returning to his office.

"Or maybe he'll decide he wants to get caught," Sarah added. "You never know about these guys," she concluded in a matter-of-fact way.

"It sounds like they're not easy to figure out," Fletcher extolled.

"Not in the least," she replied. "Not in the least."

Chapter Twenty-Three

Fletcher's progression in the House was such that his influence was becoming broadly felt across a myriad of congressional issues. His popularity among his constituents was such that he easily won re-election to a second term. While he and many of his senior staff were in Knoxville celebrating the big win, Brian Asher stayed behind in Washington to finish work on an extensive legislative agenda involving his support of the Metropolitan Governments Planning Council. This legislation would put him at the forefront of regional transportation ballot initiatives, affordable housing proposals, and a bill to promote local energy investment and infrastructure modernization.

Asher had been working practically nonstop in the months before the election and had spent a quiet Saturday at Fletcher's congressional office going through the mail and catching up on the never-ending requests for speaking engagements and appearances.

In the usual stack of constituent mail, he noticed an envelope postmarked "Bisbee, Arizona," addressed to Congressman Fletcher. Opening up the envelope, the letter contained a simple note which read:

"I know who you are. You can't fool me. You know what I want."

FK

The letter struck Asher as quite odd, and it occupied his mind for the duration of the weekend. On Monday, after Fletcher's return from Knoxville, he was in his office giving him an update on the week's schedule.

“How was the celebration?” Asher asked Fletcher.

“Great! It was good to get back to Knoxville and see so many of our supporters. It was quite a turnout, actually.” Fletcher jubilantly responded.

“What’s on the schedule for this week?” he inquired.

“More of the same weekly appointments. But don’t forget you have a meeting Tuesday, with the Budget Director of the Appropriations Committee to discuss the Omnibus Bill,” Asher replied.

“How about the Judiciary agenda?” Fletcher inquired, knowing what the response would be.

“I’ll provide you with a full-print out, but some of the highlights are today’s subcommittee meeting on the Antitrust and Competition Improvement Act amendments. Tomorrow is the Copyright and Internet Report on Efficacy and Wednesday is the Homeowner’s Bankruptcy Act hearings.”

“The normal stuff, right?” grinned Fletcher.

“Yeah, pretty much so,” replied Asher.

“Don’t forget to tell Sandy, we need to get back on that lobbying group’s request for an interview,” Fletcher added.

“Got it on the schedule already,” Asher noted.

“Anything else?” Fletcher asked, sorting through some of the weekend’s position papers.

“There was this one thing,” Asher hesitatingly answered. “Do you know anyone from Bisbee, Arizona?” he bluntly asked.

Fletcher stopped in his tracks. He looked up at Asher with an astonished look as his breathing suddenly became difficult, and his skin turned pale and clammy. His heart began palpating, and for a moment, he couldn't speak.

"Are you OK, boss?" asked Asher, clearly noticing Fletcher's sudden transformation.

Fletcher paused before he spoke. "I'm fine, just a bit of indigestion," he quickly replied. He wiped his brow as the sweat accumulated along his face. "Just a little difficulty keeping my breakfast down. Watch out for those hash browns in the cafeteria," he joked.

Composing himself, Fletcher grabbed the mysterious letter from Asher and began to read it slowly. His expression again turned pale.

"Uh . . . No, I don't know anyone from Bisbee called that," Fletcher stammered, intently focused on the letter. "Wonder what the hell that's all about?" he asked out loud.

"Who knows," replied Asher. "Probably some nut."

"That I'm sure of," Fletcher responded with an all-knowing grin.

The letter had caught Fletcher off guard. He had to act and act fast.

"Brian, cancel my appointments for Wednesday and Thursday. I forgot to tell you that while I was in Knoxville, Ambrose asked me to join him and some others in Denver for a two-day get together with some donors."

"But your legislative mark-up session is on Thursday. That won't be easy to reschedule," Asher replied.

"Just do it!" Fletcher barked.

Asher was taken back by his boss's sudden belligerent tone.

"Sure thing, Boss," he responded, leaving Fletcher's office.

"So you'll be back in on Friday?" Asher asked.

"Back in on Friday, yeah," Fletcher replied, still staring at the letter.

* * * * * * * *

This next morning Fletcher left the office for his trip to Denver. Asher was quite suspicious of Fletcher's sudden change of behavior since their meeting the day before. Around noon, he called Ambrose Cooper's office in Knoxville to confirm the arrangements Fletcher had provided.

Cooper's office not only couldn't confirm that Cooper was going to Denver, but that there were no plans to host a two-day summit with some of the big congressional supporters.

With his curiosity peaked, Asher was unrelenting in his determination to ascertain what was going on. He followed up with a call to the Congressional Travel Office to do a little more snooping.

"Travel Coordination, may I help you?" said the woman answering the phone.

"Yes, this is Brian Asher of Congressman Aiden Fletcher's office. Could you tell me the flight information for Congressman Fletcher's flight to Denver?"

"Just a moment, Mr. Asher, I'll look it up," said the woman. After an extended delay, she returned to the call.

"I'm sorry, Mr. Asher, but we have no travel plans today for the Congressman to Denver," she replied.

"Are you sure?" responded the bewildered Asher. "He was supposed to fly to Denver today."

"We don't have him on a schedule to Denver, but we do have him flying to Phoenix with arrival at 8:00 o'clock tonight."

"OK, thanks," replied the now befuddled Asher. His mind began to race.

To Phoenix? What on earth was going on with Fletcher?

Chapter Twenty-Four

It was 2:30 a.m., and Flora Kinnard was asleep in bed in an opioid-induced slumber when she heard a noise coming from the front door of her house. It was a dark, windy night in the desert and she dismissed the abrupt clatter as tumbleweed blowing against the planks of her wooden terrace.

The home was located on the outskirts of Bisbee, Arizona, off Route 80, with the nearest neighbor being a half-mile down the two-lane desert road, where her modest ranch house was located. Falling almost immediately back to sleep, she soon awoke with a startled gasp when suddenly the lights in her bedroom flashed on.

In front of her bed stood a man, and for a few moments, she strained against the glare of the lights to focus on his face. Sitting up, she allowed a slight smirk to cross her lips as her eyes fully realized who her visitor was.

"It's you!" she exclaimed in a half-hearted show of contempt and surprise. "I knew you would be back someday."

"Yes, mother, it's me," said the man in a calm, monotone voice. He was wearing nothing but surgical gloves and a plastic rain suit that covered him from his head to toe, including his covered feet, on which he wore only socks.

It had been sixteen long years since Lester Kinnard had acknowledged his real identity to anyone, but this was his mother, and there was no fooling her.

"I knew back then you didn't kill yourself,'" she murmured. "I knew you didn't have the guts to do it. Guess I was right about that, wasn't I?"

"You certainly were," admitted Lester, "but why didn't you say something to the authorities?"

"Frankly, I had more important things to worry about, like how to keep a roof over my head, plus I didn't want the goddamn police sniffing around in my affairs, so I told them I thought you were so screwed up it was just a matter of time before you killed yourself. Guess that worked, huh?"

"You always were the practical type, mother," smiled Lester.

"So who was the man in the desert you killed," she asked with great curiosity, knowing that Lester had to come up with another body to fake his suicide.

"A godsend from heaven, mother," smirked the jaded Lester. "An absolute godsend."

"Let me guess, Aiden Fletcher . . . am I right?" Flora was not so ignorant as to be unable to put two and two together to figure out how Lester had so cleanly switched his identity.

"I could never fool you, mother," admitted the smirking Lester, "but how did you find out about me?"

"I saw you on the news," she replied. "At first, I didn't believe it, but the more I looked, I knew it was you . . . Congressman Aiden Fletcher," she exaltedly proclaimed. "You shaved your moustache and colored your hair, but then I noticed that dislocated joint on your little finger; you know, the one you hurt playing basketball in high school. Then I knew, beyond any doubt," she proudly declared.

"That's when I sent you the note," she sarcastically added. "I needed some money and thought you'd be more than willing to come through for me. I figure ten thousand dollars should tide me over," she continued.

"If not, I go to the authorities," she demanded. "I doubt you'd want that to happen, would you . . . Congressman Fletcher?" She addressed him with a smug little smirk on her face . . . attempting to dominate him like he was still a defenseless little boy.

"Very observant mother," replied the admiring Lester, "very observant indeed. Your little scheme obviously worked because here I am."

"Yes. Here you are," she repeated, confident she was controlling the dialogue.

"So, tell me, you brutally murdered a young man by blowing off his head with a shotgun, leaving him in the desert for the critters and stole his identity, right?" In the back of her mind, she knew damn well the answer to her question.

"You know, mother, if you weren't such a drugged-up whore, you could have actually made something of your life, like I have," Lester dismissively responded.

"Have there been others?" Flora had hesitated to ask.

"Well, there was a little señorita who tried to hustle me across the border from El Paso," he confided with a sense of recollected joy. "She was the first bitch, and when I strangled her, all I could see was your face. I must tell you, mother. That was a pleasure like I had never known," he mischievously smiled.

"Were they the only ones?" Flora hesitantly inquired, her mind racing from the shock of what Lester had just admitted.

"Well, I could go on, but I don't think we need to go there just now," Lester dismissively replied. "We only have a few precious moments together left."

"Yeah, but how could you have murdered such innocent people?" she reiterated.

"How could I murder them?" said the incredulous Lester, his resentment now reaching the breaking point. "You're the one that killed them, you hideous tramp; them, the boy at the lake and the others."

"The boy at the lake!" she exclaimed. "I always suspected you killed that boy. I knew you had it in you to kill somebody," she replied. "But why do you say it was me who killed them . . . what in God's name are you talking about?" she yelled.

"You created me, mother," the now furious Lester asserted. "You and father created the monster I have become."

"Don't blame me for what your father did to you," she snapped back. "That was all on him," she said, trying to protect herself from Lester's growing rage.

Lester was irate. "You evil wench! You never lifted a finger to stop him. Not one goddamn time! I needed you. I was just a little kid! I think you actually enjoyed watching him sodomize me," he shrieked.

"You never called the police, and you never did anything to help me!" Lester screamed. His ire had reached a crescendo. "You're nothing but a goddamn degenerate slut!" he repeated as tears rolled down his face.

His rage continued to build as he recounted her myriad of abuses. "All the times you locked me in the closet," he screamed. "Never giving me a hug; never once saying you loved me!"

"I didn't want you to be a mommas' boy," she caustically replied, thinking as quickly as she could. "I was afraid you might turn out queer if I showed you any affection."

Lester's tirade continued. "Always telling me how evil girls were and that sex was the work of the devil. You really messed me up with women. You made me hate them, you crazy, drugged-out, bitch! You turned me into some kind of twisted pervert!" Lester screamed.

Sensing Lester's intense hostility, Flora tried desperately to calm him down as he edged closer to her.

"You have it all wrong, Lester," she implored. "I couldn't stop your father and his assaults on you, or he would have beaten me! I tried being a good mother."

That comment sent Lester over the edge. "A good mother!" he screamed, hovering over her bed. "How dare you call yourself mother! After all the emotional abuse you laid on me? You're nothing but a sick, degenerate whore!"

Trembling from Lester's wrath, Flora tried to get up, but Lester pushed her violently back into her bed.

"So how did you ever get yourself elected to Congress and from Tennessee no less," she implored, trying to change the sordid conversation.

"That's a very long story, mother, a very long story, and frankly, I don't have the time," Lester tensely responded, his patience for continuing the conversation now razor-thin.

Sensing his ominous intent, she made one last attempt to diffuse the situation. "What do you mean you don't have the time," she asked. "Where are you going?"

"Oh, I'm not going anywhere bitch. You're the one that's leaving," Lester replied, his anger seething as a demon expression crossed his face. His sneer turned into something almost alien, something she had never before witnessed.

It would be the last thing she would ever see.

Grabbing her by her long, dark hair, he repeatedly beat her in the face, then pulled out an eight-inch knife he had grabbed from the kitchen. Flora let out a muffled scream, and Lester howled like a lone wolf in the midnight desert as he plunged the knife into her chest and neck over and over and over again with a rage that had been forty years in the making.

With every plunge of the knife came a sigh of satisfaction from the boy who had been so abused by this despicable human being. As life slowly seeped out of her mutilated body, Lester dropped the knife and continued the assault by strangling her with all his might. Through his gloved hands, he could feel the last spasm of her life slip away as her soon-dead eyes stared at him in wild, horrific disbelief.

Experiencing an adrenalin rush like he had never known, there in the wee hours of the Arizona night, he lay next to Flora's body for the longest time and soaked in her demise. Running his hands through her bloodied, tangled hair, he gathered a clump of it and sniffed it deeply. The hair she had spent so much time brushing was now a wet, crimson glob of goo. The power and exhilaration he had experienced by killing the one person he had most despised was more titillating and more gratifying than he had ever imagined it would be.

Contemplating the inevitable investigation, Lester removed his rain suit and everything else he had touched, which could have contained his fingerprints or DNA from the vicious attack.

Preparing the crime scene to appear to have been the work of an isolated break-in gone askew, he walked to a gulch down the road below Flora's home where he had parked his car. He swished a tree branch along the ground by the house to destroy the outline of his foot prints from the plastic rain slippers he had worn. A blowing desert wind made the job all that much easier.

Driving off in his rental car, hanging a large trash bag of bloodied items outside the window as he drove, Lester looked back one last time on the weathered structure that had been such a house of horrors to him throughout his life. Everything around it looked dead. The old windmill looked dead; the sorrowful and lonely coos of the morning-doves sounded dead. Everything about this place was now . . . utterly dead.

A subtle smile crossed Lester's face. Nothing would ever again be as satisfying as his having vindicated himself from the foul, degenerate bitch who had so mistreated him as a boy. No one would ever again connect him to this sordid desert crossroads which had framed his miserable, horrific childhood.

He burned the clothing in a wash near the San Pedro River and buried the knife in the rugged underbrush a couple of miles deep into the open desert.

He stopped to reflect on the life he had created for himself . . . a new persona he had transformed himself into. It was an identity he had carefully crafted with great work and imagination. An identity that allowed him to forevermore escape from the terrors of his youth, and which could lead him to places he could never have imagined.

During the nearly three-hour drive to Phoenix for a late-morning flight back to Washington, Lester knew he had been destined for everything that had happened to him. The bad, as well as the good. As he had realized so many years earlier, there was simply no accounting for the capricious hand of fate.

Although he may have acquired an outward new identity, the demons from his past continued to occupy the deepest recesses of his mind. He knew he would be answerable to them whenever they called. It was who he was born to be. The persona he had been transformed into.

For that, he could always thank his now-deceased, dear mother.

Chapter Twenty-Five

Aboard the flight to Washington, safely enveloped in the protective persona of his well-established alter-ego, Lester closed his eyes. He relived in vivid detail the heady excitement of the previous night. The ghastly entity within him that his parents had fostered, and he had repeatedly tried to suppress, had once again . . . like on each of the other occasions, been satisfied. But as he knew full-well, it was only for the time being.

His exhaustion from the previous night's activities caused him to enter a deep slumber as his plane departed from the Phoenix Sky Harbor Airport. Looking down on the lifeless, primal desert below, he fell fast asleep as his mind drifted back to where it all had begun.

Even now, after, all these years, it was difficult for Lester to contain the memories of the abuse he had been subjected to as a young boy. The well-visualized flashbacks were always present. They began with his stepfather's beatings and sexual abuse, which started when he was only five. The attacks were always as fearful as Colton Kinnard could make them.

"Come here, boy!" an inebriated Colton would always say before the abuse would begin. "Get your goddamn, little punk-ass over here!"

"Please don't make me do this again . . . please!" cried the young Lester trying to hide from the father. Inevitably, he would run to the shed where Colton would come out with a belt and whip him repeatedly before ordering him to his knees to perform fellatio on him. It was beyond humiliating. It sapped Lester of his self-esteem, not only as a human being but as a male of the species.

Colton also liked to beat Lester, just to watch him cry. He loved to observe the fear that he induced in the young boy. It was a fear that Lester never forgot and one that he grew to crave as he witnessed the panic-filled screams of the bewildered victims whose lives he had so brutally taken from them.

The beatings continued for the next eight years until Lester turned thirteen. One night the drunken Colton assaulted him in yet another stupor because Lester hadn't turned on the TV fast enough. As the cursing Colton stumbled toward the frightened boy with his belt for yet another beating, Lester picked up a vase and instinctively smashed it over Colton's head.

"Don't touch me!" Lester screamed. "Don't you ever touch me again, or I'll kill you and cut you up in little pieces!" His rage was overwhelming.

Colton had never seen his son like this. His facial contortions revealed an inner demon-beast that Lester had never revealed.

Taken back by Lester's newfound sense of bravery, Colton nevertheless lunged forward.

"Why you little bastard," Colton screamed. "I'm going to whip you like a mule!" he slurred. Lester waited until Colton approached closer and kicked him as hard as he could right in Colton's nuts, wherein Colton collapsed in agony and began screaming out in pain.

"You son-of-a-bitch!" Lester yelled. "Don't you ever come anywhere near me again!"

After all the years of his stepfather's abuse, this was the end. Colton would never again lay a hand on Lester for fear he might kill him. Nevertheless, the damage he had inflicted on Lester's inner psyche had been irretrievably done.

Lester's flashbacks while making the long flight back to Washington continued, as they had throughout his life. For all the abuse his father had laid on him, it couldn't compare to what his mother had done. The scars from her neglect had shaped him in ways he could never even fully grasp.

His mother, Flora, had chosen to ignore the years of beatings and sexual abuse her husband had laid on Lester. On the one hand, she knew if Colton got off on Lester, she wouldn't have to service him herself. Sex was an activity that the couple rarely engaged in any way, given his drunken stupors and her opioid-fueled bouts of depression.

On the other hand, she didn't care much about Lester in any event. All he had ever brought to her was additional trouble, which she had more than enough of, given her otherwise despicable and badly lived life. She had completely rejected Lester's emotional needs; never any hugs or words of encouragement. He was never taken to the doctor and was forced to cook for himself if he wanted to eat. He had always been totally on his own.

One particular moment had always stuck with him. He had fallen from a friend's swing set at age ten and fractured his arm. Running home, he burst through the front door screaming for help.

"Mother! Help me! Help! I think I broke my arm!" He was screaming in pain. "Where are you?" he shouted. Flora was asleep on the sofa after yet another OxyContin binge and didn't want to be disturbed.

"Go away!" she yelled. "Can't you see I'm taking a nap?"

"Mother! I'm hurt real bad! Please help me!" Lester cried, his arm hanging limply by his side and the pain growing ever more intense with each passing minute.

"Goddamn it! Go away!" She raised up and screamed. "Can't you see I'm trying to sleep! Now get the fuck out of here, or I'll break your other arm!" Slumping back into her pillow, she began to snore. Lester was at a loss what to do. He finally ran back to a neighbor's house a half-mile up the road and got help from the mother of one of the kids he played with.

It was an episode that pretty well summed up his mother's disdainful feelings for him and his contempt for her.

During another drug-induced tirade, she had left the seven-year-old Lester home alone for fifteen hours without food or supervision. On many other occasions, she would lock him in a closet for not obeying her and only let him out after he screamed in loneliness.

"Mother! Please let me out! I'm so scared." The young boy would yell.

"You're not getting out until I say you're getting out," Flora would casually respond while working her crossword puzzles in the kitchen and engaging in her morning habit of brushing her long, brunette hair, stroke after stroke. It was a ritual that Lester had observed since childhood.

After several hours she would open the door as Lester ran out and hugged her at the waist begging for forgiveness.

"I'm sorry, mother," he would sob, "I'll do better next time." She would push him away without the slightest display of tenderness and return to the kitchen table.

"Next time, I'll leave you in there for two days," she warned. "Do you understand me?" It was a threat that Lester believed.

On other occasions, Flora would simply give Lester the silent treatment for days at a time, and when she did speak, it was to denigrate him at every opportunity.

"You little bastard," she would typically begin. "You're the biggest mistake I ever made. If I hadn't been so stupid and got knocked up by that bum in Tucson, I wouldn't have to put up with your worthless little ass."

"You've done nothing but ruin my goddamn life," she pronounced on more than one occasion.

The physical and emotional abuse continued for years as Lester withdrew from his classmates at school. His nightmares and bedwetting continued as well, which further infuriated his mother.

It wasn't until his freshman year in high school that the junior varsity basketball coach saw something in Lester he thought could be developed. Lester had always been an extremely intelligent kid but had nowhere to focus his smarts or his interests.

When his coach told him he could start for the varsity his sophomore year and possibly even earn a scholarship to college, it was all the motivation Lester needed. He began practicing seven hours a day, reading basketball training manuals and staying after practice to hone his skills.

He remembered once hitting a game-winning shot for his team at the buzzer, and his teammates and trainers rushed the court to hug him. Suddenly everyone began hugging him and jumped around. For the first time in his life, Lester had done something good for which he was commended. He began to sob.

It was the first time he had ever remembered being hugged and appreciated. After that, he would never let anyone or anything hold him down again.

His mother had left an indelible, deeply embedded scar on Lester. One which he would never be able to put behind him. For all his ability, it continued to define him in ways even he could not fully imagine.

As his flight prepared for the final approach into Washington, Lester readied himself to envelop again the role he had so well prepared for. As Congressman Aiden Fletcher stepped off the fully loaded plane, he was thrust back into a reality, far removed from the one which had occupied his inner being for so many years.

* * * * * * * *

It was several days before authorities arrived at Flora's house to investigate. Prompted by a call from her neighbor and friend, Ida Williams, who had suspected something was amiss when Flora had failed to contact her as was her daily habit, two police cruisers pulled up to the ranch house and found her disfigured body in her bedroom.

"What do we have," asked Detective McNair, arriving sometime later in the morning.

"First impression . . . looks like a break-in and robbery detective," said one of the officers who first arrived on the scene. "Front door shows evidence of tampering; drawers pulled out, and the victim's purse strewn across the living room with no money inside."

The crime scene forensics unit had just finished up when the Medical Examiner pulled up to examine the corpse. After a detailed examination of the body, he advised McNair of his preliminary findings.

"Looks like the victim was stabbed repeatedly and strangled. Hard to say which actually caused her death . . . either could easily have done her in. Whoever did, though sure looks like he held a grudge . . . it's a classic case of overkill."

"Any prints or other forensic evidence?" McNair asked.

"Nothing yet," said one of the officers on the forensic team. "Whoever did this really knows what they were doing," he added.

"Any information about the victim's family?"

"The victim's name is Flora Kinnard. No living family members. The husband died three years ago of liver cancer, and her only son committed suicide many years ago."

"Any friends?" asked McNair.

"Only the woman down the road who called it in. She stated the victim was an opioid addict with little contact with anyone else and who was always looking for money."

"That might explain a motive," opined McNair. "She may have owed somebody a lot of money, and they came to collect."

"That could also explain the rage," added one of the investigators.

"Let's wrap it up, boys," barked McNair. "We'll see what the coroner comes up with."

* * * * * * * * *

The autopsy report added nothing to the preliminary findings. It showed Flora was stabbed twenty-seven times. In addition, lesions around her neck, along with the fractured hyoid bone and absence of ligature marks, seemed to indicate manual strangulation. Follow-up forensics could produce nothing of value in identifying Flora's assailant. No tire marks nearby, no fingerprints, no DNA evidence, and no immediate family or associates with a grudge. Until someone came forward with some new leads, the case was going nowhere.

Such was often the case with a death in the desert. The large number of transients who came through the area left no evidence of their identity or motivations. Like the murder of numerous prostitutes and other down-and-out victims, there was nothing to fall back on . . . nothing to keep the case alive.

The death of Flora Kinnard fell into this category, and her case was soon relegated to the back drawer of the scores of unsolved murders which had been occurring in the area for many decades. But unlike those untold souls who were never thought about again, Flora's legacy was still alive. . .

. . . and operating with a vengeance.

Chapter Twenty-Six

Upon Fletcher's return to his congressional office on Friday, the reticent Asher met him in the reception area.

"Morning . . . how was your trip to Denver?" Asher callously asked, playing along with Fletcher's deception.

"Oh . . . uh, it was fun . . . uh, but quite busy," Fletcher stammered.

"I guess old Ambrose kept you on your toes, right?" Asher continued, playing along with the ruse.

"Are you kidding me?" replied Fletcher, now more descriptive in his deceit. "He hardly gave us a minute's rest," he laughed. "I'm glad to be back in the office just to have a break!"

The conversation continued until Fletcher had to take a scheduled telephone call.

Asher returned to his desk and dwelled on Fletcher's mysterious behavior and what it all could mean. Throughout the weekend, he continued to wonder what was going on. He googled what, if anything, had occurred in Phoenix during the previous few days that may have explained Fletcher's sudden departure to the area.

After nothing of note appeared in his Google search, he got the idea to research the latest news from the place on the strange, post-marked letter that had set Fletcher off. Where was it? . . . Bisbee, Arizona, he remembered.

As he researched the latest news from The Bisbee Observer, the newspaper of record for the tiny hamlet, the headline hit him smack in the face. On the front page was the biggest story in weeks, with a huge banner across the top:

"Bisbee Woman Brutally Murdered in Home"

The story took on a life of its own. A brief account of the incident provided:

"Last night, a local woman, Flora Kinnard, 68, a life-long resident of Bisbee, was viciously attacked by an intruder and killed in her home off Rt. 80," the article began. "Police investigators have indicated they have little information about whom her assailant might have been but suspect it may have been a transient who broke into the victim's home seeking money. Anyone with any information is encouraged to contact the police at their earliest convenience."

Asher studied the article intently, Flora Kinnard he thought . . . Flora Kinnard . . ..

And then it hit him. "Oh my God! Flora Kinnard . . . could she be the mysterious "FK" on the letter sent to Fletcher?"

His instincts took over . . . It had to be her, he thought . . . it just had to be!

Why else would the letter have so set Fletcher off? Why else would he leave immediately for Arizona? But why in the name of God would he kill her?

His head was spinning. Then the reality of what had occurred hit him full force . . . Aiden killed her! Oh my God! He murdered her! Why in God's name would he do such a thing!? Why?

The question haunted him all weekend.

* * * * * * * *

The following Monday, Fletcher walked into Asher's office perusing his appointment calendar.

"Can we get tomorrow's reception with the Attorney General's Association moved up an hour," Fletcher asked. "I'd like to get a little extra time to review the Committee markup report before the vote," he added.

"Sure," replied the subdued Asher, staring directly at Fletcher with a callous, disrespectful look. Fletcher couldn't help but notice.

"You OK, Brian?" he asked, "You don't seem to be yourself."

"Yeah," he curtly responded. "Just got some not-so-good news from back home," he lied.

"Anything I can do to help?" Fletcher offered.

"No, it'll be OK," Asher briskly said, still staring at Fletcher.

"Well, let me know if there's anything I can do, OK?" responded the uncertain Fletcher.

"Sure thing," responded the dejected Asher.

Asher slumped back into his chair. He was racked with indecision and wondered what he was going to do.

He had potential information on a brutal murder. The murderer appeared to be one of his close friends and a public figure. Should he contact authorities? Should he tell Sarah? What if he was wrong?

For all his questions, his conscience wasn't going to allow him to rest.

* * * * * * * *

It was Sunday morning over the Memorial Day weekend in Washington. It was normally a time when the residents of the District left town and the political hubbub for a few days of sun and fun, either to the Eastern Shore of Maryland or the beaches of Delaware.

Fletcher and Sarah had gone to the Outer Banks of North Carolina at the invitation of Sarah's friend, Diane Johnson, who had invited them and another couple to their weekend oceanfront cottage in the quaint little village of Duck. Fletcher's young congressional staff had mostly vacated the office by Friday morning to get a jump on the inevitable traffic jam on Rt. 50 East from Annapolis toward the Delaware beaches.

Asher had stayed in town over the weekend to finish up an array of scheduling matters for the following week. His angst over Fletcher's possible involvement in the obscure Arizona murder and how he would be able to continue to serve as Fletcher's chief of staff was nagging him day and night. He had spent most of Sunday in his office trying to make sense of it all.

Finishing up his necessary work, Asher walked two doors down from his office in the congressional suite to Fletcher's private office where staffers were under strict orders never to enter unless the boss was present. Casually pushing the massive, mahogany door ajar, Asher slowly walked in, uncertain of his purpose while surveying the surroundings with a whole new and uncertain perspective about who his boss really was.

Entering Fletcher's office with its twenty-foot-high ceiling and a giant oil painting of George Washington on one side of the room, it seemed quite different now. All the awards and certificates; the photographs of Fletcher and celebrities; the plaques and accolades posted on the walls . . . they rang hollow. Here he was in Fletcher's private domain, imagining what Fletcher thought about in his private moments alone.

Surveying the private suite and attached conference room, he felt the glow of power like never before. Everything reeked of political privilege and deference. Fletcher's office was a clutter of large bookcases and credenzas. A large sitting area with four chairs and a coffee table was situated directly in front of his desk, which was draped with the obligatory American Flag on one end and the Tennessee flag on the other. Behind the desk was a dark blue leather chair with brass rivets along the top and sides.

The walls were painted a light-yellow color which reflected the light from the ancient chandelier which hung from the middle of the room. A huge mirror hung over a non-working fireplace which made the room seem larger than it actually was. A large dark blue rug with the image of the Great Seal of the United States covered the floor under the coffee table. The books, the photographs, the mementos of his days as District Attorney were all there. His whole life was there, everything except reminders of his childhood in the California foster care system.

Being astutely aware of all that Fletcher's office represented, Asher began to wonder.

What other mementos might be present?

Slowly walking around, gently flipping through books and journals stacked in the bookcases, he sat in Fletcher's chair and hesitated before opening the drawers. He knew such a violation of Fletcher's privacy would cost him his job if he were caught. After a brief moment of contemplation, he didn't care. Given what had occurred, he had to find the truth, one way or another.

He spent half an hour sifting through Fletcher's files and paraphernalia. Nothing seemed out of place or out of the ordinary. After another few moments he walked around the office staring at the walls and the dozen or more paintings that adorned them. Fletcher's taste in art was eclectic, to say the least. Everything from western art to contemporary landscapes to portraits, there seemed to be no artistic genre to which he was particularly endeared.

Disappointed that he had found nothing to understand Fletcher's previous life, he turned to leave. As he arose from Fletcher's chair, his eyes caught a glimpse of the obscure print of an old Picasso painting entitled "Dora Maar," which hung in a hidden corner directly behind his desk over a small antique table.

Asher noticed that the print was tilted noticeably to the left. His reaction was to straighten it so that Fletcher wouldn't be suspicious that someone had been snooping around his office without his consent. Upon examining the print up close, it struck him how strangely macabre it was. It was painted in an obscure shade of yellow, and depicted an older woman in black with long dark hair and a contorted sneer on her face.

The whole thing seemed oddly maudlin, Asher thought. Grabbing the frame with one hand, Asher tried to straighten it up. As he did, the corner of a white, FedEx-type package slipped out from behind the frame and precariously hung from what remained of the tape which had secured it to the back of the print.

Instinctively, he first attempted to re-secure it to the back of the print when it fell to the floor. Grabbing the extremely lightweight envelope, he walked over to Fletcher's chair, where he carefully opened the seal . . . a seal which had clearly been opened many times before.

Pulling out a manila envelope from inside the package, Asher noticed several small plastic baggies with what seemed to be strands of human hair in them. Asher momentarily lost his breath.

. . . . *What on earth were these?*

He carefully laid the baggies down and opened the first one where the scribbled word, "Mother," was written with a red heart next to it. The graying brunette hair was matted in blood.

Asher tried to make sense of it all. He knew Fletcher had been raised an orphan and had said on many occasions that he had never known his mother. Asher was bewildered by his bizarre discovery.

He slowly counted the six remaining bags. Each were the same, each contained a lock of what appeared to be human hair. Three of the remaining six were similarly matted with blood. Each bag had a notation "L"; "M"; "A"; "G"; "MT"; and "AL." Each bag had a similar meme, depicting a smiling character or a heart.

Asher was shaken. What he was looking at was stunning in its menacing implication. What could it all mean? He dared not allow himself even to imagine, but the thought burst wildly through his consciousness . . ..

. . . . *It just can't be possible!*

The room started to spin. Asher couldn't believe something so darkly ominous was unfolding right before his eyes. It all just seemed surreal.

He stopped to collect his thoughts. His brain whirled and his heart was palpitating seemingly out of his chest.

Gathering his wits, he decided he had to try to determine the significance of it all. He went to the receptionist's desk and gathered a few envelopes and a pair of tweezers he noticed in the drawer and rushed back to Fletcher's desk.

There he carefully removed a few strands of hair from each baggie and placed them in separate envelopes. He made the identical notation on each of the envelopes as had been noted on the baggie from which the hairs had originated. When he finished, he secured the original package behind the print on the wall, exactly as it had been before he had entered the room.

Making one last survey of Fletcher's office, he made sure nothing was out of place and quietly closed the door behind him.

He left the building and returned home to plan his next move.

It was a plan that would have unfathomable implications for all involved.

Chapter Twenty-Seven

In Knoxville, Bradley Foster's long-filed appeal of Otis Stamper's conviction had finally reached the Court of Criminal Appeals. The three-judge panel had reviewed the evidence and invited the attorneys involved to present oral arguments as to why Stamper's convictions should not be overturned.

Foster had presented a limited argument for the court's consideration. His brief strongly contested the sufficiency of the evidence that led to convictions in four of the cases for which Stamper had been tried. He also asserted that the jury's finding of the death penalty for first-degree murder, was not supported by the totality of the evidence in any event.

Foster argued that the prosecution had played off the public's unabashed fear to seek convictions in all the suspected murder cases. The convictions, he asserted, were therefore tainted by extraneous factors which did not, in and of themselves, prove Stamper's guilt "beyond a reasonable doubt."

The news of the Court's decision to hear the appeal had occupied the local media's attention, but not in the way the original trial had dominated the airwaves. The way the public looked at it, whether Stamper committed three or seven of the murders was not nearly as important as the fact that he was off the streets and no longer a threat to the public-at-large. What was important was that he, in a worst-case scenario, would be behind bars for the rest of his life.

The fact that the prospective terror of repeated, ongoing murders was no longer present had greatly ameliorated the public's anxiety about a possible copycat killer. There had been the single, unsolved murder a couple of years earlier, but it was evident that there was not the recurring criminal presence haunting the streets of Knoxville as had been in the years past.

On the day of the Court's oral arguments, Foster was invited to speak first.

Foster: "May it please, the Court, I am here today to represent not only my client but, in many ways, the judicial system of Tennessee. My client admittedly has a sordid past, but that does not give the State the right to arbitrarily find him guilty of crimes for which they have presented little or no evidence."

The Court: "So tell us, Mr. Foster. What is the essence of your argument that the convictions in the four cases you assert were unfairly charged do not stand legal muster?"

Foster: "Your Honor, the DNA evidence that was presented in the evidentiary trial focused on my client's indisputable presence and his admission to the murders of the three victims previously identified. However, with respect to the four contested cases, there was no DNA evidence or any other evidence whatsoever, for that matter, linking my client to the murders of the victims involved."

The Court: "So are you asserting the convictions in the murders in question were not supported by sufficient evidence that a reasonable man could rightfully conclude that your client could have committed the crimes in question?"

Foster: "What we are arguing, Your Honor, is that the State failed to prove even by a preponderance of evidence standard that there existed sufficient evidence linking my client to the murders in question, let alone by the required standard of beyond a reasonable doubt. Therefore, the four convictions at issue cannot stand legal review, and a finding must be entered that concludes that the jury failed to apply the relevant standard by which any criminal case must be adjudged. Long-held legal precedent demands that the Court overturn said convictions and remand the case for a new trial."

The Court: "Does the prosecution, in this case, wish to respond to the Appellant's arguments regarding the sufficiency of the evidence which resulted in the Appellant's convictions?"

The Prosecution: "Your Honor, The Knox County Prosecutor's Office, by contrast, argues vociferously that an otherwise well-constituted jury of men and women who heard and considered the evidence, must be given deference over any attempt by the defense to merely seek reversal simply because they do not agree with the outcome. Our judicial system is dependent on the good judgment of our citizens to weigh what is relevant and reject that which is immaterial in order to arrive at a fair and impartial verdict, and that is exactly what happened in the case at bar. We strongly oppose the arguments presented by the Appellant and urge that the original convictions be sustained in their entirety."

The parties submitted post-argument legal briefs in support of their respective positions. After several weeks, the Court panel issued a 3-0 decision on the appellate question.

The decision read in pertinent part:

"The Court having heard the arguments of the parties, and weighing the totality of the evidence presented at oral argument, we are of the opinion that there was insufficient evidence to support the convictions in the four cases at bar. We, therefore, vacate said convictions and remand those counts for retrial on the merits presented. We sustain the convictions in the remaining three counts but vacate the resultant imposition of the death penalty and remand those cases for re-sentencing on the question of whether the prosecution met the evidentiary standard of pre-meditated murder as charged in the Complaint."

There it was. The Country Boy convictions had been eviscerated by the Appellate Court for lack of evidence sufficient to support a conviction.

The Sixth District Attorney, who had followed Fletcher, announced that they would reanalyze the evidence before making a firm decision on whether they would retry the cases in question. In the view of insiders, such a statement appeared tantamount to an admission that the prosecutors did not have enough evidence to warrant a retrial of the case.

The public reaction to the Court's determination was mixed. Still even those individuals who wanted Stamper retried, rested comfortably knowing he would be serving three, sixty years to life sentences on the cases for which the guilty verdicts had been upheld.

A reporter who managed to reach Fletcher to seek his response to the Court's ruling was given a terse reply by the man whose career was made by the original convictions.

"I'm confident that the Sixth District will retry the counts in question and again obtain convictions on the counts where the Appellate Court has confused mere arguments with the totality of the evidence," he proclaimed.

"Do you expect to see the convictions reinstated?" asked the reporter.

"Without a doubt," Fletcher replied. "Without a doubt."

Although Fletcher's public pronouncements on the case were backed by his bold bravado, both he and most of the staff who had worked on the cases were not surprised by the Court's reversal.

Asher and Sarah arrived at the same conclusion. As they had long ago argued, the case had been overcharged, to begin with, at Fletcher's insistence.

Their remaining concern was not so much whether Stamper should receive the death penalty versus life in prison but on the fundamental question that had lingered in the minds of most individuals who had followed the case.

If Stamper didn't murder the other four victims . . . then who did?

Chapter Twenty-Eight

Sarah's interest in the Court's reversal of the Stamper conviction was not just professional. She had lived through the Stamper trial, and her husband had prosecuted him. It was personal. She also had the lingering question of who else could have been involved. She, therefore, took it upon herself to personally re-assess the forensics in the four cases noted.

There must have been something that they missed, she thought.

Sitting at her desk contemplating her next move in the case, she received a call. It was Brian Asher.

"Hello, Brian . . . How was your weekend?" she asked.

"Not bad," he responded trying to be stoic after his discovery in Fletcher's office. "How was the Outer Banks?"

"Just great!" she replied. "I needed a few days just to get out of Washington and unwind."

"Tell me about it," Asher said. "I could sure use a break about now."

"You do sound a little stressed," she noted.

"Working hard . . . You know the drill, around here."

I certainly do," Sarah noted. "By the way, did you hear about the court's reversal in the Stamper case?"

"I did," he replied. "It's why I'm calling you."

"You know this opens up a whole new avenue," he said, trying not to state the obvious.

"I know what you're leading to," Sarah said. "In fact, I'm going to personally conduct a new forensic review on the four cases immediately," she added.

"Good!" replied Asher. "I was hoping you were going to pursue that."

"Listen," he added, "the reason I called is . . . I was wondering . . . I have been asked to give you some forensic evidence on a case a friend is investigating in Arizona. Would you be able to do a little analysis on it and let me know what, if anything, you find?"

"Sure," replied Sarah, "anyone I know?" she added.

"No one important," he replied. "I just thought I'd try to do a friend a favor."

"Let me know when you want to get together to give me the evidence and I'll get right on it."

"Sarah . . ." Asher paused. "It's imperative you not tell anyone about this, especially Aiden. Do you understand what I am saying?"

"Well, sure," Sarah hesitated, "I understand the need for confidentiality, but why exclude Aiden specifically?"

"I can't tell you that right now, but I will soon," Asher nervously asserted.

"But you have to promise me you won't say a word to Aiden about what you're doing . . . do you understand?"

"Promise," Sarah solemnly replied, as if she were raising her arm taking an oath.

"Can I stop by your office tomorrow and give you what I have?"

"What do you have?" Sarah asked inquisitively.

"I will show you tomorrow," Asher curtly replied.

"Sure," Sarah sighed, knowing she was not going to get any more out of him. "How about 10:00 a.m.?"

"See you then," Asher abruptly responded and hung up.

Asher's uneasiness had been palpable. It was as if he was sitting on a time bomb.

Sarah was perplexed. Why was Brian so uptight, and why was he insistent on keeping everything so quiet?

* * * * * * * *

The next day Asher arrived on schedule at the FBI building on Pennsylvania Avenue where he was escorted to Sarah's office on the fourth floor. It was a rather cramped area, as are most of the offices in the vicinity of the Federal Triangle, an area formed by 15th Street and the intersection of Pennsylvania and Constitution Avenues where numerous federal office buildings are located.

"Brian! So good to see you," gushed Sarah as Asher entered her office. They gave each other a warm hug which was a testament to all they had been through with Fletcher.

"Morning Sarah," he somberly replied. He looked tired and over wrought.

"This is the first time I've been to your office," he noted, surveying the premises.

"It's small but comfortable," she cheerfully responded. "So tell me, what is it that you wanted me to take a look at?" Her curiosity was gnawing at her.

Reaching over to grab his briefcase, Asher pulled out a standard envelope with a small baggie, within which he had placed a few strands of blood-caked hair.

He handed it to her and watched her intently as she held them close to take a good look.

"It looks like there are still follicles and roots attached," she said. "That will make it a lot easier," she noted. "Let me run this through chemical analysis and see what we find under the microscope," she advised.

"How long do you think that will take?" Asher asked.

"A few days, if I push it through," Sarah responded. "You know, these things take time," she admonished.

"Well, I'd appreciate you giving me a call as soon as you know something," Asher urged.

"I will, Brian," Sarah replied. "Listen . . . my friend. I know something is really bothering you," she added. "Care to tell me about it?"

"I wish I could," he said. "But I can't say anything for the time being. But I promise you I'm going to fill you in as soon as I can."

Sarah knew that was all she was going to get out of Asher for the time being. But she sensed that whatever was on his mind was eating him alive.

“Don’t forget what I asked you about keeping this quiet,” Asher reiterated.

“I won’t,” she responded. “I’ll tell no one.”

They hugged as Asher left Sarah’s office. She watched him lumber down the hall to the elevator looking like he was carrying the weight of the world on his shoulders. She felt sorry for him, given whatever enormous burden he was carrying.

* * * * * * * *

In Knoxville, the Regional Forensics Center, in conjunction with the Knoxville Homicide Unit, was called back to redouble their efforts in lieu of the Court’s reversal in the Stamper case. The cases of Miriam Fleming, Anna Sue Ellison, Ginger Mattingly, and Marcia Thomas were pulled out of storage and assigned to a team of forensic analysts.

Sarah Fletcher, who was heading up the forensics review for the VICAP Unit of the FBI, initiated a joint task force with the Knoxville Unit as the investigations proceeded. A conference Zoom call was organized to compare notes.

Sarah began the conversation. “Thanks, everyone, for being here; what do we know so far?”

“Well, as we initially concluded, the case files indicate that with respect to the first three victims, hair evidence was still available, but no blood or bodily fluids were present. No conclusions were therefore possible with respect to whether the victims had been sexually assaulted,” noted the lead investigator.

“The most notable feature of the physical evidence in those cases was that each of the victims had been brutally beaten and strangled which were indicators of the rage the killer felt toward the victims,” he added.

"So, what was the common denominator?" Sarah asked.

"All young women between nineteen and twenty-four, dark or brunette hair, that's basically it," said another detective.

"How about the fourth victim?" Sarah inquired.

"Well, that case is different," said one of the analysts. "There, the victim was stabbed and beaten, but as with the others, no sexual assault."

"Again, that would indicate an up close and personal killing but, let's ask ourselves, why no sexual assault?' stated Sarah. "Why doesn't this guy . . . who acts out a rage not seek to dominate his victims sexually?"

"Either he had some hang-up with sex, or he doesn't want to leave his DNA," quickly answered one of the team. "Or both. That's the only logical answer."

"Let's assume he didn't want to leave his DNA," Sarah interjected. "Apart from the most logical reason of identifying himself, why else wouldn't he want it found? Because that would prove that Stamper hadn't killed all the victims he was charged with. It would prove there was, in fact, a second killer," she added.

"So, the second killer is murdering his victims strategically," added another team member.

"So why would he stab Marcia Thomas when with the others he had beaten and strangled them?"

"To make it look like Stamper," the lead detective surmised. "He changed his pattern of killing so Stamper would get the blame. He had to keep killing because of his uncontrollable urge, but the heat was on and he wanted it to look like Stamper did it."

"That's why the stabbing but again no sexual assault," said the analyst.

"How about the Locum murder a couple of years ago on New Year's Eve? Any reason to tie her in with the others?"

"Again, she was strangled," noted Sarah, "but that case may be differentiated as it appears the motive there may have been a robbery."

"Unlike the first three," said the detective. "But even so, that doesn't rule out that her murder might be connected to the first three."

"So, our second killer stabbed Marcia Thomas to make it look like Stamper, but when Stamper is safely incarcerated, and the pressure was off, reverts to his old pattern of strangulation," noted an investigator.

"So why haven't there been any other victims in the past two years?" asked one.

"Either the killer found religion, is incarcerated, has moved, or is dead," stated another. "Has to be one of the four."

"How about the forensics on the strangulations?" Sarah inquired.

"That's interesting," said the detective. "The abrasions on the necks of the strangled victims all show almost identical thumb measurements across the esophagus, indicating the same killer."

"Anything notable about the thumb imprints," Sarah asked.

"Well, I don't know how important this may be, but the killer has a somewhat larger thumb than normal," remarked an analyst. "Take it for what it's worth."

"So, are you saying we might be able to identify the killer by the size of the tissue abrasion around their neck?" Sarah asked.

"I wouldn't go that far," replied the analyst. "Every abrasion carries its own mark, especially the circumference impression."

"Even if the killer was wearing gloves?" Sarah further inquired.

"Yeah, I believe so. What's important is the location of the abrasions around the victims' necks which would indicate the approximate size of the killer's hands and his thumbs in particular."

"OK then, let's put a little more emphasis on the forensics in the Locum murder," surmised Sarah. "I think we may have let her case get caught up in the fact that there were no further killings after her and that may tell us more about our guy than we may have first surmised."

The Zoom call was ended with a little better notion of what they were looking for, but still no firm lead on who the second killer might have been or whether he was still in their midst.

Sarah ended the call with her mind still on the ominous mystery of what Asher had so anxiously presented to her.

What the hell was that all about? She continued to wonder.

Chapter Twenty-Nine

Several days passed before Sarah received the forensic results from the VICAP lab of the hair sample Asher had given her. She immediately called him, anxious to hear his response to the information she had acquired.

"Brian . . . this is Sarah," she said. "Thought I'd give you a call to let you know I've got the results back from Forensics."

"What did you find out?" he nervously asked.

"Well, we got some good DNA from the hair follicles and our lab ran them against the VICAP database from a compilation of state and local information," she replied.

"And . . .?" he said. The suspense was killing him.

"And the hair matches the DNA from one Flora Kinnard, an older woman murdered in some little place in Arizona," she announced, awaiting Asher's response.

Asher had to utilize all his strength to maintain his composure. "That's interesting," he stammered. "Hey, can I get back with you on that? I've got something quite pressing at the moment."

"Sure," replied the befuddled Sarah. She thought for sure he would want to discuss the findings in detail. "Call me when you want to talk some more about it."

"I will, thanks" he replied, abruptly hanging up the phone.

Sarah had never seen Asher so lacking in composure. Something was clearly happening, and he wouldn't tell her about it.

Back in his office, Asher had hung up the phone gasping for breath. He paced the floor, not knowing what to do.

The forensics demonstrated what he had strongly suspected for the past week. The realization was unfathomable to comprehend.

Aiden Fletcher was a murderer!

Why would he lie to everyone and sneak off to Arizona to kill a sixty-eight-year-old woman from some little bum-fuck town out in the middle of the desert?

He returned to his desk, grabbed the letter Fletcher had received from, "FK" and read it over and over again.

"I know who you are . . . you know what I want."

What did she know about Fletcher that no one else knows? He wondered.

None of it made sense! What was he going to do? If Aiden killed the old woman, was Sarah's life now in jeopardy as well?

The questions were too difficult to formulate, but he could no longer hold it in. He had no choice. He had to act and quickly redialed Sarah's office.

"Could I speak to Sarah Fletcher, please? This is Brian Asher calling."

Sarah immediately picked up the phone, frightened by the way Asher was acting.

"Brian! Tell me what's going on . . . right now!" she demanded. Her voice was quivering in anxiety.

A long moment passed, and Asher spoke. "Not over the phone," he replied. "Meet me at the National Mall just behind the National Gallery of Art."

"I'll be there in fifteen minutes," she replied, slamming down the phone and rushing out of her office.

When she arrived at the designated spot, she saw Asher sitting on a park bench staring off into the distance, oblivious to the hoard of joggers running past.

Sarah strolled up behind him, and he jumped anxiously from the bench. She instinctively hugged him knowing whatever he was going to tell her would be difficult to accept. They sat back down on the bench together, holding hands.

"Sarah, what I have to tell you is horrible," he began, nervously shaking. "I've racked my brain wondering if what I'm going to say may somehow place you in physical jeopardy."

Sarah was taken back, then composed herself. "If it's that bad, maybe you're putting me in jeopardy by not telling me."

The comment gave Asher the strength to proceed.

"You know the hair sample I gave you to analyze?" Asher said. Sarah braced herself for what was coming.

"I found that hair sample hidden in Aiden's office, behind a painting," he stated.

"What's more, Aiden lied to us and took a secret flight out to Phoenix the day before the murder of a woman named Flora Kinnard, from Bisbee, Arizona, whom I believe had sent him a letter which had totally freaked him out."

The reality of what Asher was saying was slowly sinking into Sarah. She couldn't speak.

What he had to say next ripped her apart. "What's more," he added, "I found six other bags of hair behind the same painting."

Her expression went absolutely blank, considering what it all could mean. Sarah was shattered. She clearly understood the implication of finding Fletcher's "trophies" hidden in his office. Her distress reduced her to a quivering glob of ruin. She jumped off the park bench and ran to an old oak tree and sobbed.

Asher let her be for an extended period of time and waived off passer-byes who were concerned about her devastating condition. After several minutes he put his arm around her to comfort her and walked her back to the park bench. She hugged him and sobbed again.

She finally composed herself enough to speak.

"Oh my God Brian," she wept. "Why? How could he do this to these people?"

"I don't know Sarah," he replied. "For the life of me, I don't understand what's going on. I just don't!"

"Does he have any connections that you know about in Arizona?" he asked.

"Absolutely none that I'm aware of," replied Sarah, trying to pull herself together. "As far as I know, he's never even been to Arizona," she continued.

"He grew up in California," she added. "I can't for the life of me figure out why he felt he had to kill some old woman in Arizona."

"Sarah, I think we have to come to terms with the notion that Aiden might not be who he claims to be," concluded Asher, shaking in disbelief from his own proposition.

"The bag I found the old woman's hair in said 'Mother' on the outside," he continued. "Is it possible that he just went out there and killed his mother?"

"What about the other bags of hair?" she asked, "do you know anything about them?"

"Nothing," he responded, "I'm almost afraid to find out."

"Brian, do you think he might have had something to do with some of the murders in Knoxville?" She now wondered.

"That thought has been rattling in my mind for a week," Asher responded. "I'm afraid to let my mind even speculate what the other bags could mean."

"Are you going to let me analyze them as well?" she asked in desperation. "We have to find out, Brian."

"I know," he responded. "I know we do. Are you up for it all?" he added.

"No, but we have to know for sure," she replied.

With that, Asher reached into his briefcase and pulled an overnight-sized package out with the six other bags with locks of hair in them. Sarah looked at them and began to sob again. Some of them were still matted with blood which could only mean one thing.

"Let me have our forensics unit assess them and see what comes up," she noted. "Then we'll have a better idea what we're dealing with."

"I've been debating about whether to confront him with this or just go to the police," Asher stated. "I'm not sure what to do right now."

"Like I said, let me do the forensics on the remaining samples and then we'll figure out what to do next," she said.

"OK then," Asher responded, "I won't say anything to Aiden until we can get a better handle on it."

"I'm so sorry about all of this Sarah. I'm so terribly sorry."

The two hugged again, and Sarah walked briskly back to her office. Clutching the pouch containing the hair samples, she realized the stark reality that her marriage was irrevocably over.

The whole scenario that had just played out with Asher was surreal. She couldn't believe that her entire life had been irretrievably altered in just half an hour. Then it suddenly occurred to her:

Was she now in jeopardy like Asher had surmised? What if Aiden found out she knew about it all?

She began to tremble at the darkening threat that now hung heavy over her.

Contemplating the terrifying scenario, she found herself in, Sarah quickly realized she had no choice. She had to pull herself together, both mentally and physically. She had to play the role of a contented housewife like she had never played it before. One false step, and she might well become Aiden's next victim.

She couldn't break down; she couldn't act scared. She had to convince Fletcher beyond any doubt that she was sublimely naïve about his extracurricular affairs. One wrong turn, and it could all be over. She imagined herself as a spy operating behind enemy lines. She couldn't give him any reason, even remotely, to question what she might actually know.

She had to give the performance of a lifetime . . . Her life depended on it.

* * * * * * * *

The mystery of Aiden Fletcher now occupied Sarah's every waking hour. She tried to recall everything he had ever said about his upbringing as an orphan in Southern California. The foster homes he might have stayed in; the orphanages in which he lived. Was there anyone who might have known him back then, even some old college friends he might have palled around with? She was determined to look under every stone; uncover every lead. She researched the major orphanages around San Diego, where he said he had grown up. Only one, The Escondido Children's Center, even had a record of him that they would disclose. It proved to be of little to no value.

She decided her only hope was to try to locate someone who knew him in college at San Diego State. Researching its website and googling his name as an alumnus, she stumbled onto a list of his member associations during his time as a student. One note contained an obscure reference to a business professor who had sponsored him for a law school scholarship at the University of Tennessee.

The professor, Dr. Edwin Kirwin, had long retired from the University but still lived in the greater San Diego area. After googling his name, she came up with his phone number and gave him a call. The old professor would have had to have been in his eighties and there was no guarantee he would even remember Fletcher. It was worth a try.

"Is Dr. Kirwin available?" she asked upon dialing the number for him in the directory.

"He is," replied the elderly woman who answered the phone. "May I ask who is calling?"

"Uh . . . yes, it's Karen Boyer from San Diego State," Sarah said, sounding convincing.

"Oh yes," the old lady replied. "Let me get him," she replied.

After several moments, the old man picked up. "Hello," he garbled, "This is Dr. Kirwin."

"Dr. Kirwin. This is Karen Boyer from San Diego State. How are you today?"

"I'm fine," he replied. "I haven't heard from anyone from the University in some while," he chuckled. "What can I do for you?" he asked.

"Dr. I'm part of the alumni group, trying to put together a special alumni photo book of some prominent graduates from the late nineties," she stated.

"Do you happen to recall a student of yours named Aiden Fletcher by any chance?" Sarah held her breath, waiting for an answer.

"Aiden Fletcher," he mulled. "How old did you say he was?" he asked.

"Oh, well he's in his mid-forties now, but back then he would have been in his early twenties."

"Was he a student of mine?" the old man asked.

"Yes sir," Sarah responded, her hopes dimming that the conversation would result in useful information. "It might help you jog your memory that he went on to law school after graduation."

After a long pause the old professor came through. "Didn't he go somewhere in the south for law school?"

"He did!" Sarah replied. "To the University of Tennessee."

"That's right!" the professor asserted. I remember now because my cousin had gone there and said they had a good scholarship program for deserving college graduates."

"That's him!" Sarah regaled. "Would you know what he looked like if I send you a picture?

"I kind of remember what he looked like then, but I don't know about now," he chuckled.

"It would be a picture of him from law school," she replied.

"Well, I could look at it, but I'm not sure I'd necessarily remember."

"Dr. Kirwan, if I sent you a picture of what he looks like just a couple of years after he left California would you be able to tell me if that's the Aiden Fletcher you remember?"

"I'll try," he said.

"Dr. Kirwin I'm going to send you an email with his law school photo in it. Could you look at it and respond right back to me and tell me if the man in the picture looks like the Aiden Fletcher, you knew?"

"You mean just email you right back?"

"Yes, sir. Just tell me if that looks like him or not," Sarah replied.

"Sure, I can do that," Kirwin answered. "Hey, one more thing I just thought of that you might be interested in."

"What's that?" replied the curious Sarah.

"Now I remember him! He stopped by to see me just before he left to drive to Tennessee," the old man recalled.

"Interesting," replied Sarah. "Did he say he was driving through Arizona by any chance?"

"By golly he did!" replied Kirwin, proud that his memory was serving him so well.

"Did he say what part of Arizona he was going to be driving through?"

"Tucson, if I'm not mistaken. But I could be wrong."

"Thank you so much Dr. Kirwin. I really appreciate your help," Sarah said. "I'm sending you the photo right now."

"OK," he replied, "I'll be waiting for it."

Within a minute, Sarah emailed Fletcher's Law Review photo to the old man. She sat back and waited. No response. She waited some more, and still no response. She decided to call Kirwin back.

"Dr. Kirwin, this is Karen Boyer, again. Did you recognized the photo I sent you?"

"Well, I've been studying it for several minutes and I don't think that's Aiden," he said.

“Are you sure?” Sarah beseeched.

“I’m pretty sure,” said Kirwin. “One thing I distinctly remember about him . . . he had a pronounced cowlick,” he added. “Couldn’t keep it combed,” the old man laughed. “The man in the photo doesn’t have one at all. That couldn’t be him.”

“So, you feel pretty confident the man in the photo is not Aiden Fletcher?”

“There’s no doubt about it,” replied Kirwin.

Chapter Thirty

It was a start. Sarah now knew beyond any doubt that the Aiden Fletcher who left California was not the Aiden Fletcher who arrived at the University of Tennessee. But where was the switch made?

She called Asher to share her information with him as they began to piece together the strange odyssey of the man she had unwittingly married.

"Let's back up a minute," Asher suggested, putting his Yale law school brain to work. "Let's assume the woman in Bisbee, Flora Kinnard, was in fact, his mother like he scrawled on her hair sample."

"The article about her murder said she had lived there all her life, so it stands to reason that her son had to have grown up there to, right?" asserted Asher.

"Her obituary said she was preceded in death by her husband Colton and her son, Lester," Asher noted.

"So, let's get an old high school year book from Bisbee and see if anyone named Lester Kinnard looks like who we now know as Aiden Fletcher."

"Brian, you're absolutely brilliant!" replied Sarah. "I think you're really on to something!"

Sarah spent the next couple of hours shifting through Google searches until she found the 1992 Bisbee High School yearbook called, "The Puma." Slowly opening the pages to the senior class, she held her breath.

Running her finger down the page in alphabetical order she approached the "K's" and it hit her like a shot in the face. Under the name of "Lester Kinnard" was an unmistakable photo of her husband, Aiden Fletcher!

Quickly dialing Asher, she yelled "It's him! Oh my God! It's him." Sarah paused to catch her breath.

"Aiden's real name is Lester Kinnard! Brian you were right! "You nailed it!"

"Wow!" screamed Asher. "Just wow!"

"Where do we go from here?" Sarah asked, trying to figure out how to utilize the bombshell information she had just discovered.

Without missing a beat, Asher piped up. "The article said Lester preceded Flora in death. Search the Bisbee Observer newspaper and see when he died."

"OK hold on," Sarah anxiously stated as she googled Lester's name. "Here it is!" she announced.

"Wait a minute," she exclaimed. "Here's an article about Lester and a boy that drowned at a lake when he was quite a bit younger," she noted.

"No telling what that was really about," replied Asher. "Knowing what we know, it's obviously suspicious in any event."

Sarah continued to search for anything about Lester's death.

"Here's something!" she shouted. "It says Lester committed suicide in 2002 at the age of twenty-eight! That's the year Aiden started law school at Tennessee!" Her excitement was through the roof.

Asher and Sarah were piecing together the mystery of Lester Kinnard like fine detectives. Their minds raced as they continued to connect the dots.

"The article says he committed suicide, but that his body had suffered a devastating shotgun blast to the head and the critters had eaten up most of what was left," Sarah read.

"That's how he made the switch," concluded Asher. "He murdered the real Aiden Fletcher and made it look like he had committed suicide. By the time they discovered the body, they couldn't tell the difference, and Lester drove off under the new identity of Aiden Fletcher, whom he has been ever since. His mother must have finally noticed him in Washington and that's when she sent him the letter which caused him to sneak back to Arizona and kill her," Asher continued. "She was the only living person who knew he wasn't who he portrayed himself to be."

"She and Dr. Kirwin," Sarah interjected.

"Wow!" spewed Asher. "In many ways it was utterly brilliant."

"I'll bet you anything if you talked to some of the locals in Bisbee; they would tell you Lester grew up in an abused home," Sarah said. "That's what made him what he is today," she asserted, falling back on her psychological training.

"OK, let's get a little sleep and try to digest what we've come up with," Asher suggested. "We'll talk about what to do in the next few days after we get back the analyses of the rest of the samples."

"Oh, and Sarah," Asher added.

"What?" she countered.

"Be careful, OK? Now you know what kind of monster he really is," warned Asher. "Don't worry, I think I have it under control," she replied. "At least for the time being."

* * * * * * * *

That night as she went to bed, Fletcher leaned over to give her a kiss good-night.

"Good night, Sarah," he softly said, giving her an uncharacteristic kiss on the cheek.

The sensation made her shudder. It sent a psychological chill through her like she had never known.

* * * * * * * *

The next day Sarah called her friend Diane to invite her to lunch.

"Hey, baby-cakes," said Diane. "How's it going?"

"Uh . . . could be better," answered Sarah, with an anxious tinge to her voice. "Tell me you're free for lunch today."

Diane could detect that all was not right with Sarah and lied about her schedule to accommodate her luncheon request.

"Sure," Diane responded, hoping to find out what was bugging Sarah. "Where to?"

"How about the Capital Grille? Say around noon?" Sarah sputtered.

"Of course," Diane responded, always pleased to have lunch at her favorite, upscale spot-on Pennsylvania Avenue, just down from Capitol Hill.

Diane couldn't wait to try to ascertain what was going on with the obviously troubled Sarah. "Are you OK?" She asked. "You don't sound like yourself."

"Oh, I don't know, Sarah nervously replied. "It's always something, isn't it?"

"Well, whatever it is, we're going to talk about it," Diane declared, offering Sarah some best-friend support.

"See you then . . . thanks," stated Sarah, hanging up the phone.

During lunch at the Capital Grille, the two dined over chardonnay and a cold shellfish platter with crab bisque. The conversation soon switched to whatever was bothering Sarah, who was still exhibiting the same anxiousness that she had displayed on the phone with Diane earlier in the morning.

"So, what's wrong, dear," Diane insisted in a terse, but compassionate way.

"It's Aiden," Sarah replied, not quite able to say all that was on her mind.

"What about him?" Diane inquired, curious where Sarah was coming from.

"It's just something about his past," Sarah said, still hesitant to share. "I discovered some things about him that I'm not sure whether I should approach him about."

"Do you want to tell me what it is specifically?" Diane exclaimed.

"All I can say is it has something to do with his having maybe grown up in Arizona," Sarah remarked.

"I thought he was from California?" Diane responded, having heard about Fletcher's orphaned childhood on more than one occasion.

"Well, that's what I've always believed, but now I'm not so sure," Sarah replied.

"You're not so sure?" Diane asked quizzically. "What aren't you sure about?"

"Just a few little things have popped up recently that I can't talk about just yet," Sarah offered, with a slight tear in her eye.

"Is he cheating on you?" Diane sternly asked.

"No, it's not that," Sarah said. "I wish it was that simple."

It was clear Sarah was not emotionally able to say anything more about the issue for the time being. Reaching over and grabbing her hand, Diane offered her a comforting thought.

"Look, sweetheart. You know I'm always there for you, don't you?"

"Yes, of course," replied Sarah, with a whimpering look, squeezing Diane's hand and reaching over to give her a hug.

"Whenever you need to talk, just let me know, OK?"

"I will," said Sarah, with a ray of hope in her now lightened expression.

* * * * * * * *

In the following days, the hair samples that Asher had provided Sarah were being analyzed by the forensics unit at the VICAP. The process was tedious and the results could only be as good as the quality of the samples provided. Typically, hair samples gathered from a crime scene would be analyzed against samples collected from the victim or the suspect, depending on which was being tested. In addition to a visual comparison against the VICAP database, the real analysis was performed using liquid chromatography-mass spectrometry.

Under such a process, microscopic comparison is utilized to determine the protein patterns which are unique to every individual. Once individual DNA is identified, it is compared against records in the CODIS database which is shared by both state and federal investigative agencies.

The seven total hair samples provided to Sarah by Asher, including the one marked, "Mother," were thus analyzed and summaries prepared in a report to Sarah's office. The results were stunning.

Sarah anxiously awaited the results in a briefing from the Director of the CODIS laboratory, Dr. James Hazelett.

"Dr. Fletcher, we have conducted a meticulous review of the seven hair samples provided," Hazelett began.

"What were your conclusions?" replied the visibly anxious Sarah.

“Well let me be blunt and just say that wherever these samples originated from, they have provided a strong causal link to five homicides in our database from the Knoxville, Tennessee area.”

His words had sent a quiver up Sarah’s spine. It had confirmed her worst suspicions. “Go on,” she cautiously urged, nervously awaiting the rest of the Hazelett’s conclusions.

“The best way I know how to organize these findings is to present them to you as they were presented to us,” Hazelett continued. “One sample at a time.”

“Let me just preface what I am about to share with you by saying you will find these results stunning,” said Hazelett, taking a deep breath. “Let’s begin with the sample marked by the initial “M” he began.

“After complete chemical analysis and a liquid chromatography assessment, compared to the records contained in the joint database, we can confidently conclude that the hair sample provided is a perfect match for the victim known as ‘Miriam Fleming,’ of Knoxville,” concluded Hazelett.

Sarah was crestfallen by what she had just heard. She gasped to catch her breath while she tried to process what she had just heard.

“Are you OK?” asked the concerned Hazelett, noticing her difficulties.

“I’m OK,” Sarah shakily responded after a moment. “As you know, my husband and I worked on these cases while we were in Knoxville, and to finally get some definitive findings is quite a lot to process,” she added.

“I understand completely,” Hazelett replied. “Do you wish for me to continue?” he said. “Yes, definitely,” Sarah replied. "I just needed to gather myself for a moment. Please proceed."

Hazelett continued. "The next sample was marked "A," and our analysis concluded that it is a match for the victim known as 'Anna Sue Ellison,' also of Knoxville."

"Similarly, the sample marked 'G,' matched the DNA of the victim known as 'Ginger Mattingly,'" he continued.

As the rollcall of victims proceeded, Sarah's mind raced. It was an affirmation of her greatest fears.

"The next sample, which was marked 'MT,' matches the DNA in the database for a 'Marcia Thomas,' and the sample designated 'AL,' is a perfect match for the victim known as Annabelle Locum, both also from Knoxville," Hazelett offered.

"What about the other sample which was noted by an 'L'?" Sarah asked. "Any findings there?"

"I'm afraid we simply drew a blank on that one," he stated. "That one was a bit different. We found no comparable DNA in our database to confirm or deny a specific identity."

"Why do you believe that was?" Sarah queried.

"I can't even speculate. It simply wasn't in our database." Hazelett responded.

"Then of course, we had previously analyzed the seventh sample marked 'Mother,' which was identified as having come from a Flora Kinnard of Bisbee, Arizona, which we previously discussed."

Sarah sat silently as Hazelett concluded his gruesome findings.

“I assume you will be initiating a communication with the respective task forces both here and in Knoxville?” Hazelett asked, assuming the answer.

“Most definitely,” replied Sarah. “We’re just going to have to tie up a few loose ends first. Thank you for your work, Dr. Hazelett. It has been exemplary.”

“My pleasure,” replied Hazelett, placing the formal reports on Sarah’s desk.

“One last question, Dr. Hazelett,” Sarah asked. “Would you agree that it is significant that not only did the samples indicate a match with the victims noted, but that whoever procured these samples had direct and intimate knowledge of who the victims were, as indicated by how he marked the containers they were found in?”

“I don’t think there’s any question about that,” Hazelett concluded. “Find whoever put these samples together, and you’ve got your killer.”

* * * * * * * *

Hazelett’s parting words sent a cold, reverberating chill up Sarah’s spine. Not only had it been revealed that Aiden had most-likely killed the previous four victims in Knoxville, but now the forensics showed him to be implicated in the death of Annabelle Locum, who had been murdered just two days before Fletcher had left Knoxville for Washington!

Asher had found the samples hidden in Aiden’s office, obviously precious trophies from the unfortunate victims of his horrific crimes. Trophies that he most likely returned to whenever the moment seemed right, and he wished to re-live the monstrous thrill of having brutally taken their lives.

For Sarah, there was now no longer any point in denying the reality of the situation. What had seemed at first to be a frightening assumption which she had still hoped could be rebutted, the unvarnished, undeniable truth lay bare in front of her. There was no escaping it.

Her husband, Congressman Aiden Fletcher . . . was a full-blown serial killer!

Chapter Thirty-One

After Hazelett left the meeting, Sarah began pacing the floor of her office. She knew what she had to do. Aiden had left for work that morning in a surprisingly jovial mood and said he would be tied up in party meetings most of the afternoon and was preparing a speech that night for an awards dinner.

Asher had been unavailable all morning. He had staff obligations for the Judiciary Committee hearings on the markup of amendments to the Controlled Substances Act and would to be out of his office all day.

She tried again to reach him at his office but only got his voicemail.

"Brian. This is Sarah. I've received some very disturbing information about Aiden. Call me as soon as you get this message. It's extremely important."

Her angst was rapidly escalating. They had to call the authorities.

It was later that afternoon before Asher could get back in touch with Sarah and the conversation was short.

"Brian. I was just briefed by our VICAP lab team," she anxiously gasped. "The hair evidence on the other six samples you gave me can be tied directly to five victims in Knoxville," she exclaimed.

"My God!" Asher replied. "It's worse than we even imagined," he replied.

"I'm going to give the Bureau a full briefing and get back to you on how they intend to proceed," Sarah stated.

"Wait just a bit before you do that," Asher urged. "I want to have a chance to at least test Aiden on this. Maybe just get a reaction if I can tweak him a bit on what we've discovered. Who knows, maybe he has some kind of weird explanation," he added, hoping against hope that most of it wasn't true.

Sarah wasn't so sure, but Asher's instincts on everything so far had been right on point. She agreed to wait to hear from him before briefing the Bureau on Fletcher's involvement in the murders.

"I'll call you back when I know something," Asher stated, abruptly hanging up the phone.

"Talk to you then," Sarah replied to the now dead phone line. All she could do was wait.

Asher spent the rest of the day anticipating his conversation with Fletcher. How would he approach him? What exactly would he say? The tension was building inside him.

Around 4:00 p.m. Asher got a call. It was Fletcher.

"Hey Boss," Asher cryptically began, trying not to disclose his disdain for what he now knew about Fletcher's secret life.

"Brian, listen. I'm going to need you to contact Mark Borden on the Joint Committee and have him give us a realistic time frame on when we can get these mark-ups facilitated," Fletcher said.

"I'm afraid I won't be able to do that," Asher replied, his contempt now obvious.

Fletcher was taken back. Asher's attitude was disarming.

"What do you mean you won't be able to?" Fletcher responded, becoming a bit testy. "Are you tied up with something I don't know about?"

"You might say it's something like that," Asher caustically remarked.

"Do you have a problem that I'm not aware of?" Fletcher replied, now quite attentive to Asher's sudden change of demeanor.

"No Aiden, I think you're the one that has the problem," Asher callously replied.

"What on earth is bugging you Brian? You're acting like someone I don't even know."

"Funny you say that," Asher said, with a contemptuous laugh. "You're the one that no one seems to know."

Fletcher became a little more subdued with Asher's last comment. A staffer suddenly interrupted.

"Congressman Fletcher, your wanted back in the Committee room," the young intern chided.

"Something has come up," Fletcher replied. "Tell them I'm going to be momentarily delayed."

"Yes, sir," the staffer replied, walking away.

Turning his attention back to Asher's comment, Fletcher responded.

"What on earth are you talking about Brian?"

"I'm talking about the fact that you aren't who you say you are . . . are you, Lester?" Fletcher was utterly and completely dumbstruck by the words he had just heard Asher express.

How did Asher possibly know? Fletcher's mind was racing. What else did he know? The questions were piling up in Fletcher's mind faster than he could assimilate them.

"Sorry, what did you call me?" he demanded in a quizzical tone, acting very confused by Asher's comment.

"You know what I said," Asher continued. "I know about your past and what you've been doing these many years," he added with a tone of belligerence.

Fletcher's brain was in overdrive. He had to play it as cool as possible to try to get a grip on what was happening in the flash of this perilous moment.

"I don't know what you mean . . . What I've been doing,'" Fletcher repeated, grasping at straws and stalling for time.

Asher was pumped. He had Fletcher where he wanted him, and his sudden disdain for the man he had worked with for so many years suddenly burst through like a dam. He hadn't planned on confronting him, but it happened . . . suddenly and without warning.

"I found your little hair trophies behind the Picasso in your office," Asher blurted out. The temptation to face up to Fletcher had simply overwhelmed him. He anxiously anticipated his reaction.

The words caught Fletcher completely off guard. For the briefest of moments, he was totally speechless. He couldn't process his now, jumbled thoughts.

His brilliant mind came to his rescue.

"Oh, those"! Fletcher suddenly laughed. His sincerity seemed convincing. Asher was taken back by the unexpected, light-hearted response.

"Brian, those things are not what they appear to be and certainly not what you think they are!" He laughed even louder. "I can explain those! They're gags and it's a long story!"

At that moment, Fletcher's intern again intervened and distracted his attention.

"Congressman Fletcher, they told me to tell you they need you right now!"

"OK, OK, I'm coming," Fletcher snapped.

Turning on his considerable charm, Fletcher turned to Asher.

"Brian, listen, I have to run. I'm attending that civil rights awards dinner tonight. Are you going to be home later?"

Confused by the question, Asher played along. "Sure, why?" he asked.

"What if I were to stop by at your place for a few minutes after the dinner," Fletcher proposed. "I can explain everything to you very easily. Believe me, it isn't at all what it appears to be," he assured.

Asher was skeptical, but Fletcher's sincerity seemed beyond genuine.

Asher paused, but relented. "OK, I'll see you later tonight then," he replied as Fletcher scurried down the hall to his meeting.

* * * * * * * *

The dinner and reception that night was at the Phoenix Park Hotel, on North Capital St. N.W., just north of the U.S. Capitol Building. It was to honor various congressional members for their contributions to civil rights initiatives and international immigration achievements.

Fletcher was slated to be one of the speakers. The cocktail reception began at 6:30 p.m., with dinner at 7:15 p.m.

After the dinner was well-underway, Fletcher temporarily excused himself, leaving his cell phone at his place setting. At the same time, his tablemates continued their conversations, hardly noticing his recusal from the table.

"I'll be right back," he told one of the officials seated next to him. "I'm going to the restroom."

Cutting quickly around the back of the hotel, Fletcher hailed a passing cab. "First St. S.E. and Independence," he said. The taxi sped to its destination less than five minutes away. It was 7:35 p.m.

Brian Asher's apartment was situated down a stairwell of a two-story, brownstone building which was painted red with black trim. A small little courtyard fronted the street, enclosed by a black, wrought-iron fence.

He knocked on the door, and Asher soon answered.

"Hey man, mind if I come in for a minute?" Fletcher's greeting seemed warm and genuine. He was wearing a disposable rain jacket to protect against the light evening sprinkle which had just begun.

"Yeah," replied the reticent Asher, uncertain about the real reason for Fletcher's visit.

Fletcher found his way into the tidy little apartment as Asher turned to mute the sound on the TV.

"That won't be necessary," Fletcher said as Asher turned around.

Fletcher was holding a .22 caliper Beretta LR pistol he had long-ago purchased on the street in a surgical-gloved hand and pointed it directly at Asher's head.

"What the fuck . . . are you doing?" Asher screamed in utter astonishment.

"Oh, just tying up a few loose ends," Fletcher calmly responded.

"I was right!" Asher exclaimed. "I knew you killed those women."

"You're a smart boy Brian," Fletcher replied. "Maybe a little too smart. How did you find out about me?" Fletcher asked quite curiously.

"It all came about with the murder of your mother in Bisbee," Asher responded. "I knew you hadn't gone to Denver with Ambrose like you said. The strange letter from Bisbee just set you off."

"Ah, dear old Mother," Fletcher noted. "Such a memorable bitch."

"But how did you figure it all out?" Fletcher asked, genuinely curious as to how his complex little scheme had come undone.

"We tracked you back to an old college professor in San Diego, who told us the law school photo of you wasn't the Aiden Fletcher he knew in college. Then an article on Flora Kinnard's death in Bisbee led us to you, Lester," Asher recanted.

"You say 'us.' I assume you mean you and Sarah," Fletcher supposed.

"She knows everything," Asher confirmed.

"Ah, well, I'll have to deal with her later, I suppose."

"Don't hurt her. She hasn't done anything to you," pleaded Asher.

"We'll have to see about that," said Fletcher.

"So, how did you come across the hair samples," Fletcher asked Asher.

"Just snooping around your office and noticed the Picasso was tilted a little bit. I went to straighten it out and out fell the whole package."

"Quite a surprise, I'm sure," replied Fletcher with a sneer.

"Why did you ever keep those macabre things?" asked Asher. "Some kind of sick trophies?"

"You might say that," replied Fletcher. "Sometimes when the mood strikes, there's nothing more titillating than to sit down with a good glass of Scotch and play with my little mementos," he added.

"Sniffing them always gave me such a rush," Fletcher added. "Something you'd probably never relate to, my friend. So, you took some of the hair samples and had an analysis done, I take it," said Fletcher.

"We sent the samples to Sarah's lab. They've got all they need on you," said Asher.

"Oh, I wouldn't be so sure about that," Fletcher responded with a smile.

"I decided it would be prudent to take my little sweethearts somewhere and give them a new home in case anyone else got too nosey," replied Fletcher. "You know, I'm really going to miss them . . . each and every one."

"It won't matter," Asher replied. "Sarah knows it was you!"

"All she knows my dear friend, is what you told her," Fletcher corrected him. "And you aren't going to be around to back her up."

Suddenly, Asher realized the depth of what Fletcher was planning to do. It was beyond comprehension. He had removed the incriminating evidence, and but for Sarah's tiny samples, there was nothing left to connect Fletcher whatsoever to any of the murders.

Without me, there wouldn't be anything tying Fletcher to any of it!

It was diabolical, Asher thought.

"Don't do this Aiden," Asher pleaded. "Let us get you some help."

"Now, why would you think I need any help, Brian?" Fletcher responded. "I'm just doing what I was born to do, that's all."

"NO!" screamed Asher. "Your mother did this to you! You can stop! Please, Aiden!"

"Turn around!" snapped Fletcher. The reference to his mother made him seethe with anger.

As Asher complied, Fletcher walked Asher over toward the kitchen.

"You'll never get away with this you sick fuck!"

"Oh, you might be surprised," responded Fletcher.

They were the last words Brian Asher would ever hear.

Fletcher ordered Asher to place his right hand along-side his head. With the barrel of the .22 pointed at a precise angle to his hand, Fletcher squeezed a single pull of the trigger and sent a bullet through Asher's right temple. The muffled sound of the small caliper weapon hardly resonated over the noise from the TV.

He quickly placed the gun in Asher's bloodied right hand and rubbed it in the trickle of blood seeping out of Asher's head. Then carefully stepping around the body to ensure he didn't leave a print of his shoe. Fletcher made his way into Asher's bedroom and then to his computer, where he put on another pair of gloves and typed the following note on Asher's social media page.

"I can't do this anymore.

The thrill was sublime. I killed them.

I couldn't stop myself.

Now I join the ranks of the dead."

After ensuring everything was nice and tidy, including the computer's keyboard, Fletcher gingerly stepped outside of Asher's apartment and closed the locked door behind him. Looking both ways down the deserted street, he quickly removed the rain jacket and walked a block where he disposed of it and the gloves in the sewer and caught a cab back to the hotel.

As he walked into the conference room where dinner was still underway, he glanced at his watch. It was 8:00 p.m. He had been gone a mere twenty-five minutes. As Fletcher resumed his seat at the table, he turned to one of his dinner companions and said "My goodness, this sea bass is really quite tasty, don't you think?" Without missing a beat, he resumed the conversation with the group as if he had never left. Toying with his dessert, Fletcher grabbed his phone and made a call as he contemplated the excitement that the last half hour had brought.

. . . Join the ranks of the dead, he thought. That was divine!

Within a half hour or so, he was called upon to make his speech. He received a hearty round of applause from a crowd that saw him as a future party leader. Stepping to the podium, he began his presentation.

"Ladies and Gentlemen, welcome to Washington," he began. "I can't tell you what a pleasure it is for me to have had the opportunity to share such a lovely dinner and address you on such a fabulous evening . . ."

The event continued for another hour or so and Fletcher made his way back home. It was 11:00 p.m. when he walked through the front door to find Sarah watching the late news.

"How was your dinner?" she stiffly asked, playing the role of the unknowing wife to the hilt.

“Quite enjoyable,” he replied. “It was one of the few times I actually got to relax and enjoy the festivities rather than being so occupied all evening long,” he smiled.

Sarah glanced ever so slightly his way and detected the slightest hint of a smile cross his lips.

“What’s so funny?” she said, trying to play the game until bedtime.

“Oh, it’s nothing,” Fletcher responded. “I was just thinking about something someone said tonight.”

“What was it?” she wondered.

“Oh, nothing really,” Fetcher replied, “Something about joining the ranks of . . . you know, honestly, I forget now.”

The line had delighted him.

Such an eloquent sentiment, Fletcher thought, as he made himself a scotch at the bar.

Chapter Thirty-Two

Fletcher came to the office the next day at his usual time. By 9:30 a.m., Asher had not made an appearance. He buzzed his personal assistant and remarked, "Is Brian in yet? I want to go over today's schedule with him."

"He hasn't arrived yet, sir," replied the assistant.

"Well, buzz me when he does," Fletcher responded. "We got a lot on our plate today."

By 11: 00 a.m., Asher had still failed to arrive at the office.

"Did anyone try calling him?" said Fletcher.

"Yes, sir," replied one of the office staff. "We've tried calling him several times, but he hasn't answered," came the reply.

"That's odd," said another. "Brian is usually so punctual," said another.

"Check his calendar," ordered Fletcher. "Make sure he's not on leave today."

"We checked his leave schedule, and there's no indication he was supposed to be off today," stated Fletcher's assistant.

"Strange," Fletcher said. "I wonder why he hasn't contacted anyone."

"Probably got caught up in something unexpected," said one of the staff. "You know Brian, always trying to wrap things up."

It was 2:30 p.m., and still no word about Asher.

"Do you think he's OK?" someone asked. "Maybe one of us should go by his place and check on him."

Before the words left the aide's mouth, another staffer came running into the office.

"Oh my God!" he said. "I think Brian has done something to himself!"

"What do you mean?" said the surprised Fletcher.

"Here look," said the aide sitting at his desk and scrolling down the page to Asher's Facebook entry from the previous evening."

"Quick!" Fletcher said. "Someone, call the police and get them over to his apartment! Cathy, let's take your car. I'm going over there myself," said Fletcher, his voicing filling with anxiety.

Within twenty minutes, two police cars arrived at Asher's home and rang the doorbell. No one answered. Finally, a specialist forced opened the locked door, and several officers made their way inside.

Lying face down on the kitchen floor in a pool of blood was Brian Asher with a wound in his right temple and a pistol next to his body.

The medical examiner surveyed the body and found no bruises or abrasions on the torso or lower extremities. Nothing to indicate a struggle, and the TV was on. In fact, there was nothing amiss in the apartment that would indicate anyone else had even been inside. Forensics did a sweep for fingerprints or other evidence that would have indicated Asher had been robbed or assaulted. Examining the wound and the blood splatter in the kitchen, nothing indicated that anything other than the obvious had occurred. The powder residue on Asher's temple and hand were consistent with a weapon fired by him at close range. His body temperature indicated he had been dead less than twenty-four hours.

The preliminary judgment would have to await a formal forensics review. Still, to the seasoned officers at the scene, the conclusion was inescapable . . . that Brian Asher had committed suicide, most likely the night before.

The evidence team dusted for fingerprints on the computer and the pistol, and nothing showed up other than Asher's own set of prints. After an hour and a half of forensic analysis, Asher's body was bagged up and sent to the Medical Examiner's Office for an autopsy. Just as Fletcher pulled up, authorities were removing his body in a black, plastic bag to the awaiting coroner's ambulance. A special investigations unit pulled up and prepared to do a complete sweep of the house, looking for anything that might assist in understanding the motive for the killing.

Fletcher ran into the house in a panic.

"What's going on here!" he demanded, frantic by what he was witnessing.

"Who are you?" demanded an officer.

"I'm Congressman Fletcher. Who is in that body bag?"

"Someone named Brian Asher," replied the officer. "Do you know him?"

"He's my chief of staff," Fletcher answered. "He works for me . . . oh my God!" Fletcher cried out. "What on earth has happened?"

"Looks like he committed suicide," responded the officer. "Shot himself in the head with a pistol."

Fletcher was devastated and hugged his assistant Cathy who had driven over with him. Together they embraced and sobbed loudly.

"I guess we'll need to call the office and tell everyone what has happened," Fletcher said to his assistant.

"I'll do it right now," Cathy obediently replied. She stood outside under a large oak tree by the sidewalk and started sobbing as she made the first call to the office.

Fletcher sat in the front seat of one of the patrol cars and called his wife, Sarah, to break the news. "Sarah, this is Aiden," he said.

"Aiden," she replied with a tinge of surprise. He rarely called her at work, and she was not expecting a call from him in any event.

"Sarah, I've got some terrible news," Fletcher began, preparing for the shocking disclosure. "It's Brian . . . I'm afraid he's dead!" he exclaimed, breaking out in tears. "It looks like he committed suicide."

The words struck Sarah with stunned disbelief. She refused to accept what Fletcher had just told her. She was in abject denial. Her fear was pulsating throughout her body. There was no way . . . no way Brian would have killed himself! Not with all they had going on with Aiden. Her first and only thought was that it had to have been Aiden who had murdered him. No other explanation at this point could be possible.

Had Aiden found out Brian knew about his secret background and his trophies?

Did Aiden also suspect that she knew about it all as well?

Now Sarah's fear had ratcheted up to where she couldn't think straight. She had a tremendous emotional dilemma. She needed a shoulder to cry on . . . an outlet to mourn the tragic loss of her friend. Now, Sarah was convinced her own life was in jeopardy, like Brian had warned.

She didn't know what to do or who to turn to. "What happened, Aiden?" Sarah cried, finally responding to Fletcher's notice of Asher's death.

"Oh my God, Sarah! I don't know how to say this," Fletcher began. "He shot himself," he sobbed.

Sarah was in a panic-stricken, emotional tail-spin. How could all this be happening? She wondered. Did Aiden find out about Brian's discovery? Did Brian confront him, and things turned bad? Her mind was swirling. She had to get a grip. She had been testing herself to the limit to maintain outward control of her life with Aiden. Now, with the news on Brian, she was losing it.

Sarah thought, this just can't be possible! What is going to happen next?

"Why don't you come home, Sarah," Fletcher softly urged. "I'm stopping at the office to console the staff, and then I'll be coming home as well. It'll probably be a couple of hours."
"OK," Sarah replied, struggling to speak. "I'll see you then."

As she hung up the phone, it was as if she had been disconnected from the very life she had always known. Her independence . . . her friendship with Brian . . . all erased in a moment's time.

Reflecting on the moment, she was grateful to have at least some time to console herself before seeing Aiden. Her fear was eating her up and she didn't know if she could handle it. She wasn't sure about anything at this point. She trembled, trying to piece the nightmare together.

What could possibly await her next? Her dread was beginning to overwhelm her.

* * * * * * * *

As Fletcher returned to his Capitol Hill office, a mob of staff aides greeted him and others who had worked with Brian and knew him well. Fletcher hugged and sobbed with each, one after another, as the disbelief permeated the very building itself. The mass of mourners spilled out into the hall as others tried to make their way into the dispirited wake. Several congressional members with offices nearby joined the sad and dejected cluster of aides weeping outside of Fletcher's office. They were speechless, overhearing the startling news. Others who were merely walking down the corridor observed the commotion and were soon apprised of the heart-breaking development.

It was a stunning moment in all their lives. A moment none of them would ever forget.

* * * * * * * *

Fletcher arrived home after 6:00 p.m. to find Sarah curled up on the sofa, almost in a fetal position. She was wearing nothing but her bathrobe and slippers, and judging by the Kleenex tissues beside her, had been crying her eyes out. His appearance at the door gave her a start. She didn't know what might come next but was too deeply enveloped in fear to move. For a fraction of a second, their eyes locked on the other, like predator and prey on the open savannah. Both suspected each other of knowing something but not entirely sure of what.

"Sarah, I'm so terribly sorry," Fletcher said, approaching Sarah to give her a hug.

Her body recoiled ever so slightly at his touch, but she had learned not to overtly display her anxieties around him. For Fletcher, he had to comport himself as if he had no inkling as to what Asher may have told her about him.

"What happened?" Sarah managed to cry out.

"God only knows," Fletcher replied, holding his emotions in check. "They say it looks pretty clearly like he killed himself, but I guess we won't know anything for sure until the forensics come back."

"Had you noticed any changes in him recently?" Fletcher asked his wife.

Thinking back . . . of course, she had! Asher had been terribly upset before he told her of Fletcher's involvement in Arizona and shown her the hair trophies he had found in Fletcher's office. But she never dreamed that the whole incident could drive Asher to suicide. No way! Whatever changes had come over him were about Fletcher . . . not himself! Nothing that would have caused him to take his own life!

"Not really," she sadly replied, not giving Fletcher anything that might portray her actual feelings on the matter.

"I just don't understand it," Fletcher stated. "Come think of it, Brian had been acting a little strange lately, but I never dreamed it might be something that could drive him to this."

Fletcher continued, noticing he had garnered Sarah's complete attention.

"He did mention the other day that something had happened at home that he was concerned about, but he never explained what it was . . . at least not to me."

Sarah had no idea what Fletcher was referring to and wondered whether he was just fabricating a storyline.

She sat in silence for the rest of the night while Fletcher repaired to his study to make phone-call after phone-call talking to an endless stream of people about the tragic events of the day.

When she finally went to bed, well past 1:00 a.m., she let her mind drift. She still couldn't believe what had happened, but more importantly, she wondered HOW it all happened.

Looking across to Fletcher, now sound asleep, she pondered the unthinkable:

Did Aiden kill Brian? If so, what kind of monster could he possibly be?

Chapter Thirty-Three

The day after the discovery of Asher's body was difficult indeed. Fletcher had closed his congressional office and given the non-essential staff the day off to grieve. That left a core of about six individuals who had to be there, no matter the circumstance. The police investigation was still ongoing, and detectives were conducting interviews with a few of Asher's friends and senior associates at work.

Some of them did mention that in the days preceding his death, Asher appeared to be highly agitated, but no one had an inkling why. Fletcher expected to hear from the DC police and he wasn't disappointed.

The phone rang at the Fletcher residence. "Is this Congressman Fletcher?" asked the voice.

"Yes, it is," Fletcher affirmed. "May I ask who is calling?'

"This is Detective Gagnon from the DC Metropolitan Police Department. How are you, sir?"

"I'm fine, thanks," replied Fletcher. "I've been expecting your call."

"Good," responded Gagnon. "I was wondering if my partner and I could stop by and speak to you and your wife about Mr. Asher's death," he pithily added.

"Certainly," replied Fletcher. "Anything we can do to shed some light on this tragedy."

"Would you be available right now?" asked the detective.

"Sure," said Fletcher. "Come on over."

Within twenty minutes, a dark gray, unmarked Ford Taurus police car pulled up in front of Fletcher's brownstone, and two detectives knocked on his door.

Fletcher answered, looking for all the world like he had been grieving for the past couple of days.

"Congressman, I'm Detective Louis Gagnon and this is my partner, Detective Phil Miller. May we come in?"

"Of course," responded Fletcher. "Have a seat and make yourself comfortable."

As the officers were getting seated, Sarah walked in.

"Gentlemen, this is my wife Sarah," Fletcher announced.

"Nice to meet you," Sarah responded. "I guess you're here to find out anything you can about Brian," she surmised.

"Yes, ma'am," responded Gagnon. "Anything you can tell us would be quite helpful at this point."

"We've been interviewing most of the Congressman's staff and several of Mr. Asher's close friends, and the general consensus seems to be that he was usually a happy-go-lucky guy, but in the last few days, didn't seem to be himself," Gagnon asserted.

"Do either of you have anything that might help to explain what may have been bothering him these past few days . . . money, girlfriend problems, health . . . anything like that?"

Sarah was internally perplexed. She wanted to tell the full story of how Asher had told her of Fletcher's trip to Arizona and the hair trophies he had found in his office and how those shocking revelations had made Asher quite anxious indeed.

She couldn't bring herself to taking that tact right then. On the other hand, by saying nothing, she could see this playing out as a classic suicide case and giving the investigators even more reason to conclude that was in fact, what it was.

It was the internal dilemma she had been fighting for days. She feared for her life but didn't want to offer any evidence to make it look like Asher's death was a suicide. She decided that preserving her health was her first priority.

Fletcher spoke first. "Well, I noticed he seemed to be acting a little strange the past few days, but I had no inkling he was capable of killing himself."

"The only thing that gives me pause was that when I asked him the other day if he was OK, he merely said he had gotten some bad news from home," Fletcher offered.

"Oh wait!" Fletcher added. "He did mention something about the court case in Knoxville reversing some of the murder convictions of the guy we prosecuted down there. That seemed to cause him a great deal of angst," Fletcher surmised.

"I wish to God that I had had the slightest inkling he might do this to himself," he anguished, burying his head in his hand. "I would have definitely tried to help him through whatever it was that was tormenting him. I will never forgive myself for that," he concluded as his voice began to fade.

"Mrs. Fletcher, we understand you and Mr. Asher had a good relationship," began Gagnon. "Is there anything you could offer that may shed light on all this?"

She paused to measure her words. What Fletcher had just said about Asher's reaction to the Knoxville murders was beyond her ability to rationalize.

Why would that have bothered him? She wondered. Was Fletcher just making it up?

Addressing the detective's question, she chose to play it down the middle.

"Like most of what you have heard from the staff, I too noticed his behavior was a little off, but I'm confident that whatever was bothering him, it wasn't the reason for his presumptive suicide."

"Can you speculate what else it might have been?" asked Gagnon, looking directly at Sarah, sensing perhaps she wasn't telling all she knew.

Sarah paused ever so slightly.

Was this the time to tell the detectives about Aiden? She was torn but had to protect herself at this critical moment.

"Uh, no . . . nothing else," she stammered.

"Anything you'd like to ask us?" Gagnon asked.

"Could you give us the latest on the forensic findings?" asked Fletcher.

"Sure, I was getting to that," Gagnon replied.

"The Medical Examiner looked at the location of the wound and the path of the bullet," he began.

"He concluded based on the inter-cranial trajectory of the bullet that the gunshot entrance wound to the upward right temporal area was right-to-left and back-to-front, which is consistent with a right-handed victim pointing a gun to his temple."

"Moreover, the close-range of the gunshot wound should have left gunpowder residue on the victim's head and hand, which it, in fact, it did," Gagnon explained.

"Combined with the blood splatter on the victim's right hand and gun, together offers all the hallmarks of a suicide. When we consider his apparent suicide note on his social media page, then the inevitable conclusion that he took his own life seems increasingly clear."

"Anything else you could update us on, detective?" asked Fletcher.

"We've basically ruled out foul play, as there is simply no forensic evidence that anyone else was in his apartment. No fingerprint evidence, no fibers . . . nothing. The evidence is telling us that Brian Asher was in his house alone and took his own life. It's that simple."

"There is one more significant finding that I will share with you," Gagnon stated, "on the condition you don't leak it to the press."

That comment captured the full attention of both Sarah and Fletcher.

"We did a full sweep of the house and found a package in his bedroom with what appears to be several hair samples; some caked with blood," Gagnon revealed.

Sarah audibly gasped. "What!" she yelled, "that's not possible!"

Sarah was stunned. This can't be. None of what she was hearing was making any sense. How could they find hair samples at Brian's house? He had told her he had found them at Fletcher's office. Could he have been lying to her all along? This was absolutely crazy!

The detective seized on her outburst. "What do you mean that's not possible?" he queried.

Sarah stammered. "What I mean is the implications are staggering," she answered.

"Damn right," added Fletcher. "This might well mean that he's been associated with these murders all along. I just can't believe it!"

Sarah hesitated and then made an admission that she could no longer hold back.

"I have something to confess, detective," Sarah began.

Both detectives and Fletcher were riveted, waiting to hear what she said next.

"Brian came to me several days ago with several minute hair samples which we had tested for DNA," she asserted. "I assume they came from the samples you say you found at his house."

"Did he say where he got them?" Gagnon asked.

Sarah had prepared for the answer. She just couldn't bring Aiden's name into play yet. Given that Brian's death was all but officially ruled a suicide, she couldn't put the pieces together yet. She had a lot to sort out before she was ready to formally accuse Aiden of the murders in question. It was all still a gigantic puzzle, and her mind couldn't process it.

"He didn't say," Sarah coyly answered, "He was going to get back to me, but I guess it didn't work out that way."

"I'm guessing you'll find the samples in question will match what our VICAP Lab analyzed previously," she said. "If so, you'll see that they come from several of the victims in Tennessee."

"Was Mr. Asher in Knoxville during the time that the murders in question took place?"

"Yes, he definitely was," Fletcher interjected. "He worked for me as my Deputy when we prosecuted a big serial murder case. He knew everything that was going on down there."

"Might he have had access to the hair evidence?" Gagnon asked.

"There WAS no hair evidence," Fletcher emphatically asserted. "This is the first I've ever heard of any hair evidence. Only Brian would have known about that." The implication was clear.

"And he's no longer with us," Gagnon sarcastically replied.

"I suggest you coordinate with the Knoxville investigators on this," Sarah urged. I think it will save you a lot of time."

"I'll do that," Gagnon assured. "But folks, stick around. I may be back with some more questions."

"We'll be here whenever you need us, detective," Fletcher politely responded.

As the detectives left Fletcher's home, their unmarked car pulled out into traffic as the detectives compared notes.

"So what's your take Phil?" asked Gagnon.

"Doesn't seem overly difficult to me," Miller candidly replied. "All the forensics point to suicide. No evidence anyone ever entered the house. Now we have a prime suspect in several other murders. Seems like it became too much for the guy to deal with. Seems fairly straightforward when you add it all up."

Gagnon added to the sentiment. "Yeah, I guess you're right. It seems to be the only logical scenario we have right now," replied Gagnon. "It all points to Asher, I suppose."

"I'll get these hair samples to VICAP. Sounds like they've already done the work for us. We'll have them contact the Tennessee authorities; then, if nothing else pops up, I think we'll be ready to write it up."

"Where are we headed next?" Gagnon asked.

"To Southwest DC," responded Miller. "We've got to interview the ex-employer of a suspect in that convenience store murder a few months ago. He might be able to give us some updated information."

"No rest for the weary, right partner?" chuckled Gagnon, referencing the nearly seventy unsolved murder cases in the District that year alone.

* * * * * * * *

Once the door closed, Fletcher turned to Sarah and laid it all out.

"I don't know about you, but I'm absolutely stunned," Fletcher began. "Who would have ever believed Brian would have been capable of doing such horrible things?" Sarah just sat on the sofa and stared blankly out the window.

"What on earth would have possessed him to kill all those people?" he cried. "How could we have not noticed at least some kind of sign that he wasn't right?" Sarah was almost too mentally exhausted to answer.

"Maybe, because we had no reason to," she curtly replied, not knowing what to think.

"Sadly, it's always the person you don't suspect," Fletcher added. "I blame myself for all of this," he continued, dropping his head into his hands and weeping. "I should have been more observant, but God, we were just so busy all the time."

"I just feel so bad for all those women," Sarah glumly blurted out.

"Not to mention what their families have been through," Fletcher sympathetically added.

His sincerity seemed completely genuine. Sarah was now beyond confused. Nothing made sense to her anymore . . . absolutely nothing. The events of the last two days had put her life in abject turmoil. She was on a bizarre merry-go-round, and she wanted off.

She was dumbstruck. She didn't know what to think or what to believe. Everything had now turned upside down, and she was an emotional wreck. The implications surrounding the whole situation were beyond rational interpretation.

It all began with Brian bringing her the hair samples. Could it all have been a ruse? Did he have a grudge against Aiden after working for him all these years? Was he trying to set Aiden up? Why? Did it just become too much for him to bear?

All these questions and so very few answers. The stress was driving her to delirium.

She just wanted to shut her eyes and make it all go away.

Chapter Thirty-Four

"Diane, this is Sarah."

The call came through late that night, well after Fletcher had gone to bed. Sarah was at her wit's end and desperately needed someone to talk to. She was calling from the small porch outside the utility room on the side of their house.

Glancing at her watch, Dianne hastily answered her phone. "Sarah? Do you know what time it is? Is everything OK?"

"I don't know," Sarah whispered. "I'm scared. I don't know what to think."

"Calm down," Diane replied. "Take some deep breaths. Now, what happened?"

"The police were here this afternoon, and they said they have evidence they found in Brian's apartment that may tie him to some of the killings in Tennessee," Sarah exclaimed.

"What?" Diane replied, not believing what she was hearing. She had known Brian quite well. "That's not possible!"

"That's what I thought," said Sarah, but they said the forensics showed Brian killed himself and they found some evidence at his apartment that might tie him to some murders."

"What kind of evidence?" Diane inquired.

"Some human hair samples," Sarah answered. "We call them 'trophies' in the psychiatric literature. It's something personal of the victim that a serial killer keeps as a memento."

"Gross!" replied the friend. "So, what does it all mean?"

"I don't know," cried the confused Sarah. "I personally don't believe Brian did these things. I really don't, but the evidence is what the police say it is."

"Is it possible someone could have killed Brian and planted the evidence at his place?" Diane questioned, trying to apply logic to an otherwise incoherent situation.

"That's what I was wondering!" Sarah exclaimed. "On the one hand, that would seem perfectly logical to me, but on the other, that's not what the police are saying occurred. It's especially confusing given what Brain told me the other day before he died," Sarah revealed.

"What was that?" Diane gasped.

"He admitted he had some hair samples but said he found them hidden in Aiden's office," Sarah disclosed.

"Sarah! I can't believe what you're telling me! That is impossible!" shrieked Diane.

"Now you know why I had to call you. This is driving me stark-raving mad," cried Sarah.

"I don't know what to think, but deep down, I just can't believe Brian would do these things. He just couldn't."

"So do you think Aiden might have been involved in some way, despite what the police are saying?" Diane asked.

"I don't know!" Sarah replied, tears running down her cheeks. "I'm just really scared."

"Listen to me, Sarah, listen good," Diane counseled. "You have to maintain yourself like you fully accept the police findings. You can't give Aiden any inkling that you may suspect him. Do you understand what I'm saying?"

"Yes, I've been trying to play that role for the last several days," Sarah conceded. "Frankly, I don't know how much longer I can do it."

"You have to stay strong. Do you hear me?" asked Diane.

"Yes, I hear you," Sarah calmly replied.

"Call your office tomorrow and tell them with all the tragedy surrounding Brian's suicide that you need a couple of days off to grieve. OK?"

"That's the truth," Sarah honestly replied.

"After Aiden leaves for work in the morning, you've got to comb your house inch by inch and see if you find anything . . . anything at all that might tie Aiden to any of this. Understand?"

"Yeah, that's a good idea," Sarah agreed.

"I mean, inch-by-inch, don't leave anything uncovered, OK?" Diane re-affirmed. "It may take a couple of days but be meticulous about it."

"I will," Sarah agreed. "I'll let you know whatever comes up."

"Call me if you need anything," Diane urged: "Anything at all!"

"I will," Sarah assured her.

"Oh! . . . and Sarah . . . take care of yourself. We'll get to the bottom of this."

"God, I hope so!" Sarah responded. "It's just a horrible nightmare!"

* * * * * * * *

The next morning Fletcher and Sarah shared a cup of coffee over the kitchen table with scones and a bit of fruit.

"I've decided I'm going to take a day or so off," Sarah announced. "I just need some time to recover from all of this."

"Good idea," Fletcher replied. "It's been a lot to absorb. More than anyone should have to deal with."

"Get some rest today. I think it will do you some good," Fletcher added with a sympathetic smile.

"I plan to," Sarah replied.

"I'll give you a call around lunch and see how you're doing," he added.

"OK, talk to you then."

Sarah peered out from behind the window curtain and watched Fletcher enter his car parked on the street a few yards down from their house. He drove off and was soon out of sight. She quickly began to implement her plan which involved systematically examining anything and everything within the house; under carpets, behind paintings, on top of bookcases . . . everything.

She poured through long-forgotten files; turning the pages of books in the study; looking in lamp fixtures, under cushions, and behind window shades. She even looked in Fletcher's golf bag imagining where she might hide something if she were being investigated. After four hours, she had uncovered nothing and was beginning to believe her idea would not prove fruitful.

Her cell phone rang. It was Diane.

"How's it coming?" she asked, trying to present an air of optimism.

"Nothing," replied Sarah, "absolutely nothing."

"Well, don't give up until you've looked everywhere," insisted Diane. "If there's something there, it will be in the last place you would think of."

"How are you feeling today?" she continued.

"Hard to say," said Sarah. "I'm still trying to digest all that has happened. It's like being in the twilight zone . . . none of it seems real."

"I can't imagine what you're going through," confided Diane, "but hang in there. This thing is going to resolve itself one way or another."

"That's what I'm afraid of," Sarah replied. "Talk to you later."

"Anytime," Diane said. "Got that? Call me any time."

"I will," replied Sarah, preoccupied with her task.

Sarah continued her search going through all of Fletcher's clothes, one piece at a time. It wasn't until she got to the closet rummaging through his twenty or so suits that she came across something odd.

In the inside pocket of one of his suit jackets was a slip of paper with a foreign telephone number and the name of Ileana Worden of Trident Trust Company on it. She looked up the exchange of 345 and discovered it was for the Cayman Islands. Her mind was racing with the myriad of possibilities such a contact might represent.

She was determined to find out more.

* * * * * * * *

Fletcher returned home for dinner a bit early, in part to check on Sarah and how she was coping with the remarkable news of the last couple of days. He entered the house with the look of a dejected soul, having lost his best friend and compatriot.

"How was your day?" Sarah timidly asked trying to maintain an air of normalcy. In her mind, she was sizing up his every movement, trying to glean his true persona and how it was reacting given everything that was happening around him.

"Pretty rough day," he replied. "Everyone who was at work was still in a daze, just moping around. It's all terribly sad, actually," he said with a pained expression on his face.

"How was your day?" he countered, trying as well to get a feel for her demeanor after a day of revelation.

"I didn't do much actually," Sarah replied. "I couldn't bear the thought of turning on the TV and hearing about Brian, so I tried to straighten up around the house and get a few things done."

"Any luck?" Fletcher responded.

“Yeah, I pulled together some clothes for the laundry and found this,” she matter-of-factly replied, handing Fletcher the slip of paper from his suit jacket.

With a composed bearing, she extended her arm and handed him the paper, and calmly asked, “Is this important? I was going to throw it away but thought you might need it.”

Fletcher took the slip of paper from her hand and paused ever-so-briefly before he answered. Sarah noticed the hesitation.

“Oh, that,” he calmly began. “That’s the name of an executive at a Caymans Island bank who our committee is trying to work with on some new reporting proposals,” he glibly remarked. “One of our staffers gave me this number from the committee documents and said I might want to call her for some inside perspective.”

Fletcher flipped through his newspaper as he sat on the sofa, paying little heed to the inquiry. It was a smooth response, he thought.

Sarah didn’t press the point; after all, it didn’t seem overly suspicious. It may have been just what Fletcher said it was.

In fact, however, it was far more than it appeared.

* * * * * * * *

Fletcher had created an offshore bank account a few years earlier and had steadily diverted campaign funds and Committee appropriations to a false-front contractor called The Triad Group. In so doing, he had established a fictitious name . . . Mr. Leopold Mintor, as a director of the corporation, which allowed Fletcher to access the account whenever necessary.

The Caymans had over 200 banks on the island; foreign, domestic, and otherwise. The islands were small, located 150 miles southwest of Cuba, but represented the sixth-largest offshore banking center in the world.

Fletcher had the bank invest the money in stocks, bonds, mutual funds, etc., and wasn't even seeking to evade taxes, as much as to create a legitimate account from the diverted funds that he had control over. The scheme had worked beautifully, and Fletcher had profited handsomely from his devious venture.

He had grown the account to nearly $4 million in his relatively short time in Congress. It had been one of his proudest achievements.

A couple of years earlier, there was one occasion when he thought it might all come crashing down. The Government Accountability Office (GAO), pursuant to public outcry after a congressional scandal, came in to conduct a large-scale audit on the Judiciary Committee and the political donations to several of its members.

Auditors who interviewed Fletcher asked about the Triad Group and its role as a subcontractor for the Committee, one of over 2,500 contract workers or firms that provide services to Congress.

"Specifically, Congressman, what is the role of the Triad Group with respect to the mission of the Judicial Committee?"

Fletcher, as usual, was exceedingly good at thinking off-the-cuff.

"The Triad Group provides a wide range of administrative services to us," replied the confident Fletcher. "Specifically, they oversee many of our compute operations, procurement, financial oversight, and human resources," he stated.

"Have you ever had any indications that they might not have been performing the services for which they have billed the Committee?" asked an auditor.

"Never," replied Fletcher. "Tell you the truth; they have been one of the more responsive contract entities we've worked with. I would have no reluctance to sponsor them for future Committee needs."

"So you're satisfied with the services the Committee has secured from them?"

"Absolutely," Fletcher responded.

"And you could provide us with whatever invoices, etc., that might bear out their work for the Committee?"

"Sure, that wouldn't be a problem," Fletcher said, knowing that was a lie.

"Thank you, Congressman," replied an auditor. "We may get back to you if we have some more questions."

"Anytime," said Fletcher.

The GAO never returned for further information. Fletcher knew based on past precedent that he and Triad would be free of further investigations for several years to come.

* * * * * * * *

Sarah resumed her search of the house the next day after Fletcher left for work. He had been a bit jovial, cracking a joke before he walked out the door. His dour demeanor from the evening before had lightened; perhaps in response to Sarah having found a bit more balance to her mental state. Picking up where she left off, Sarah combed through the guest rooms, the utility room, and even into the attic where she went through the crawl space, flashlight in hand. She rummaged through the computer desk in the study, hoping to find a wayward drawer or something out of place which might tip her off to something that wasn't quite right.

She took a break at mid-day and pondered whether the whole investigation was an exercise in futility. She began to question herself again like she had done for the umpteenth time in the past several days. What was she doing? What was it she was looking for? She had no answers, and her frustration was starting to mount.

Was it Brian who was the bad guy, or was it her husband? Even now, despite having no evidence to the contrary, she clung to an innate feeling that things had not gone down with Brian as the police had concluded it had.

There was still the notion of what Brian had said about Fletcher coming out of Arizona, and there was Aiden's photo in the Bisbee yearbook and Flora Kinnard's murder. Still, everything else was merely based on what Brian had told her. The only real thing was the hair samples he had brought to her lab, but how could she prove they came from her husband's office? Again, it was just what Brian had said.

She felt her mind spinning yet again. The circuitous logic she was trying to employ just kept returning to the same place over and over, and just like all the other times, it offered no firm conclusion. She was simply not going to figure any of it out, she thought. It was a riddle, wrapped in a mystery, inside an enigma. Calling her friend Diane again, they chatted for a bit before Sarah felt compelled to return to her task.

"Keep at it," Diane urged. "Sounds like you're almost done."

"I don't think there's anything here," Sarah dejectedly offered.

Then she got an idea, it was probably stupid, but she had nothing to lose. She simply had to do it. Fletcher told her he would be in Annapolis all day at a party conference and probably wouldn't be home until 7:00 p.m.

Catching the Metro to Capitol Hill, Sarah went to Fletcher's office, staffed only by a handful of dispirited aides. Walking into the reception area, the receptionist Amy greeted her politely.

"Hello, Mrs. Fletcher," she said. "What a surprise to see you here." Sarah gave her a hug as the two commiserated over Brian's tragic death.

"The Congressman isn't in today if you were looking for him," she politely offered.

"Oh, no," she replied, "I just stopped in for a moment to get a book to take home. I forgot to tell Aiden to grab it this morning before he left. I'll just be a moment."

"Sure," said Amy, having no reason to question the Congressman's wife.

Sarah walked hurriedly into Fletcher's office toward the back bookcase and grabbed the first book she saw, "The Making of a President," Theodore White's 1960 classic on John F. Kennedy's election. She approached the Picasso in the back of the room that Brian had earlier described. Taking a glance around, she subtly pulled the frame out from the wall and looked behind **. . .** there was nothing.

She returned the frame to its place when Amy strolled in.

"Find what you were looking for?" she asked.

Holding the book up, Sarah replied. "Yeah, right here," and began walking toward the door to leave.

"I'll tell the Congressman you stopped by," Amy stated.

"No, please, don't bother him. It was just a little thing," Sarah replied.

"OK, no problem, see you again before too long," she said, with a wave goodbye.

"Next time," said Sarah leaving the office.

Chapter Thirty-Five

Returning from her husband's office, Sarah sat and pondered the significance of her little investigation. She didn't know, what if anything, she was hoping to discover. It wasn't like Sarah expected anything to be behind the Picasso. Still, in the recesses of her mind, she was perhaps hoping something might yet confirm Brian's version of the horrific events of the past several days so she wouldn't have to accept the reality that he was a killer who had taken his own life.

Not that she wanted Aiden implicated either. She wished with all her heart that he would be found to have had no involvement whatsoever in the murders in question.

The whole scenario was still racing in her mind. It was as if the real truth would never see the light of day. She didn't even know what the truth was anymore. She thought that maybe she should quit trying to solve the Rubik's cube mystery and just let events take their course. Then it hit her yet again that her life might still be in jeopardy.

Back home, she picked up where she left off with her search. She finished except for a utility room closet where Aiden kept his tools and various paraphernalia that couldn't be stored anywhere else. It was generally referred to by the couple as the "junk room," and that pretty much described it to a tee.

She pulled out a couple of brooms, a vacuum, folding chairs, a ladder, and a myriad of cleaners and household items.

It was an effort just getting all the crap out of the closet to inspect. She combed through everything and found nothing.

The only thing left was a gun case that Fletcher kept on the bottom shelf behind some cans of paint. She wasn't about to touch that. She was deathly afraid of guns and had told Aiden on numerous occasions she wanted nothing to do with guns and would never go near one.

As she continued to try to find something that might address her concerns about Aiden, she was becoming more and more doubtful about whether Brian had told her the truth about him. The fact of the matter is that there was absolutely nothing to tie Aiden to anything!

Exhausted from her two-day search of the house, she began to question whether she had been overreacting and whether or not she should just come to grips with the fact that Brian, by all appearances, had been responsible for everything that had happened.

The next morning, she returned to her office and tried to resume a normal routine. In the back of her mind, however, her lingering doubts about it all just wouldn't leave her alone.

She was done agonizing. Her life had been a living hell ever since Brian had come to her with the hair samples. She was through with the bewilderment. She had now made a decision . . . unless something else came up to implicate her husband, she was going to treat the subject like everyone else was treating it . . . as the suicide of her friend whom she apparently did not know as well as she thought.

What else could she possibly believe?

She simply could not continue the agony of being caught in the middle, spinning in confusion as her constant apprehension was destroying what was left of her sanity.

She needed to share her feelings with her friend.

"Diane . . . its Sarah. I thought I'd just touch base."

"Sarah! What did you find?" Diane exclaimed.

"Nothing, absolutely nothing," Sarah replied.

"Did you look everywhere, and I mean everywhere?" Diane asked.

"Every freaking place in our house," Sarah responded with confident assurance.

"Now what?" her friend asked.

"I've decided I'm going to back off for a while," Sarah replied. "I've been an emotional wreck over this. Until someone comes up with something that specifically implicates Aiden, I'm going to try to reclaim my life . . . the life I had before all this happened."

Diane wasn't expecting Sarah's sudden change of heart but understood why she had arrived at her newfound attitude.

"Good for you," Diane responded with a tone of support. "I understand where you're coming from. I really do. I don't know how you've stood it this long."

* * * * * * * *

While the police report on Asher's death was being finalized, Fletcher was pleased with the way everything was playing out . . . just as he had planned it. The whole set-up, beginning with his discreetly excusing himself from the dinner that night with no one noticing, to the meticulous staging of

Asher's death and the police assessment of it as a suicide, had been nothing short of brilliant.

But the coup de grace had been the planting of the hair samples . . . his "sweethearts," in Asher's apartment. That was going to change the direction of everything, including any suspicion that might have been building toward him.

Now with Asher out of the way, the biggest threat was removed. His one concern was about what Asher had said the night he was killed . . . that Sarah "knew everything." That was still a huge problem for him.

He had a dilemma he couldn't yet resolve. On the one hand, would Sarah be dissuaded from suspecting him once the police report became official, or would she see through the set-up and turn him into the police? The conflict was quite vexing. How could Sarah suspect him of killing Asher, knowing he had an airtight alibi for the evening in question? The anxiety of the situation was beginning to get to him as well.

He had to play his cards right, yet again. There were two options before him, he imagined. If he were to kill Sarah, even by making it look like an accident or another routine murder, the timing would be too suspicious. To lose his chief of staff and wife within a matter of a few weeks would be too coincidental. Unwanted attention would undoubtedly be cast upon him anew.

On the other hand, what was keeping her from going to the police and telling them the whole story that Asher had related? She was Deputy Director of the very office within the FBI that ran the databases on this very type of thing, for Christ sakes! He now had deep regrets about having her appointed to that position. How stupid! He thought. What could he possibly have been thinking?

The one thing he had going for him was that he was a US Congressman, and the authorities would be very reluctant to approach him without some exceedingly firm evidence to implicate him in the murders.

It all came down to Sarah and what her apprehensions were directing her to do. He knew she was an emotional wreck given the shocking events of the past several days and couldn't predict whether she would respond in a rational manner or not.

Should he be exploiting her anxieties so she would appear to the authorities as being an unreliable witness, or should he help calm her fears, so she could perhaps accept the reality of the situation based on how the police had interpreted the evidence?

He was torn on how to proceed. If he made the wrong move, it could put him in a perilous situation.

Maybe the best thing would be to scare her enough so she wouldn't dare say anything to authorities. Then again, that might only be a short-term solution to a much longer-term problem. Fletcher had to assess her level of fear. That might well indicate her mindset in relation to how she saw him in the whole affair.

How would he be assured that she wouldn't rat him out at some point in the future? The answer might be that after all the accusations, she still had no concrete evidence to implicate him, only what she was told by someone who now isn't even alive and who is presumptively deemed to be the killer himself.

He would spend the next few days sizing her up and deciding what his course of action should be. One thing was certain; nothing would prevent him from doing anything and everything necessary to protect himself and his own self-interest.

That was the way it had always been.

* * * * * * * * *

Fletcher took a rare evening off from his congressional duties and arrived home from work at 6:00 p.m. He was growing a bit anxious about Sarah and the investigation into Asher's death and attempted to enjoy a much-needed drink in his study, as he awaited her arrival from a late-afternoon business conference.

He had given the situation a lot of thought and had come up with a plan. He would play the role of a grief-stricken husband who wanted to get their life back on track. How Sarah reacted to the overture would be a good indicator of how he should proceed next.

He continued to hone his long-thought-out scheme for what he would do if Sarah freaked out and tried to have him arrested. It wasn't what he wanted, but in his mind, it might be the last resort. It all came down to her and how he thought she was handling the situation. It promised to be a potentially stressful evening.

Sarah arrived home from her conference and was a little surprised to see Fletcher waiting. She tried not to show her surprise as he sat somewhat uneasily awaiting their encounter.

"What are you doing home so early?" she abruptly inquired, genuinely surprised by his early evening appearance. She looked around to see if anything was out of order.

"I wanted us to have some time together," he earnestly replied. "Things have been so awful; I just wanted us to try to decompress a bit from all the stress we've been under."

Whether he intended it or not, Fletcher's words provided a soothing balm to Sarah's otherwise tormented psyche. For just a moment, she allowed herself to imagine being free of all the anguish she had been experiencing.

Walking toward her, he gave her a gentle hug. She reacted a bit stiffly but absorbed the embrace as she imagined what it would be like to be free of all the conflict in their lives.

"Can I get you a drink?" he asked.

"I'll have a Manhattan," she calmly responded, in dire need of something to help relax her.

Returning from the bar, he handed her the drink and sat down in an overstuffed chair in the living room.

"Sarah, things have been really terrible around here. I don't know how either of us have been able to bear it," he began.

His words went straight to Sarah's soul. Was he feeling as bad as she was? She wondered. Her attention was completely on what he was saying as she took a long, soothing sip from her drink.

"Sometimes things happen in life that hit us out of the blue," he continued. "Things so horrible that we can't digest them. I know that's how it's been for me," he added, looking at her genuinely grief-stricken.

"I don't know how all of this plays out," he stated. "I guess the only thing we can do is accept what has happened and try to move on with our lives the best we can."

Sarah was invigorated by Fletcher's words. They were everything she needed to hear to calm her restless emotions. His words sounded as if they came from her own tortured psyche and were a soothing elixir for her fragile state of mind.

“Aiden, I don’t know what to think anymore,” she admitted. “I don’t know how to go forward without some kind of resolution.”

Fletcher could feel her deep-seeded pain. It was the vulnerability he was looking for.

“Sarah, I know we don’t have a lot of answers right now, but I want us to get back to the way we were . . . the way it was before all this came into our lives,” he urged. His sincerity was authentic.

“How do we do that?” Sarah pleaded. “Things are so upside down right now. I don’t know which direction to go in.”

Fletcher knew he was making the inroads he had hoped to make with her.

Gently caressing her hand, he continued.

“Sarah, what do you think of taking a long weekend and going somewhere to try to unwind . . . just you and me?”

“Like where? She answered.

Fletcher knew he was being persuasive. If she were deathly afraid of him, the conversation would not be going in this direction.

“I don’t know . . . maybe the Greenbrier,” he suggested.

The Greenbrier was an exclusive resort situated on 11,000 acres in the Allegheny Mountains, 250 miles out I-81 from Washington in White Sulphur Springs, West Virginia. It was a highly desirable destination for Washingtonians, with its quiet country ambiance, golf, a casino, and five-star dining. It had long been considered the pre-eminent escape from the rigors of life in Washington and a memorable experience to all that had been fortunate enough to enjoy it.

"The Greenbrier?" Sarah responded. "That would be nice, but can you get away?"

"I'll tell the office I won't be in Friday. We'll leave Thursday afternoon and come back Sunday. What do you say?"

The idea of getting out of the boiler room of Washington, especially now, was enough on its own to convince Sarah. Whatever the immediate future might hold for them, she had decided to make the mental leap to accept the prevailing position on all that had occurred with Brian. At this point, it's all she had to hold on to in any event.

She needed to pursue clarity at this point, no matter how it was presented. It was the beginning of her journey back to what she hoped was some kind of normalcy.

"OK, then," she cheerfully replied. "Let's do it!"

By Thursday afternoon, Fletcher picked up Sarah at her office at the FBI building in his Audi and got on I-66 in Arlington for the four-hour drive to West Virginia. They had left early enough to avoid the HOV restrictions and the worst of the rush hour traffic and found themselves soon traveling through the serene countryside of The Plains, Virginia. They soon merged onto I-81 South toward Roanoke and then on I-64 toward Charleston.

The drive had been pleasant enough with Fletcher sometimes holding Sarah's hand as they commented on how peaceful things were in the Virginia countryside.

"This was just what I needed, Aiden. You're a real sugar pie. Thanks for doing this for me," Sarah remarked.

"Thank you, Sarah," he replied, smiling at her "sugar pie" reference, which was a term of endearment she occasionally used when she was feeling particularly appreciative of him. “It’s what both of us needed.”

His subtle smile reflected his satisfaction with how everything was working out. Getting Sarah back on board was the key.

Arriving at the grounds of the iconic resort was inspiring in and of itself. The vast, tree lined white structure with beautiful gardens and its array of horse-drawn carriages was indeed something to behold.

“It looks like the U.S. Capitol without the dome,” Fletcher commented.

“It’s bigger than the U.S. Capitol,” Sarah replied.

The multi-colored floor-to-ceiling curtains with a palette of red and green fabrics dominated the interior of the resort. It was like stepping back in time when things were easier and a lot more elegant.

The weekend accomplished what both of them were hoping for. Sarah was able to pretty much let go of the demons that had been haunting her since Brian’s revelations and shocking death.

Fletcher had manipulated the time together with his wife to better get a feel as to whether she might be a threat to his well-being. Driving back to Washington, they both arrived with a more trusting sense of each other and a newly found determination to get on with their daily lives.

That night, after Sarah had gone to bed, Fletcher sat around a slow-burning fire finishing the last few draws from his cigar.

Things were back to where they needed to be; he smiled . . . at least for the time being. He had gotten himself out of a tight spot and accomplished what he intended to.

But then again, he always did. If there was one thing, he did well . . . it was surviving.

Chapter Thirty-Six

The weekend had brightened Sarah's spirits. She and Aiden had shared a few restful days together in a tranquil environment which both had badly needed. The time spent allowed them to reassess the other's attitudes, specifically their perspective on each other.

"How was your weekend?" Diane asked upon Sarah's return.

"It was fine," Sarah responded. "Nice couple of days of doing nothing but sitting outside and talking."

"What was the topic of conversation?" asked Diane.

"Oh, pretty much about moving on with our lives and trying to put all our anxieties behind us," Sarah replied.

"Did he show any anxieties?" said the curious Diane.

"Most definitely," replied Sarah. "I think he was as nervous a wreck as I was," she added.

"So you're not afraid that he may hurt you anymore?"

"I'm just taking it one day at a time now," Sarah stated. "I'm not as fearful about it as I once was. I think things have pretty much run their course."

"Well, just keep an eye on him," Diane warned. "Don't assume anything . . . OK?"

"I won't, Sarah said. "I definitely won't."

* * * * * * * *

The following weekend, the Washington area had its usual complement of shootings and violent criminal assaults. Among the casualties were four homicide victims, three by shootings and one by strangulation. The three shootings were all pretty much in the traditional places, Anacostia and the Third and Fourth Districts of the city.

In Arlington, where the famous Iwo Jima Marine Corps Memorial is located, the fourth victim was found. Early Saturday morning, a jogger discovered the body under a grove of trees not far from a small parking lot near the memorial.

The victim was a twenty-two-year-old receptionist for a lobbying group on K Street. She had been brutally beaten, as evidenced by her fractured skull and severe abrasions around her neck, indicating that she had been strangled as well.

In the aftermath of the murder, a friend identified the victim as Maureen Bickell, age twenty, who lived in Crystal City, in a high-rise apartment, a short metro ride from Rosslyn, Virginia, just across Key Bridge from Georgetown.

The friend had called the Arlington police the day after the body was discovered when she had heard about the murder on TV. She told police that a bunch of friends from Capitol Hill, including the victim, had been partying late into the night on Friday in Georgetown, hopping from bar to bar until nearly 1:30 a.m., when several of them decided it was time to call it a night.

She told police that Maureen was more than a little tipsy as she made her way down Wisconsin Avenue to pick up her car near the Georgetown Waterfront Park off the Whitehurst Freeway near the Potomac River. Three of the young women had been walking together until the other two veered off to get into their own cars, parked on M Street, just a short distance from where Maureen's car was parked.

"We asked her if she wanted a ride to her car," the friend had told police, weeping as she recalled events from the fateful evening. "But she said she was fine and could make it the rest of the way, no problem," the woman recalled.

"Was there anything else that you recall after dropping her off?" the officer had asked.

"Well, I'm not sure, but it seems like after she kept walking, I noticed her getting into a car with a man just a block or so from where we left her," she asserted.

"Did you notice what the man looked like?" asked the officer.

"I didn't get a very good look, to be honest," she said, "it was dark, and I wasn't in the best of shape myself," she added. "But I would guess he was in his mid-forties or so."

"Could you identify him if we showed you some photos?" she was asked.

"No, I just caught a slight glimpse."

"How about his car?" Questioned the officer. "Could you tell what kind it was?"

"Well, it was a dark car, maybe blue or black," she replied. "I don't know my cars very well, but it was an imported car like a Volvo or BMW."

"Anything else?" asked the officer.

"No, that's it," she said, crying through her Kleenex. "I feel so bad! If only she would have let us drive her to her car."

* * * * * * * * *

In a continued effort to escape her troubles, Sarah had been away that weekend hiking through the Shenandoah Mountains with a couple of friends. Fletcher had encouraged her to go. He was pleased she was getting out for the first time in months with friends. He was hopeful it would get her mind off the Asher affair, and that he could return to his normal life as well.

Upon her return on Sunday afternoon, the couple sat on their terrace and enjoyed a glass of Chardonnay.

"How was your hike," Fletcher asked Sarah.

"Oh, it was fun," she said. "We drove down Skyline Drive and spent our time getting on and off the Appalachian Trail to hike some of the smaller trails throughout the Park. We did several of the classics . . . Old Rag, White Oak, Hawksbill Summit," she eagerly added.

"Great!" replied Fletcher. "Sounds like you had a fun weekend. I'm glad you could get away and clear your mind," he added.

"How was your weekend?" she asked.

"Oh, pretty uneventful," he responded. "Stayed late at the office on Friday and pretty much worked at home the rest of the time."

"I wished you could get out more," she said. "It would do you some good just to get away from DC more often."

"The weekend at the Greenbrier should hold me for a while," he said. "Besides, there's enough here in town to keep me interested," he said, with the slightest of grins.

"Anyway, hope things can settle down to normal," he added, staring at Sarah to judge her reaction.

"Me too," she replied, heading back into the kitchen. "Me too."

After several tedious weeks had passed since Asher's death, it appeared that things were indeed resembling some modicum of normalcy.

The couple returned to their routines without incident for a few days until she was approached by an assistant at the FBI with some startling news.

"Just thought I'd update you," he said. "While you were out of town, there was another suspicious murder."

"Oh really!" she replied, curious about what she was about to be told.

"Another young girl found beaten and strangled at Iwo Jima Memorial last Friday night," he said.

"What!" Sarah exclaimed. "Do they have any suspects?"

"None," replied the assistant. "Nor have they come up with any kind of forensic evidence at the crime scene,"

"Sounds very similar to those two murders from several months ago," she stated.

"Yeah," he replied. "All three in their early twenties; beaten and strangled; no sexual assaults, no knife wounds, nothing else to give us a lead."

"Do you think it's the same guy?" asked the assistant.

"I don't know, Jimmy. I honestly don't know, but it certainly could be," she said.

"I want you to flag these cases, and if you find out anything more . . . and I mean anything, you get back to me as soon as possible. Understand?" Sarah announced.

"Sure thing," replied the aide.

The case didn't set off any new alarms in Sarah, but it did get her thinking. So far, they had received no leads on the three suspicious DC murders. They all seemed to have the same MO, but there didn't seem to be an overt pattern between them.

And then it occurred to her. Picking up her phone, she called Jimmy back.

"Yes, ma'am," he replied.

"I want you to contact the Arlington Medical Examiner's Office and ask them if they have any indication as to whether the victim in the latest strangulation death had any evidence that a lock of her hair had been cut off," she asserted.

"Do you think the killer cuts off the hair of his victim and keeps it as a trophy?" Jimmy inquired.

"It's entirely possible," replied Sarah. "There was no indication on the previous two victims one way or another, but if there is evidence on the third victim that that's the case, the killer might be establishing a pattern. We'll just have to wait and see."

"In any event, I'd like to get an answer to that as soon as possible, OK?"

"Sure," said Jimmy. "I'll let you know what they say."

Returning home that night, Sarah was feeling confident enough about Fletcher that she brought it up over dinner.

"By the way, I saw where another young girl was strangled last weekend in Arlington," she said. "Did you hear anything about that?"

Looking up from a text he had just received, Fletcher's reaction was indifferent.

"I may have heard a snippet about that on the radio but haven't kept up with any of it," he replied. "Did your office come up with anything?" His comment was joined by a conspicuous, disinterested look.

"No, not really," she answered. "It's just another case that seems to have some similarity with those other two."

"Do you think it's the same guy doing it?" Fletcher asked, now genuinely absorbed by her comments.

"It's hard to say," she said. "If it is, he's pretty smart. He's not leaving any DNA or other forensic evidence at the crime scene, which is in and of itself pretty unusual."

"Maybe he's just lucky, or most likely they're unrelated," replied Fletcher, losing his interest in the topic.

"Anyway, whatever the outcome, I'm sure it will resolve itself before long," he asserted.

Not even Fletcher realized how prescient his comment would be.

* * * * * * * *

The next day Sarah was at her office when her assistant knocked on her door.

"Come on in, Jimmy," she said. "Do you have anything for me?" curious to know the answer to the assignment she had given him.

"I'm not sure exactly," he responded.

"What do you mean you're not sure?" she inquired.

"Well, I spoke to the medical examiner's office and asked them if they could determine whether the last victim's body showed any evidence that the killer may have clipped a lock of her hair from her."

"And?"

"And they said it's quite possible, but they couldn't say definitively," Jimmy responded.

"What specifically did they say?" queried Sarah.

"They said that there appeared to be an abrasion on her scalp in the back of her head where someone might have pulled a few hairs from her head, but there was nothing definitive." "On the other hand, they said it was possible the killer might have just clipped a lock of her hair, and it simply wouldn't be noticeable. Either way, they can't make a definitive determination," he concluded.

"Did you ask them what their best guess might be?"

"I did!" he proudly replied. "They said with the irregularity of the natural fall of her hairline; they think it's entirely plausible that the killer did, in fact, take at least some of her hair, especially from the back where it tended to be quite a bit longer."

“Thanks, Jimmy. I’m going to proceed on that assumption . . . at least until we have something else to go on.”

Chapter Thirty-Seven

Several days passed, and nothing was developing on any of the three suspected DC murders. Sarah had all but given up trying to find a common connection between them and didn't know where to turn.

Maybe her imagination was getting away from her, she thought. Just because they were all strangled didn't necessarily mean they were all killed by the same perpetrator. Maybe, like many of the other DC murders, they would simply go into the unsolved file, and that would be it.

Fletcher and Sarah went about their business and were beginning to establish a semblance of a routine. One evening, after tedious work schedules, the two called it a day and went to bed at 10:00 p.m. Several hours later, in dead of the night, Sarah looked over and noticed Fletcher was not in bed. Usually a very sound sleeper, rather than roll over and go back to sleep, her curiosity was perked.

Anxious as to what he might possibly be doing, she tiptoed to their bedroom door and peered down the hall where she could see a dim light on in his study and heard him utter subtle whimpers which she could not make out.

She soon saw the light in the study suddenly extinguished. She hopped back into bed and kept her ears attuned to the slightest of sounds. Within moments, she heard the creak of the utility room closet door closing. Fletcher soon returned to bed and slipped under the blanket. Sarah feigned a deep sleep.

As she lay on her side, she could only imagine what might have been going on with Fletcher at that hour in the morning. He soon fell fast asleep.

The next morning over coffee, she asked him about the late-night occurrence.

"Trouble sleeping last night?" she asked.

"Huh?" he responded, not knowing how to answer.

"I heard you get up last night," she expanded. "Were you having trouble sleeping?"

The question continued to catch Fletcher off guard.

"Oh!" he stammered. "Yeah, I couldn't sleep," he abruptly replied, not wishing to elaborate. Sarah's questions were making him increasingly uncomfortable.

"What were you doing in the study at that hour?" she persisted.

Again, Fletcher couldn't come up with an adequate explanation. His suspicion of Sarah's motives was now growing in intensity.

"Just sitting there," he offered. "Actually, I don't even remember what I did." He was doing everything he could to dismiss the conversation.

Sarah found his response to her questions a bit puzzling but didn't pursue the matter any further.

The next day at work, she couldn't get the episode off her mind. The more she thought about it, the more dubious she was of his explanation. It wasn't like him to do such a thing or act as he had in response to her questions about the incident. She remained skeptical of the whole thing. There had to be more to it than that, she thought.

She needed to confide in her friend as her angst continued to grow.

"Diane," she said, placing a call. "Do you have a moment?"

"For you, of course," her friend replied. "What's up?"

"I'm not sure it's anything, but something happened last night that seems a little weird," Sarah replied.

"Like what?" Diane asked, her curiosity perked.

"Well, it may just be my imagination running wild, but it seems like Aiden's behavior last night was very out of sorts," Sarah began. First, he got up at 3:00 a.m., which he never does. Then I heard him in the study kind of moaning."

"Weird," said her friend. "Think he was looking at porn? That might explain it."

Sarah pondered the comment for a moment. It all made some sense.

"Anything else?" Diane said.

"I don't know," Sarah stated. "Maybe this sounds a little paranoid, but I heard him going into the utility room closet next to the study. It probably doesn't mean anything, but it just seemed weird to me. He never gets up like that."

"Do you think he's hiding something?" Diane asked.

"I don't know what it could be," Sarah acknowledged. "I combed every inch of the house, including that closet. If there were something in there, I would have found it."

"Go back and check it again," her friend advised, "You might have overlooked something."

Sarah thought about what her friend had suggested but was convinced herself that her curiosity was now bordering on being delusional.

She pondered the situation for the rest of the day.

By 1:00 p.m., she couldn't get it out of her mind. She had to go check it out one more time.

"Cathy, I'm going to take off a little early today. Something came up that I need to take care of at home," she told her administrative assistant.

"Sure thing," the assistant replied. "See you tomorrow."

Sarah arrived home and went straight to the study. After searching every inch to no avail, she again pulled out everything in the closet, one item at a time. Still, nothing appeared out of the ordinary.

She noticed however, that the gun case had been moved since she had last inspected the closet. In the interim, Aiden hadn't taken the gun case out to clean or anything; her curiosity was now heightened.

She hated guns, and it caused her great anxiety to even handle the case in which it was contained. Nevertheless, she squeamishly pulled down the locked case where Aiden kept his .38 special revolver and took it into the kitchen. She couldn't figure out how to open it but finally used a knife to flip the lock.

Prying open the case, she noticed the silver revolver and several bullets in a small container resting on a patterned foam pad, custom fit to the gun. Checking the case further, she saw nothing, but something told her to keep digging. With great disdain, she removed the gun with her two fingers and laid it carefully atop the kitchen table. She then ran her hands along the outer edge of the foam bedding and lifted it out of the case. Under the padding was a sealed envelope which she carefully opened and therein were three plastic bags . . . each containing human hair!

Her heart jumped out of her throat! She screamed out loud at the heinous discovery. She wanted to throw up; the shock was beyond intense.

She cried out uncontrollably as she paced the kitchen with her horrendous find. She knew it had to be hair trophies from the three women killed in DC. She just knew it!

It's Aiden, she shrieked! Oh my God! It's been Aiden all along!

The reality of the situation was immediately brought to the forefront of her brain. Brian was right! It had to have been Aiden who killed all those women, she realized. Brian had found the hair samples in Aiden's office behind the Picasso just like he said, she reasoned. Then Aiden must have somehow found out and killed Brian and then covered it up to make it look like a suicide!

But what about the hair samples found at Brian's? They had to have been planted by Aiden. Somehow, he had pulled it off to make it look like Brian had been the killer. How did he do it? The police investigation had gotten it all wrong!

The moment was overwhelming. Sarah could hardly breathe. The room was spinning as her brain tried to compute this newest horrendous twist in the nightmare that had become her life. She was in an abject panic.

She had to confirm to whom the hairs belonged. It couldn't wait. But assuming they proved to be the three DC women . . . what came next? She knew from this moment her life was truly in jeopardy.

The horror was overwhelming.

* * * * * * * *

Sarah sprinted out of the house after frantically returning the contents into the closet. She grabbed the hair samples and ran in the opposite direction just in case Aiden might happen to pull up in his car. Grabbing her cell phone, she quickly dialed her friend.

"Diane, I have to talk to you now!" Sarah screamed over the phone. "I found something.
It's terrible!"

Diane realized from her friend's excitement that her search had come up with something that was going to blow everything wide open.

"Meet me at the Hotel Washington," said Diane, "on the rooftop terrace."

"Be there in fifteen minutes," Sarah replied.

She grabbed a taxi to the hotel and arrived in a mere ten minutes.

The Hotel Washington was an institution. It was built in 1918 and listed on the National Register of Historic Places. Located on 15th Street, N.W. between Pennsylvania Avenue and F Street, N.W., it was renowned for its view of the White House across the street and for its intimate rooftop garden where a discreet lunch could always be assured.

Getting off the elevator on the terrace level, Sarah was greeted by Diane, who gave her a warm and extended embrace. Sarah was quivering in fear.

"It's going to be OK, sweetheart," she assured the shaking Sarah, without even knowing the extent of her discovery. "We'll make everything OK. Don't worry."

After being seated at their table on the far end of the terrace, which assured their privacy, their conversation began.

"Tell me everything," Diane anxiously urged, straining across the table to ease as close as she could to Sarah.

"I don't know how to say it," Sarah began. Visibly nervous, she began to cry.

Diane reached out to comfort her as Sarah collected herself.

"I found something in Aiden's gun case," she stated. "He probably put it there of all places, knowing I would never dare touch it."

"So, I opened it up and found these," she exclaimed, discreetly placing the three bags containing the hair samples on the table.

"What are these?" Diane replied, recoiling at the sight.

"They're undoubtedly human hair," Sarah responded. "The only question is to whom did they belong?"

Diane was dumbstruck by the discovery. She didn't know how to respond to what she was being shown.

"It changes everything we've been told," Sarah remarked. "It would seem to confirm what Brian told me before he died," she added.

"So now you don't think Brian killed all those women?" Diane asked.

"No, not in the least. It puts whole a new spin on everything that has happened," Sarah replied.

"What are you going to do now?" Diane wondered.

"Well, one thing is for sure. I'm going to get these analyzed at the lab as soon as I leave here. I'll be shocked if they don't match the three women here in DC," Sarah responded. "After that, we'll play it by ear."

"Are you afraid of Aiden?" Diane questioned; her face was torn with concern.

"I'm scared to death," she replied. "I can't stay at home, because very soon he's going to know I found his trophies. Now that we know what he's capable of, what would keep him from killing me?" she questioned.

She knew the answer . . . nothing.

Suddenly Diane took on a quizzical look on her face. "What happens if the forensics on the hair comes back with no matches, then what?"

Sarah paused. The question stopped everything.

"My God, you know, in my zeal, I hadn't considered that," she pondered. "I'm just assuming they belong to murder victims . . . one way or another. If these samples don't point to anyone, in particular, we're back to square one. We'll have absolutely nothing."

The thought brought Sarah to a new, dizzying low. After all that had occurred, everything would again culminate in a dead-end, with Aiden in his position as a congressman, not being suspected and the police report on Asher most likely remaining the definitive version of events.

The thought was chilling. Sarah couldn't bear to live her life not knowing.

On the other hand, what if the evidence now demonstrated that Aiden was the killer?

That would blow everything open, and it would all be up for grabs . . . including her own safety.

The nightmare wouldn't end, she thought.

"Call me the moment you find out something," Diane urged, getting up to leave.

"I will," Sarah replied. "Believe me; I will."

* * * * * * ** *

Sarah rushed back to FBI Headquarters and ran into the VICAP Director's office.

"Frank, I have to talk with you right now. It's an emergency," Sarah gasped.

"What on earth?" Director Frank Hayden began to respond.

"Listen to what I have to say," Sarah began. "I know this is going to sound bizarre, but I have reason to believe my husband is a serial killer," she stated bluntly.

The Director was flabbergasted. "You mean Aiden?" He couldn't believe what he was hearing.

"Bear with me," Sarah replied. "What I have to tell you is going to be hard to process."

She spent the next half hour capsulizing everything that had occurred since the Knoxville murders and the trial of Otis Stamper. She outlined what Asher had told her about the hair samples found in Aiden's office and his subsequent suicide and framing him as the killer.

She then handed Hayden the three hair samples she found in Fletcher's gun case.

"We have to expedite the analysis of these samples," Sarah directed. "We have to know their origin before anything can happen."

Her boss picked up the phone and direct-dialed the forensic lab.

"This is Director Hayden," he began. "I need a tech to come to my office ASAP and pick up some hair samples for analyses," he barked.

Within a couple of minutes, a senior lab tech burst into his office.

"Peter, I want these samples cross-checked against the database for possible matches. How long would it take to get the analyses completed if we gave it top priority?"

"Two days at the earliest," the tech responded.

"Good. I want you to contact me the moment the results are in. Understand?"

"Yes, sir," said the tech, grabbing the samples and heading back to the lab.

"OK," said the Director, that's all we can do for the time being. I'm going to call the Criminal Investigative Division and have them find you a secure place to stay for the night, just to make sure. I don't want to take any chances with your well-being. We'll soon have a better idea what we're dealing with, and we'll go from there."

"Until then, I'm not doing anything rash. I've seen things in this job that I was convinced had dire implications, but upon further inquiry, it proved to be a false alarm. So, let's just see what the hair samples tell us before we put anything in motion, OK?"

"Oh, and Sarah," he added, "I want you to take the next few days off. The agency will provide you with a car. I think you need to get out of town until we can get a clearer picture of what is happening and assess Aiden's involvement in all that's going on. OK?"

"Thanks, Frank," Sarah stated. "I think that's a good idea. "We'll stay in contact. Let me know the moment you hear back on the hair samples."

"Don't worry," said the Director, "that's a promise."

* * * * * * * *

Fletcher had not been particularly worried about Sarah's inquisitive questioning about his late-night activities until he called her office that afternoon.

"Is Sarah there?" he asked the receptionist, whose office was on a different floor from the Director's office.

"I'm sorry, Mr. Fletcher, she's not in. She left the office today around one o'clock," came the reply.

"Did she say why?" Fletcher exhorted.

She said something came up at home she had to take care of," was the response.

Fletcher was now curious. He was more than curious . . . he was alarmed. Her persistent questions that morning of his late hour activities in the study had caused him angst, but this put him on full alert.

"Marcia, cancel the rest of my schedule for the day," he told his assistant. "I've had something come up at the Justice Department that I need to attend to. Call me if anything important arises. Otherwise, I'll see you in the morning."

"Yes, sir." came the response.

It was late afternoon as Fletcher made his way to Dupont Circle and investigated what, if anything, was going on with Sarah. His gut told him that something was very wrong. His gut, as usual, was right.

Entering the house, he just sensed that things were not in their usual place. He could see from the front entrance of their home that the door to the utility closet area had been left wide open. The chair to the study had been pulled out. Neither he nor Sarah ever left things like that. Walking to the kitchen, he could see tiny shreds of the gray foam padding from the gun case scattered on the table, where it seems someone had ripped it out, examining it.

He immediately went to the closet and pulled out the gun case. The lock had been broken. Opening the case, he noticed the gun had been sloppily thrown in, completely unlike how he usually placed it.

Lifting the foam, to his horror, he noticed the thing he feared most . . . the hair samples were gone.

His mind raced as the apprehension set in. He couldn't think clearly. Considering the situation, he had to contemplate his options and quickly. Thinking logically, he asked himself . . . What did he know for sure?

He knew his wife had found the "sweethearts" that he had pleasured himself with the night before.

Why did he allow this to happen? What a fool he had been! How arrogant had he become to bring the very evidence into their house that could send him to death row? He had come to believe after the Asher murder that he could get away with anything . . . anything at all! He pounded his fist into the table in absolute disgust of his stupidity. His seething anger toward his wife was becoming all-encompassing.

Pausing to think, he knew that it would take a minimum of a couple of days to have his trophies analyzed at Sarah's lab to determine once and for all that the hairs she had found in their home were a match to three murder victims in the DC area. Once confirmed, he knew he would be arrested for those murders and mostly likely implicated in the Asher murder and those of the several victims in Knoxville.

He looked at the gun in the case. For a brief moment, he considered using it on himself. His situation was dire, but one he had planned for over a very long period of time. His mind was pulsating with uncertainty. Then he came to the realization that he truly had no other choice.

Like Icarus, he had flown too close to the sun and he now had to accept the only alternative left, even if it brought about his demise . . .

. . . or at least the demise of Aiden Fletcher.

Chapter Thirty-Eight

Whatever else one could say about him, Lester Kinnard was indeed a survivor. He had overcome adversity all his life and had used his innate intelligence and daring to lift himself out of the abyss and create a life for himself that most would certainly envy.

Lester had the one weakness that he was powerless to restrain. When his inner entity wanted satisfaction, he had to provide it, no matter the risk. The demon had struck on numerous occasions and undoubtedly would strike again.

He had long planned for such adversity in order to continue to live in the free world. Without a plan to survive, he would inevitably be discovered and spend the rest of his life behind bars . . . a proposition he could not abide. He would do virtually anything; eliminate anyone who was a threat to his freedom . . . including Sarah.

Contemplating the situation, he now found himself in, he realized he had to make an immediate decision; a decision that would change his life forever.

He knew he could no longer finesse events as he had with Asher. That had proven to be an especially fortuitous turn of events. He couldn't count on such luck again.

Lester made his decision. It would prove costly, but it was the only one that now made any sense. He had no other options in front of him. He had to exercise his long, thought-out plan. It would take daring and a great deal of bravado, but it was the only avenue left for him.

He was ready.

* * * * * * * *

Quickly leaving home, Lester caught the Metro and made his way toward a self-storage facility a block from Union Station. Along the way, he was fortunate to notice a moving van preparing to depart and struck up a conversation with the driver. Ascertaining that the van was headed west to Colorado, he discreetly secured his cell phone to the undercarriage and continued toward his destination.

He had maintained a small 5’ X 5’ cubicle at the storage facility since his earliest days in Washington. It was a day just like this, for which he had long prepared.

Opening his tiny receptacle, he reached in and pulled out a fully packed suitcase. Inside were several days of clothes, disposable cell phones, disguises, and a taped package with $30,000 in cash. It also contained a gun.

Gathering his suitcase, he walked briskly for half a block. He slipped into the Union Station parking garage, where in an obscure corner of the structure, he deftly applied an artificial mustache and a beard from his suitcase to disguise his identity.

Admiring his work in an automobile mirror, he was surprised how much different he looked, especially with glasses, but then again, given the price he had paid for the cosmetic items, he had better look good.

He proceeded to Union Station as darkness was beginning to settle in. It was mid-week, and the normally busy train station was operating at just a trickle of its regular traffic.

Washington Union Station was an iconic DC institution. Built at the turn of the century, it was one of the country's major railway depots and the headquarters to Amtrak. Its main façade faced the U.S. Capitol building and was half a block long. The main terminal was a sight to behold, with high ceilings, marble and stone engravings, and sculptures evocative of the Italian Renaissance.

The busy intersection of its numerous railroad tracks made for a vibrant destination for those waiting for their train or merely wanting to enjoy lunch in a beautiful setting.

The station served several routes, notably the Northeast Regional, which serviced the northern corridor from Boston to Washington and the Silver Service Route from Washington to Miami. It was the latter that was of interest to Lester.

The rail journey to Miami would take approximately twenty-three hours, with stops in Virginia, the Carolinas, Georgia, and Florida. It would allow Lester to get some rest after days of uncompromising stress.

He knew he would have at least one day, probably two, before authorities would come looking for him. He had arranged to send a text to his office before ditching his phone to advise that he would be taking an unplanned trip to Ohio to attend a close friend's funeral who had died very suddenly but would most definitely return to the office by the end of the week.

Purchasing his ticket on the Silver Meteor, Lester found his compartment and stared out the window as he pondered the formidable journey that was yet to come.

As the train pulled out of the station, he watched the passing lights of the city and observed the Capitol dome fade quickly from view.

He reminisced about his relatively short time there as an elected official. He had done exceedingly well, he thought. There was no telling where he would have gone if he had been able to keep his demons in check.

But as the lights of the District slowly dimmed behind him, he thought about what was next. His plan was solid, and the means to carry it out were readily available.

He looked back on his time in Washington as an experience to help prepare him for the next chapter of his incredibly fated life. He thought everything he created was meant to be. Without the bad times, he wouldn't have achieved what he had already accomplished.

It was his destiny to be at this place, at this time.

Despite the chaos that was about to ensue, Lester was already transitioning to his next persona.

Aiden Fletcher. . . Lester Kinnard's alter-ego and rising star in Washington, D.C., was no longer. He was, from this day forward and forevermore . . . dead and gone.

* * * * * * * *

Once aboard the train, Lester relaxed in his private sleeper car, known as a Roomette. The accommodation was a private compartment with the benefit of a bed, a large picture window, and a private shower. All meals included, and such passengers enjoyed the service of a private attendant.

For what would be the following twenty-three hours, Lester watched the myriad of train depots come and go . . . from Richmond, Virginia, to Rocky Mount, North Carolina, to Charleston, South Carolina. The stations all became a blur as countless passengers embarked while others departed the train.

Repairing to the lounge car, Lester enjoyed a couple of much-needed drinks. Just about the time he was ready to return to his compartment; a pleasant older man engaged him in conversation.

"Where are you headed?" said the man.

"To Savannah," Lester replied. "Going to see my mother who hasn't been very well lately."

"Sorry to hear that," said the man. "One's mother is the most significant person in your life."

"She certainly was . . . uh is," stammered the careless Lester.

"Where did you board the train?" the man inquired.

"Oh, I got on in Boston," Lester responded. "It's been a long trip."

"Did you stop and spend any time in Washington," the old man queried.

"No, I just passed through. I'd like to go there sometime," replied Lester. "I hear it's an interesting place."

"Just a den of thieves if you ask me," the man opined.

Lester chuckled. "You know, you're probably right about that."

"They should all be locked up," the old man persisted. "Nothing but a pack of criminals."

Again, Lester nodded his head in agreement as he arose to return to his compartment.

"Nice meeting you," Lester acknowledged.

"Nice meeting you too," said the man. "Say hello to your mother for me," he added.

"I will," replied Lester.

. . . . *The next time I'm in hell, he thought.*

The encounter gave Lester pause. He decided it wouldn't be wise to continue to mingle among the passengers in case one of them might yet recognize his disguised face from what would soon be national coverage of his exploits. For the duration of the trip, he would take his meals and his libations in his compartment, he decided.

The train had traveled all night and the next day, making innumerable stops along the way as it made its way to Miami.

He mentally patted himself on the back for having prepared so far in advance should a day like this ever occur. Without having done so, he dreaded to think where he would be at that very moment.

Lying in his surprisingly comfortable pull-out bed, Lester soon became enthralled by the rhythm of the rails during the late-night journey. He flashed back on the rekindled Jim Croce "Railroad Song" lyrics he had memorized during his embattled youth:

When I was a boy in the days of the train

I'd sit by the tracks on a long summer day

And I'd wave to the brakeman

And he'd wave back to me

While the thunderclouds rolled out of East Tennessee

But the dreams of the boy disappear when you're grown

And though I may dream, the railroads are gone

The ties they are rotten and the tracks shot to hell

Along with my dreams and the old railroad bell

In my dreams I ride the rails

Or I'd hop a ride to hide across the border

With a black-eyed girl beside me all the way

But the train whistle shrills out her memories to me

While the thunderclouds roll out of East Tennessee

The journey during the long night gave Lester plenty of time to shore up his plans with respect to his next move. It had also proved to be, in some ways, quite cathartic.

He was once again leaving behind all he had been and all he had known. Despite his uncertainties about what the future would hold, he knew beyond any doubt that his unique odyssey could only be made by himself.

Sarah had been a good cover for him, and she had played the role beautifully. But he knew she would turn on him and destroy him if she had the opportunity . . . and the opportunity had just presented itself.

His innate animus toward women in general began to show itself. He didn't know how, but he was going to get back at her . . . one way or another.

* * * * * * * *

At approximately 8:30 pm the following evening, Lester's train pulled into Miami Station, located northwest of the city and adjacent to Hialeah. It was the southern terminus for Amtrak's Silver Service Line. Leaving the station, he caught a taxi to the Port of Miami on Dodge Island off the MacArthur Causeway.

PortMiami was one of the largest passenger ports in the world; and one of the largest cargo ports in the United States. Located on Biscayne Bay at the mouth of the Miami River, it connected downtown Miami by Port Boulevard, a thoroughfare over the Intracoastal Waterway. It was known as the "Cargo Gateway of the Americas."

Directing the taxi to pull up to the South Florida Container Terminal, Lester already knew the schedule of the cargo ship on which he was going to try to catch a ride. It would take all his finesse to pull it off.

It was approaching 9:30 p.m., and the container ship in question, the LAC Costa Agata, was making final preparations for its 1:00 a.m. departure for Buenos Aires, Argentina. Approaching the onboard cargo Chief, who was overseeing the loading of the final containers from the pier onto the massive deck of the ship, Lester made his pitch.

"Excuse me," Lester remarked as the Chief was finishing his tasks. "Anyway, I can catch a ride with you?"

"This is not a cruise ship, my friend. You'll have to go to Terminal D to catch one of the ocean liners," he replied.

"Yeah, I know, but that's not what I'm looking for," Lester continued. "In all sincerity, I was really hoping I could join you on this ship," he added.

"Like I said, we don't take passengers," the Chief asserted, starting to walk away. "Good luck."

Lester paused as the Chief took a few steps. "I'll make it worth your while," he offered, waiting to see the Chief's reaction. He turned around and looked directly at Lester.

"How about $2,000 cash," Lester stated.

Now he had the chief's attention. "Do you know how long this voyage is?" asked the Chief.

"I understand it's about twenty-eight days," replied Lester, having done his homework on all aspects of the ship's journey.

"The only people on this ship are the crew," the Chief added, hoping to yet, dissuade Lester. "Besides, you'd have to eat and have a place to sleep."

"Make me part of the crew," Lester proposed. "Just give me a bunk and let me eat with the crew. They won't know the difference, anyway."

The Chief contemplated the unusual offer. "I don't think that's a good idea," he asserted.

"OK," replied Lester. "How much do you want to make this happen? Remember, it's all going into your pocket."

"$3,500" was the reply. "And I'll make sure you get clean uniforms and a bunk off by yourself. We happen to have a few extra on this cruise."

"You got a deal," responded Lester, pulling out a package of money from his suitcase.

"Just try to stay out of the way," the Chief barked.

"That won't be a problem," Lester replied. "You'll never see me."

The Chief took out a notepad and scribbled a note. "Give this to the First Officer at the top of the ramp," the Chief directed. "He'll take care of you."

"Much obliged," said Lester handing him a wad of cash, and headed up to the main deck.

Being guided to his cabin, the First Officer quoted Lester the rules. "No smoking on deck. Breakfast is served between 6:30-7:30 a.m. After that, lunch is at 11:30 a.m., and dinner at 6:00 p.m. You're allowed on the main deck when ship operations are not being undertaken. Ask the crew if you have any questions. They'll tell you what to do."

"By the way, what's your name, Mister?" he asked.

"George," replied Lester, tugging at his mustache. "Just plain old George."

"OK, George, enjoy the ride. You've got a long voyage ahead of you."

"I intend to," Lester responded. "Believe me, I intend to."

Finding his way to his cabin, Lester was surprised by his small but decidedly comfortable quarters. It had a toilet and shower and a small desk. Most of all, it had a fairly large port window that looked out across the marina.

He cleaned up and found his way to the main deck to watch the ship depart its moorings.

It was an exhilarating feeling knowing what was soon to occur. At the prescribed time of 1:00 a.m., the massive vessel fully loaded with cargo containers stacked eight high, set free from its moorings, and headed into open water.

The 6,700 nautical mile journey Lester was about to undertake would be long and arduous. After leaving Miami, the ship headed for a string of ports situated along the Straits of Florida, the North and South Atlantic, the Rio De La Plata Gulf, and finally, the Port of Buenos Aires.

Heading out to sea, he couldn't imagine a better place to escape the inevitable firestorm that was about to erupt.

For all practical purposes, he had disappeared off the face of the earth. He cracked a faint smile as he contemplated his brilliant ingenuity.

* * * * * * * *

Back in Washington, Sarah had made arrangements, with help from Diane, to stay in a small rental house on the Chesapeake Bay near Queenstown, Maryland, just off Rt. 50 from Annapolis and the popular boating community of Kent Island.

The little hamlet of less than a thousand people in and of itself did not have a lot of attractions other than an outlet mall and a few seafood restaurants. It was usually just a stopping point to refuel for young Washingtonians fighting traffic on their way to Dewey Beach, Delaware, for summer weekend celebrations.

Just across the Kent Narrows Bridge on Kent Island, Queenstown was exactly the kind of place Sarah was looking to escape to. Off by itself on a half-acre of land, the old rambler with tin siding had a small, screened-in porch and backed up to a channel with a pier and a boathouse. Alongside the deck, which peered across the blue-green waters of the Chesapeake, the bulkhead was lined with rocks, against which the constant splash of the waves made for a gentle lull as she slept at night with the rear window to her bedroom partially open.

It was the perfect place for Sarah to calm her frazzled nerves. The events of the last few weeks were beyond belief. Her nervous system had tolerated about all it could without her having to check into a sanitarium to regain her nearly destroyed emotional stability. It was convenient as well. She could always drive into DC from Annapolis when matters necessitated it, and she was close enough to FBI headquarters that she could solicit assistance whenever the need arose.

Moving in most of her clothes and personal belongings, she waved goodbye to a couple of her FBI assistants who had assisted her with the move. This would be her home for the foreseeable future. If Aiden proved to be the killer, she believed him to be, he would have a difficult time finding her in this remote, backwater burg. Whether he was still in the DC area or not, she had little doubt that he would eventually come after her and if he found her, she would undoubtedly become one of his numerous victims.

Despite the many advantages of her newfound residence, it couldn't alleviate the fear that gnawed relentlessly at her perpetually restless mind. Would she ever be free of the monster she had so unknowingly married?

Her constant and escalating distress provided the answer in no uncertain terms.

Chapter Thirty-Nine

It was mid-morning on Friday when Sarah's telephone rang.

"Sarah Fletcher," she answered.

"Sarah. This is Frank. We just got the analysis back from the lab from the hair samples you gave me."

Sarah could hardly breathe. This was it, the answer, one way or another, as to whether her husband was a wretched psychopath, or if he merely had some stupid fetish that he had yet to account for.

"What's the result?" Sarah anxiously replied.

"I don't know how to tell, you this Sarah, but the hair samples you submitted match three of the unsolved District of Columbia and Arlington murders," Hayden stated, stoically waiting for her response. After several moments, she had yet to say anything.

"Two samples have been positively identified as matching the more recent victims here in the District," Hayden tersely continued. "Selina Thornton and Elise Baker. The third positively matched the victim's body found near Iwo Jima . . . Maureen Bickel," he added.

His words had caught Sarah completely off-guard. She was beyond stunned. For the first time, it hit her that Aiden had not only been killing people in Knoxville, but now it appeared that he had been responsible for murdering women right under her nose in Washington!

She had never fully allowed herself to imagine that such a scenario could be true! Now, the reality of it was more than she could cope with.

She was dazed and having trouble concentrating as Hayden's words reverberated through her brain.

"So wha . . . what are we to make of it all, Frank?" Sarah stammered, finally attempting to speak.

"I know you think it's probably Aiden, but whomever our killer is, he has clearly migrated out of Tennessee and has landed in Washington," was his unfiltered assessment.

Despite every bone in her body telling her that this was in fact, the outcome she had dreaded, she was shaking with apprehension. She couldn't speak for several moments as her worst fears were culminating right before her.

"Frank . . . I'm speechless . . . I don't know what to say." She broke down in tears as her boss tried to soothe her devastated psyche.

"I know," he softly said. "I know how hard it must be for you at a time like this. Do you need me to send anyone out there to give you some emotional support?"

Gathering her thoughts and professional bearing, she responded. "No, that won't be necessary," she soberly responded. "So, what's next?"

"I just got off the phone with detectives from both the District of Columbia and Arlington police departments, and they are heading as we speak to your husband's office to take him to the station for questioning. I would expect if he doesn't have a fairly strong rationale at this juncture, and I'm not sure what that would be, he'll be arrested for their murders."

This was it! She thought. It's happening right now! The weeks of anxiety were culminating in the arrest of her husband. Only then would she even begin to feel safe again.

"I'll call you as soon as we have him in custody, OK?" said Hayden.

"Please do Frank. Thanks for everything," replied the grateful Sarah.

She could only wait.

* * * * * * * * *

As Sarah ended her call with Hayden, detectives from the two local police departments and an FBI agent walked casually into Suite 204 of the Longworth House Office building.

"Is the Congressman available?" asked one, flashing his badge and expecting to have to interrupt a meeting in Fletcher's private office.

"I'm sorry, sir, but Congressman Fletcher is not in the office yet," announced the young receptionist.

A bit surprised, the detective proceeded. "Do you know what time you expect him in?"

"Well, not exactly," replied the young woman. "He called a couple of days ago and said he was suddenly called away to attend the funeral of an old friend in Ohio and would be back in the office today."

The detective smelled a rat. "Would you try calling him for me?" he asked.

"You mean right now?" she said.

"Right now, if you don't mind. Tell him this is an emergency. Now please."

Dialing Fletcher's phone, there was no answer. She left a voice mail and asked him to call the moment he received the message. It was an emergency, she said.

Handing the young woman his card, the detective spoke. "If he calls back, I want you to ask him where he is and then call me immediately. Understand?"

Turning to one of his associates, he whispered, "Something tells me he isn't showing up today or any other time."

The FBI agent called the news into his office and was instructed to situate himself in the hallway and bring Fletcher into custody, if he happened to show up. The two detectives returned to their offices to prepare for what each of them knew was coming.

Four hours passed, and still no Fletcher. After several more attempts to reach him, an all-points bulletin was issued concerning his whereabouts. The dragnet was about to expand.

* * * * * * * *

By two o'clock that afternoon, the mainstream media had gotten hold of the story. Like a wildfire spreading across the prairie, news of the search for Aiden Fletcher hit every major news wire and organization in the United States.

The media couldn't keep up with the whirlwind of breaking events.

On CNN, broadcasters were handed a slip of paper and began to announce to the world what was happening.

"Ladies and Gentlemen, we interrupt our present programming, as we have breaking news from our CNN affiliate in Washington that Congressman Aiden Fletcher of Tennessee is the subject of a nationwide manhunt and is being sought on fugitive charges for his possible involvement in a series of murders from Arizona, Tennessee, and here in Washington."

"Police investigators have been presented with evidence from the Congressman's home which appears to be from several of the victim's bodies that might indicate he is somehow involved in their deaths."

"This is coming on the heels of the recent death of the Congressman's Chief of Staff Brian Asher, who was determined to have killed himself two weeks ago with evidence from numerous other killings which police had concluded were committed by him. With the new evidence uncovered today, it is now strongly suspected that Asher did not kill himself after all and that his death most likely resulted from him being murdered, quite possibly by Fletcher."

Soon all the major news networks were cutting to the story as droves of news crews flocked to Fletcher's office to interview his staff.

The corridor outside his office soon became a madhouse as reporters pushed to get interviews with whoever was standing by.

Cornering one of his legislative aides, a news reporter asked a bottom-line, inane question.

"Have you noticed anything peculiar in the Congressman's behavior recently that might lead you to believe he had killed some people?"

"Well, of course not," replied the staffer. "How is one supposed to act after they have killed people?"

TV crews set up outside Fletcher's home in Dupont Circle, hoping to interview neighbors about anything and everything pertaining to Aiden Fletcher. "Was he a nice guy? Did he seem to act peculiarly lately?"

The frenzy was everywhere. At the Hawk & Dove restaurant on Capitol Hill, an iconic political watering hole, the place was a madhouse of activity despite one's party leanings. As television sets overhead pumped out the latest, scores of aides and lobbyists on the Hill shook their heads in total disbelief over what they were hearing. Many of them knew Fletcher personally and could not accept the news broadcast.

"This cannot be happening," said one. "How did Fletcher ever get away with these things?"

Nothing had impacted Washington like this since 9/11 when the plane flew into the Pentagon. This wasn't just a national news story; it was personal to many people who had worked and associated with the Congressman.

A couple of hours later, the major networks broke into their nonstop coverage of the story to listen to a press conference with the FBI Director, the District of Columbia Police Chief, the Speaker of the House, and Sarah Fletcher, who had volunteered to appear and try to talk Fletcher into turning himself in.

"We have today issued warrants for the arrest of Congressman Aiden Fletcher, who is wanted for his alleged involvement in as many as ten murders stretching from Arizona, Tennessee, and the District. We urge anyone who had seen Mr.

Fletcher or might have knowledge of his whereabouts to immediately contact Chief Hayes of the Washington Metropolitan Police Department. Be advised the suspect might be armed and is considered extremely dangerous."

Next, the Speaker of the House took to the podium.

"This is an extremely sad day in the history of this venerable institution," the Speaker began. "At no time in its long and glorious past has a member of this body been accused of such heinous crimes. Let me assure you that the Congress will utilize every resource in its arsenal to bring Congressman Fletcher to justice."

The speaker continued and turned the event into a political speech for him and his party. Finally, at the urging of the crowd, Sarah Fletcher took to the podium to speak. Despite the scores of people assembled, you could hear a pin drop.

"Come home, Aiden," she softly began, weeping into her handkerchief. "Whatever you've done, come home, and we'll get you some help. You can't keep doing what you're doing to innocent people. Come home and turn yourself in so that others can assist you in understanding your demons. Please, Aiden . . . please."

Her relatively short comments had moved the crowd.

As the assembled speakers stepped down from the dais, Sarah was mobbed with reporters pelting her with questions about what did she know and when did she know it. The FBI Director put his arm around her and handed her off to a special agent who took her back to the waterfront house on the Chesapeake.

Her boss, Frank Hayden, assisted her into the car for the drive to Queenstown.

"I'll keep you abreast on everything that's going on," he promised. "Just take care of yourself for the time being, OK?"

He didn't give her time to answer before he slammed the door shut and pounded on the roof to signal the agent to quickly drive away.

Sarah sat in the back seat, alone with her thoughts.

"Just take care of myself," she pondered . . . and how am I supposed to do that? She had no idea where Aiden was hiding. He might be right there in Washington as she imagined him being. Surely, he was going to come after her. She couldn't get the image out of her head of him standing over her in the middle of the night at her safe house with a knife ready to cut her to pieces.

She dropped her head into her hands and didn't say a word the rest of the trip to Queenstown.

It was all a horror! One like she could never have imagined.

* * * * * * * *

The media onslaught continued unabated. The TV talk shows interviewed historians trying to find previous examples of congressional representatives who were ever charged with murder. Others interviewed prominent psychologists who described the psychopathology of serial killers and why they did what they did.

One TV channel showed Fletcher's blue Audi parked on the street in front of his Dupont Circle home, with reporters peering inside as if some critical piece of incriminating evidence might still be visible to the naked eye.

The Washington Post ran its initial online headline proclaiming:

"Congressman Wanted by Police for Multiple Murders"

Every media outlet attempted a retrospective on Fletcher's life but ran into the same dead-end that others had previously discovered. He had no known background information. Everything dug up painted him as a wayward orphan with no fixed address or connections.

Like Sarah had previously unearthed, it was only a couple of people who remembered him in college who could even offer any insight at all on him.

Sarah was torn as to whether she should volunteer the results of her investigation which showed Fletcher was raised in Arizona and was connected to Flora Kinnard's death. Through the hair samples found in his office, Sarah was nevertheless convinced there would be plenty of time to release her findings as the investigation expanded and he was safely behind bars. After all, that might be just the thing that set him off against her, and she was not about to jeopardize her well-being any further.

In Tennessee, the story broke and dominated local broadcasting like nothing ever had. In Knoxville, WBIR was producing nonstop coverage with a critical bent. After all, their favorite son, who had made his name prosecuting a serial murderer, is now being accused of being one himself!

It was a stain to all Tennesseans who prided themselves first and foremost as being honest, truthful people. Fletcher had taken advantage of their goodwill and citizenship to advance his own career, not to mention his treacherous agenda. They felt as if they had been betrayed, especially by someone who was not one of them but who had come from California!

Even more shocking, Fletcher was now accused of murdering some of the same victims that Otis Stamper had been charged with killing. The public just couldn't wrap their head around what they were hearing. It was incomprehensible.

"How could this be?" seemed to be the typical refrain coming from man-in-the-street interviews. "This is impossible!"

"Why didn't anyone know about him earlier?" asked numerous others.

The old refrain "We Got Him!" seemed to have lapsed into comic spoofs.

"We Don't Got Him!" said several Facebook entries.

At the Riverbend Maximum Security Institution in Nashville, Otis Stamper, watching the TV coverage with fellow inmates, burst out into a dance. As he had declared since his incarceration and certainly after the appellate court decision, his reaction was over-the-top predictable.

"I told you bastards I didn't kill all those people!" he screamed to whoever was listening. Many were laughing at his antics and ridiculing his crazy responses.

"Hey Otis, maybe you should run for Congress!" one inmate laughed.

"You ought to," yelled another. "You're certainly qualified for it!"

The appellate court had vacated four of his convictions, and ordering a new trial had represented one of the biggest embarrassments in the history of Tennessee jurisprudence. Now with the incomprehensible news about Fletcher, it seemed anything was possible. Stamper certainly thought so.

Hell, I may even be let out on bail for a while, Stamper imagined, thinking about the copious amounts of whiskey and women he might consume if his freedom was granted.

* * * * * * * *

Over the next couple of days, reports were coming in from all over the country alleging locations where Fletcher had been spotted. In Coeur d' Alene, Idaho, someone called in saying that a man that looked like Fletcher was seen at the boat ramp trying to get a boat in the water. Police, obligated to respond, checked it out, and the man in question was the owner of the little pub where the ramp was located.

Near Versailles, Kentucky, someone called to say they saw a strange man near a horse barn on one of the upscale Bluegrass farms outside Lexington that resembled Fletcher. The man turned out to be a local vet there to administer some medications to a barn full of horses.

False leads began appearing all over the country, each of which however, had to be checked out. The FBI was working overtime to separate the screw-ball sightings from those that might have some real merit.

One old man called in to say he had seen Fletcher on a train from Boston, saying he was going to Savannah to see his mother. Authorities declined to follow up knowing that Fletcher's mother was long dead and concluding that given the man's advanced age, the account couldn't have had any merit

The hunt for Aiden Fletcher was becoming a national obsession, both for serious law enforcement agencies spending valuable time and resources and those not-so-serious who were taking advantage of the situation . . . for money.

One video game popped up overnight, portraying Fletcher as a fugitive rat pursued by the US Army, the Chinese, and God knows who else. Killing hundreds of people in his wake; the object was to find him before he took over the world. The game, called "Fled Fletcher," was a huge hit on the video game circuit and undoubtedly made its creator a good chunk of money.

After initial attempts to locate Fletcher had proven unsuccessful, a break in the case appeared and ratcheted up attention in those pursuing him.

A cell phone tracker used by Verizon in connection with its communication towers showed that Fletcher had not made a call since the preceding Tuesday but was suddenly showing the phone's whereabouts out West near Colorado.

An all-points bulletin was put out and law enforcement units near Littleton, Colorado, outside Denver, closed in on a weakening signal in the approximate location of a moving van stopped at a home in the Cherokee Ridge neighborhood.

With a well-coordinated maneuver, the local police department zoomed in and, with guns drawn, surrounded the van and entered the home with the expectation of confronting Aiden Fletcher, surprised and unprepared.

In its place, they found an older couple and their pet Yorkie resting in the living room after having worked strenuously to unpack some of the myriads of boxes that were being delivered.

Convinced that Fletcher was nowhere in the vicinity, communications back to Verizon suggested the van itself was the source of the tracking signal. Redirecting their focus on the moving crew and the remaining boxes on board, the officers were stumped as to what was happening.

It wasn't until their search of the van's undercarriage was made did they discover a cell phone wedged under the frame of the semi.

After numerous calls to the Verizon network, someone placed a call to Fletcher's known cell phone number and discerned that the phone placed on the van was indeed Fletcher's and that the van had left Washington the previous Tuesday; the last time Fletcher had been seen.

"It's all a ruse," the special agent-in-charge back in Washington snapped. "He intentionally threw us off his track," he concluded.

"It's frustrating," said another, "it frustrates me, my department and anyone working on this. I mean, I'd like someone to come up with a few answers."

"No doubt," replied another, "but where in God's name, is he?"

"Christ knows," said the other. "But he clearly had a plan in place. There's no telling what happened to him. He could be anywhere."

He could be anywhere . . . was exactly right.

Chapter Forty

It had been three days since the Costa Agata had set sail from Miami bound for its twenty-eight-day voyage to the Port of Buenos Aires. It had made a stop at the Puerto de Matanzas in Cuba to take on more cargo. Lester's disguise had become a permanent part of his appearance now, and no one questioned him about anything.

He had spent the eight hours during the ships' reloading venturing into Mantanzas to explore the city's cultural attributes, architecture, and bar life. Located on the northern shore of Cuba and known for its Afro-Cuban folklore, it was approximately 56 miles east of Havana.

Mantanzas was the birthplace of the music and dance tradition known as the rumba, a dance still openly performed at many restaurants near the port. While strolling through the city, he stopped and had a leisurely lunch at Bar Corrida, where he enjoyed the local rum and seafood in a leisurely, laid-back atmosphere.

Lester enjoyed his few hours in Mantanzas so much that it made him feel like he was on vacation instead of fleeing from the law. He made a mental note to perhaps return someday and stay a few days. That along with a couple of days, in Havana, would make for a great little vacation, he imagined.

Back on the ship, Lester helped some of the crewmen take a count of the recently loaded containers for the Master of the boat. He often volunteered to help out with some of the crew's chores to help pass the time, and with his good humor and pleasant persona, he was making friends with several of the crew members.

The highlight of the day was the nightly poker games over rum and Cuban cigars. Lester had been a fairly good poker player in college and had kept his skills sharp during his occasional Friday night poker nights with his friends in Knoxville. The games usually produced a great deal of laughter and braggadocio about the crew's various conquests of women, a topic that Lester did not often contribute to.

The ship's advanced communication network, including internet and cell phone service, was outstanding. Every evening before dinner, the crew would relax in the lounge and watch whatever was taking place on the evening news out of Miami, usually with a cold beer in hand.

The nonstop broadcasts of Congressman Fletcher being wanted in a nationwide manhunt fascinated the crew, given the scope of the coverage and the crimes for which Fletcher had been accused. To Lester's great fascination, most of the crew were cheering for him not to be caught, reasoning that one man pursued by thousands made him the underdog, and thus a natural empathy had evolved.

"That guy has balls, that's for sure," said Carlos, watching the coverage intently.

"Why do you say that?" asked Lester, curious to hear Carlos's logic.

"I don't know," Carlos replied. "You think after killing all those people, you'd figure he'd eventually get caught, but he keeps on doing it. That takes big balls."

"Whatever is driving him must be a real rush," added Antonio. "To risk so much. It must offer a thrill that he couldn't get anywhere else."

"I think you're right about that," replied Lester, with a sly smile.

It had indeed offered a thrill that he couldn't get anywhere else.

* * * * * * * *

Within a few hours the ship had edged its way out of the Puerto de Mantanzas back into the North Atlantic Ocean. The day offered the crew a fairly light schedule and one where most of them caught up on their personal business. Lester was no different.

Sitting at his desk, Lester began to get serious about the next phase of his great escape. Picking up his burner cell phone, he called a number he had long ago jotted down for future use should the occasion ever arise.

Listening patiently for the party to answer, Lester took a big draw on his Hoyo de Monterrey, Epicure No. 2, one of the finest Cuban cigars made.

"Banco de la Republica," said the female voice. "How may I be of service to you today?"

"Buenos Dias, Señorita," Lester exclaimed. "Cómo estás esta mañana?"

"Muy bien gracias," came the reply. The young woman was flattered by Lester's soft manner and easy fluency in Spanish.

"I was calling to open up a couple of accounts with you," Lester continued. "Can I do that over the phone?"

"Certainly, Señor, what kind of accounts did you have in mind?"

"I wanted to open both a checking account and a money market account if that's possible," Lester replied.

"Absolutely," the young woman responded. "May I ask whose name the accounts will be opened in?"

"The accounts should be in the name of Javier Castillo," replied Lester.

Detective Marty Castillo had been Lester's favorite character as a young man growing up watching the TV show "Miami Vice." He had always admired Castillo's cool, detached and authoritative persona and aspired to one day be like him.

"Thank you, Señor Castillo. Are you wishing to make any deposits today?"

"I will make only modest deposits today Señorita, but I fully intend to wire substantial funds into them very shortly."

"In that case, I will give you the account and routing numbers so that you can make the wire transfers at your leisure," she said.

"That would be just fine, Señorita. Gracias."

"You're welcome. Do you have a pen? Here are the numbers you will need."

After Lester wrote down the account numbers, the young woman spoke again.

"Anything else I can do for you today, Señor?" she said.

"You can tell me your name." Lester cheerfully replied.

"Sofia," she said with a soft giggle.

"Well, Sofia, you've certainly made my day so delightful. Perhaps I will see you in person one day when I come to visit my accounts," he chuckled.

Sofia laughed. "Perhaps you will, Señor Castillo. Have a nice day."

"Ten un dia maravilloso!" Lester replied.

"Gracias Señor Castillo."

* * * * * * * *

The Banco de la Republica, or BROU, was the largest bank in Montevideo, the capital city of Uruguay, with a population of 1.3 million people. The city was located on the southern coast of the country on the northeastern bank of the Rio de la Plata, an estuary formed by the confluence of two major rivers, which empty into the Atlantic Ocean. The rivers formed part of the border between Buenos Aires, the capital of Argentina, and Montevideo and provided an easy ferry crossing between the two capitals.

Montevideo maintained one of the highest-quality of life ratings in Latin America, with a rich arts and music culture and an active nightlife. Described as having a vibrant, eclectic environment with a rich, cultural life, it was also known for being a thriving tech center with an entrepreneurial focus. With a rich European heritage and a moderate, subtropical climate, it was truly one of the jewels of Latin America and an exceptional locale to engage in many activities.

It was also a wonderful place to disappear.

Lester had thought long and hard about where he would go if the day ever came that he would have to flee to evade detection of law enforcement. Uruguay was his top choice, and every aspect of his new life would be centered on its myriad of services and the ability to maintain his anonymity.

He soon wired $1.5 million of his Caymans funds into his Banco Republica accounts, which would sustain him for as long as necessary. He had already made initial arrangements with high-end, black-market merchants who could provide him with a Uruguay passport and a birth certificate.

Once he had those, it would be easy to apply for anything else he needed to begin life as Javier Castillo, his new identity. There were many more aspects to disappearing into the city that would soon become his new base of operations. He would however, have to be prudent about controlling his inner urges until he felt fully and securely situated.

As he peered out over the blackened South Atlantic Ocean from the deck of the Costa Agata, he tacitly imagined a new life, a new appearance, and a new opportunity to satisfy that which his inner entity had deemed so insatiable.

In Uruguay, he would have a remarkable opportunity to begin his life all over . . . yet again.

* * * * * * * *

It had been three weeks since Aiden Fletcher had been implicated in the murders of the three local women in DC and Arlington. Although the media was still touting the storyline on its evening broadcasts, the lack of any substantive leads caused the public's intense focus on the story to slowly begin to dissipate.

Sarah was still living in her waterfront rental away from the hustle-bustle of Washington but was in touch with colleagues at the Bureau on a regular basis.

Receiving a call from Director Hayden, she asked yet again whether progress had been made on locating, and more importantly, apprehending her husband.

"Hey Frank," she laconically addressed her boss as he patiently waited for her to answer the phone.

"Sarah. How's it going?" he asked, trying to be upbeat for her benefit, but knowing her anxiety about Fletcher still being on the lam was turning her into an emotional recluse.

"Any leads?" she asked, hoping he might offer something new.

"We're still pursuing every angle we can think of Sarah," he honestly answered. We won't give up until Aiden is apprehended and brought to justice."

"Frank, can I ask you a question?" she stated.

"Sure, fire away."

"How do you think he's managed to stay invisible like he has?"

"That's a damn good question," Hayden responded. "I've wondered the same thing myself. He hasn't fallen into any of the normal traps. No usage of credit cards or ATM withdrawals, no cell phone calls, no contacts with former associates. He has no family to communicate with. If I didn't know any better, I would almost suspect he was dead."

"Do you think that's possible?" Sarah queried.

"It's possible but highly unlikely," Hayden responded. "Don't take this the wrong way, Sarah, but it would be a lot better for everyone if he were."

"I wish that were truly the case," she replied. "It would make my life exponentially better. By the way, are we seeing any more murders with his signature on it anywhere else in the country?"

"We've looked hard at that, and it appears the answer is no."

"So, what does that tell you?" she curiously inquired.

"It tells me that given the publicity, he's either too scared to pull this shit again, or he's no longer even in the country," Hayden responded. "I don't know; I've never quite seen anything like it."

"Do you think it's possible he's never even left the area?" Sarah asked. Her question emanated from the nadir of her deepest-held anxiety.

"Sarah, anything is possible at this point," Hayden said matter-of-factly.

"How's it going over on the Eastern Shore?" he asked, trying to lighten the conversation.

"Good, I suppose," she replied. "I try not to venture out much. I still have this creepy feeling Aiden is watching me and is just waiting for the right time to strike."

"If it makes you feel any better," Hayden said, "I doubt seriously he would want to be anywhere close to the DC area right now. The scrutiny here is so intense."

"I hope you're right, but somehow, I don't think the normal rules apply to him. From a psychological point of view, I think he might feel he has some unfinished business here, and that business is me."

"Care to expand on that?" Hayden asked.

"I think his psychological gratification is the power he exercises over his victims. His psychotic breaks won't allow him to merely quit because there's an increased likelihood he might be caught. He's driven to murder no matter what the risk. It's just a power trip, and honestly, that's what has me so concerned."

"I'm afraid he views me as someone who must be punished because I turned him in and ruined his life. I fear I've become the substitute for the mother he so despised. The one we strongly surmise he brutally murdered." She continued with her analysis.

"The rage exhibited in her killing was overwhelming. It's like he's mission-driven. His first goal is to rid the world of women he sees as being like his abusive mother, whatever characteristic he sees in them that sets him off. His next goal is to punish those whom he perceives as having done him wrong, and I would certainly fall into the latter category."

"So, you think in his mind, you have replaced his long-hated mother?" Hayden inquired.

"It's what keeps me up at night," she solemnly responded.

"Let's just hope we catch a break and can bring him in," Hayden asserted.

"Hope is all I have right now," Sarah said, her words dripping with apprehension. "I'm not confident this is going to end well."

Chapter Forty-One

The Costa Agata was twenty-five days into its voyage and approaching the Rio De La Plata Gulf, the final stage of its journey to the Port of Buenos Aires.

Lester had essentially become one of the crew during the nearly four weeks he had worked, slept, and eaten with the men who managed the massive cargo ship's daily operations.

Among the twenty-odd crew members onboard, Lester had become close to a few, especially the two or three who regularly played poker after hours in the crew quarters of the ship.

One such individual was a man named Tomas Morales, a Spanish-born seaman who made his home in Sitges, Spain, a small town just south of Barcelona. It was a beautiful beachfront area often compared to St. Tropez for its mix of tradition and glamor. Lester was well aware of Tomas' hometown, as he made it a constant topic of conversation during the nightly get-togethers with the crew.

Lester had a plan, and he needed Tomas to help pull it off. One night after several drinks and a few hands of blackjack, Lester spoke to him as the two were headed back to their compartments.

"Tomas, I was wondering if you might be able to do me a small favor," Lester asked.

"Certainly, Señor George," Tomas replied, "anything at all."

Reaching into his desk next to his bed, Lester pulled out an addressed envelope and handed it to Tomas.

"When will you be going home next?" Lester asked, already knowing the answer.

"As soon as we unload the ship, we'll be putting back to sea and headed to Barcelona," Tomas enthusiastically responded. "I'll have three weeks off after that. Why do you ask?"

Lester handed him the envelope and kindly responded. "Would you mind mailing this for me once you arrive in Barcelona?" Lester requested.

"Sure," replied Thomas, "but you can always mail it from Buenos Aires."

"Oh, I know," Lester responded, "weird as it may sound, my friend for whom this is addressed has a thing about collecting postmarks from all over the world. She doesn't have one from Spain, and I thought I'd help her out."

"No problem," said Tomas, taking the envelope from Lester. "I'd be happy to help you out," he replied.

"Oh, and here's a little something for your troubles," Lester stated, handing Tomas a hundred-dollar bill.

"Oh, that's not necessary," Tomas asserted, "I'll be happy to do it for nothing."

"No, I want you to take it," Lester responded. "Besides, I want this mailed in Barcelona, not before . . . understood?"

"Absolutely," Tomas said. "I'll mail it as soon as we port in Barcelona, not before."

"Thank you, Tomas; I greatly appreciate this. My friend will be so very surprised."

* * * * * * * *

After a relatively brief journey up the Rio de la Plata Gulf, the Costa Agata arrived at its destination . . . the Port of Buenos Aires, the terminal operated by the state-owned General Port Administration.

Saying his goodbyes to the crew, Lester made his way to the ferry station that offered a direct route to Montevideo, Uruguay, across the vast expanse of the Gulf. It gave Lester time to think about the final phase of his plan.

The trip took a little over two hours, and Lester arrived in the heart of the city. A short taxi ride deposited him in front of a stately apartment building in Parque Rodo, a popular neighborhood district named after the massive park located in the center of the community, which surrounds a lake with pedal boats for rent. It was there that he finalized arrangements he had made on the ship to rent a furnished flat for three months, so that he could get situated and establish his new identity.

The Parque Rodo, was known for its bustling night life with scores of bars, restaurants, and nightclubs while hosting an array of outdoor shops and activities. The southern side of the community faced the Rio de la Plata and was situated on the Playa Ramirez, one of the city's most popular beaches. Many University departments were scattered throughout the streets, ensuring the near-continuous crowds of students and tourists alike.

Checking into his "el apartamento," Lester threw his weary body on the bed and soon fell fast asleep. The last month had been an incredibly arduous journey, both physically and mentally. As he lay in the queen-sized bed, he stared intently at the whirl of the overhead fan.

His mind drifted back on all he had achieved in order to have eluded authorities and prepare the foundation for his new, adventurous life.

It was arduous, but a journey he had been through before. He was confident he could make it work again.

With all he had accomplished, there was still much to do. Nevertheless, he was proud of his ingenuity and, most of all, his courage under fire. The very attributes that had always served him well.

* * * * * * * *

Over the next few days, Lester made connections to secure the services of a plastic surgeon in an effort to establish a new appearance. One that would easily blend in with the masses of Uruguayan nationals, but more importantly, would forever mask the visage of the now-departed Aiden Fletcher.

He had already dyed his hair and eyebrows nearly black and soon wore the Latin American designer clothes so popular with the affluent in his trendy new community. An expensive Panama hat and dark sunglasses gave him a finished look so integrated into the local culture that no one would think to look twice as he walked down the street.

He soon underwent a rhinoplasty procedure to reshape his nose and additional surgery to enhance his chin. Combined with Botox treatments to his cheeks and lips, within a short time, he was unrecognizable from his former self. With his new appearance, he was ready to secure identity papers establishing himself as a Uruguayan citizen.

Between the high-end black markets of Buenos Aires and Montevideo, Lester was ready to complete the last but most important aspect of his transformation . . . procuring the necessary official documents to pass as a full-fledged citizen of Uruguay.

The underground market for such services was quite extensive and extraordinarily good. Lester soon finalized his previous arrangements to acquire an official passport and birth certificate establishing his new identity. With such, he had the ability to obtain a driver's license, an ID, and credit cards, all through legal channels, which provided him with the necessary documentation sufficient to do anything a natural-born Uruguayan citizen could do.

The clandestine services he utilized were so proficient he was even able to acquire professional background documents, which showed him as having graduated as an honor student with a Master's degree in business from the University of the Republic, the largest and best-known college in the country.

Thus, within a month after his arrival into the country, Lester had fully and legally established himself as a prosperous and legitimate Uruguayan citizen . . . Señor Javier Castillo.

Standing in front of his mirror, he allowed a self-satisfied smile to cross his newly enhanced lips. His scars from the surgeries were barely noticeable. His appearance was now completely transformed and was indistinguishable from a native-born Latino.

He had done it . . . acquired a new appearance, a new identity, and a new financial profile for a little more than $15,000.

More importantly, despite all odds and with little prospect of success, he had outmaneuvered the law enforcement agencies of the United States and had virtually disappeared from the North American continent. He had found a new base of operations, and it suited him exceedingly well.

South America offered a whole new world for Javier Castillo's taking . . .

. . . . and take it he would.

Chapter Forty-Two

The hunt for Aiden Fletcher was still alive, both in Washington and elsewhere. However, after two months of virtually no leads, the media had grown weary of the story, no matter how compelling the publicized account had been.

The FBI had made little progress on the case since the revelation of the victims' hair having been discovered at his home by his wife. She had disappeared from public view, and the story was no longer dominating the headlines.

The Aiden Fletcher story took on almost mythological status, reminiscent of the DB Cooper saga from the early 1970s, where an unidentified man hijacked a Boeing 727 aircraft after stealing $200,000 and parachuted somewhere over southwestern Washington airspace.

Despite an extensive manhunt and a forty-five-year FBI investigation, no conclusions had ever been reached regarding the culprit's true identity or his ultimate fate. Numerous theories of widely varying plausibility had been offered over the years, none of which ever brought investigators closer to the truth.

But Cooper's bold and adventurous crime inspired a near cult-like following over the years that was noted in film, songs, and written articles. An extensive documentary on him had achieved record ratings.

The accusations against Aiden Fletcher had been so astonishing, they were hard to believe, yet his sudden disappearance had lent credence to the presumption of his guilt. All it would take would be one substantial lead, and the story would burst open again with all the fury it had initially generated.

Editors and media types of every genre frothed at the prospect of Fletcher's eventual capture. They could only imagine how the resulting coverage would send their ratings through the proverbial stratosphere

It was like a time bomb waiting to go off, with the clock clicking ever-steadily downward.

* * * * * * * *

Sarah Fletcher had not been doing well in the intervening weeks after Fletcher's disappearance. She began to suffer from generalized panic attacks, not knowing where her husband was or when he was going to strike next. She had become a recluse and would only venture out of her little waterfront rambler to obtain essential goods or services.

Her neighbors hardly ever saw her other than when she would sit out on her porch with a shawl and stare at the Bay for hours at a time.

She had been seeing a psychiatrist in Annapolis who was treating her for anxiety and prescribed Xanax to treat her ongoing fear and apprehension. She simply could not get the thought out of her head about her husband finding out where she was and what he would do to her when he did. Her treatments didn't provide much more than moderate relief in any event.

Nevertheless, she was working remotely from home and had been keeping up with her responsibilities at work. She maintained contact every day with her office and constantly hoped to hear something new regarding her fugitive husband.

She elected not to go out socially for fear of being discovered, but would allow certain friends to come visit her and spend the day.

Diane Johnson had been one of those friends.

* * * * * * * * *

It was a busy Tuesday morning at Diane's K Street office. The House had just passed an Omnibus spending bill that had included a provision for one of her clients that would bring them approximately $400 million in government contracts over the next five years. Passage of the bill in the Senate was a foregone conclusion.

She had been exhausted from the effort, but her firm's fee for having secured the legislation was enormous. She had received a $350K bonus for her work on the project, and she was feeling good about herself and her future with the firm.

Late in the morning, her assistant brought in the morning mail, which she left unattended until she had a free moment in the afternoon to go through it.

One letter, in particular, caught her attention. The address had been handwritten, and it bore a postmark from Barcelona, Spain, of all places.

Why would anyone be sending her a letter from Barcelona? She wondered.

Carefully opening it up, she began to read the handwritten note and screamed in horror.

"Oh my God!" She shrieked. "Oh my God!"

Her associates came running into her office as she visibly began to shake from the shock of what she had just read.

Gathering her composure, she assured her colleagues she was OK but needed some privacy to make a call. Shutting her door, she dialed Sarah's number, uncertain of how her message was going to be received.

"Sarah, it's Diane," she anxiously uttered. The angst in her voice was not lost on Sarah.

"What's wrong?" Sarah urgently asked.

"I got something in the mail today from Barcelona you need to know about," Diane curtly responded.

"Barcelona? Why would that have anything to do with me?"

Diane paused . . ." because I think it may be from Aiden," Diane reluctantly answered.

"What!" Sarah screamed. After two months of hearing nothing, now came a shocking correspondence from the very man who was the subject of a nationwide manhunt; her murderous husband.

"What does it say?" she pleaded.

"Sarah, I'm not sure I should tell you. It's pretty scary," Diane hesitated.

"Tell me!" Sarah insisted. "I have to know!"

"Sarah, as your friend, I don't want to alarm you. I'm very scared to tell you what the message contains," Diane admitted.

"Diane . . . you have to tell me," Sarah asserted in a much calmer voice. She was now thinking like the professional she was.

"I have to be able to analyze whether, in fact, it's from Aiden and if I can draw anything from it psychologically. No one can do that as well as I, if we're going to apprehend him. Do you understand?"

Diane knew she was absolutely right. It was more than just passing on a message from husband to wife. It was evidence that had to be analyzed and examined.

"Can you send it to me . . . right now . . . this moment?" Sarah asked. "I have to be able to look at the handwriting and scrutinize the words used. Would you transmit it right now?"

"Sure," responded Diane. "Let me scan it and I'll send it over."

"Oh, and Diane? Call this number. I'm going to have a couple of agents come over and pick up the document from you and take it to the lab for analysis. OK?"

"Sure thing," replied Diane. "I'm going to call you shortly."

"Thanks much," I'll talk to you then."

Diane scanned the message and emailed it to Sarah and immediately called the number she had been given.

"VICAP, Sarah Fletcher's office," came the reply. "May I help you?"

"This is Diane Johnson," she stated. I'm a friend of Sarah's, and I just talked to her. She told me to call you and tell you I have received a letter that I believe is intended for her, and it may have been sent by her husband. I need to have someone come over and pick it up ASAP."

"I'll send an agent over immediately," replied the assistant with an urgency to her voice.

Within twenty minutes, two FBI agents arrived at Diane's office and shut the door. She handed them the letter and watched their faces as they turned to the other in utter dismay.

"We're going to take this right to the lab for analysis," said one. "We'll call Sarah as soon as we have anything. Thanks for contacting us."

"Thank Sarah," she replied.

* * * * * * * *

Within minutes, Sarah's laptop abruptly engaged as Diane's email suddenly appeared in her inbox. Staring at the subject line which contained the brutally riveting words "The Letter," she paused. With great trepidation she opened the message. The moment seemed eerily surreal . . . in a chilling, Hitchcockian sort of way.

Sarah braced for what she knew was coming.

Quickly making a copy, she sat down in the chair nearest her make-shift office and began to scrutinize the unsettling document meant for her and only her. The letter was calculated and affirmed her greatest fears:

Sarah/Bitch!!!!

I am closer to you than you can imagine.

You will know my wrath as my blade

Plunges into you over and over.

I will never rest until you have joined my mother in the depths of burning HELL!!!!!

Don't shut your fucking eyes.

I am coming for you.

Sugar Pie

The emotional devastation she experienced at that moment was hard to quantify. The nightmare she constantly had been living with was coming true right before her eyes! It was obvious Fletcher maintained a sickening, psychopathic hatred of her for having exposed his secret life. Clinically speaking, it was clear he was deeply obsessed with her and wouldn't be satisfied until she was stone-cold dead.

She broke down and sobbed as her latent fears overtook her. She was scared like she had never been before . . . like she could never have imagined.

It was now all very clear to her. She knew she could never escape Aiden's fury until he was captured or he had murdered her . . . one or the other.

The culmination of her anxieties was laid bare by his letter, and she realized without a doubt that there was nothing she was going to be able to do about his hideous threats.

She held her head in her hands and wept.

"God help me," she murmured as she tried to regain her bearing.

At that moment her phone rang. It was Director Hayden.

"Sarah, I just received word about the letter," he began. "How are you holding up?" he asked.

"Not well," she replied, tears rolling down her cheek. "This just solidifies all that I've been apprehensive about. He's coming after me."

"Don't worry," Hayden stated. "We're not going to let anything happen to you. You have my word."

"Thanks," said Sarah, "but you don't have to placate me."

"Can we talk about the specifics of the letter?" Hayden asked, curious to get any insights she might offer.

"Are you convinced it's actually from your husband?" Hayden said.

"Yes," she responded. "I know beyond any doubt it's from him because he signed it 'Sugar Pie'. That's a term of affection I used with him that no one else could possibly know about."

"Any connection to Barcelona?" Hayden inquired.

"None that I know of," she replied. "What do you think about that?"

"I think he either screwed up by inadvertently disclosing his location, or it's a diversion to throw us off. In any event, we're going to have to refocus our efforts in Spain and see what we can come up with," replied Hayden.

"Why do you think he sent it to your friend instead of to your office?" Hayden continued.

"I am guessing it's because the words "Fletcher," "FBI," and "Washington, DC." have been all over the news and if someone noticed the envelope, it might draw unwanted attention to himself," she said. "Besides, he knows where Diane works and that anything addressed to her would find its way to me."

"Let me ask you this," Hayden queried. "Some of the staff think it might not actually be him because he made reference to stabbing you when it seems his other victims were beaten and strangled. What's your take on that?"

"I think unquestionably it's him," she responded. "Even though he might not have used a knife on his earlier victims, I think that was done intentionally to preclude us from finding any evidence of his DNA. He's an organized killer. Everything he does is meticulously planned out."

"His mother, however . . . that was a different story. He viciously stabbed her repeatedly. It's a special kind of rage that he saves for those he most despises, which now, unfortunately, includes me."

"Listen, Sarah," said Hayden, "I don't want you worrying about this. I'm going to have an agent monitor your home for a few days, just in case Fletcher tries to make a move. Would that make you feel better?"

"That's very kind, Frank," Sarah responded. "That wouldn't hurt, but Aiden may not make a move for some while yet. You can't protect me from him forever."

After her conversation with Hayden concluded, Sarah stepped out on her deck to try to compose herself. What she had just gone through amounted to an unspeakable nightmare. Her mind raced as to how she could grasp the demonic threat that now lay directly before her.

He would come to her in the middle of the night when no one was around to hear her screams. His furor would be maniacal and his obsession terrifying. She imagined the shock of being stabbed over and over again as her blood seeped slowly out of her body onto the floor of her bedroom.

Her eyes would slowly begin to close as he thrust his blade into her chest and screamed his demonic rants, knowing that would be the last thing she would experience before she passed from this life. The unspeakable, frightening end to a life she had always treasured.

Chapter Forty-Three

Javier realized more than ever, that he had landed in an environment incredibly well suited for his needs. In addition to providing him with an invisible presence where he could come and go as he pleased, it offered a wealth of artistic, business, and cultural opportunities.

He could be himself without anyone asking questions or growing suspicious of his activities. With his recently established affluence, he could embrace the best of his newfound Latin urbanity, which he was quickly beginning to prefer to the one-dimensional commonality of the United States.

Montevideo was everything he could have hoped it would be. Historically considered a quiet, out-of-the-way South American urban center, it offered perhaps the highest quality of life in Latin America. It provided an eclectic, civilized lifestyle with a vibrant nightlife, alive with Latin music, tango dancing, and other forms of social entertainment. It's Spanish and European influences permeated every aspect of the city and provided a rich, cultural diversity that allowed for a broad array of opportunities for young and old alike.

Despite historical economic unrest and years of civil dictatorship, Montevideo enjoyed in recent times uninterrupted and sustained economic growth. The country was politically stable and developing into one of the most desirable places to live on the South American continent.

In addition to its economic prosperity, Montevideo offered Javier something else that would serve him well.

The city suffered from an inordinately high incidence of violent street crimes, particularly homicide, due principally to gangs seeking to control drug traffic routes and operations. As a result, the public had grown anxious about the deteriorating security situation in the streets of Montevideo. At the same time, the local police were ill-equipped to handle the influx of weekly killings that were becoming more and more commonplace.

The local environment thus provided Javier with everything he required . . . including a rich bounty of young, available women.

He didn't have to wait long to satisfy the demonic urge that for so long had been his dark and ghastly companion.

* * * * * * * *

Pocitos was an upscale beach district along the banks of the Rio de la Plata. It was populated with high-rise apartment buildings, storefronts, and numerous bars, most located on quiet little avenues off the beaten path.

Javier had been frequenting many such drinkeries in the weeks gone by.

The Café Hermosa Noche was one such establishment, situated near a waterside pedestrian sidewalk known as The Rambla, which went 14 miles along the entire coastline of Montevideo. Arriving one evening just before 11:00 p.m., Javier took a seat at the old-world bar and ordered a Clerico, a popular Sangria-like local drink consisting of wine and fruit juice.

He saw her at the end of the rail with one of her friends. Tall and lanky, she reminded Javier of Sarah, who now occupied a growing and increasingly sinister corner of his not nearly forgotten memory. After subtly watching the women enjoying their several drinks with accompanying laughter, he quietly observed as she and her inebriated companion proceeded to leave the tavern. It was nearly 2:00 a.m.

After her friend jumped into a taxi parked at the curb near the front of the establishment, the young woman proceeded to walk the one block across a park to where she had left her car. It was there that Javier caught up with her behind a grove of trees fifty yards from where she had parked the car.

"Buenas noches señorita," Javier politely asserted walking up behind her.

The young woman was at first startled, but recognized Javier from the bar and paused while he continued.

"Puedo acompanarte a tu coche?" ("May I walk you to your car?") the debonair Javier politely asked. The woman hesitated but soon decided that such a prosperous looking gentleman did not pose a threat to her.

"Ciertamente señor," ("Certainly sir,") she exclaimed, relieved that his offer seemed genuinely sincere.

As she turned to continue toward her car, she suddenly felt Javier's arm wrapped tightly around her neck and shoulders. Before she could scream, Javier let out an enraged, horrific howl as he plunged his serrated knife into her torso.

"Bitch!!" he angrily exclaimed. "Fucking bitch! Enjoy your journey to hell!"

The young woman recoiled and managed to turn as Javier buried his blade into her chest over and over again. The entity within him continued its gruesome assault for several more moments before he dropped the knife and began to strangle her with all his might. Through her bloody gurgling, her nearly lifeless body took on an expression of abject terror and her eyes fixed their gaze at the demonic face of pure evil.

It would be the last thing she would see in this life.

Thrilled with the exhilaration of the moment, Javier looked around the nearly deserted streets and proceeded to drag the young woman's body a few feet back into the treed area of the park. For a few brief moments he laid down beside the corpse caressing her hair in his hands and inhaling the perfumed scent of his freshly dead young victim.

He imagined the woman to be Sarah, begging for her life and replayed the young woman's agony in his invigorated mind as he used the knife to cut off a locket of her hair and got up to leave.

"You fucking bitch!" he exclaimed, icily staring down at the body and mentally channeling his now detested wife. "You will never escape my wrath!"

Placing the locket of hair and knife in his suit jacket, he nonchalantly strolled out of the park . . . into the dead of the night.

* * * * * * * * *

The news channels the next day described the murder of the young woman in startling detail. As Javier sat on his balcony and basked in the sensuous afterglow of his late-night escapade, he felt incredibly alive. Just like he had all the other times before.

Smoking a cigar, Javier looked out over the green space of Parque Rodo and felt a satisfaction like he had never known. He had escaped the massive manhunt of the US authorities and was now permanently ensconced in a place that offered him everything he could ever want.

Looking back on his astonishing life, he had confronted his unfathomable, but inevitable fate and pursued it, no matter where it had led him. No matter the hardships . . . no matter the pain . . . no matter the loneliness.

Through his unrequited ambition and dazzling ingenuity, he had carved his own destiny and arrived at the place where he was meant to be all along.

With his feet propped up on the railing of the balcony, he gently puffed on his cigar while enjoying a freshly squeezed Mohito. The contentment of the moment overcame him.

After decades of incredible struggle, Lester Kinnard was truly at a place he could call home.

Chapter Forty-Four

The pure black of the late-evening sky was punctuated only by the specter of an emerging full moon. As it crept ever-so-slowly across the dark and sinister expanse, the blustery cold wind off the Chesapeake gave the lonesome night a bone-chilling feel, terrible and fierce to the core.

The branches of a large oak tree brushed noisily across the side of the house as the gale blew violently across the waters and made its presence known to the modest inland community.

It was perhaps appropriate that Sarah Fletcher would be forced to endure such an ominous and disquieting scene as the foreboding, darkened clouds blew swiftly by as if trying to escape the menacing horror of what was yet to come.

This was how it was going to be on the last night of her increasingly disconsolate life.

She had gone to bed early, but like most evenings since receiving the letter from Aiden, her sleep had been fitful. Lying in bed, she looked at the clock on her nightstand. It was nearly 3:00 a.m., and her senses were adjusting to the eerie silence that had completely enveloped her.

She heard an abrupt, distinctive snap of a twig from outside her bedroom window and the sudden bolt of a startled rabbit across her back terrace. Moments later, the almost imperceptible squeak of the back door slowly opening shocked her senses into a full and disquieting alert.

Her breathing became labored, and her fear overwhelming.

She could hear the creak of the old house's floor as someone was cautiously making their way to her rear bedroom. Her heart was in her throat as all the oxygen in the room seemed to have suddenly dissipated.

Experiencing terror like she had never known, she grabbed her phone, and with hands quivering uncontrollably, tried desperately to call for help. Her eyes glaring, she then made out the ever-so-faint, but distinct outline of a sinister shadow on the wall approaching her room.

Suddenly the hallway lights flashed on, and standing at the darkened doorway of her bedroom was the worst fear she could ever imagine.

"Hello Sarah," Aiden Fletcher announced in the coldest, deadest voice she had ever heard. "Are you ready to die?"

Sarah began to scream as loud as she possibly could, but the sound couldn't carry over the gusting winds whirling all around her. As he approached her bed, the edge of a huge serrated knife glimmered in the wicked moonlight peeking through her bedroom window.

"No, Aiden, please! Please don't do this!" she beseeched.

The thrust of his knife into her chest shocked her system, and her bed-gown soon became saturated in her rich, red blood. He plunged his knife into her again as the blade entered her neck.

"Stop! Please stop! I beg of you!" she screamed as Fletcher stood over her, shrieking with maniacal groans.

"You bitch!" he howled. "You evil fucking bitch!" His rage seemed to emanate from the depths of hell itself.

With one last burst of strength, she suddenly bolted upright out of bed, and in the blink of an eye . . . he was gone.

Sarah looked at her gown, and there was no blood, no knife, no anything. Then it hit her . . . it had all been a dream! A horrible, ghastly nightmare!

She quivered with fright. It had been so real . . . she had felt the moisture of his beastly breath across her cheek as he laid atop her. The demonic look on Fletcher's face was so terrifying she would never be able to get it out of her mind.

Sitting on the side of the bed with her head cupped in her still trembling hands, she sobbed uncontrollably as the fiendish, psychological vision lingered. She tried to comprehend what she had just so savagely experienced.

Then the realization hit her full force. Like all the previous, ill-fated women who had tragically crossed his path, Fletcher maintained an all-encompassing power over Sarah's diminished and haunted soul . . . a fractured power which she could not, in any way, control.

She realized that the psychiatric literature and the scores of forensic case studies she had spent her career analyzing could never have fully prepared her for the horror of the demonic force that was now so indelibly seared into her devastated psyche.

The ghastly entity that was Aiden Fletcher, wherever he was and whomever he now portrayed himself to be, would never leave her, nor could she ever escape his diabolic hold over her now solitary and shattered life

Acknowledgments

It was a great joy and challenge to write this novel. I would like to thank three people in particular for their invaluable assistance in making it a reality. First to my beloved wife, Doris, whose numerous storyline suggestions, editing and marketing proved most valuable; to my good friend Hency Bunner, who provided a great sounding board and offered many insights into the development of the plot twists and characters; and finally, to Emilie Lorenzi, whose tireless efforts in the formatting and editing of the book made it all the better. Without them, this book might not have been written and I am grateful to all of them for their tireless efforts.

About the Author

Steve McGuire is a native of Louisville, Kentucky, and a retired federal judge who had a 32-year legal career in Washington, DC. He has traveled extensively throughout the world and enjoys classic cars, fine wine, golf, and writing novels. He resides in Naples, Florida, where he enjoys life with his wife, Doris; their golden retriever, Henry; and mini golden-doodle, Alfie.